KU-331-505

JOSEPH R. GARBER

VERTICAL RUN

SIMON & SCHUSTER

A VIACOM COMPANY

First published in Great Britain by Simon & Schuster, 1996
A Viacom Company

Copyright © Joseph Garber, 1996

This book is copyright under the Berne Convention
No reproduction without permission
All rights reserved

The right of Joseph Garber to be identified as
author of this work has been asserted in accordance
with sections 77 and 78 of the copyright designs
and patents act 1988

Simon & Schuster
West Garden Place
Kendal Street
London W2 2AQ

Simon & Schuster of Australia Pty Ltd
Sydney

A CIP catalogue record for this book is available
from the British Library.

0-684-81648-2

This book is a work of fiction. Names, characters,
places and incidents are either the product
of the author's imagination
or are used fictitiously. Any resemblance to actual events
or locales or persons, living or dead, is entirely coincidental

Printed and bound in Great Britain by
Butler & Tanner Ltd, Frome and London

VERTICAL RUN

For Steve Oresman, known as Magpie,
a better sort of bird than those found herein.

Dessencions, discordes, contencions, stryfe, great manslaughter, murmuracions, feares . . . noughty enterprises . . . moch pyllage, theftes, robberies, lyes, great noyses, tumultes, comocions . . . great mischiefe, hatred and wrath . . . deceite, treason, burnynge, adulterye . . . warre, envy, hatred, rancour . . . and finally all kinds of wickednes.

—Vaughan's *Almanacke and Prognostication for 1559*

Man, biologically considered, and whatever else he may be into the bargain, is simply the most formidable of all the beasts of prey . . .

—William James

VERTICAL RUN

PROLOGUE

Then we began to ride. My soul
Smoothed itself out, a long-cramped scroll
Freshening and fluttering in the wind.

—Robert Browning, "The Last Ride Together"

Two young men on horseback.

The taller, David Elliot, is lank and dark and long of limb. His brown eyes are solemn, but he wears a subtle smile. The shorter, Taffy Weiler, is squat as a bulldog; his wiry hair is as startlingly red as the tie-dyed T-shirt he wears, and his blue eyes sparkle with no small deviltry.

Dave comes from Indiana. Taffy is a New Yorker born and bred. They met in San Francisco, which, this summer, is the only place to be. Now they are fast friends.

In September Taffy will start to work for a medium-sized electronics company near San Jose, an outfit called Hewlett-Packard; not many people at NYU have heard of it. Dave, having passed through Indiana State's R.O.T.C. program, is entering the Army; he will report for duty the third week of August. It is certain that he will be sent to Vietnam.

This ride is their last journey together. Adulthood awaits them at summer's end.

Today they are in the high Sierras, more than two hundred miles east of San Francisco. They crossed the mountain divide yesterday, picked up their horses and pack mule from a leathered-looking man who was waiting for them in a pickup truck, and began riding west into the mountain fastness.

Here, on a cobbled slope well above nine thousand feet, their horses have become short of breath. There is no trail; the mountainside is steep. The ground is granite, grey shot with streaks of black. Small white quartzes tumble beneath the animals' hooves, and are so bright with afternoon sun that they cannot be looked at.

From time to time, Dave brushes a hand across the extravagant moustache he has grown this summer. He's proud of it, thinking that it makes him look older. It does not.

Taffy leers at him. "You gotta give me one thing, compadre. You gotta give me that the day you show up to take the oath, you've still got the moustache."

"The moustache goes. I'll be a crewcut, clean-shaven, all-American boy."

"Oh man!"

"Oh man, yourself, and pass me a brew. Arguing with you makes me sooooo thirsty."

Taffy pulls a lukewarm can of Ballantine from his saddlebag. He passes it to Dave together with a churchkey. Dave opens the beer and swiftly lifts it to his mouth, catching the foam on his tongue. Then he lifts the brim of his floppy straw hat, using a handkerchief, one of the six that his mother made him pack, to wipe away a line of sweat. "How much further?" he asks.

Taffy shoots him a lopsided grin. "According to my sources, we should have already been there. Of course my sources were stoned at the time."

Dave snickers.

The two ride on.

It is nearly sunset when they arrive, a holy hour in which the heavens glow, and upon which a sacred mountain silence falls. They breast a small rise, and look down. Dave catches his breath. The loveliness is heart-stopping.

"It's perfect," Taffy whispers. "Just like they said, the perfect place. Am I right, or am I right?"

Dave doesn't answer. He is rapt at what he sees, a small valley, five, perhaps six times larger than the stadium at Indiana State. It is nearly a perfect circle, bounded by steep white cliffs on three sides, a towering stand of conifers at its farthest reach, a small green lake, emerald green, greener than a green bottle, in its center. Soft evening shadows lie across it. Nothing moves. The air is wine. Dave feels something that he has never felt before, and does not expect to feel again. He is uplifted; he is whole.

With a sudden rush, the sound of a feathered arrow through the air, a red-tailed hawk explodes from the sky. Its talons snatch a small grey animal. The hawk screeches in triumph as it flashes out of sight. All in a matter of seconds, here and gone, with only a burnished pinion floating in the air to mark its passage. Dave's horse backs up nervously. Dave pats its neck.

"We camp by the lake, right, compadre?"

"Fine by me," Dave answers. He is not really paying attention. Rather, he is cloaked in wonder, lost in dreams. Shangri-la, Bali Hai, Avalon, Armenia-in-the-Sky, Oz, Wonderland, Barsoom— everyone has a private place of dreams. This valley is his. The beauty of the place has seized him, and made him its own. He knows that he'll never forget this valley, knows that for the rest of his life, no matter what troubles may come, the remembrance of this moment and this spot will comfort him and bring him peace.

This one moment has been the finest in his life, the finest he shall ever experience, and down all his days he will remember it with longing. He knows this, and the knowledge makes him sad.

1.
A BAD DAY AT THE OFFICE

Though fraud in all other actions be odious, yet in matters of war it is laudable and glorious, and he who overcomes his enemies by stratagem, is as much to be praised as he who overcomes them by force.

—Machiavelli, *The Prince*

CHAPTER 1
HOW DAVE LOST HIS JOB

1.

On the morning of the day he disappeared, David Elliot awoke, as he did every weekday, at precisely 5:45 A.M. Twenty-five years earlier in a hot, green place, he'd learned the trick of waking whenever he wanted. Now it was just another habit.

Dave slid his legs out from beneath Pratesi sheets. He glanced neutrally at where his wife, Helen, lay curled into a small, tight ball, on the right-hand side of the bed. The Panasonic clock radio on her nightstand was set for 8:20. By the time she awoke to her more cultured business day, he'd be in his midtown office, hard at work.

He stepped into the closet and swept his Nikes, sweatsuit, socks, and headband off a shelf. Then, padding over to the long, low, far-too-modern bureau—the most recent fruit of Helen's obsessive re-decorating—he fumbled a fanny pack out of a drawer, dropping a rolled-up change of underwear and his wallet, keys, and gold Rolex President watch into it.

After visiting the guest bathroom to relieve himself and brush his teeth, he went to the kitchen. The Toshiba coffee maker's brew light glowed green. The timer's digital display read 5:48. He decanted the pot into a large enameled mug decorated with a picture of the 47 Ronin, the souvenir of a visit to the Sengakuji Temple during a business trip to Tokyo. He emptied the grounds from the brewer basket, filled the machine's reservoir, and reset the timer for 8:15. Helen needed her morning coffee just as much as he did. Or maybe more so—Helen was far from sociable upon rising, and it was not until she opened the doors of her Lexington Avenue gallery that she put on her best behavior.

Warm, thick coffee slid down Dave's throat. He shivered with pleasure.

Something soft brushed his pajama leg. Dave reached down to tickle the cat's chin. *"Bon matin, ma belle,"* he said, knowing that all cats speak French of preference. The cat, who was named Apache, arched her neck, stretched, and purred.

Helen loathed Apache's name. She had insisted more than once that Dave change it. Second marriages produce more compromises than first marriages. Dave knew that, and knew that he should accede to his wife's request. But a cat's name is a cat's name; it has nothing to do with its owner's wishes. And so after five years of marriage Dave still called the animal "Apache," while Helen (who, being blonde, was used to having her way) icily referred to it as "that cat."

Apache padded away on her morning rounds. *"Au revoir,* Apache," Dave whispered, thus satisfying in some small way a sense of honor sullied by too many concessions.

Thinking improper thoughts about the difference between cats and cattiness, Dave retrieved the morning's *New York Times* from outside the apartment door. For the next several minutes, he sat at the dining room table nursing his coffee and flipping through the newspaper. He did not read it closely. His early morning ritual of scanning the paper was merely an excuse to enjoy the day's first cup of coffee.

As he turned to the business section he noticed that, quite unconsciously, his right hand had crept up to pat the left side of his chest. Dave grimaced. A sly, sardonic inner voice—Dave always thought of it as his guardian angel—whispered, *Still looking for a pack of cigarettes. Twelve years after you quit, and the body still wants its morning hit of nicotine. Say, pal, maybe you should get back into tobacco stocks after all.*

"Mornin', Mr. Elliot. Nice day for a run." The doorman believed it to be his duty to assure the building's joggers that every day was a "nice day for a run."

"Good morning, Tad. Anything in the papers today about Lithuania?"

Tad's ancestors had migrated to the United States in the 1880s. As far as Tad was concerned, it had been only yesterday. He was staunchly nationalistic about the land of his ancestors. Dave did not think that one day had passed, in the three years since he and Helen had purchased their apartment, upon which Tad had not had something to say about Lithuania.

"Nothin' in the *News* or the *Times*, Mr. Elliot. But I get the papers from Vilnius, you know, by mail. They usually show up on Wednesday or Thursday. I'll letchya know what's happening tomorrow."

"Great."

"Say, whatchya do to your hand?" Tad pointed at the gauze pad taped around Dave's left palm.

"An employee bit me."

Tad blinked. "Ya gotta be kiddin' me."

"Nope. We . . . my company that is, bought a research outfit out on Long Island. I was there yesterday on a tour. One of the . . . production workers expressed its disapproval of the new management." Dave grinned wryly. "And it wasn't even a hostile takeover."

Tad guffawed as he pushed the front door open. "You're makin' this up, right?"

"Nope. You get a lot of that in corporate life—biting the hand that feeds you."

Tad chortled again. "I guess I'm glad I'm just a doorman, Mr. Elliot. Have a nice day."

"Same to you, Tad. See you tomorrow."

"Sure, Mr. Elliot. Have a nice day."

On Saturdays and Sundays, Dave ran west, jogging across Fifty-seventh Street to Fifth Avenue, then north to Central Park. On those days, the running was purest pleasure. There were fewer menacing crazies on the street—or so it seemed—and the runner could concentrate on the running. Best of all, it was on the weekends that Mark came down from Columbia University to run at his father's side. Mark, his son, his and Annie's, was Dave's special pride. Running with Mark was the best part of Dave's week, the thing to which he most looked forward.

Dave always made a point of asking Helen to join them on their weekend runs. She never accepted. Helen found a jogger's sweat lacking in gentility, favoring instead chic perspiration extracted by pricey exercise centers, by even pricier private trainers.

No matter. Mark was with him, and, rain or shine, the running was a delight.

Less so the weekdays. No matter how you ran, no matter where you ran, watchfulness was called for. Certain blocks were to be avoided; alleys were a risk; none but the reckless jogged beneath bridges and overpasses; nor did the prudent begin their runs before dawn. On a morning run even a man like David Elliot, a man who did not have an enemy in the world, sometimes glanced warily over his shoulder.

His workday route took him east on Fifty-seventh to Sutton Place, then north on York Avenue until he reached a pedestrian bridge across FDR Drive. He ran up the path by the East River until he reached the high Nineties. Once there, he turned south again, retracing his steps. After crossing the bridge a second time, he

jogged west to Park Avenue, and then south to the corner of Fiftieth and Park.

It usually was just after 7:00 A.M. when he entered his office.

As an executive vice president of his company, David Elliot was
entitled to, and enjoyed, the perquisites of rank. His forty-fifth
floor suite consisted of eight hundred square feet of expensively
understated space, a walk-in closet, a discreet wet bar, and a full
bathroom with tub and shower.

Dave liked his water hot. Steam filled the bathroom as he lath-
ered himself from top to bottom twice over. Still in the shower, he
took a Gillette safety razor and a can of shaving cream from the
shelf above the spigots. He never used a mirror when shaving, and
hadn't for so long he couldn't remember. It was another habit he
had picked up in a war unwillingly remembered.

7:20 A.M.

David Elliot, with a towel around his waist, stepped out of the
bathroom and into his office. On the mahogany credenza behind
his matching mahogany desk, a Toshiba brewer, the twin of the
model at home, beeped three times, signaling that his coffee was
ready. Dave filled a chocolate-brown mug with it. The cup was
decorated with a raised, angular, silver-enameled design: the Senterex corporate logo.

Dave took a sip and sighed. Life without coffee is too awful to
contemplate.

He noticed, *damnit*, that the watercolor over his credenza was
askew. Every week or two, some dust-rag-wielding vandal from
the nightly cleaning crew knocked the thing sideways. It was a minor irritation, but one that was growing in its power to annoy.

He put his coffee cup on a brass coaster (also embossed with the
Senterex logo), and straightened the painting—Hua Yen, a portrait
of a sleeping tiger dating from the mid-1700s—quite lovely, quite
valuable, one of the nicer perquisites of working for Senterex. The
company's chairman, Bernie Levy, savvier than most corporate

moguls, let the purchase of executive artwork fall into the hands of neither high-priced interior designers nor, worse, his corporate officers' wives. Rather he demanded that quality art, only the work of masters, decorate the company's headquarters offices. For this reason a sextet of Leonor Freni chalks decorated the forty-fifth floor reception area. Orozco, Rouault, Beckmann, Barlach, and Ensor could be found in the hallways. Elsewhere, on the walls of various corporate offices, a visitor could find Picasso, Munch, Thomas Eakins (in the office of Senterex's chief counsel, of course), a most expensive Matisse, and a startlingly abstract Whistler. Bernie himself had a special affection for Camille Pissarro, two of whose oils hung on proud display in the corporate boardroom. Of course Bernie, being Bernie, denied that Senterex acquired art for aesthetic reasons; rather, when guests commented on the company's collection, he boasted of how much it appreciated in value, and the cash the company could accumulate were it sold. But Bernie lied. He'd never sell the Senterex collection, not a single piece of it. He loved it too much.

Dave stepped back, eyeing the tiger. It was straight again, or straight enough.

And now for a little music. He switched on his stereo. The opening bars of Ding Shan-de's *Long March Symphony* came softly through the speakers. Idly, Dave wondered why the American music establishment ignored the Chinese romantics.

Having no answers to his own question, and caring about cultural politics even less than he cared about the civic kind, Dave put the thought out of his mind. Instead, he reached for his coffee cup and took another sip. *God, that's good!*

Almost invariably Dave was the first person in the office—or at least the first in the executive suite. Bernie Levy, master of the corporate ship, didn't show up until 8:00 or so, his limousine leaving Short Hills, New Jersey, at 6:50 sharp. The rest of the executive cadre drifted in between 8:15 and 8:45, depending on what train they caught from Greenwich, Scarsdale, or Darien, and always much conditional upon that train running on time. The first of the secretaries arrived at 8:30 punctually.

For this reason, Dave knew he could, as was his unvarying morning habit, lounge buck naked (but for a towel) at his desk, savoring the day's second cup of coffee, and studying the pages of *The Wall Street Journal.*

Several peaceful minutes later, with a third cup of coffee in his hand, he ambled into his walk-in closet to select his suit for the day.

Today he chose a lightweight tan, almost khaki, number. Although the brutal humidity of the past summer had broken, the late September weather was still warm. Dave's wool suits would remain on their hangers for a few weeks longer.

With suit pants donned and belted, and feet comfortably placed in soft, glove leather Bally loafers, Dave unwrapped a fresh, starched white shirt. He put it on, and after some consideration selected from his tie rack a pale yellow tie with a blue motif. A full-length mirror backed Dave's closet door. He pulled the door three-quarters closed so that he could study himself.

Never learned how to knot a tie without a mirror, did you? his guardian angel asked.

He looked himself over carefully. *Not bad. Not bad at all.* His waistline hadn't changed since college. Forty-seven years old, but looking younger than that. *Oh, you handsome dog, you're going to live forever.* Dave nodded as if in agreement. The daily jogging, the two nights a week workout with weights, no smoking but for an occasional and much prized cigar, a diet about which even Helen couldn't complain, alcohol consumption that was modest by any . . .

"Davy?"

The questioning voice came from the office behind him—Bernie Levy's voice, its gruff Brooklyn accent unmistakable. Dave glanced at his Rolex. 7:43. Traffic must have been light this morning. Senterex's chairman and CEO was in the office well ahead of schedule.

Dave shrugged on his jacket, nudged his tie knot imperceptibly to the left, and gripping his coffee cup, pushed open the closet door.

"Yes, Bernie. What's up?"

Bernie was facing away from the closet. Dave didn't see his gun until he turned around.

2.

Here in the jungle there are two kinds of time—long time and slow time. Long time is what you usually get. You sit beneath a tree or in a hooch or in a field tent, or maybe you're tiptoeing Indian file through the boonies, and nothing happens. Hours pass, and nothing happens. Then you look at your Timex and discover that it has only been five minutes since the last time you looked at it. Long time.

The other kind of time is slow time. There's a flat metallic snap, the receiver of an AK-47 chambering a round. Then there is fire and explosions and screams and the whine of bullets all around and each one aimed at you for unending eternity. And when, after hours of hot terror, and no little rage, the shooting stops, you come back from hell and glance at your Timex.

Guess what? Five minutes have passed since the last time you looked at it.

Slow time. The clock gets choked with molasses. Men weep at how slow the seconds pass. They are MACV-SOG. Their shoulder patch is a fanged skull wearing a green beret. They are the hardest of the hard, the baddest of the bad. Nothing fazes them. They look at their watches. They weep.

One afternoon, the smell of cordite and hot brass still fresh in the air, First Lieutenant David Elliot places his blued-steel Timex on a rotten tree stump, slaps a full magazine into his Model 1911A Colt .45 automatic, and blasts the watch to fragments.

The pistol in Bernie Levy's hand seemed preposterously tiny. Bernie was five inches shorter than Dave and twenty pounds heavier. His hands were large and fleshy. The gun was almost lost in his grip. It was nickel-plated. Dave was willing to bet that the grips were ivory. *Small caliber*, Dave's guardian angel whispered. *Twenty-five? Maybe a .22. Not much stopping power. Enough at this distance, though.*

"Bernie, why do you have . . ."

Bernie looked exhausted. His eyes were red and ringed with dark smudges, as if he had been too long without sleep. His face, once all sharp and hawklike, had gone flabby with age. His jowls quivered with some emotion that Dave couldn't read. *How old is he? Sixty-three, isn't it?* Dave thought he should know precisely.

". . . a gun?"

Bernie's eyes were empty, the lids half closed. They looked reptilian, cold and empty. There was nothing in them at all. Dave expected to see something in them. He didn't know what.

"Why, in God's name?"

Bernie inched his hand forward, lifting the pistol.

Holy Christ, he's going to pull the trigger!

"Bernie, come on, speak to me."

Bernie rolled his lips, tightening them and then loosening them. Dave watched his hand tense.

"Bernie, you can't. Not without saying something. Bernie, for the love of God . . ."

Bernie's shoulders twitched. He licked his lips. "Davy, this is . . . If I only had a choice . . . You don't know, Davy . . . Bernie Levy blames himself, and God will not forgive. Davy, Davy, you can't know how bad this makes me feel."

Oddly enough, Dave almost felt like snickering. Almost. "This is going to hurt you more than it will me, huh? Is that what you are trying to say, Bernie?"

Bernie sighed and pursed his lips. "Always with the funny stuff,

Davy, always with the *wisenheimer spritz*." The hand holding the gun went tense again.

Slow time. Though the coffee wasn't scalding, it was hot enough. It seemed to take forever to reach Bernie's face, his wide-open eyes. The coffee burned right into them. Bernie yelped. Dave took one, two, three steps forward, his left arm low and straight. It took him hours to do it, walking straight into the muzzle of Bernie's wavering gun.

He swept Bernie's arm up, wincing at the pain in his bandaged hand. He drove a knee into Bernie's groin. Bernie made a noise like a punctured tire. The pistol tumbled loose. Dave snatched it from the air. Bernie was bent forward, his head at Dave's waistline. Dave brought the pistol butt down on the back of his skull. Hard. Twice.

Bernie lay still on the floor. David Elliot stood above him, gasping for air, waiting for the clock to recalibrate itself to normal time, but most of all wondering what the hell to do next.

Corporate office life is not without its moments of excitement. There are villains and heroes, triumphs and defeats, and clashes of eager ferocity. Friendships are made, and later broken; hard words are exchanged; there are bitter rivalries, and even open animosity. However, political infighting, not the physical kind, is the stuff of executive conflict; only on television, and then only in the sillier kinds of programs, do business people pull guns on one another.

Such thoughts, in a highly abbreviated form, flashed through David Elliot's mind as he tried to regain his breath. He spun through the past few seconds, finding in them no clue as to why his boss, a man whom he counted as a friend, would come after him with a loaded firearm.

Unless this was some sort of stupid joke.

A joke? Uh-oh . . .

Dave's stomach sank. Then he glanced at the pistol. A baby Browning. No toy. No ivory grips either. He ejected the magazine.

Eight rounds full. He racked back the slide. A bullet popped from its chamber and rolled to the floor. He picked it up. Hollow point, .25 caliber.

No joke.

What then? What could have driven Bernard Levy, whom Dave knew to be as even-tempered an executive as was ever born, to point a gun at one of his corporate officers?

Nothing. There was no reason in the world that could account for it. The very morning of the previous day, shortly before leaving to tour the new Long Island acquisition, Dave had sat in Bernie's office and reviewed a series of marketing reports with him. It had been a good meeting, warm and cordial, and had closed with Bernie endorsing Dave's recommendations.

There had not been a negative word. Not even a hint of one.

Something earlier? Not likely. Dave ran a handful of Senterex's two dozen divisions. He managed them smoothly, and the results were always as expected. There were no sources of conflict there.

Not that he and Bernie always agreed. Bernie was a deal-maker, a grand conglomerator of the old school. He had come up from the streets of Brooklyn, the son of immigrants. With no assets other than nerve, a nose for opportunity, and a flair for canny acquisitions, he had built Senterex from the ground up.

And Bernie still made acquisitions. He couldn't resist them. They were his life's blood. He loved finding smallish companies— sometimes marginally profitable, sometimes not—that he could buy on the cheap and then improve. Some he kept as part of the Senterex portfolio. Some he sold, but never at a loss. All fit his vision of financial synergy. Every now and then other Senterex executives didn't concur with Bernie's acquisition targets, and argued with him. Dave himself had strongly challenged Bernie's decision to purchase Lockyear Laboratories, and even more strongly resisted Bernie's subsequent assignment of responsibility for the operation to him once the deal was consummated.

But was that worth killing someone over? Never in a million years.

Could it be something personal? Had Dave done something outside the office to affront Bernie, to insult him, to humiliate or betray him? Not likely. Bernie lived a quiet, almost wholly private life. Dave never saw him socially. Although their relationship was more than merely friendly, it was largely limited to the confines of the forty-fifth floor.

Now Bernie wanted to kill him. Not a word of explanation. Just a gun, and mournful Bernie saying, "Bernie Levy blames himself, and God will not forgive."

"Hell, Bernie," Dave whispered, although he was only speaking to himself, "if you want to shoot somebody, for Christ's sake shoot somebody special. Not an ordinary schmuck like me."

Ordinary—David Elliot knew himself, knew precisely who he was, knew he was an ordinary man, devoutly committed to the ordinary predictability of an ordinary life. Sure, when he was young, little more than a boy off an Indiana farm, he'd wanted more than farm boys should—gallant deeds rewarded with medals and great renown. But he soon learned that those things came at a price. And so now, and for a very long time now, he was just an ordinary, ordinary guy. Hell, more than merely ordinary, he was a statistic. What is the profile of the average, upper-income corporate executive? David P.-for-Perry Elliot, that's what. Two marriages, one divorce, far from religiously ardent, a fiscal conservative and social moderate, ethnically hybrid, physically fit, fond of football, bored by baseball, reads less than he should, watches more television than he should, is boringly monogamous and slightly prudish, is nonetheless occasionally tempted, works an average of fifty-six hours a week, worries about the stock market, complains about his taxes, doesn't gamble, doesn't take drugs, and doesn't look forward to his annual physical exam. He vacations in the ordinary places. He socializes with the ordinary companions. He adheres to the ordinary codes. For twenty-five years, he's devoted himself to ordinariness. He has positively embraced it, wanting nothing else from life than what is ordinary. It is how he defines the word "good." He is, goddamnit, just an ordinary man and nothing more.

So why, Bernie, why the hell did you try to kill me?

David Elliot, an ordinary man, could conceive of no answer to the question.

Dave looked at his watch. It was 7:45 A.M. exactly. Two minutes. Slow time had ended. The thing to do, he realized, the only thing to do, was to get help. Maybe Bernie had suffered some sort of attack. Maybe brain damage or . . .

. . . *or whatever,* his cynical angel growled. *It's irrelevant. My friend, you've just cold-cocked the pistol-packin' chief executive of an $8 billion NYSE-listed company onto the floor of your expensively carpeted office. By definition, you now have problems that lie well beyond your competence as a businessman. Besides which, let me point out, you hit Bernie kind of hard. What happens if he is more than merely out cold? Like, for example . . . oh hell . . .*

Dave dropped the pistol into the pocket of his suit coat. He stepped out of his office, took one deep breath, and began to jog down the long carpeted corridor that connected his corner office with the rest of the executive suite. He was hoping that one of his fellow corporate officers had come in early. Or one of the secretaries. Or the receptionist. Or anyone.

He got as far as the reception area at the end of the hall. Two cold-eyed men were standing there, just around the corner. As soon as they saw him, they began reaching beneath their jackets.

David Elliot's clock slowed down again.

3.

Dave forced his face into a smile. "Good morning. I'm Pete Ashby. Can I help you?"

Both men froze. The eyes of the taller one narrowed, studying Dave's face.

"Are you waiting for Dave Elliot? He's usually the first one in, but I just walked by his office and his door is still closed."

The two men relaxed, but only slightly. Neither was as tall as Dave, but both were, by any measure, big—*real big, the kind of big that makes you think of weight lifters, professional wrestlers, and jackhammer operators.* The collars of their off-the-rack wash 'n' wear shirts were at least size 18. Their suit coats, brown and grey respectively (and not, Dave observed, entirely natural fiber), were of the sort of loose cut muscular men prefer—albeit neither was cut loosely enough to disguise the silhouettes of their shoulder holsters.

They don't know you, pal. Lucky you. They don't know what you look like. At best they've seen a photograph, and not a very good one. Stay cool, you may just be able to pull this off.

The taller of the two, a square-faced man whose close-cropped hair was turning grey, spoke. "No, Mr. Ashley . . ."

"Ashby, Pete Ashby. I'm vice president of engineering."

"Excuse me. Mr. Ashby, then. My colleague and I are here to see Mr. Levy." There was a trace of the Appalachians in his voice—eastern Tennessee, western North Carolina, somewhere in the mountains. It was an accent that many found musical, but that made Dave's skin prickle.

"Bernie's office is down the hall to your left. He usually gets in just about now. Do you want me to check for you?"

The taller man flicked his eyes left. It was the first time they had left Dave's face. "No need. He said he'd meet us here."

Dave felt sweat break out on his palms. The doors to the Senterex executive reception area were locked until 8:30. No one could get in without a key. "Can I get you some coffee or something, Mr. . . . ahh, I don't think I caught your name."

"John." There was a pause. The man didn't like to give his name. "Ransome. And my colleague is Mark Carlucci. We are . . . accountants. We're here . . . to go over the audit report with Mr. Levy."

Right. Coopers Lybrand is recruiting retired NFL linebackers to balance its clients' books. That'll be the day.

"Pleased to meet you." Dave observed that neither man offered to shake hands. "Now about that coffee? Let me get you some. We all have our own coffee makers on this floor. Most companies, you know, have a kitchenette or . . ."

Shut up, shut up, shut up. You're babbling. You'll blow it.

". . . well, mine's brewed up. I can . . ."

"No thanks, Mr. Ashey."

That was your second try, you cunning bastard.

"Ashby."

"Sorry. I'm terrible with names."

Dave's mind was racing. The two men had to be involved with what Bernie had done—or tried to do—minutes earlier. There could be no other explanation for their presence in the executive reception room at this hour. But how were they involved, and who were they? The holsters outlined beneath each man's suit coat told him . . . What? Were these guys cops? Mafia? The KGB? What kind of thugs had Bernie gotten himself involved with?

"Well, I ought to get to work. Bernie should be here any minute now. So if you'll excuse me . . ."

"Certainly. Don't let us keep you."

The reception area lay at the intersection of four corridors. Dave's office, like those of the other divisional executives, was at the distant end of the south hall. Bernie's suite was on the opposite side of the building, occupying the northeast corner and commanding the best view. The corporate staff officers—finance, legal affairs, human resources, and so forth—had their offices to the east. A short hall led west through double glass doors to the elevator bank.

Dave started to turn west.

Wrong, you idiot, wrong! You said that your coffee maker was on this floor. You said you were a corporate officer. You can't go to the elevators. . . .

He jerked himself to a stop. Both men were looking at him now. Their expressions had changed.

Dave tried to improvise a smile. He didn't succeed. "You didn't happen to see a stack of *Wall Street Journals* by the elevator, did you? They usually leave them right outside the glass doors." Weak, but it was worth a try.

The man who called himself Ransome slowly shook his head. His eyes had gone flat.

Dave nodded, and turned east. He walked across the reception room toward the hall. There was a small hot ache in the center of his back. He hadn't felt that particular sensation for twenty-five years, not since he was on patrol in Indian country. *Charlie's here. Charlie's got a gun. Oh my, now Charlie's leveling his sights. He's drawing a bead. He's tightening his finger. Hey, man, Charlie's getting ready to smile. . . .*

Every nerve in his body was on fire. Sweat broke out from his forehead and trickled down his cheeks. His throat scalded with rising vomit.

In the hall now. *Almost home free. Another ten seconds and you're out of sight.* He wanted to scream and run. He felt his knees quiver. The pounding of his heart was deafening. *Keep cool. You can make it same as you did in the old days. . . .*

There was a small nook two dozen feet down the hallway. It had been built to hold a photocopier that was never installed. As Dave passed it, he heard Ransome's softly drawling voice behind him. "Oh, Mr. Elliot, there's just one other thing."

"Yes."

Aw shit!

4.

Dave hurled himself into the nook. His shoulder butted hard against the wall. Four ragged holes burst open in the plaster.

Chalky fragments exploded into the air. The dust stung his eyes. He slid to the floor, fumbling Bernie's pistol from his pocket. Two more holes opened. The only sound he heard was the thud of bullets tearing into Sheetrock. Ransome and Carlucci were using silencers.

He tucked his feet back, seeking purchase against the wall behind him. He pulled back the slide on the small automatic and, as he released it, thrust himself forward into the corridor.

Carlucci was just entering the hallway, a step ahead of Ransome, his gun cradled in two hands. The muzzle was aimed high, well above where Dave lay. Dave fired twice, and two times more. Carlucci stopped. A bouquet of flowers, blood roses, bloomed on the pocket of his shirt. His mouth fell open. He whispered, "Mary, mother of God have mercy . . ." Dave rolled back into the nook.

Ransome, still in the reception room, snapped off a badly aimed shot, then dodged left and out of sight.

Dave looked curiously at the small, shiny pistol in his palm. *My, my,* his guardian angel opined. *Just like riding a bicycle, isn't it? Once you learn how to do it, you never forget.*

Ransome's voice, low but not inaudible, came from the reception area. "Partridge, this is Robin. Thrush is down. I have incoming. Repeat. I have incoming."

Great, he's got a radio and he's got a friend.

Ransome paused, listening to a reply that Dave could not hear.

"Affirmative on the weapons team, Partridge. Negative on the medic, it's too late for that. Negative on sealing the premises. This is supposed to be a private party. Let's keep it that way." He paused again. "For the record, six foot one, 170 pounds, medium build and very trim. Hair: light brown, parted on the left, expensive cut. No facial hair. Eyes: brown. No glasses, no distinguishing marks. Belay that. No distinguishing marks except for a gauze bandage on his left hand. Khaki-colored lightweight suit, two-buttoned jacket, no vest. White shirt, yellow tie with blue pattern. Gold cuff links with an onyx setting . . ." A second of silence. "An onyx is a shiny black stone, Partridge. Jesus, where do they find you guys? Continuing: black loafers, plain, with no bangles or tassels. Gold watch worn on left wrist. Wedding band on ring finger. One more thing—add an 'armed and dangerous' to the description." Ransome stopped again, then replied, "Right now? Right now he's cocky as a nigger with a knife. He thinks he's in control of the situation. But he's not." Ransome paused one last time, then said, "No problem. We can wait. Neither of us are going anywhere. Roger, forty-fifth floor, that's an affirmative. Robin out."

Ransome's voice was cool, without a hint of emotion in it, and his hill country accent made the small hairs on the back of Dave's neck rise. His heart was beating faster now, and his breath was coming short. That voice, that goddamned Appalachian voice . . . so much like the voice of Sergeant Michael Mullins . . . the very late Sergeant Mullins . . .

Now is not a good time for reminiscing, pal. Now is the time you've got to think. Think fast, and think . . .

". . . sharp, gentlemen." The survival training instructor is a slender, intense colonel in perfectly tailored fatigues. There is something about his bearing, the way he stands and the way he moves, that tells his audience that he knows his subject firsthand. The colonel is not talking about abstract theory. The topic of his lecture is hard-won personal experience.

"Gentlemen, would you like to know what we call a man who panics under fire? Let me tell you. Gentlemen, the technical term for a man who panics under fire is 'target.' That sort of soldier is the sort of soldier who gets chalked up on the other side's scoreboard before the end of the first inning. Accordingly, when you hear a round coming your way, you must not panic. You must not cringe. You must not feel the least apprehension or agitation. Instead, you must think. Thinking is the only way out. Only logic and reason will preserve you. And what do logic and reason tell us, gentlemen? What they tell us is this: when someone shoots at you, the only rational response is to—with dispassion and dispatch—render that enemy incapable of shooting at you again. There is, gentlemen, no reasonable alternative to this course of action."

Dave mentally reviewed the layout of the forty-fifth floor. The corridor in which he was trapped led east, passing a half dozen inner offices—cubbyholes occupied by the executive cadre's aides and assistants. The doors to those offices were spaced about twelve feet apart. At its far end the hall intersected another corridor—one that ran around the perimeter of the building. That's where the executives lived.

One other thing. The fire exits. There were three of them, heavy metal doors that opened on stairwells. One of them was . . . off this hall . . . where? Twenty or thirty feet away, he supposed. If Ransome was as good as Dave guessed he was, Dave would be dead long before he reached it.

But then, you're going to be dead anyway, aren't you? Ransome just said something about a weapons team. They're probably in the lobby, an elevator ride away. High side, pal, you've got maybe three, maybe four minutes of breathing time left.

Dave winced at his inner voice's jibe. Ransome, he thought. The only way out was through Ransome. Cupping his hand to the side of his mouth Dave called out, "Hey, Ransome."

"Yes, Mr. Elliot. How can I help you?" Ransome's tone was neutral, flat. He sounded, if anything, relaxed.

"I'm sorry about your friend Carlucci."

"No sweat. I barely knew the man."

"Good. Besides, I think you have to agree that it was your fault."

"Really, why is that?" Ransome did not sound the least interested.

"You're the senior man. Besides, you should have known that if I got past Bernie, then I almost certainly would have gotten his weapon."

There was a short pause before Ransome replied, "Point taken." His voice was still utterly unemotional.

Well, that idea's not going to work. You're not going to make him lose his cool. By the way, I bet the weapons team is in the elevators by now.

(Think, gentlemen. Think fast, and think sharp.)

Dave glanced around the nook. It was a little more than three feet deep with walls like all those in the executive suite, papered with a stiff, beige fabric. In six places, the covering was gouged open, jagged, and showing the empty places behind. There was nothing else to be seen except a small red box marked ALARM— FIRE.

Reaching up with his bandaged left hand, Dave yanked open the fire alarm box and tugged down the lever. A harsh siren blared through the halls. It sounded like a buzzsaw on sheet metal, and made the fillings in Dave's teeth ache.

Ransome raised his voice over the shriek. "No good, Mr. Elliot. We'll just call it in as a false alarm."

Dave shouted back, "Think about it, Ransome."

"What do you . . . Ah! Very good, Mr. Elliot. You've stopped the elevators, haven't you? The law requires they automatically return to the ground floor when an alarm goes off. That's just outstanding, truly superlative."

"Thank you."

"Congratulations, you've bought yourself some time that I didn't think you had. However, be assured that my people will use the stairs."

Ransome seemed to go silent. No . . . not silent. Dave could make out his voice, smothered by the sound of the alarm. He probably was on the radio explaining the situation.

Uh-uh. No good. You don't want him talking to his men, you want him talking to you.

"Ransome!"

"Yes, Mr. Elliot." As Ransome replied, the alarm shut off. The disappearance of the noise made Dave jump.

(You must not panic. You must not cringe.)

"Is Ransome really your name?"

"No."

"How about John?"

"No."

"Do you want to tell me what your name is?"

"No."

"Mind if I keep calling you Ransome? Or would you prefer John?"

Ransome thought about it. "Ransome is better."

"Okay, Ransome it is. Mr. Ransome, I've got a favor I'd like to ask."

"Go ahead."

"Tell me why you're here. I mean, what's this all about?"

"Sorry, no can do. All I can tell you is that it's nothing personal. I hope you appreciate that."

(You must think. Thinking is the only way out.)

Dave let a little bitterness creep into his voice. "Thanks a lot. So why can't you tell me? What is it, don't I have a need to know?"

"Something like that."

He's sniffing the bait. Now try a little whining.

"All right, then. What are my options? Can't we cut a deal or something?"

"I'm afraid not, Mr. Elliot. There is only one way to end this thing. The best I can offer is to make it easy for you. Reflect upon your military experience; you will understand what I mean."

Dave bit his lip. What did this man know about his Army record? And how dare he bring it up?

"What are you talking about?"

Ransome's voice warmed. The change in inflection was almost unnoticeable, but it was there. "Last night I read your old 201 file."

Just last night? What the hell . . . ?

Ransome continued, "It turns out that we went through the same school and the same classes, you and me. Uncle Ho's elite academy of elegant etiquette. You were an R.O.T.C. boy. Me, I was a 90 day wonder. Not that how we got there matters. What matters is that even though I was there ahead of you, we were in the same units, and the same places, and the same dire hell. We even reported to the same C.O. . . ."

"Mamba Jack," Dave blurted. This was bad, very bad.

"Yeah, Colonel Kreuter. I was on his team just like you were. And Jack only hired one kind of man—my kind of man, your kind of man. That kind of man."

Dave forced himself to laugh. "Ransome, are you trying to tell me you think I'm some sort of hard case?"

"You know it, buddy. They don't issue you a green beanie unless you are. You wore one. I wore one. We are who we are."

Dave didn't want to hear this. "Maybe. But I've been somebody else for a long time now."

"I don't think so. Once you're one of us, you're *always* one of us." Ransome's hill country voice was vibrant now, and he spoke with a warrior's pride. "It's like being a communist or being a Catholic. You can't ever quit. Not really. Think about it—you still have all the moves; you're still a pro. If you don't believe me, just ask Carlucci."

"I got lucky."

"I think not."

(Only logic and reason will preserve you.)

Dave raised the pitch of his voice, speaking faster and with calculated nervousness. "Okay, okay, what's your point?"

"My point is very simple. You pulled an honorable tour of duty, at least until the end . . ."

Dave snapped, "Some people would say that was the only honorable part."

"Yeah," Ransome drawled, "but we both know what kind of people *they* are. But my point is that you wore the colors, did the tour, and served with the best."

"So?"

"So, that buys you something in my book."

Dave sent his voice higher. "What?" He sounded almost shrill.

"One favor. Only one. First, you toss me that little sissy peashooter of yours. Then you come out and assume the position. You remember the position, don't you? On the knees, hands under the fanny. You put your head down, and I handle the rest. No muss, no fuss. That's the best deal I can offer you, Mr. Elliot. Clean, quick, and painless. Otherwise—well, hell, buddy, we're going to have us a messy morning here."

"Jesus!" Dave made the word sound like a squeak of terror. He wanted to sound almost—but not quite—hysterical. "That's your best offer? Jesus!"

"Think about it. It could be worse."

(And what do logic and reason tell us, gentlemen?)

Dave sluffed off his suit coat and counted to fifty. "Uhh . . .," he groaned.

"Come on, Mr. Elliot, be reasonable. Make it easy on yourself."

"You can't . . . I mean, we can't . . . ahh, talk this over? If you'd just tell me what the problem is . . ."

Don't lay it on too thick. He'll get suspicious.

"I wish I could, but I can't. Look, Mr. Elliot, way back when, you and I were in the same line of business. Remember how it used to be? Well, I'm sorry to say that's the way it is now. So, come on, Mr. Elliot, we both know how these things work, the same as we both know there's no other way. Face the facts, man: the longer you wait, the worse it's going to get. Please, Mr. Elliot, I'm asking you—wouldn't you rather make it easy on yourself?" Ransome's voice was soft, sympathetic, encouraging.

(The only rational response is to render the enemy incapable of shooting at you.)

"Uhh . . . I mean . . . uh . . . But can't we . . . uh . . ." Dave cocked his arm for a hard throw, and tossed his wadded-up jacket into the hall. A small hail of silent slugs shredded it to ribbons while it was still in the air.

Dave smiled, mentally tallying the number of times Ransome had fired. His inner voice, his guardian angel, sneered in a Daffy Duck voice, *Of courth you realithe thith meanth war. . . .*

5.

He hadn't hated war. Twenty-five years earlier he hadn't hated it one little bit. Other men did. But not Dave Elliot. Dave Elliot rather enjoyed it—or at least he enjoyed it until he realized what it was turning him into.

He especially enjoyed it when his enemies were good. The better they were, the happier he was. There was something about knowing your opponents were hardened, smart professionals that made it . . . that made it . . .

. . . almost fun.

"Ransome, I consider that to be a pretty goddamned unfriendly gesture."

"I understand your perspective, Mr. Elliot, but try to look at the situation from my point of view. I'm just trying to do my job here." There was not the least hint of an apology in Ransome's voice.

Come on, Ransome, do it. Please, Ransome, please. You know you have to do it.

Dave's heart was thundering. He forced himself to take long, deep breaths, hyperventilating, keeping his adrenaline high, pumping himself up for what he was about to do. Get psyched, get psyched, get psyched! That was what Mamba Jack had always barked just before the lead began to fly. Get psyched!

Yeah!

"I thought we were supposed to be comrades-in-arms."

"I want you to know that I was sincere about that, Mr. Elliot."

Listen for it. Get ready. The muscles in Dave's legs tingled. His face burned red with anticipation. He obsessively rubbed his thumb rapidly back and forth against his index finger.

"You know I'm not going to believe another word you say."

"I can respect that."

Any second now. Any second . . .

The sound was very faint. Just a tiny click—the noise made, Dave prayed, by a magazine being ejected from a pistol butt.

That has to be it. If it isn't, you're about to die.

He jerked down hard on the fire alarm lever, using it to pull himself to his feet. The siren squalled, filling the hallway with its grating shriek. Dave spun out of the nook, stretching his legs, pumping his elbows, running headlong as hard and as fast as he could, running as he ran every morning but running faster, running toward where, if the gods chose to smile on David Elliot, the man who called himself John Ransome crouched with a temporarily empty gun.

And the gods did smile. Ransome was stretched prone on the reception room floor, his head and shoulders angled into the hallway in a classic shooter's sprawl. An empty clip lay under his chin. He was off balance, rolled sideways to reload. As Dave hurtled forward, he saw anger flit across Ransome's face. The man knew that he had been suckered.

Well, thank you, Mr. Ransome. It was most kindly of you to lie down in that position—excellent for target practice, but a little lacking when it comes to mobility.

Ransome snaked back, raising his arms defensively. Dave was five feet away. Ransome pulled into a crouch, started coming out of it.

It was going to be close. Too close. He'd have to use Bernie's gun, and he didn't want to do that unless he had to. And he'd have to unless . . .

The one thing, his instructors at Fort Bragg had told him, the one thing you never, *never* do in hand-to-hand combat is kick your opponent. Forget everything you've ever seen or heard or read about karate, judo and kung-fu. Forget Batman and forget Bruce Lee on that *Green Hornet* TV show. That's Hollywood stuff, not the real world. In the real world, there are twenty different things your opponent can do to you if you've got a leg up in the air, and nineteen of them make you dead. *Never kick!* The drill sergeants had screamed it over and over again. *Never kick!*

He kicked Ransome in the face.

Same school and same classes? Is that what you said, Mr. Ransome? If so, you weren't expecting that particular move, were you?

Dave's heel caught Ransome squarely under the left cheek, snapping his head back and spinning him over, belly-up. Dave cocked his right elbow into a spear, dove forward, came down hard onto—into—Ransome's solar plexus. Ransome's face went white. Dave drew his arm back, flattening his palm, aiming a killing stroke at the tip of Ransome's chin.

He never delivered the blow. Ransome's face went slack, and his eyes closed.

Dave levered his right arm across Ransome's neck with choking force. Ransome didn't move. Dave peeled Ransome's right eyelid open. Only white showed. Most people can roll their eyeballs back. A trained man can fake unconsciousness persuasively. Dave flicked a finger against the white of Ransome's eye. There wasn't the slightest twitch. No one can fake that. Ransome was out cold.

David Elliot wanted a cigarette more than anything else in the world.

According to the contents of his wallet, John Michael Ransome was a vice president with something called The Specialist Consulting Group. The late Mark Carlucci was a senior associate with the same organization. Neither of the two men's business cards showed an address, only a phone number: area code 703—Virginia. Nor was there a home address on either's driver's license, only a post office box number—the same box number for both Ransome and Carlucci.

Now there's a little coincidence for you. Dave's inner voice, at least for the moment, was sounding a little smug.

"Sparrow, this is Partridge. Report." Carlucci's radio was miniature, black, and bore no manufacturer's stamp or other indication of who produced it. Carlucci had worn it clipped on his belt. Now Dave wore it clipped to his.

"Roger. This is Sparrow. There are one goddamn lot of stairs in this sucker."

"Where are you and what's your E.T.A.?"

"We're on thirty-four in the south stairwell, and the men need a breather. Give us three, Partridge."

"Is three more minutes acceptable to you, Robin?"

Dave answered, trying to mimic Ransome's soft Appalachian drawl, "Affirmative on that."

"Roger. Take a break, Sparrow. Partridge out."

Whew.

Dave backed away from Ransome. Even though the man was unconscious and bound with his own belt, Dave didn't want to take his eyes off him—nor the sights of the very odd pistol he had removed from the late Mark Carlucci's hand.

You gotta give that shootin' iron some thought.

Later. Not now.

He lifted the telephone on the receptionist's desk, punched 9 for an outside line, and dialed the number on Ransome's business card. There was a pause while the call connected. The phone at the other end of the line rang once before a mechanical voice answered, "Enter authorization code."

"Hello, I'd like to speak to Mr. Ransome's secretary."

"Enter authorization code now." It was some sort of a robot, a computer telephone operator. Dave pushed a few of the telephone buttons, entering a random number. "Access denied." Click.

Dave shrugged. If he was going to get answers, he would have to get them somewhere else. In the meantime . . .

He stepped back to where Ransome lay. The man was still unconscious. Even if he was awake, Dave doubted if he would tell him anything. Ransome was not the kind of man who could easily be made to talk. It would take hours of interrogation—MACV-SOG-style interrogation—to break him down.

Dave started to drop Ransome's wallet onto the man's chest. He stopped, frowned, and opened it. He fingered the bills inside. Eighty-three dollars. He really didn't like doing this.

Aw, go ahead. How many times can they hang you?

If he was in as much trouble as he thought he was—*what better definition of trouble is there than having a team of bad attitude gunmen on your case?*—then he would need cash. It would be suicide to use his credit cards. Every card transaction in America is captured electronically. Buy something in a store, and the sales clerk slides your card into one of those little grey Verifone terminals to log your purchase into a distant computer. The Verifone box automatically registers the identity of the merchant entering the transaction. If someone wants to know where you are—precisely where you are—all they have to do is tap a few computers. And if you're stupid enough to use a cash dispensing machine, the job is even easier.

Dave folded Ransome's bills over twice, and put them in his pants. Then he emptied Carlucci's wallet. Sixty-seven dollars. He knew he should have picked Bernie Levy's pocket as well, but it was too late to do it. He'd already been back to his office preparing a little surprise for Ransome's weapons team. It wouldn't be a good idea to enter it again.

Instead he walked to the west fire door, and entered the stairwell. With any luck, he'd find help only three flights away.

6.

Fire stairs—every office tower has them. Usually they're concrete, but sometimes steel. It all depends on the building code. Dave's were concrete.

The stairwell reminded him of a prison movie—Cagney and Raft circa 1939. The walls were featureless, uniform, grey. The cold monotony was broken only by insulated pipes and, every five floors, by a red-enameled cabinet containing an emergency fire hose.

The stairs themselves were wide enough for three people to walk side by side; they wound from the top of the building to its ground floor, quite perfect in geometry, a spiral in cement. There was a seven-by-twelve-foot concrete platform at every floor, and another halfway between each floor. Fifty floors, one hundred platforms, and twelve stairs linking each platform to the next. No landmarks but for enameled metal plates announcing the floor number.

At every platform, the stairs turned 180 degrees. Twelve stairs up, turn. Twelve stairs up, turn. Twelve stairs up, turn. If you ran too fast, you'd become dizzy.

Dizzy . . . If you've got a problem with heights, you don't want to look over the railing and down the stairwell.

Dave gnawed his lip. The gap between the spiraling stairs was wide enough for a man. If you wanted an easy way to end it all, you need do nothing more than step through a fire door, cross a platform, straddle your legs across a cold iron banister, and . . .

My, aren't we in a cheerful frame of mind this morning?

The top five floors of the building housed Howe & Hummel, attorneys-at-law. Harry Halliwell, senior partner and Dave's lawyer, occupied an oversized corner office on the forty-eighth floor. Like Dave, Harry was an early riser and a committed jogger. The two often arrived at the corner of Fiftieth and Park Avenue at the same time, Harry running north from his Murray Hill townhouse, Dave coming from the opposite direction.

He counted Harry not only as his lawyer, but also as his friend. Five years earlier, when Dave and Helen wed, Harry had been the best man and his wife, Susan, had been matron of honor. At least once a month, and sometimes more frequently, the two couples went out together for a night on the town. Once they had gone on a vacation to Hawaii together, although Harry had spent most of his time on the beach with a cellular telephone glued to his ear.

If there was anyone who could help Dave now, it was Harry. Shrewdly logical and disarmingly soft-spoken, Harry Halliwell was a lawyer's lawyer. More than that, he was one of those rare men of unquestioned integrity whom both politicians and corporate potentates term "an honest broker." He was called upon to arbitrate conflicts between unions and management, between business and government, and sometimes even between nations. No matter how bitter the disagreement, Harry always managed to negotiate a compromise that both sides felt was fair.

Harry seemed to know everybody, and everybody seemed to know him. His clients ranged from Forbes 400 moguls to Mafia chieftains. There was no problem that Harry Halliwell couldn't handle.

Including, one hopes, counseling a client who suddenly seems to have a contract on his head.

Dave raced up the stairs, taking them two and three at a time, running as he had all his life, and running perfectly. When he reached the forty-eighth floor, he wasn't even breathing hard.

He pushed the fire door. It didn't move.

He jogged the handle. It was locked. A fire alarm was supposed to unlock all the building's doors automatically. Either something had gone wrong, or Ransome's men knew their business.

The fire doors are one-way only. They open from the inside, but are locked on the outside. In this town there are too many desperadoes to do it any other way.

No problem. Dave might not be able to use his American Express Platinum Card to buy his way out of trouble, but that didn't mean he couldn't use it at all. His instructors—not the Special Forces trainers at Fort Bragg, but the other ones, the ones who never mentioned their last names—had taught him, among other less-than-licit skills, how to shim a lock.

The latch clicked. The fire door swung open.

Moments later he was outside Harry's office. Harry's door was cracked. The lights were on. He could hear Harry's muted voice on the telephone.

Dave tapped on the door and then entered. Harry was stretched out in his chair, still dressed in his running gear. His feet were resting on top of the cluttered, much-scarred Parsons table that he used as a desk. Behind him, his bookcases overflowed with loose paper, bound volumes, and an astonishingly untidy collection of bric-a-brac accumulated, who knows how or why, over the course of his thirty-plus year career.

The lawyer looked up at Dave, raised an eyebrow, and spoke into the telephone. "Yes. Yes. I do understand. Really. Don't worry, Congress will come around. I've spoken to Bob, and I think we can find a common ground. No, I think not. Really. Indeed. Well, now I have another appointment I must move on to. Certainly. Oh, and sorry I missed Chelsea's birthday party. I trust she got my gift. Good. Of course. Think nothing of it. Yes, good-bye."

Harry sighed as he set the telephone down on the cradle. "Ahh, me." First he frowned, then he looked up smiling. "It's that time of year again. Appropriations hearings. One would think that after two hundred years of practice the executive and legislative branches would have learned how to reach accommodation." He gestured at a silver Tiffany decanter. "Coffee, David?"

"Thanks. I need it."

"Have a seat, and tell me what brings you to my chambers at this unholy hour?" Harry hefted the decanter. He looked at it and grimaced.

Dave pulled up a chair. He tried to frame some appropriate way to say what had to be said. He couldn't. Instead, he blurted out, "Harry, this is nuts, but Bernie just tried to kill me."

Halliwell's eyebrow shot up again. He removed the decanter's lid and peered inside. "You are joking of course."

"No joke. And he wasn't alone. There were these two other guys—gunmen, Harry."

Halliwell shook the coffee pitcher and frowned. "Hmpf. I seem to have emptied this in rather less than a half hour's time. No good for your heart drinking that much coffee. Gunmen, you say? Well, they couldn't have been very competent, could they? Not if you're . . ." He stopped, holding the decanter in mid-air, and studied Dave's face.

Dave nodded. "It's not a joke, Harry. There's a dead body on the forty-fifth floor. Maybe two. I'm in trouble."

Harry pulled his feet off the desk. He stood and whispered, "You *are* serious, aren't you?"

Dave nodded again.

"How did you, ahh, manage to . . . well . . ."

"Good luck, Harry. Old reflexes and good luck. And if I wasn't in the kind of shape I'm in, I think I'd be dead."

Harry's eyebrows reached their ultimate height, hovered for some few seconds, and then fell into a frown. "Uh . . . well. My, my, my . . ."

"I need help."

Harry smiled his most practiced and professional smile, the one that made his clients feel better. "And you shall have it. But first you shall have some coffee. As shall I." He walked out from behind his desk. "Whatever this . . . well . . . problem is, Dave, it strikes me as one that shall involve the consumption of rather more caffeine than is good for either of us. I will go fetch a fresh pot."

So saying, he walked past Dave and toward the door. He didn't time his next act correctly. If he had, Dave would not have caught the arc of heavy silver out of the corner of his eye.

Dave lurched left. The coffee pitcher smashed down on the back of his chair, missing his skull by less than an inch. It tumbled from Harry's hand and rolled across the carpet.

"Harry! What the hell . . . ?" Dave was on his feet. Harry, his face contorted and red, was backing toward the door.

"You're a dead man, Elliot! A dead man!"

Dave stood stunned, his mouth open. Something made of acid and ice uncoiled in his stomach. "Harry . . ."

But Harry turned and ran.

7.

So far, he had been operating on intuition and no small amount of luck. Now he needed a plan.

Ransome was a professional, and so were his people. There would be men in the lobby watching the elevators and fire stairs. Ransome had told them what Dave looked like and how he was dressed. At this time of day, the lobby was empty. Ransome's people would spot him in a second if he tried to escape from the building.

Nor was there any question of finding a phone and calling for help. He couldn't call a friend, call his wife, call his brother. He couldn't even call the police. At least not right away. Not until he knew why—why, why, why—his boss, his best friend, and several people he didn't even know seemed to want him dead.

Because if they wanted him dead, they might want some other people dead too. And David Elliot had no intention of putting any-one he cared for in harm's way.

Besides, he could make it on his own. At least for a little while. Maybe longer than that. After all, in the old days they'd trained him well—gratifyingly well. It seemed his body had not forgotten the lessons that his mind had long rejected.

That scared him. It scared him more than Bernie had. Or Harry. Or Ransome. Or the sound that bullets make, close, too close, to where you cower.

Beneath the skin, after all these years, it seemed there still lived the man he had almost become. And no one—neither Ransome, nor anyone else—terrified him more than *that* man.

Dave had to find a place to hide—to hide and reflect and plan. He thought he knew where to find it.

Now he was on the fortieth floor, Senterex's working class district and home to the corporation's lowest echelons. There was no high-priced artwork in this part of the corporate castle. Most of the floor was given over to a maze of partitioned cubicles occupied by junior accountants, order entry clerks, and other worker bees. They were strictly nine-to-fivers. The entire floor was sure to be empty.

The fortieth was also the floor where the employee cafeteria was located, a white-walled room furnished with Formica-topped tables, and containing a bank of vending machines. Dave walked past it, stopped, and turned around. He wanted something from the cafeteria. *Two things, actually . . .*

He slid a stolen dollar bill into the change machine. Four quarters jingled into the change slot. He pumped two of them into the coffee machine. A paper cup tumbled into the dispenser. The machine burped and spat steaming brown liquid into the cup. Dave lifted it.

Ouch! It's damned near boiling!

He took a sip. It was scalding, far too hot, and . . .

Blah! Ugh! Terrible! Christ, that's the worst coffee you've had since the Army. If I worked in this joint, I'd file a complaint with the Environmental Protection Agency!

He hesitantly took a second taste. *Nope, it isn't going to grow on you, and you don't want it to.*

Dave walked over to the counter where the cafeteria's condiments and tableware were stored. He thought momentarily about dosing his coffee with a suspiciously colored substance labeled "Imitation Coffee Creamer Substitute," but decided against it. Instead, he selected two stainless steel forks and a table knife from the collection of utensils. Then he walked briskly back to the corridor.

Now where is it? It used to be just around the corner and . . .

The door was painted a scuffed off-white. There were two locks set in it, one the standard lockset used in all Senterex office doors and the other a heavy-duty deadbolt. A grey embossed sign hung next to the door: ROOM 4017, TELEPHONE ROOM.

The deadbolt would be a problem. Dave pursed his lips, remembered lessons from long ago, and set to work with the forks.

CHAPTER 2
THE OLD
SWIMMING HOLE

1.

In every business and in every corporation there is at least one high-ranking executive who, no matter how competent his or her people may be, believes that they are not quite competent enough—but that they can be made so. Easily. Overnight. All it takes is a little training, a little inspiration, a little exposure to the right motivational training program.

Ahh, but which one is the right one? There are, after all, so many.

Such executives know deep in their hearts that the "right" program really does exist. It is a magic elixir that, once found, will alchemically transmute ordinary corporate drones into nonpareil paragons of productivity. This one simple thing, this philosopher's stone, is perhaps to be found in a book, or on a videocassette, or in a computer software program, or, most likely of all, is the surefire result of a three-day seminar staged by some oddly named company headquartered (inevitably) in Northern California.

No matter. Wherever it is and whatever it is, it exists, and once located will have on the staff the same effect the word "SHAZAM" has on Billy Batson—a clap of thunder, a bolt of celestial lightning, and behold: Captain Marvel!

It was David Elliot's misfortune that in Senterex, the chief acolyte of this particular dogma was also the chief executive, Bernard E. Levy. Bernie's enthusiasm for the latest rages in chic managerial theory was unquenchable. He embraced them all, each and every one, with religious zeal. Worse, having been born again in the church of this, that, or the other new high priest of corporate productivity, he insisted that his entire executive cadre join him among the ranks of the converted.

During his six-year tenure on the forty-fifth floor, Dave had been subjected to the ministrations of quite nearly a dozen motivational ju-ju men, managerial messiahs, and behavioral gurus. He had sat through interminable weekend seminars staged by temporarily popular business school professors, wallowed with his fellow executives in hot tubs at the Esalen Institute, and sweated with them in saunas at the Aspen Institute. He had jogged side by side with his wheezing and purple-faced boss at an *In Search of Excellence* "skunkworks bootcamp," and, a year later, had helped carry him down from the mountain upon which, during an Outward Bound "team-building adventure," Bernie had sprained an ankle. On another occasion, Bernie locked the entire managerial cadre in a windowless room at the University of Arizona, demanding that they spend a day silently typing "brainstorming" ideas into personal computers. There had even been something called a "Wolverine Management Seminar," a program that, as far as Dave could tell, consisted principally of sitting around the conference room and growling an ardent desire to eat the hearts of Senterex's competitors raw.

Just a few months earlier, Bernie had recruited the services of a self-styled "organizational psychologist." The man, who, like most of Bernie's pet witch doctors, operated out of California, came to . New York to subject Senterex's top managers to an interminable regimen of pattern recognition tests and elliptic question-and-answer sessions.

Dave remembered the only one of these sessions from which he'd learned something about himself—or, for that matter, about anything else.

The psychologist had subjected Dave to a series of free form association-preference questions.

"What's your favorite color?"

"Green."

"Any particular shade?"

"Emerald green."

Green as a green bottle.

"What's your favorite car?"

"What I drive? A Mercedes."

"No, what would you like to drive?"

"A Porsche."

"An emerald green Porsche?"

"No. I think a yellow one."

"Yellow is a sexual color. Did you know that?"

"No, but I'm not surprised."

"If you were reincarnated as an animal, what animal would you like to come back as?"

"A sea otter."

"Why?"

"They just float with the tide, don't they?"

"What animal would you expect to come back as?"

Dave didn't answer.

"Come, Mr. Elliot. What animal would your fate—your karma, as it were—cause you to be reincarnated as?"

Dave shook his head. "I have no idea. I like to run. Maybe I'd come back as some sort of deer or something."

"Ah, the hunted not the hunter."

"If you say so." But the answer that formed in Dave's mind, the karma he feared himself to have, had nothing to do with herbi-vores.

"Do you have fantasies?"

"Of course."

"Power fantasies?"

"Don't we all?"

"Achievement fantasies?"

"Certainly."

"I don't mean success."

"I know that."

"What achievement do you fantasize about? What ultimate achievement? The pinnacle of your dreams?"

Without thinking Dave blurted, "Mark Twain." Then he blushed.

The psychologist looked perplexed. "Mark Twain? Would you explain that for me, please?"

Dave felt uncomfortable. He had never mentioned his Mark Twain fantasy to anyone, not even to Helen, who would not have appreciated it anyway. In fact, he had barely admitted it to him-self. He stuttered, "The achievement I dream about is . . . well . . . I'd like to write a book . . . a book about Mark Twain. In fact, I'd like to write a study of his life and works. That's what I dream about."

"A best-seller?"

"No, not necessarily. But critically . . . well, acclaimed would be nice, wouldn't it?"

"Now this is very interesting, Mr. Elliot. Most business people of your seniority fantasize about sports—buying a baseball team, be-coming a PGA champion, sailing around the world, and things like that. But you, Mr. Elliot, you dream about something else entirely. You dream of becoming an erudite literary figure. This is excep-tionally peculiar."

Once upon a time, David himself would have agreed that it was, indeed, exceptionally peculiar.

2.

Once upon a time, a young man wants to be a lawyer, but his ultimate goal is more ambitious than that. Becoming a lawyer will be only a step along the way. In the end, he wants to be in politics. The Senate, the governor's mansion, a member of the Cabinet, perhaps even . . . well, who knows how far he can go.

He'll need a degree from a prestigious law school, Harvard or Columbia of preference. And, he'll need grades good enough to clerk for a Justice of the Supreme Court—or, at a minimum, a Court of Appeals judge. Then he'll spend a few years working for the state government, making contacts, building relationships with the right people. After that, he'll be ready to run for office. First, the state legislature. Later something higher. The public life is what he has been made for.

He grins as he frames the witticisms he'll make during televised debates. Already he can see his smiling photograph in the newspapers, on campaign posters, on magazine covers . . . standing in the spotlight, on the platform, behind the rostrum . . . proud and upright and popular and dynamic and respected and a leader of men . . . and, of course, a champion of the people. Always that. That more than anything else. He will be the man they call "the conscience of the Senate," or something similar. Just like Jimmy Stewart in that old movie, he will be the one who . . .

These are daydreams, of course. He uses them to keep awake while, at a wage of seventy-five cents an hour, he works the graveyard shift in an aluminum extrusion plant some twenty miles from the university. Between classes and homework, between R.O.T.C. drill and the job he holds to pay his tuition, he usually manages to get four hours of sleep on weekdays. He catches up on the weekends.

He is shooting for cum laude. He almost makes it, but not quite.

He doesn't mind R.O.T.C. Drill is relaxing in a mindless sort of way, and the classwork is undemanding. His only objection to the Reserve Officer Training Corps is that—in this year when more American boys enroll in it than ever before—it obliges him to associate with the jocks, frat boys, and engineering majors who actually enjoy playing soldier. It is a minor objection, easily outweighed by the stipend the program pays, and, when he reflects on it, by the certainty that an honorable military record—ideally with a decoration or two—will be an important asset for a rising young politician.

He gets his decorations, all right. One of them is a Bronze Star.

But by then the medals are irrelevant, as is a record of military duty bravely served. He abandons his political dreams before the court-martials even begin. Instead of yearning for a public life and political power, David Elliot decides that he wants to live his years as comfortably, even prosperously, as he can; but regardless of comfort and regardless of prosperity, to slip through the world as silently as possible, leaving no footprints behind.

The village of My Lai is still fresh in the Army's mind. Four or five hundred civilians, they never can quite agree on how many, methodically slaughtered by the baby boys of Company C. It being war, and the victims being blameless and unarmed civilians, all the time-honored traditions are followed. Torture. Rape. Scalp-taking. The conventional customs of war.

Enough of it has leaked into the press that the powers that be are mightily embarrassed. But they're even more embarrassed by Lieutenant David Perry Elliot.

So when the time comes for the court-martials, They (with a capital "T") decide to move slowly, cautiously, and with a great deal of secrecy.

The protracted procedures involved result in Dave having nothing but time on his hands. He is confined to base, forbidden to communicate with the outside world. Apart from his daily—some would say obsessive—workouts, the only recreation open to him is reading.

He's never been much of a reader. High school had seen him consume the obligatory works—all carefully selected to demonstrate that reading is, or at least should be, dull. In college, between his night job and his classes he had little time for anything other than textbooks. Nor has his subsequent career, involving as it did the practice of covert warfare, lent itself to leisurely reading.

However, for these months of waiting for the trials to begin, he has little to do but read. What he reads is what he finds, largely such worn and much-thumbed volumes as are stored in the day room of the Bachelor Officers' Quarters.

Two passages that he reads make upon him a singular impression. The first is by Hiram Ulysses Grant, later, due to a clerical error at West Point, renamed Ulysses S. Grant. The second is by Mark Twain.

Here is the first, written while he was dying by possibly the greatest, surely the most reluctant, general America ever produced: "Experience proves that the man who obstructs a war in which his nation is engaged, no matter whether right or wrong, occupies no enviable place in life or history. Better for him, individually, to advocate war, pestilence, and famine, than to act as obstructionist to a war already begun."

And here is the second, good Sam Clemens speaking: "Patriotism is patriotism. Calling it Fanaticism cannot degrade it; nothing can degrade it. Even though it be a political mistake, and a thousand times a political mistake, that does not affect it; it is honorable—always honorable, always noble—and privileged to hold its head up and look the nations in the face."

David Elliot has been reading, and re-reading, Mark Twain ever since.

3.

Safe behind the telephone room's locked door, Dave talked things over with his cynical guardian angel.

Let's tally up the facts in the case of the likely to be late David Elliot, shall we, pal? Maybe there's some sort of sense you can make of this mess. Maybe you'll even find a clue as to how to save your butt.

Probably not.

True, but it's not like you've got anything better to do with your time. So, first question: Who is Ransome and who are his pals?

Dave answered silently: All I really know is who he was and where he came from. Special Operations. Covert warfare. Just like me—in Army uniform, but not entirely under Army command. Not merely raw muscle either. They never recruited muscle just for muscle's sake.

And what else?

A survivor. No kamikaze pilots need apply. We don't do heroes and we don't do Custer's last stand. That's what Mamba Jack kept telling us.

Brains, brawn, and an instinct to survive. Your basic sine qua non for the biz. So now what do you know?

Not much. After the war ended most of us in that line of business simply came back home, hung up our spurs, and tried to get on with our lives. Those who didn't—well, some of them stayed in, or so I heard. Not necessarily in the Army, but still on active duty.

So maybe Ransome is a Fed?

No way. Why would someone from the government want to kill me? I don't have anything to do with politics. I don't sign petitions. I don't join causes. Hell, I don't even vote.

Still, the Feds have been known to . . .

Nuts! I doubt if I have so much as spoken to a government employee in twenty-five years.

What about year twenty-six?

Not possible. If they had wanted to shut me up, they would have shut me up then. Not now. It would be crazy to wait all this time. Besides, those days are ancient history. Nobody cares anymore.

Maybe. Maybe not. And if Ransome isn't one of Los Federales, then what is he?

Who knows? A merc maybe. After the war some people took their skills elsewhere. Became mercenaries—trusted advisors to the local dictator in Singapore, Iraq, Ecuador, or wherever. One year I'd see them mentioned in some story about Chile or South Africa, and the next year I'd hear they were in Ethiopia or Guatemala. Colonel Kreuter, good old Mamba Jack himself, started his own company. War Dog, Inc., he called it.

You think Ransome comes from Kreuter? That after all these years Mamba Jack is settling his bill?

No. If Jack ever decides to pay off old debts, he'll do it personally. Not that that's any consolation.

So?

So, I'm still in the dark.

What about the mob?

Not possible. Businessmen don't do deals with gangsters except in the movies. Least of all does Bernie Levy deal with them. He wouldn't touch anything the mob was involved in. He's the most ethical businessman I've ever met—the original Straight Arrow.

Straight Arrow just tried to shorten your life span with a Browning.

I'm aware of that.

What about Harry? He defended that guy, Joey whatshisname, the Mafia kingpin from New Jersey.

Harry Halliwell might defend a gangster, but he'd never go into business with one.

Not the Feds, not the mob. Maybe it's Con Ed, mad because you forgot to pay the light bill.

Oh, give me a break! I don't have enough information to even guess what's going on.

You have some information. Like for instance, Ransome saying that he read your 201 file.

My military personnel jacket. That crack he made about my service being honorable until the end means he knows what's in it. But no one is supposed to know that. They sealed the records. They're stamped "Top Secret," and buried in the vaults of the Army Judge Advocate General. Nobody could read my 201 file unless he carried a high-level security clearance. Or knew someone with a clearance.

Another puzzle: It was Bernie rather than Ransome who came to pull the trigger. What do you make of that?

Ransome is a pro. My guess is that he's been in the business—whatever his business is—all his life. He's good at it, and killing people doesn't bother him one little bit. So, why did he send Bernie to do it? If the contract was on me, and Ransome was there, why did he let a civilian like Bernie Levy try to do the job?

Think about the mise-en-scene, pal.

Right. Right you are. I'd almost missed that. They tried to do it in the office. Why there? Why didn't they just take me out from a moving car while I was jogging, or put one behind my ear while I was walking home at night? There's only one answer to that. The answer is that early in the morning on the forty-fifth floor of a Park Avenue high-rise, there aren't very many people around. Nobody to watch. Nobody to ask questions. It would have been very quiet, and no one ever would have known. Remember Ransome said, "This is supposed to be a private party. Let's keep it that way."

And, therefore . . .

Colonel John James Kreuter is slouched behind a field table in a candlelit hooch. No one calls him Colonel Kreuter. They call him Mamba Jack. The nickname pays tribute to the Black Mamba, a snake whose venom is a neurotoxin, the most swiftly acting and lethal poison in the world—one bite and ten seconds later, you're history.

Mamba Jack is proud of his nickname.

A three-quarters-full bottle of Jack Daniel's Black Label sits before the colonel. The stub of an unfiltered Lucky Strike dangles from his lips. He takes one last, deep drag, and flicks the butt to the dirt floor. He smiles at Dave. His teeth are phenomenally white, and he has the longest set of canines that Dave has ever seen.

"Well now, here's our young Lew-tenant Elliot lookin' all bright-eyed an' bushy-tailed." Mamba Jack speaks with a long East Texas drawl, the accent of a redneck born and bred. Unless you had been told, as Dave has been by the company clerk, that Colonel Kreuter had graduated third in his class at West Point, you would think him to be an ignorant hick.

"I think the time done come for yew to loose yer virginity, Lew-tenant."

"Sir?"

Kreuter leers. It makes him look like Disney's Big Bad Wolf, and he knows it. "I got a li'l job for yew. Seems like Charlie's got hisself this ol' Roosian KGB major up there north of the Dee Em Zee. Now this here Roosian he's become a bit of a botheration. Seems like he's a-passin' out guns an' he's a-passin' out supplies an' he's a-passin' out advice. Now, I don't much mind the guns, an' I don't much mind the supplies, but that advice—why, son, that just irks the living hell out of me. Become a real burr beneath my saddle, as it were. So what I want yew to do, Lew-tenant, is yew take some men up 'cross the Dee Em Zee an' communicate to this aforementioned Roosky Mamba Jack Kreuter's sincerest displeasure with the sit-e-achyun."

"Sir. You want me to bring him back?"

"Naw. What for? Hellfire, what would I want with a smelly ol' Roosian? Can't speak to him. Don't know the language. 'Sides which, nobody don't need no live, palpitatin' Rooskies lyin' around. Got enough po-lick-tickle trouble as it is."

"Termination, sir?"

"Yessir, Lew-tenant Elliot, that is the accepted terminology. But y'ain't a-gonna do it messy. No bodies, an' no evidence. What we want, Lew-tenant Elliot, is for that ol' KGB major's boss to worry some. Want him to worry that his boy done cut an' run. Worry that he's down our way a-talkin' an' a-gabbin' an' a-singin' his li'l heart out. Want him to have nightmares 'bout that there major showin' up on teevee a-talkin' to Mike Wallace an' good ol' Walter Cronkite. Yew got that, Lew-tenant, yew know what we want yew to do?"

"Yes, sir."

"An' that is, what, Lew-tenant?"

You remember what you answered, of course? Dave's sarcastic angel asked.

David Elliot, slumped on the linoleum floor of the Senterex telephone room, smiled ambivalently at the memory of his answer: "Yes, sir," he'd said. "You want the major to get disappeared."

Right. And now somebody wants you *to get disappeared.*

4.

In the early 1970s, when Dave was beginning his business career, telephone equipment rooms were large, noisy places. All the equipment was electromechanical—endless banks of chattering relays and clicking switches. It took work to maintain the PBX systems in those days, and a team of telephone company men usually would show up to tinker with the hardware once or twice a week. Dave, whose first position was in the administration department of what was then called the First National City Corporation, remembered them. They always seemed to be big guys, a little overweight, with cigar butts clinched between their teeth. They all wore heavy grey work pants and answered to Irish or Italian names.

Most important, they kept lockers in the telephone rooms. Spare clothes, overalls, jackets, sometimes workboots. Dave had hoped to find something similar in the room containing Senterex's switching equipment. No such luck. The days of the electromechanical PBX had gone. Modern telephone systems are small, compact, and computerized. The only sound they make is the whir of their cooling fans.

Yes, there was a locker in the room. But all it contained, apart from shelves of miniature electronic parts and spools of colored wire, was two back issues of *Hustler* magazine, a tool belt, and a pair of gloves. Only the belt and gloves would be useful for what Dave had in mind.

The one other useful thing in the room was a wall-mounted beige telephone. After more than an hour of hard thought, Dave had decided to use it. He'd call his brother. Not Helen. Helen didn't handle crises well, and was swift to assign him blame for anything that went wrong. Dave had long since decided that if his second marriage was going to work (and he badly wanted it to), he and he alone would have to handle the rough spots.

Rough spot? A category into which the present moment fits nicely, don't you think?

Better to call his brother than to deal with Helen. Frank would be flabbergasted, but at least he could be relied upon to act. All Helen would do was . . . *"bitch" is the word you're looking for . . .* complain. That and ask accusatory questions he didn't have the time to answer—didn't have answers to anyway.

Dave eyed the phone, checked his watch, and was ready to make the call when Ransome's Appalachian drawl crackled over the radio. "This is Robin."

"You okay, Robin?" Dave recognized the voice—the man called Partridge. His accents were crisp and military. Perhaps he, like Ransome, was a former officer.

"More damage to my pride than anything else, Partridge." Dave nodded approvingly. Ransome's answer was just right. Exhibiting a little chagrin (but *never* apologizing) is the smartest thing a commander can do after screwing up a mission.

"All right," Ransome continued, "I want a full status, but before you give it to me, I want you to get on the horn to homebase and order up taps and traces. I want the subject's little black book of phone numbers locked up and locked down. His wife, his ex-wife, his kid, his brother, his doctor, his dentist, his broker, and the guy who shines his shoes. His neighbors and his friends. Everyone he knows. Bug them all, and bug them now. If the subject calls anyone, pull the plug. I do not, repeat, do not, want the subject uttering one single word to anyone. Copy that, Partridge?"

"Affirmative. I'm on it."

"Sir?" Another voice. Not Partridge, and not as professional.

"Yes, Bluejay," Ransome answered.

"Sir . . . uh . . . given the situation, the subject escaping and so forth, do you think we could be given some background on the . . . uh . . ."

"Negative. You know what you need to know."

"But, sir, I mean . . . like, why are we after this guy? Wouldn't it help if we knew the reasons for . . ."

"NFW on that, Bluejay. Don't ask questions. Trust me on this, you're better off not knowing."

"Sir . . ."

"Robin out." The radio went silent.

Dave chewed his lip, drew his hand back from the phone, and changed his plans. But later he used the phone anyway. He called 411—information.

His watch read 9:37. It was almost time to go.

He sipped the dregs of his now tepid coffee and grimaced. There is little art and less expense involved in making a halfway decent cup of coffee. He wondered why the distributors of coin-operated dispensing machines couldn't master the job.

Dave rose, hitching the tool belt around his hips. It was made of wide, tan leather, and was hung with screwdrivers, pliers, a pair of wire strippers, a soldering iron, a holstered blue telephone test set with dangling leads, and one or two odd-looking implements whose functions he could not fathom. The belt had been a nice find; it would help alter his appearance. He stuffed a pair of thick work gloves over the front of the tool belt, hiding the distinctive buckle of the Gucci belt that held up his tan trousers.

Nobody looks at the telephone man. He's part of the furniture.

Dave had changed the part in his hair, sluffed off his tie, removed his collar stays, untaped the bandage on his left hand, and rolled up his cuffs. His watch and wedding ring were in his trouser pocket. Thick wedges of dirt were caked beneath his well-manicured nails. He planned to walk with lips slightly parted, breathing through his mouth. Just another blue-collar worker trying to do his job.

His shoes were his biggest problem. They were far more expensive than a telephone repairman could afford, and looked it. He prayed that no one would notice them, and cursed himself for not having the sense to retrieve his Nikes from his office closet.

Another problem: he needed to use the bathroom. He thought momentarily about leaving his bolt hole and trotting down the hall to the men's room, but decided it wasn't worth the risk. The pressure on his bladder was sufficiently uncomfortable that he did not wish to wait the fifteen minutes or so before he intended to leave the telephone room, the fortieth floor, and the Senterex building itself. The planned circumstances of his impending departure left little leeway for a trip to the head. And, once out on the street—well, there aren't very many public toilets on the island of Manhattan, nor do prudent people use them.

Reluctantly, he urinated in the paper coffee cup, filling it to its brim.

A new voice came over Carlucci's radio. "Robin, do you read me?"

Ransome answered. "Robin here."

"This is Myna. Robin, there's been a screw-up."

"Seems to me there's been more than one." Ransome spoke without inflection.

"Affirmative. However, this one is a current issue. Homebase just took Thrush out of his body bag and started the procedures."

"So?"

"Inventory reports his weapon is missing."

"No surprise."

"So's his radio."

There was a long moment of silence. Then Ransome muttered flatly, "I am exceptionally disappointed to hear that."

"The subject has been listening to every word we've said."

"I already worked that out, Myna. Attention all stations. All right, ladies, listen up. I have something to say. I want our Mr. Elliot to hear it too. Mr. Elliot, please acknowledge."

Dave's thumb twitched toward the transmit button. He didn't push it.

Ransome took a deep breath and blew it out. "Mr. Elliot?" he said. "Mr. Elliot? Very well, have it your way. You have so far. The rest of you people, pay attention. I am going to outline the agenda for the rest of this little soiree."

Ransome's tone was smooth. He spoke slowly and clearly, with not the least trace of emotion. "I want double teams on the ground floor. I want extra watchers on the elevators and the stairs, and two reserve teams on call outside. Partridge, tell homebase to order those people up here ASAP. Mr. Elliot, I imagine that your current thinking calls for attempted exit during the lunch hour or at the end of the business day. You are, I presume, hoping that you won't be noticed in the crowd. But you will be. Bank on it. You are *not* going to get out of this building. Now, as you have no doubt deduced, there is a security blanket on this operation, and we really don't want to alarm the civilians. It will be business as usual for all the good folk and gentle people who work in these premises.

Tonight, after everyone has cleared out, we'll run a floor-by-floor sweep. Partridge, alert homebase that I will be requiring dogs. Dogs, Mr. Elliot. I am confident that they will get a good solid taste of your scent from the running gear you stow in your office. Unless I miss my bet, it will be over well before midnight."

Ransome paused, waiting for a reaction. Dave gave him none. Instead he stood still, his head cocked slightly to the left, listening to an unwelcomely familiar vocabulary and vocal rhythm.

"No comment, Mr. Elliot? So be it. Let me say with all candor, that I find your conduct this morning to be unseemly. However, in light of your service record, I suppose I should not be surprised. You know, I trust, the portion of the record to which I refer?"

Dave winced.

"Well, you surprised me. Perhaps you even surprised yourself. And speaking of surprises, you may rest assured that the booby trap you rigged in your office performed as per specification. It cost us ten minutes figuring that one out."

Dave had gimmicked Bernie's .25 automatic so that it would fire into the floor as soon as someone opened his office door. He had hoped Ransome's people would think he was in there, making his last stand. Apparently they'd fallen for the trick.

"Another thing, Mr. Elliot. I have examined my weapon. What you did to it was a nice touch. Please accept my compliments. If I hadn't found that paper clip you wedged in the muzzle of my pistol, the next time I fired a round I would have had a nasty surprise, wouldn't I?"

If that's all you found, you still *may be in for a nasty surprise, you jerk!*

"Now I'm thinking that there is more to the merry hell you are raising with this operation than your fine training—the best Uncle Sam could provide—can account for. What I'm thinking, Mr. Elliot, is that it's in your blood. I think what you are doing just comes naturally. That makes you an especially dangerous man."

Ransome paused again.

"But then, so am I."

Dave felt his lips tighten. Ransome was turning up the heat. He had something in mind . . . something drawn, no doubt, from one of the standard psychological warfare textbooks.

"I've lost two of my troops so far, one to your marksmanship and one to an unfortunate accident outside your office. I do not wish to lose another. Therefore I am going to offer you a proposition. Given your present circumstances, you would be well advised to accept it. I hope, therefore, you will do the reasonable thing, and cooperate."

Reasonable? Good God! The man is trying to kill you, and he wants you to cooperate!

"The deal is as follows. I will contact my superiors and I will seek their approval to communicate certain facts to you. I hope to persuade them that, if you are made aware of these facts, an accommodation can be reached. It may be possible to negotiate a revision of my current orders. Those orders, as I am sure you have concluded, are of a sanctionary nature. To do that—for you and I to discuss the terms upon which the sanction can be canceled—we will have to speak. So, Mr. Elliot, please do as I tell you. It really is quite important. Momentarily we will be changing the encrypt codes on our radios. Once that is done, you will be unable to descramble our transmissions. Indeed, you will hear absolutely nothing. However, do not, I repeat, do not discard your radio. Keep it with you at all times, and keep it activated. Should my superiors determine that we might arrange an amiable conclusion to this affair, I will reset the encrypt codes so that you can hear me. Let me reiterate that. Keep your radio on. I will be using it to contact you again, relatively soon I hope."

Ransome halted, then added, "I really would appreciate an acknowledgment, Mr. Elliot."

Aw, go ahead, say something. Get it out of your system.

Dave depressed the transmit button and spoke. "Ransome?"

"Yes, Mr. Elliot?"

"Up your poop with an ice cream scoop."

Ransome inhaled sharply. "Mr. Elliot, I am coming to believe that you lack the maturity one expects of a man of your age and experience. Nonetheless, and despite your unseemly comment, I am going to give you a very important piece of information. It is something that I should not say, but I'm going to say it anyway. Right now you think your best case scenario is to get out of this building and into the streets. Well, Mr. Elliot, I'm here to tell you that it is *not* your best case scenario. Indeed, it is your *worst* case scenario. If you get out of this building, what will happen is worse than any worst case scenario you ever dreamt of."

5.

The radio went dead, just as Ransome promised. Dave shrugged, slipped it into his shirt pocket, and reached for the phone. His call was answered on the first ring. "WNBC-TV, Channel Four Action News. Can I help you?"

When he first concocted his plan, Dave thought it would be best to speak with an accent—Irish or Arabic or vaguely Hispanic. But for the scheme to work, he would have to sound credibly foreign, and he wasn't sure he could manage that. It was simpler to sound like an ordinary, conventional lunatic. New Yorkers were used to those.

Babbling as fast as his tongue would let him, Dave spewed out the words: "Can you help me? No. But I can help you. I can help everyone. And I will. I've had enough. *Enough!* Now I'm going to do something about it. Remember that movie. 'I'm mad as hell, and I'm not going to take it anymore.' Well, I'm not going to take it anymore. That's why they're going to die!"

"Sir?"

"Rivers of blood. The opening of the seventh seal. Behold a pale horse, and his name that sat on him was Death. I am Death, and I am come today upon the unrighteous. Thus with violence shall that great city Babylon be thrown down, and shall be found no more. I bring the fire of the Lord this morning, and it will purge evil from the earth!"

"Sir, I'm not following you."

"Without are dogs, and sorcerers, and whoremongers, and murderers, and idolaters, and whosoever loveth and maketh a lie. That's what I'm saying, and I'm saying that today they are cast into the pit!"

"Yes. Yes sir, but can I . . ."

"The corner of Fiftieth Street and Park Avenue. Send a camera crew. Just tell them to point at the middle of the building. They'll see it. This morning. Soon. Satan and his legions are going out of business. They are going out of business with a bang. Do you take my meaning? With a bang!"

"Sir? Sir? Are you still there?"

"I am. They won't be! They'll be in hell!"

"Please, can I ask you a question? Just one . . ."

"You cannot." Dave hung up the phone. He allowed himself a satisfied grin.

6.

Minutes later he heard the sounds of the evacuation. A moment after that someone rattled the handle of the telephone room door and called out, "Is there anyone in there? Hello? We've got a bomb threat. Everyone has to get out of the building."

Success, Dave's acerbic guardian angel crowed. *The television people called the cops. The cops sent the bomb squad. Ransome couldn't stop them from ordering an evacuation if he tried. And he wouldn't dare try— because, if you were a guy like Ransome, you'd know that it just might be true. Some loony-toon actually could have planted a bomb in this build-*

ing. The odds might be a hundred to one against it, but it could happen. And you'd know that if you did try to stop an evacuation and if a bomb did go off, then you, a.k.a. John Ransome, would be swimming in a sea of sorrow.

The doorknob rattled again. "Anyone there?" Dave didn't answer. He heard whoever it was walk away.

He forced himself to wait. After a little time, it became quieter outside. Only a few hurried footsteps passed. Then it was silent. He flicked the thumb latch and pushed the door open. He stepped out, looking left and right. The corridor was empty. He peered down it, studying the distant wall of the intersecting hallway. He listened for the echo of heels on linoleum, looked for a shadow against the beige painted plaster.

It's not really beige, is it? More of a light taupe or a café au lait, don't you think?

Who gives a damn what color it is?

Just trying to be helpful.

Satisfied that everyone had left, Dave sprinted up the hall, turned right, and ran past the cafeteria. Empty. Everyone gone. Next stop . . .

The accounting department's bullpen. Five thousand square feet of commodity office space, separated into eight-by-eight cubicles by grey . . .

More of a dove color, I'd say.

. . . fabric dividers. Each cubicle contained a small desk, a chair, and a two-drawer file cabinet.

The dividers were low enough for Dave to peer over. He hurried by them, glancing into each cubicle as he passed. In an environment carefully designed to eliminate individuality, each cubicle's occupant had injected a small personal touch. Here a Garfield doll crouched on a file cabinet; there a flower vase with fresh cut irises; elsewhere photographs of children or their crayon drawings tacked to the grey, or rather dove-colored dividers. One or two art posters; a photograph of a castle in Bavaria and another of a man and woman, their arms around each other, standing on a bright gold beach; an amateur oil painting; a model plane; a framed piece of pseudo-needlework reading, EMPLOYEE BEATINGS WILL CONTINUE UNTIL MORALE IMPROVES.

But nowhere could he find what he needed. And time was short.

There! Whoops. No. Not those. They're a woman's.

Dave ground his teeth in frustration. It was such a simple thing. So simple, but so important. It should have been easy. There is always someone who . . .

Aha!

A pair of reading glasses. Wire-rim, a man's style, about the right size. Somebody farsighted had set them down before evacuating the floor. Most bomb scares are false alarms. The owner of the glasses wouldn't need them, wouldn't want them while he walked down the stairs. He was sure he'd be back in a few minutes.

Dave put the glasses on. His world turned tiny, slanted the wrong way, and out of focus. He removed them and popped the lenses out. From a distance no one would notice—he hoped—that the frames were empty.

Bound to work. In a crowd, you'll just be another big galoot with glasses. No tie, no jacket, tool belt, wearing glasses and a pair of slacks that could pass for khaki workpants—yeah, you'll make it. None of them but Ransome has ever seen you face-to-face. Pal, you're out of here!

And indeed he was—down the hall, around a corridor, through a fire door, into a stairwell and then . . .

Aw, hell.

There were people on the stairs, and not merely stragglers. The occupants of the upper ten floors were still coming down. Hundreds of them. The stairs were packed.

First the good news: Some of those people might come from the forty-fifth floor. They could be your friends. Now the bad news, you thought Bernie and Harry were your friends. . . .

Dave glanced at faces. Nobody looked familiar. He stepped into the pack. Nervous, alert, he listened to every voice, trying to catch the tones of someone he might know or who might recognize him.

". . . probably the Arabs, again."

"No, I was in the office when the call came in. They think it's the damned stupid Irish."

"I'm Irish."

"Oh. Well, then . . ."

Nope. He'd never heard those voices before.

Just ahead of him. Two women. ". . . so he says he thinks he can move me out of the word processing pool on a direct report to him. But, I don't know, he's so creepy."

"Honey, he's a lawyer. They're *born* creepy!"

He knew neither of them.

Two more voices, even farther ahead. Dave strained to hear them. ". . . with a formal proposal letter in two weeks. Not that they'll accept our proposal or pay our fees. That particular company never does."

"Why? They know somebody has to do the job, don't they?"

The speakers were two men, one younger, one older, both impeccably attired and expensively coiffed. Dave guessed they were management consultants from the firm of McKinley-Allan, headquartered on floors thirty-four to thirty-nine. Charging price tags of $3,000 and up for a day of professional time, McKinley-Allan was, if not the bluest of the blue chip consulting organizations, surely the most expensive.

The older man, probably one of the senior partners, answered in a voice reminiscent of Orson Welles, "The reason, as our more insightful partners will allow, is that in the final analysis the consultant's profession is not dissimilar from that of the common prostitute—the competitor we must always fear most is the enthusiastic amateur."

The younger man guffawed a little too loudly. The older shot him a look. Dave recognized his movie star profile. It was Elliot Milestone, one of McKinley-Allan's best-known partners.

You've only met him once. He probably doesn't remember you. Be careful anyway.

Another voice, this one behind him. It spoke a language only heard in boardrooms and executive suites—mellifluous multisyllabic corporate executive-ese: ". . . tell Bernie that we ought to seriously consider moving the company out of New York." Dave jerked. The speaker was Mark Whiting, Senterex's chief financial officer. "The taxes are horrendous, the commute is unspeakable, and who the devil needs to put up with walking down forty-five flights of stairs every time some lunatic decides to phone in a bomb threat?"

"I couldn't agree with you more." It was getting worse and worse. The answering voice belonged to Sylvester Lucas, vice chairman of Senterex. "We've received development proposals from Arizona, New Mexico, Colorado, New Hampshire, and Ohio. . . ."

"Forget Ohio."

"Most assuredly. Nonetheless, they all afford appreciable benefits in taxes, labor costs, and other expense categories. Accepting any one of them would drop better than one additional point of margin to our bottom line. At the current P/E, that would bump our market cap by an appreciable sum."

"The P/E would go up too."

"Just so. Those of us whose compensation package involves a healthy spicing of stock options would enjoy certain gains."

"Well, hell. Why don't you bug Bernie? Bring it up at the next Board meeting."

"Indeed. I would be bugging Bernie, as you put it, at this very moment, were it not for this unfortunate business with Dave Elliot."

"Em. Yes. I was told—strictly on the QT, you know—that it was some sort of flashback episode. Vietnam. I gather it is not unknown among those who had the misfortune to serve."

"Oh? That would explain it."

"And some other things as well. This Ransome chap told me quite a lot about our good colleague. It was not a pleasant story. Apparently there have been other episodes. I intend to bring the whole matter before the Board."

"Ah. Well, Bernie has called for a meeting later. . . ."

The eighteenth floor landing was just ahead. As Dave reached it, he drew back, facing the wall and fiddling with his belt until Whiting and Lucas passed. He was having trouble breathing, although he was not at all out of breath.

7.

The closer the evacuees came to the ground floor, the less they spoke. Many were winded and gasping. A handful slumped against landing walls, massaging out-of-shape thighs.

David Elliot's legs felt fine. His runner's muscles could take more punishment than forty flights of stairs could dish out.

There was a door just ahead of him—dull, matte green, and dented. A large "2" was painted on it. Just in case someone missed the point, a sign overhead read SECOND FLOOR.

This is it. Last stop coming up. All off, please. Please be sure to check the overhead bins for your personal belongings. . . .

The worst that could happen was that Ransome would be waiting on the ground floor, standing next to the door from the fire stairs, scrutinizing every face that passed. If he was, then someone was going to die. Ransome wouldn't have his gun out. Dave was sure of that. But he also was sure that Ransome's hand would be close to his pistol, that he wouldn't hesitate to use it, and that he'd make his apologies to the witnesses later. If Ransome was waiting, Dave would have only a second or two to . . .

Kill him.

Right.

With a screwdriver.

Through the heart.

Then you run.

Then I run.

Dave tightened his hand around a long Phillips screwdriver. He drew it out of his tool belt, holding it flat against his leg. The muscles in his right arm coiled, tense and ready.

He reached the bottom of the stairs. Ahead of him the crowd shoved through the fire door and into the ground floor lobby. Dave pushed behind them, his eyes flicking right and left, his screwdriver ready.

Ransome was elsewhere. Dave wiped his palms against his trousers. He could feel the dampness through the fabric. That was bad. The screwdriver could have slipped out of his fingers.

So far so good. You really didn't want to shiv him anyway. You're out of the shivving business.

And have been for a long time.

Dave took a slow, deep breath and tried to concentrate on what was going on around him. Something was wrong. The lobby was packed. No one was moving. The crowd was pushing forward, but not getting anywhere. And tempers were rising.

It does not matter whether he or she is a Harvard-trained lawyer or a Queens-born cabby. New Yorkers are New Yorkers, and when their voices are raised in the very special anger that only frustrated New Yorkers can muster, all speak with the same accent. "Come on, move it, toots." "Who you calling 'toots'?" "Whadsdamatta up dere?" "You think I'm in charge of this Chinese fire drill or something?" "Hey, jerk, get yer hand off my butt." "It wasn't me, lady." "My ass, it wasn't." "Let's go up there!" "Put out that cigarette before I put it out for you." "Try it." "Quitchyershovin'." "Look, youse, some Ay-rab is plannin' on torchin' dis joint any minute now, so get the lead out." "Who you callin' a Ay-rab, you wop?" "In your ear, guy." "Yeah?" "Yeah!"

The bottleneck was at the bright, glassed front of the lobby. Four of the six revolving doors leading to Park Avenue were out of order. That left two sets of revolvers and a pair of regular doors as the only exits.

I bet those doors didn't jam by accident.

The crowd surged forward across the lobby. Dave was still at the rear, and still a long—too damn long—way from the street and from safety. His height was sufficiently above average that he could see over the heads of the packed mass of bodies in front of him. He searched across it, looking for points of danger.

There they are.

Four teams of men stood clumped by the exits, off to the side where the crowd wouldn't jostle them. They were big, like Ransome, and wore the same kind of off-the-rack suits as he. Each man's arm was bent at the elbow, resting across his chest, ready to reach beneath his jacket.

Pushed from behind, Dave had no choice but to move forward. He kept his eyes fixed on the watchers. The watchers kept their eyes fixed on the faces of the evacuees nearest the exit.

The man beside Dave growled, "Goddamned landlord can't maintain the goddamned doors in the goddamned building. Welcome to goddamned New York goddamned City." Dave ignored him.

Just behind him a woman yelped, "Ouch, you're on my foot!" Dave lifted his shoe. "Sorry, lady."

"Geez, some people . . ." Dave tuned her out.

Now he was at the rear elevator bank. The building was served by two sets of elevators, one for the top twenty-five floors and one for the lower twenty-five. Each bank was set in its own dead-ended corridor off the lobby. Between them was a third, shorter corridor housing the building's newsstand.

He heard something. At first it didn't register on him. It was just another voice in the crowd, albeit a little louder than most. He almost missed it. His attention was focused on the men by the door. If she hadn't repeated herself, he would have ignored her.

"There he is! Over there! Look! Over there! Look!"

Then it registered. He turned his head. He saw . . . he was confused . . . he couldn't believe . . .

"That's him! There! There he is! Get him!"

8.

In every boy's life there is, or should be, a pond. Ideally, this pond is to be found in a remote and private place, far from the eyes of adults. It should be deep (for diving), cool (for the heat of summer), and surrounded by tall, leafy trees (for meditative loafing).

In the best of all possible worlds, it also will be a little dangerous.

Dave's pond is perfect, a nonpareil. It lies beyond a low string of hills—just steep enough to be spared plowing and planting—and down a shallow valley. Three miles of bicycling among tall corn and toasty blowing wheat brings him to the hills. Fifteen minutes more, straining and pushing his bike every step of the way, and he is standing by its shore.

It is three quarters of a mile wide, and a half mile across. Most of it is fringed with green-brown cattails and pussy willows. A wobbly, ill-built raft—no more than planks and rusty fifty-gallon drums—drifts in its center. No one but boys of a certain age ever visit it.

Perfect.

Dave first was invited to its sacred precincts when he reached the age of ten. It is understood that those of younger years are not welcome at the pond. And it is understood that those older than fifteen are, in their growing maturity, expected to find other summer recreations. It is a place for boys, and intended to remain eternally thus.

Not that the adults don't know of it. Far from it. They all are aware of its existence, and all, to a man and to a woman, forbid their offspring to go there. "That pond—you'll get tetanus if you swim in it. Besides, it's full of cottonmouths, and the bottom is nothing but quicksand."

Great! Quicksand! And snakes! Wow!

Although, in truth, Dave and all his friends have never seen so much as a grass snake in the hollow. And as for the quicksand . . . well, the boys know that if any of their number had ever been lost to quicksand, the story would have resounded for a hundred miles around, and lasted for a hundred years. Since no such story is current, the quicksand theory can be discounted.

Except . . .

Except that one of the most notable allures of the pond is its depth, which is very great indeed. Try though they might, none has ever dived deep enough to reach bottom. Thus, the existence (or lack thereof) of quicksand cannot be confirmed. Maybe the peril is real after all. Maybe the bottom of the pond is treacherous muck that will grab hold of your legs like a gigantic, slimy octopus and suck you screaming and thrashing down, down, down . . .

Or, maybe there is something else at the bottom of the pond. Something alive. Something that gets you and leaves no trace. Something with teeth and appetite that gives rise to rumors about quicksand, but in reality is a gigantic . . .

. . . pike, with fangs . . .

. . . squid like in that movie . . .

. . . clam like in that other movie . . .

. . . dinosaur, an ichthyo-whatchyamacallit . . .

. . . snapping turtle, five hundred years old and so big . . .

Well, they have to dive, don't they? It is essential. It is the done thing. No boy can resist it. One of them will succeed. Certainly. Someday, someone will. And when he does, his heroic name and brave achievement will ring down the ages.

Dave dives. The other boys do cannonballs off the raft, or push off its side, or plummet in a deadman's fall. Dave dives. He works on it, perfecting his spring up, his fold over, his straightening into a perfect jackknife that slices down through the water, deep, and deeper still.

One day he triumphantly makes it to the bottom.

The pond water is brown, thick, muddy. You can't see your hand before your face. The deeper you swim, the darker it becomes. Eventually, there is nothing, no light at all except for a dull bronze glow way away and far above you.

On the day he reaches the bottom, even that bronze is gone. Dave has passed beyond where the light can penetrate. He claws downward blindly, knowing that he has made it farther than anyone else, into a realm no boy has ever reached. Satisfied at this accomplishment, and despite the fact that he knows he should turn back, he pulls another stroke, straight down, cocking his arms forward. His hand brushes something.

Slime. Slippery. His heart is in his mouth. *The squid!* No, strands of something. What? Weeds. Weeds on the bottom. *I made it!* He wraps his hands around them and pulls himself down. Careful now, it really could be quicksand. No, just ordinary mud. He jerks at the weeds. He wants evidence, proof that he, David Elliot, has finally done the thing to which all aspire. The weeds come away easily.

Time to go now. Been here too long. Need air.

He kicks up. He has pushed his luck going so deep, staying

down so long. His face feels red with the strain of it. Saliva fills his mouth. He really needs air. The surface can't be far, can it?

He swims harder, taking long powerful strokes. This is getting bad. There is a sharp pain around his sinuses. His lungs are aching.

He can see the bronze glow. Brighter now. Not far to go. *Everyone on the raft is going to go nuts when they see what's in my hands.* Red spots, match flames in the dark, dance before his eyes. Bright. Very bright. Any moment the air . . .

His hands smash into something. If he hadn't been pulling into a stroke, he would have cracked his head into it. He does anyway. But not hard. That doesn't matter. What matters is that he needs air now. *Now, please, God, now!* And something is holding him down, keeping him from the air, trapping him in the cold dark water, killing him, drowning him. Brass bands tighten around his chest. He has never known anything to hurt as much. Any moment now his mouth will open, water will rush in, his lungs will fill, he will drown and die. He pushes and struggles against the thing holding him in the water, in the dark, away from life and air. It is malevolent and active and evil and hatred personified and it wants him to die and he can't get past it and he will open his mouth and scream and . . .

It is the raft. He is beneath the raft. He shoves away and bursts gasping, blue-faced and empty-handed, into the air.

Until he reached the age of forty-seven, that moment beneath the water marked the greatest despair that David Elliot had ever known, and the greatest fear. He could not imagine anything more horrifying or more blackly agonizing than to be utterly out of breath, and held prisoner beneath some—God knows what—thing in the water. The immediacy of death paled in comparison to the sickening, hopeless, and bleak terror involved in knowing that fate has set its hand against you and there is *no* escape.

However, at the age of forty-seven, which is not a good age for such revelations, Dave discovered that there was a kind of despair that was even worse. He discovered it as he watched Helen, his wife, a woman whom he sincerely tried to love, point at him and shout, "That's him! There! There he is! Get him!"

CHAPTER 3
AN ONION NOT FOR EATING

1.

Later, Dave's ill-tempered inner voice would berate him for behaving precisely as Ransome unquestionably had hoped.

The shock of Helen's betrayal immobilized him. He couldn't handle it, couldn't move. He saw her standing near the high lobby windows, surrounded by sullen gunmen, and could not believe the evidence of his eyes. She was looking at him, pointing at him, aiming Ransome's trained killers his way. It was unthinkable. His mind rejected it. Helen would never do such a thing. Dave was hypnotized, a rabbit petrified before a snake.

He would retain only a blurred recollection of what followed. Shoulders jostling him from behind. A nasal voice growling, "Push ahead, youse." Ransome's goons wading into the crowd, forcing themselves through a tide of irritated New Yorkers. Someone thumping his back, "Come on, fella, we gotta get outta here."

His body saved him. His mind had nothing to do with it. A

cramp shot through his midriff. He gasped. In the crush of the mob he was unable to bend or turn. His gorge began to rise. He gagged and choked and made a long wet sound.

"Wassamatta, mista?"

Vomit spewed out of his mouth and through his nose. Someone screeched, "Oh shit!" The crowd surged away from him. As the people nearest him shouted and pushed to escape his retching, those nearer the exit doors were crushed forward.

Someone screamed. New Yorkers know that when the screaming starts, it is time to move on. Fast.

The mob in the lobby surged toward the blocked exit. A high plate glass window next to one of the revolving doors shattered outward. A male voice shrieked in pain. Another window burst. People bolted through the falling shards, running for the street. Ransome's men were washed back; one went down, bellowing; the bellows turned to whimpers; shortly silence.

Dave stumbled away from the pack, into the elevator corridor.

Some few moments later he found himself dazed and shaking, and no longer on the ground floor. He wasn't quite sure where he was or how he had gotten there. The elevators had been standing open, idle until reactivated by the authorities. Each elevator car had, as mandated by the building code, a trapdoor in its ceiling. All it took to open them was twisting four thumbscrews. He had—he thought he had—he wasn't sure he had—what . . . ?

Just like the movies, pal. You and Tarzan.

I didn't do that.

Oh yeah, take a look at the grease and grunge on your clothes.

The numbness had begun to fade. He bent over, placed his hands on his knees, and forced himself to take deep, gulping breaths. Jesus! It had been bad. It had been the worst. He hadn't frozen like that since . . .

Don't think about it.

Helen! Why? How? What could . . .

Don't think about that, either. Think about something else. Like maybe how cruddy your mouth tastes.

He wanted a drink of water. Badly. A little soap and a washcloth wouldn't hurt either.

He looked around dully. It seemed he was . . . where? . . . it didn't look familiar, but . . .

The second floor. That had to be it.

What was on the second floor? What the hell occupied the second floor of *any* New York office building? Most Park Avenue high-rises don't even have second floors. Their elevator lobbies, all marble and modern sculpture, extend up two or three stories. And, as for those few buildings that do make use of their second floors, it is the least desirable office space on the premises—eye level with roofs of buses, sitting atop the cacophony of New York street life, cursed with perpetually dirty windows that have no view. The second floor is an unrentable albatross around every landlord's neck.

In Dave's experience, *real* business people didn't have offices on second floors. They were always higher—up in the aeries where corporate eagles nest. No one would be caught dead with a second-floor address—at least no one who was not engaged in some odd and arcane form of endeavor, wholly alien to normal New York business practices. *DO-do-DO-do DO-do-DO-do. You are traveling in a different dimension. . . .*

Suddenly it came back to him. He *had* been on this floor. New York landlords use their second floors for temporary space, renting offices like rooms in a hot pillow motel to people who need (don't ask why) an office for an hour or two or a day or two. Or alternatively, the landlords put luncheon clubs on their second floors—private restaurants available on a members-only basis to the elite tenants of the upper floors. Mediocre foods, overpriced wines, but decent service and convenient privacy when you want to impress that out-of-town customer ("I've asked Suzy to make us lunch reservations at the club. . . .").

Like all Senterex executives, Dave held a membership in his building's club. He hadn't used it in years. He wasn't even sure he remembered what the landlord called the place. It was something British. It was *always* something British. The Churchill Club? The Windsor Club? The Parliament Club?

No matter. There would be water in the club, and a washroom. Dave was grimly eager to visit a washroom. One with soap and hot running water.

He stepped out of the second floor elevator corridor and turned left. The hall was papered with a dark scarlet design and hung with gilt-framed oil paintings of deceased prime ministers, Tories to a man.

Right, the Prime Minister's Club.

The entrance was a thick, heavy-looking door, veneered to give the appearance of improbably venerable Tudor oak. A small brass plaque was nailed at eye level: MEMBERS AND GUESTS ONLY.

The door swung open to a velvet-lined anteroom and more pictures of dead English politicians. The maître d's podium, with leather bound reservation book and brass inkwell—*complete with quill pen, for God's sake*—stood to the left. Heavy plush draperies with ridiculous golden tassels separated the anteroom from the restaurant proper.

The toilets are at the far end of the restaurant.

The dining room was large, and brightly lit. The tables were covered with snowy linen, laid with gleaming silverware. At a center table, facing the door, a half-empty glass of orange juice resting near his left hand, sat Ransome. His right hand held his gun level and well-aimed at Dave's chest. The expression on his face was as neutral as ever. He didn't say a word, but simply pulled the trigger.

2.

The firing pin snapped. A wisp of smoke drifted out of the automatic's silenced muzzle. The bruise beneath Ransome's eye—a souvenir of Dave's shoe—reddened. A look of faint irritation flitted across his face. He lifted his left hand to pull back the slide and chamber another round. By that time Dave had drawn his own weapon. Ransome dropped his hand back to the table.

The two men looked at one another in silence. Dave felt a small smile grow on his face. Ransome's expression did not change.

Ransome broke the ice. "Mr. Elliot, you are truly a bird of rare plumage. I am beginning to develop a certain affection for you."

"Not to be rude, but I feel exactly the opposite."

"Mr. Elliot, I sympathize with you completely."

"Thank you." Dave made a small gesture with his gun hand. "By the way, I'd appreciate it if you would drop your piece. Just let it slide out of your fingers. And then . . ."

The weapon, a twin of the pistol in Dave's hand, thumped on the carpet. Ransome spoke before Dave could finish his thought, "Kick it away, Mr. Elliot? That's traditional, and I am, if nothing else, a believer in the traditional values." He shot out the toe of his shoe. The pistol skidded three yards forward. Ransome continued, "Just as a matter of curiosity, would you mind telling if you gimmicked all the rounds in the magazine?"

"Only the first one. When you don't have the right tools, it takes a lot of time to jimmy the slug out of the case and empty the powder."

"As I well know." Ransome seemed thoroughly relaxed, a quiet man having a polite chat with a distant friend. "However, given the direction our relationship has taken this morning, I believe I'll inspect the rest of my bullets when I have the chance."

His control is amazing. The man must be the coolest dude on the planet. "What makes you assume that you *will* have a chance?"

Ransome arched an eyebrow at the muzzle of Dave's pistol, now pointed at the center of his midriff. He shook his head. "You don't have it in you. Oh, certainly, in the heat of combat you can kill a man. I've seen you do it. But in cold blood? I think not."

Right on schedule Ransome casually began toying with a table knife. His expression was poker-faced, but his pupils dilated. The muscles in his neck tensed. He was ready to move. "No, Mr. Elliot, you won't shoot me."

Dave shot him.

The silenced pistol made a small thump, sounding like a fist punched into a pillow. Ransome howled. He clutched his thigh where, just below the groin, blood welled out. "GODDAMN YOU SONOFABITCH YOU SHOT ME YOU SONOFABITCH RATFUCK BASTARD!"

Dave ignored him. He was on the floor, had begun to drop while squeezing off the shot. He rolled left, once, twice, three times, looking for where Ransome's backup man should be.

And was.

Dave aimed, breathed, squeezed. Another fist punched the pillow. Twice. Three times. The sound was so soft. The backup man's face disappeared in a red rain. He never even managed to lift his gun.

"I'M GOING TO KILL YOU YOU COCKSUCKER YOU BASTARD YOU SHOT ME!"

"Shut up, you're behaving like a baby." Dave had rolled one more time, bringing his pistol around toward Ransome.

"FUCK YOU JACK THAT'S WHAT I HAVE TO SAY YOU MOTHERFUCKER!" Ransome was doubled over, pressing both hands against the wound. His face was turned up, and his lips were drawn back. His eyes rolled, and he looked like a Doberman gone berserk.

Dave blew through his lips with no little disgust. "Come off it, Ransome. It's a flesh wound. I doubt if I nicked more than a millimeter of meat. If I'd wanted to do you any real damage, you know I could have."

"JUST FUCK YOU FUCK YOU FUCK YOU MAN HOW DARE YOU FUCKING SHOOT ME!"

Three tables—four counting Ransome's—were set for breakfast. Someone had been having a morning conference when Dave called in his bomb threat. Dave snatched a beaker of ice water off one of the tables and flung its contents in Ransome's face. "Ransome, take a table napkin, hold it up against your thigh, and shut the hell up. The way you're acting, you'll die of a heart attack before you die of that wound."

The ice water plastered down Ransome's hair. Rivulets dripped down his cheeks. The look on his face made Dave shiver. It was First Sergeant Mullins's face, just before the end. In a voice low and very, very cold, Ransome hissed, "Elliot, you lousy shit, you could have blown my balls off."

"Risks of the game, my friend. Besides, you said you read my 201 file. You should remember my marksmanship rating."

"I'm going to kill you for this."

Dave sighed with exasperation. "So what else is new?"

"How I do it, asshole. How much it hurts and how long it takes. That's what's new."

"Thank you for defining our relationship. Meanwhile, don't sit there like a jerk dripping blood all over the place. Put a piece of ice up against the cut. It'll ease the pain and slow the bleeding."

Ransome snarled, pursed his lips, and swiveled to fumble an ice cube out of a water glass. As he turned, Dave whipped the gun against the back of his skull. Ransome sprawled across the table and slid gently to the floor.

A caesura of the clock. Time at full stop. He had (hello, old friend) a loaded firearm in his hand. His enemy was unconscious at his feet. Merely out of curiosity, no malice in his heart, Dave aimed the muzzle at the base of Ransome's skull. The gesture felt comfortable, felt right. He thumbed back the hammer. That felt even better.

It would be a very, very easy thing to do.

It is the easy things that damn you, not the hard.

Twenty-five years earlier, David Elliot, not entirely sane at the time, stood in the heart of horror and promised God that he would never, *never*, again fire a gun in anger. I will, he prayed, hurt no one, never again, no act of anger, no deed of violence, oh God, I will war no more. . . .

Now, in the course of a single morning, he had killed two men. It had been easy—easy as it ever was—and quite automatic. He hadn't felt a thing.

However, now, at just this moment, a pistol in his hand and a worthy target in his sights, he *was* feeling something—feeling a sense of accomplishment, the comfortable emotion of a skilled man who has exercised his skills with perfection. With two fresh deaths on his hands and the perfume of cordite on his fingers, he knew he was at no small risk of feeling fine, quite fine, and feeling better every minute.

Never again, he thought. Never. He'd almost lost. They'd almost won. Now it was happening again. If he let it. But he wouldn't, he couldn't, let himself be turned back into the kind of man they once had wanted him to be.

Ransome expected otherwise. Ransome and his people. They'd think they knew what he'd do. Take a civilian hostage or two. Set up an ambush. Build up the body count. Start a firefight. Try to shoot his way out of the building.

Dave smiled grimly. He lifted the pistol's sights from Ransome's head, flicked on the safety, uncocked the hammer, and slid the weapon beneath his belt. Although he knew his enemy could not hear him, he spoke to Ransome anyway: "How many people have you got watching the exits, buddy? Twenty? Thirty? More? Whatever the number is, I'm not going to get by them, am I?" Dave glanced down at his trousers, torn and thick with grease. "Nope, I'm a real eye-catcher. Hell, looking the way I do, they'd shoot me on general principle. But I will get out, Ransome. Count on it. Also count on me doing it *my* way, not *your* way. I'd sooner take a gun to my head than do anything *that* way."

3.

It was dark, warm, cozy, and safe. Nearby, the equipment made a soothing humming sound. The air was a little stale, but not bad. Dave lay on his side, curled comfortably. His stomach was full and he felt like taking a nap. He liked it here.

Always wanted to go crawl back into the womb, didn't you, pal?

The perfect hiding place. Dave was delighted to find it, and a little surprised. Senterex had long since moved its Management Information Systems department out to suburban New Jersey. He had thought that just about every other company in New York, including the Wall Street brokerages, had done the same. Manhattan office space was too expensive to waste on computer hardware. Besides, programmers are a delicate sort of breed, and more productive when removed from the pressures of city life.

However, at least one New York company hadn't relocated its computers yet. The outfit was a subsidiary of American Interdyne Worldwide. American Interdyne, perpetrator of one of the 1980s' last great kamikaze junk bond raids, was operating under the protection of the bankruptcy courts and an especially senile federal judge. Maybe that was why the company still had its computers located on the twelfth floor of a very expensive Park Avenue office tower.

What does space in this joint rent for, anyway? Forty bucks a square foot, plus or minus.

American Interdyne's computer room was in the grand old style—weighty with heavy-duty mainframe computers, whirring peripherals, and blinking consoles. Other companies were dismantling their enormous centralized systems empires, replacing banks of balky $15 million IBM behemoths with sleek worksta-tions and high speed client/server networks. American Interdyne had not. Its systems department sprawled across an entire floor, a quarter of which was given over to the sort of ponderous main-frames that most executives, Dave among them, thought of as di-nosaurs.

He was happy to see them now, though. The nicest thing about the monsters, he thought, was their finicky complexity. The pam-pered giants demanded endless care and feeding. Legions of high paid technicians to coddle them. Custom power systems. Heavy-duty air conditioning. Endless rows of peripherals. Special moni-toring and control equipment.

And wire.

Lots of wire. More wire than you can imagine. Large mainframe instal-lations consume oodles of cabling. And you don't simply hook these suck-ers up once and then forget about them. No way. You always have to fiddle with the cabling, reconnecting ports, plugs, and interfaces. Oh, the DASD's connected to the mainframe, and the mainframe's connected to the frontend, and the frontend's connected to the multiplexer, now hear de word of de lawd!

Which meant raised flooring. American Interdyne's computer room, like that of every other big mainframe user, was built on a raised floor. The wires and the cables snaked beneath. The floor was paneled so that, as was required every so often, the computer staff could open it up and reconfigure the wiring.

Dark, warm, and cozy. It really was quite peaceful under the floor.

Dave needed the peace. Twice after leaving the Prime Minister's Club he had almost bumped into members of the NYPD Bomb Squad. If they had seen him . . . tattered, filthy, stinking of vomit, his arms full of stolen food and supplies, and with a brace of ex-ceptionally illicit pistols stuck in his belt . . .

Would've had a little trouble talking your way out of that one, pal. Es-pecially explaining the shootin' irons.

The pistols were automatics. One belonged to Carlucci, and one to Ransome's backup man. They were the same make and model, although what that make and model was, Dave could not say. Neither bore a manufacturer's stamp nor a serial number. Both had lightweight polymer fiber frames, factory silencers, laser sights, and staggered clips holding twenty-one rounds of ammunition.

Those rounds were cause for reflection—TUGs, they were called, short for *Torpedo Universal Geschoss*. Dave had never known that pistol versions were manufactured. The bullets were hunting ammo, designed to penetrate deep, mushroom inside the body, rip a target's heart out. A man hit in the torso with one of those rounds would die where he stood; even a grazing wound would render him immobile.

Just above their safety levers, the pistols had slightly recessed slide bars. Dave guessed that pushing these slides forward converted the pistols to fully automatic operation, turning the pistols into handheld machine guns.

Room brooms. Not quite your old Ingram MAC with the WerBell Sionics suppressor, but wicked enough. Thirty-eight auto, 130 grains for a muzzle velocity just a skosh below the sound barrier. Optimal silencing that way. Punches your target up with a bit more than three-hundred foot pounds of energy. Ouch.

Also ouch if the authorities ever caught a civilian carrying one. Dave suspected that even *thinking* about such a gun was a violation of the Sullivan Law.

Which raises a few questions about where they come from—and the people who carry them.

Safe beneath the floor, his head pillowed on a nest of comfortable, rubber-clad 22 AWG wire, Dave tried to doze. His argumentative guardian angel wouldn't let him. The issue was Helen, of course. Why had she materialized at the side of Ransome's men? How had they persuaded her to turn on her own husband?

Dave doubted that she'd betrayed him intentionally. Ransome's people probably had told her some godawful lie (*or worse,* cautioned his inner voice, *some godawful truth*) to trick her into identifying him.

What lie? he asked himself. *What truth?* the angel countered.

He could find answers to neither question. Nor could he—not quite yet—allow himself to explore the alternative explanation to Helen's behavior. *Maybe she is on their side. Maybe she wants you dead the same as everybody else.*

Nonsense. He'd spent five years working as hard as he could to turn the marriage into a success.

How hard has she worked?

Shut up! I don't need this!

You know what they say about guys who argue with themselves, and then lose. . . .

Dave growled and rolled over, trying to find a more comfortable posture. As he turned, the radio that he'd taken, together with sixty-seven dollars, from the corpse of Ransome's backup man, slipped away. He retrieved it and placed it close to his ear. The volume was low. Sooner or later American Interdyne's technical staff would be coming back to the computer room. Dave didn't want them wondering where that odd noise—*sounds like a walkie-talkie to me, Frank*—was coming from.

A conversation was in progress: ". . . like someone had dropped a ketchup sandwich and smeared it all over the floor. Half of New York City must've stepped on the poor bastard's face."

Another voice answered. "Aww, man, that's nasty. That's just a nasty way to go. Somebody's gotta call Don . . . Robin and get us some goddamned orders around here."

"Negative. Robin's on personal radio silence. We don't speak to him until he speaks to us."

"Aww, man. The cops are letting people back into the building. I don't know what the hell we're supposed to do, but I think we should get our hairy asses out of here."

"Not without orders."

"Screw the orders, man. And another thing, screw only Robin and Partridge knowing what this happy horseshit is about. I mean, man, so we're supposed to ice this guy, right? No big deal, they say. Just an honest day's work for an honest day's pay, right? Yeah, no big deal. Well, man, if it's no big deal, then why the hell won't they tell us what it's all about? Christ, it ain't like we don't all have clearances or something. But, uh-uh, no questions, Robin says. No answers, Robin says. Well, bullshit is what I says. You know what I think? I think this guy, the subject, has got something on somebody. I mean he knows some bad shit about one of the big boys. And whoever that big boy is . . ."

"Belay that!" Dave knew the voice. It belonged to Partridge.

"No, man, listen . . ."

"At ease, Warbler. And don't call me 'man.' "

Hmm. Sounds like Partridge is as much of a hard case as Ransome.

Warbler's voice dripped sarcasm. "Well, excuse me. *Sir.*"

"Warbler, if you've got a problem with the chain of command, I am the man to resolve it for you. And if any of you men have a problem with your duty, I'll be pleased to discuss it with you one on one. Otherwise, you know what your job is, and that's all you need to know. Am I understood, gentlemen?"

Second-in-command. Partridge is Ransome's second-in-command.

Someone mumbled, "Yessir."

"I didn't quite hear that, soldier."

"Sorry, sir. I said yes, sir."

"Clear the channel." It was Ransome's voice, cool enough, but not quite as cool as it had been. "This is Robin. Our friend has got another radio."

"Son of a . . ."

"I said clear the channel. In case you have forgotten, that translates as zip your lip."

Sounds a mite touchy, doesn't he.

"Point number one: Momentarily, I will be issuing a code change. On my mark we will go to Xylophone Delta Niner. Point number two: I want everyone back to their assigned stations immediately. Point number three: I require a medical kit for personal use. Point number four: We need a cleanup team on the second floor, in the restaurant. A body bag will be required."

"You tagged him, Robin?"

"Negative. The bag is for Oriole."

"Aww, man . . ."

"Zip it!" Dave heard a snap. Ransome inhaled deeply and blew out. He'd just lit a cigarette. *Well, we all have our little weaknesses.*

"Mr. Elliot, I trust you are listening to this. I am immediately declaring a unilateral cease-fire."

To quote Mark Twain, I suspect our friend is somewhat economical with the truth.

"I repeat, it's truce time, Mr. Elliot. We all will return to our posts and take a little breather. As I promised, I will communicate the current status to my superiors and urge them to authorize a negotiated settlement. In the interim, my people will stay on watch where they are. You, I presume, will do much the same. Given the coverage I have on the exits, that is your sole rational course of action."

Ransome stopped, waiting for an answer. "A confirmation would be useful, Mr. Elliot."

Dave pushed the send button on his radio and whispered, "I copy, Robin."

"Thank you. I have one more thing for you. We will direct the management of this restaurant to take an inventory of their supplies. If some quantity of pepper is missing, I will revise my earlier orders accordingly."

Three bags of pepper rested near Dave's feet. He had always been skeptical when waiters politely asked, "Some fresh ground pepper, sir?" New York being the sort of place it is, he didn't really believe that those oversized wooden pepper mills really had fresh peppercorns in them. They were, he conjectured, merely elaborate reservoirs designed to make the customers believe they were getting what they paid for. In the kitchen of the Prime Minister's Club Dave had found a row of open quote pepper mills unquote, a funnel, and three bags of pre-ground pepper. Welcome to New York.

"Which means, Mr. Elliot, that you won't have to waste your time spreading it around for the dogs."

Too bad. If you use enough pepper, the dogs go berserk and turn on their masters.

"All right, men, reset to Xylophone Delta Niner. Do it now."

Dave expected the radio to go silent as Ransome and his men activated a code change. But, after a moment, Ransome's voice continued. "I have one other thing to say, Mr. Elliot. Now that the troops are off the air, I can say it in confidence. You're a former officer. You know what a commander can and cannot say in front of his men."

"I copy, Robin."

Ransome inhaled, then exhaled a long slow hiss. Dave was willing to bet he'd taken an extra heavy drag off his cigarette. "Okay. Here goes. I lost it down here, Mr. Elliot, and therefore owe you an apology. I don't lose my cool easily. But, when I saw the blood between my legs, I thought you'd gotten my equipment. That's why I behaved as I did. Now let me confess that I'm sorry. I know I was out of line, and I know you did what was only right. You were one of Colonel Kreuter's people. He taught you the rules, the same as he taught me. No one-man bands and no solo pilots. Even the Lone Ranger has got a faithful Indian companion. You knew that. You knew I'd have a backup man with me. And you handled it just the way you were supposed to. I respect that. I hope you'll forgive my behavior and my remarks. I mean that sincerely. You have my word the episode won't be repeated."

Not bad. Right out of the psych-warfare books. Credible, sincere, level-headed—you know, for an absolute psycho, Ransome almost sounds like a nice guy.

"Mr. Elliot? Are you reading this, Mr. Elliot?"

"I copy, Robin."

"Over and out." The radio went dead. Ransome had changed codes.

Dave pushed his head back into the wire, making himself comfortable. He burped. The food he'd taken from the Prime Minister's Club had tasted as good as any meal he'd ever eaten. But that was not surprising. After all, the first law of soldiery is: stolen food tastes best.

"Always take a chicken when you get a chance, because if you don't want him yourself you can easy find someone that does, and a good deed ain't ever forgot." Huck Finn said that.

And the second law of soldiery is this: once the shooting has stopped it's time to take a nap.

Shortly, David Elliot was asleep.

4.

The instructor's tweed jacket gives him an appropriately professorial appearance. He is of average stature, but seems taller. The way he holds his head, nose lifted slightly, adds to the illusion of height. His hair is a little on the long side, but well-trimmed and fashionable for the late sixties. Nonetheless, it seems slightly out of place in a room full of military-issue brushcuts.

He speaks with a pronounced New England accent—not the lace curtain Irish burr of the Kennedys, but something more aristocratic. "Good afternoon, gentlemen." Lieutenant Elliot and his fellow students—there are only a dozen of them—have spent the morning touring the facilities. They are a big improvement over Fort Bragg. "My name is Robert. You can call me Rob if you so desire. I, like everyone whom you will meet here, prefer to be addressed by my first name. As for our family names, well, I fear we all have developed a slight amnesia."

The class gives an appreciative titter.

"The training you will receive here at Camp P may come as a surprise to you. It is not this institution's goal to further the lessons you have already learned. We assume that you have mastered the honorable arts of soldiery. You would not be here if you had not. Rather, our curriculum is devoted to a different craft. This craft has two dimensions. The dimension you doubtless yearn to hear of is our craft's outer manifestation—uncommon arms, infernal devices, devilish pranks, and the other rather feral skills demanded of saboteurs, subversives, and assassins. Certainly we shall be teaching you those things. But not immediately. First, we shall focus on the second dimension of the craft, the psychological dimension, the inner dimension, the dimension of the mind. In the end, gentlemen, it is in the mind that the game is played, and it is in the mind that it is either lost or won. Do you take my meaning?"

A few people nod. A Marine officer behind Dave barks, "Yes, sir!"

"Do try to forget the word 'sir.' We are a college of equals here. Now, to begin, as good Americans, you gentlemen have grown up in a culture that holds team sports in high esteem. I am sure you all have gone to many games and spiritedly cheered your home team. Like as not, you yourselves have been on the fields, good team players each and every one of you. Perhaps you have even had a moment or two of sporting glory. If so, then you are justly entitled to take pride in it, for surely team sports are affairs of honor. But, alas, they are also matters of a certain primitive simplicity and structure. Consider: the field has but two goalposts. The teams have but two sides. The game is played out over a designated period of time, as governed by a single, simple rule book that is known and respected by referees and players alike. Some have said that sport is a metaphor for war, and war a metaphor for sport. This is not, I fear, the case, although it is a common American mistake to believe so. During the coming few weeks, I hope to disabuse you of this unfortunate error, because, you see, war, and most particularly the sort of warfare for which you gentlemen will be preparing yourselves, has rather more than two sides and rather more than two teams. Nor is there a single set of rules. The game you seek to learn is layered like an onion. Peel off a strip, and another awaits you. And another, and another. The man who seeks to find the secret heart of an onion, gentlemen, is a man who will be bitterly disappointed. For when he has peeled the onion to its heart, he will hold in his hands nothing. The psychology of that particular truth can be most unsettling. It is my mission to ready you for it. I hope to teach you how to look beneath the surface of things, how to perceive how many layers the onion has, and how to recognize that it is the layers that are the soul of the onion. This is a matter of some urgency, gentlemen, because once you are out of the classroom and into such fresh hells as we will dispatch you, you will swiftly discover that beneath the surface of the game, another game is being played, and beneath that game another still. And their rules, gentlemen, ahh, all their rules will be very, very different."

Mamba Jack Kreuter is too smart to send a green lieutenant, three weeks in-country, as officer in charge of an assassination mission across the DMZ. Dave Elliot works this much out while he is still in the colonel's hooch. The fact of the matter is that the good colonel regards Dave as little more than a sacrificial lamb.

Not that Jack isn't fair about it. He's given Dave enough—just enough—information to reason his way to the truth.

Kreuter let slip the fact that the Russian Dave is supposed to kill is a KGB major. Kreuter also made it clear that the issue with the major is not his provisioning the VC, but rather the advice he's giving them.

Question: What sort of advice would a KGB major be giving the Vietcong?

Answer: Advice based on KGB intelligence, intelligence being the stock-in-trade of the good old *Komitet Gosudarstvennoy Bezopasnosti.*

Question: Where does the KGB get its intelligence from?

Answer: From agents and informers.

Dave sits in his own hooch, drinking warm beer as he puzzles it through. The Russian major is being fed his material by an informer—maybe one of the Vietnamese officers attached to Kreuter's command, or maybe somebody else. Whoever it is has to be highly positioned and delivering quality material. Neither Mamba Jack Kreuter nor any other commander would risk an incursion across the DMZ unless the intelligence loss was serious.

Question: How would you go about catching this particular traitor?

Answer: Set a trap to bag a senior Cong—or better yet, the Russian.

Question: What bait?

Answer: A team of expendable grunts led by an equally expendable lieutenant.

Dave is being sent north to lure the enemy out of his lair. Kreuter expects that he'll blunder up through the boonies, get close enough to the Russian's headquarters to attract some attention, and draw enough fire to cause some confusion. Meanwhile, a second American team—a larger one with more experienced leaders—will be flanking around the Russian's base of operation. Once the shooting starts, they'll move in and seize their prey. That is what the mission is all about. *"Beneath the surface of the game, another game is being played. . . ."*

Question: What do they call the bait they stake for the tiger?

Answer: A Judas goat.

Question: How many Judas goats get to eat tiger cutlets?

Answer: There's always a first time.

5.

Although he did not dream of onions, David Elliot awoke thinking of them. Or rather one in particular. Its top layer, he said to himself, was named Bernie Levy.

Tell me more.

People like Ransome don't send people like Bernie to do their dirty work for them. They do it themselves. That's what they're paid for. The only way that Ransome would have—could have—sent Bernie to kill me was if Bernie made a case, convinced him, argued him down. He and Ransome probably battled it out. Bernie Levy is a stubborn man. God knows he is a stubborn man. Once he decides that something is right, he sticks with the decision.

That's only part of the answer.

The other part is what he said. "Bernie Levy blames himself, and God will not forgive."

So?

Somehow Bernie thinks that he is responsible for Ransome wanting me dead. If he believes this nightmare is his fault, then he'd believe that killing me was his job. More than his job. His duty. Bernie's an ex-Marine. *Semper Fidelis.* Duty has always been a big deal with him.

You think Bernie is behind this mess?

Maybe not. He might be just another victim, same as me. My guess is that he is. He had a choice between letting Ransome ice me or shooting me himself. When he came into my office, he was muttering and stammering about not having any alternative. That's what he meant. He thought he owed it to me. I had to be killed because of a mistake *he* had made. He owed it to me to be the one who pulled the trigger. He owed it to me to not let a stranger do it.

Nice gesture.

Honorable, I'd say. Bernie was taking the sin on his own soul. It would have been a point of conscience with him.

Okay, so what kind of ungodly hell has Bernie gotten himself into and how are you involved?

I don't know. I can't even guess.

You sure you didn't witness a mob hit or something while my back was turned?

What have I seen? What have I heard? What do I know?

6.

Someone walked overhead, across the raised floor of the computer room. A voice, male, tenor and unaccented, called out: "It's almost 3:30, people. El Supremo wants all of the ops staff in the conference room. He's got a new decree that's come down from on high."

Someone sighed. "More salary cuts."

"Yeah," another person added. "To offset the growing burden of top management bonuses."

"Look, people," the tenor said, "I know it's been rough around here, but at least we've still got our jobs."

"At least until 3:30."

The tenor ignored the wisecrack. "El Supremo says he needs an hour with you. Have we got anything major scheduled between then and now?"

A woman answered, "Nothing big, but there is an RJE run on the receivables that's supposed to init at 4:00. It's for Fort Fumble, our esteemed corporate headquarters."

"Okay, Marge, you're the one who runs that job anyway. You skip the meeting and handle it. I'll stick around in case you need some help. El Supremo and I ride home together on the train. He can fill me in then. Everyone else, head 'em up and move 'em out. You know how much the boss hates people to be late for his meetings."

A chorus of three or four voices broke into the opening chorus of *Showboat*, "Niggers all work on de . . ."

"Cut that out!"

Heels and soles clicked across the flooring tiles. Dave heard a door open and slam shut. It was quiet for a moment. Then steps came his way. Light, tapping—a woman's shoes, the woman named Marge. She stopped just above his head.

The tenor spoke. "Do you run it from that console?"

"Em, yes."

The man's heavier footsteps thumped over Dave's head. "That's a 3178, isn't it?"

"Yup."

"I didn't even know they still made those. Not exactly the right terminal for the job, is it?"

"Make do or do without. That's the American Interdyne way."

"Well, how do you . . ."

"Look, Greg, I've been handling this run all by my little lonesome for seven months. You don't need to hang around. Why don't you trot off to that meeting? Make El Supremo happy."

Dave heard Greg scuff his toe across the tiles. "Well . . . Marge, the thing is that I didn't really stay here to help you with the job run."

"Oh?" Dave thought that Marge's tone of voice turned a little sharp.

"Uh, yeah. Well, the thing is, Marge, that I . . . Look, I've said this before. You're a good-looking girl, and I don't think I'm a bad-looking guy."

"So are Ken and Barbie, but they don't come in the same box." Dave guessed that these were the words of a woman who had held this particular discussion before.

"Come on, Marge. I'm your sort of guy, and you know it."

"My sort of guy doesn't have a wife and a kid in Great Neck."

"I've already told you that's history. You want evidence? Fine! I can show you the lawyer bills!"

"Thanks, but no thanks."

"All I'm asking is that we go out together once or twice. Loosen up and have some fun. Have a few drinks, eat a nice dinner. Maybe take in a movie. Just get to know one another a little better. What's wrong with that? Why won't you even think about it?"

"Greg, let me make this very, very clear. I have thought about it. A lot."

"Good. I knew that it couldn't . . ."

"And I decided no."

"What? Why?" Greg's voice was a little louder than was polite.

"There aren't any 'whys,' Greg. Just a plain old no."

"You're not taking me seriously. Listen, Marge, I am serious about this. Very serious. You've become important to me, and I won't have . . . Hey! Don't you walk away from me, lady!"

There was a scuffle. Marge's voice was raised too, higher than Greg's. "Let go of me, Greg. Let go of me now!"

"Not until you settle down and listen up! Just who do you think you're dealing with here anyway? I'm your boss, Marge. Have you forgotten that? I'm the guy who fills out your appraisal form and decides what kind of raise you get. I'm the one who kept you off the last round of layoffs. And if you want to be off the next round, lady, you'd better clean up your act!"

"What? Greg . . ."

"Forget what the White House says about the economy, babe. It's a cold hard world out there, and good jobs aren't that easy to find."

"No, Greg. There's some . . ."

"Especially if you've got a black mark on your record. On the other hand, Marge, if you stay with American Interdyne, there are opportunities. You might even get promoted if you play your cards right."

"Someone else, Greg . . ."

"Screw him! Just screw your boyfriend, babe."

"No. I mean behind you."

Greg, who was holding Marge's arm twisted behind her back, glanced over his shoulder.

David Elliot smiled at him, although not in a friendly way.

7.

Nudging Greg with his toe, Dave confirmed that lover boy was down for the count.

He shook his wrist, trying to throw off the pain. The knuckles of his left hand were bruised, and blood beaded along his unbandaged wound.

Your hand is filthy. Along with everything else you're going to get gangrene.

After a last look at the quite unconscious Greg, Dave glanced up at Marge. His first thought was: great cheekbones. His second thought was: she's going to scream any second now. He blurted, "Hi, I'm Dave Elliot and I've been having a bad day."

Marge's jaw—square, firm, attractive—fell. Her green (deep green, emerald green, green as a small mountain lake) eyes, large behind oversized, rectangular, red-framed glasses, goggled. She opened and closed her mouth twice. No sound came out.

"Actually, a very bad day."

Humor her. Act a little boyish, a little chagrined.

Marge backed away. She made a limp gesture with her right hand, as if trying to push something away.

"I guess I look like a mess."

Marge finally managed to mutter something. "Buster, you don't know the half of it."

"A really, really bad day."

"And you smell." She wrinkled her nose. Dave liked the way it wrinkled.

"Actually, it's been the worst day of my life. Look, Marge—that's your name, isn't it?—Marge, if you back away any farther you'll bump into the wall. What I'm going to do is to move over here, away from the door. So if you want to sort of sidle over to the exit, I'll understand."

Marge pursed her lips, giving him a narrow look. "Really?"

"Yup, really." She was an attractive woman. Greg had gotten that part right. A little short, perhaps five foot three, but well proportioned. Black hair, glistening like polished coal, trimmed in an oriental bell cut. In her mid-twenties. Humorous green eyes and lips made to smile. A cute Jewish nose that was sort of, well, saucy, and . . .

Hadn't you better drop that line of thought, pal? The lady's already had to deal with one masher today.

Marge kept her back to the wall and her eyes fastened on Dave. She edged around the perimeter of the room until she reached the door. Once she had her hand firmly on the knob she spoke again. "I guess I'm supposed to thank you or something. I mean about that slob Greg. So thanks."

"You're welcome." Dave glanced down at his once white shirt. He brushed at its coating of dirt. No improvement.

She looked at him, cocked her head, and put her hands on her hips. "That's it? You say, 'You're welcome,' and that's it?"

"Pretty much, I guess." *Soft'y, soft'y, catchee monkey.*

"You come up out of the floor like some Stephen King thing, kung-fu lover boy here, and then heigh-ho Silver and who was that masked man, is that what you're saying?"

Time for a boyish smile. Come on, pal, make her believe you.

He sighed and looked down. "It sounded like you needed a hand. With Greg, I mean. And . . ." He looked up and grinned. ". . . anyway, I needed to do something to . . . I don't know . . . cheer myself up or prove I'm a nice guy or something. So . . . maybe the reason I belted him is . . . that I sort of did it as much for myself as for you."

"What?" she growled. "Do you always solve your self-image problems by punching people out?"

"Can't say. I haven't had any self-image problems until just to-day."

She studied him. The way she did it was almost clinical, inch by inch, top to bottom. Dave suspected she was trying to decide what he looked like beneath his coating of grime and filth. Finally she spoke. "Are you in . . . I don't know . . . some sort of trouble or something?"

He heaved another sigh. "An understatement."

She put her hands on her hips, puffed her cheeks, and cocked her head. Dave found her expression utterly adorable. "Okay. I know I'm going to regret this, but okay. I suppose I owe you something for . . ." She waved a disdainful hand at Greg's prone form.

Perfect. Now give her one last out.

"Marge, I need a hand. I'd like to ask you for it. But I don't want you to feel like you owe it to me."

Marge blew out between her lips. "Okay, Mr. . . . what did you say your name was?"

"Elliot. Dave Elliot."

"All right, Mr. Dave Elliot. You've got five minutes, wall clock time. Let's hear what you've got to say."

She tapped her foot on the tiles and fingered her lower lip. Finally she spoke, "I'm supposed to believe this, huh?"

Dave shrugged. "There's a phone on the wall there. Call Senterex. My extension is 4412 and my secretary is named Jo Courtner. Her extension is 4411. Tell her that you're my dentist's assistant and that you're calling to reschedule the appointment I had for to-morrow. The dentist is named Schweber, by the way. See what happens."

"What's the main number?"

Dave gave it to her. She dialed, asked for extension 4412, and spoke. "Good afternoon. This is Marge from Dr. Schweber's office. Mr. Elliot has an appointment tomorrow that we need to change." She paused, listening. "Oh. Well, do you have any idea when he'll be back?" Another pause. "Several weeks. Well, why don't I call back the middle of next month? Okay. Good. Thank you and have a nice day."

She set down the phone. "You're out of town. Family emergency. No one knows how long you will be away."

"Now call my brother. If there was a family emergency he'd be back in Indiana too. Say you're calling from my attorney's office—Harry Halliwell is his name—and you need to speak to him about the revocable trust I set up."

Marge made the call. Her eyebrows arched as she heard the answer. After hanging up the phone she said, "Your brother says you're on a business trip to Tokyo. He says you won't be back for a month."

Dave turned on his best, his warmest smile. "I sure could use some help, Marge."

She shook her head and stared down at the floor. "Look, I'm just a simple working girl. People with guns . . . Mafia or whatever . . . and besides, you've . . . I mean . . . you've hurt people."

Marge stopped speaking, licked her lips, and glanced at Greg's unconscious form.

Careful, pal, you're losing her.

Dave brushed his fingers through his hair. "Only to stop them from hurting me."

Her eyes were still on Greg.

"Do you know anything about guns, Marge?"

Her lips thinned. "When I was eight, my family moved to Idaho. NRA country. Everyone's a hunter. I've seen every kind of gun there is."

"Good. Look at this." Dave reached behind his back and removed one of the pistols hidden beneath his shirt. He squatted, placed it on the floor, and sent it spinning toward Marge. "I took it off of one of Ransome's men."

She bent down and picked the weapon up. She held it with the respect of an experienced marksman. After a moment or two of studying it, she nodded. "High-tech stuff, right? I've never seen anything like it."

Dave didn't say anything. He simply waited for her to make up her mind.

She did. She checked the safety on the pistol, turned it butt first, and walked away from the door. She held out the gun to him. "I think you're in real trouble, mister."

He took the pistol and slipped it beneath his shirt. "I need some help. Just a little. Nothing that could get you involved. I promise. Word of honor."

Liar!

"No, I . . ."

"Three things. That's all I ask. One: find me a roll of duct tape or something—whatever it is you guys use to wrap the wire under the floor. Two: find me a tape recorder or a dictation machine. Three: watch in the hallway while I go to the men's room and wash up and change."

"Use the ladies'."

"Pardon?"

"The only women on this floor are in this department. They're all in a meeting now. The ladies' will be safer."

8.

Dave—freshly washed, materially less odorous, and dressed in the amorous Greg's slacks and shirt—was back in the computer room.

Marge eyed him approvingly. "You look like a computer nerd. Lopsided glasses, pants too short, shirt untucked. All you need is one of those plastic pocket protectors."

"Thanks. If I had white socks and a pair of sneakers, my disguise would be perfect."

Even though Greg was two inches shorter than Dave and one waist size larger, his clothes weren't a bad fit. The looseness of the shirt was a definite plus. It made the guns easier to conceal. Greg's shoes, unfortunately, were another matter. They were too small. Dave was still wearing his obviously expensive Bally loafers. He wanted to get rid of them.

Marge hefted the handheld dictation recorder that Dave had given her. "Are you sure this is going to work?"

"I hope so. It's my best shot."

"And you're certain you've got this radio set right?"

Dave had taken two radios—the first from Carlucci and the second from the man he had shot in the Prime Minister's Club. While hiding beneath the computer room floor, he had examined them. Both had small, removable panels on their backs. Once the panels were taken off, Dave found a row of miniature red LEDs displaying what were undoubtedly encryption codes. A bank of toggle switches was set directly below the LEDs. It had taken him only a moment to reset the second radio to the same codes as those displayed on Carlucci's radio—the radio that Ransome had said he would use to call Dave.

"Yes, Marge, the radio is the way it should be."

"So all I do is I push down this transmit button and play your tape?" She pointed with a long, slender finger. Dave liked long fingers. He hated stubby ones. Marge, he thought, really had excellent fingers. Other things too. She was, he thought, the very antithesis of his wife—pleasantly rounded where Helen was New York thin; petite where Helen was, well, let's face it, too tall; street-smart where Helen was coolly sophisticated; and unabashedly sexual where Helen . . .

Hey, pal! Yeah, you!

He forced his mind back to the business at hand. "Right. As soon as you hear a voice—any voice—you play the tape. But only if you're out of the building. If you hear a voice while you're in the building, just ignore it. If Ransome calls before you get out of here, I'll have to come up with another plan."

She took a deep breath and flashed him a smile. "What about Greg?"

Nice smile!

"Somebody will hear him sooner or later. Either that, or the janitors will find him tonight when they're cleaning up. Until then he isn't going anywhere."

She studied her shoes. "By the way, I meant to ask you—why did you wrap so much of that stuff around . . . well, you know . . . his little thingie?"

"When it comes time for someone to pull the duct tape off that bozo, I want him to say 'ouch.' "

She giggled. "You're a mean guy, Mr. David Elliot." Her grin lit up the room.

And she had a look in her eye. Or at least Dave thought she had a look in her eye. Or rather, perhaps it was that he *hoped* she had a look in her eye. "Yeah," he smirked, "that's me, mean as a junkyard dog."

She tilted her chin up. The tint of her cheeks brightened. "But not mean to everyone?"

Marge's voice had softened. Quite the contrary, Dave's was husky. "No, not everyone." He took a step forward. It was pure reflex. Marge did the same. There wasn't anything reflexive about it. Dave observed that the air-conditioned computer room had become warmer. Not an unpleasant kind of warmth. More like a languid summer breeze.

She stood closer to him. Her eyes sparkled. Only a foot of space separated them. Either he was reading the signals wrong, or she *liked* having him closer. He was drawn to her, and she to him. There was a magnetism—real, instantaneous, unavoidable. It was rare, but it happened. Some people call it love at first sight, although, of course, it's not.

An especially foolish thought flashed through Dave's mind. He liked the thought, and he liked the foolishness, and most of all he liked Marge, and so . . .

He brought himself up short—a jerk on his psychic reins so abrupt as to be painful. To even *think* what he'd been thinking was so utterly wrong as to be insane, if not suicidal. And to involve this woman, who was already too deeply involved . . .

Nice to know you've still got at least a few morals left, pal.

Dave snatched Marge's hand, shaking it as he would the hand of a business colleague. "Thanks for all your help, Marge. Really, really, really thanks. But I'd better get moving. Your friends—the other people in this department—will be back from that meeting pretty soon, I think."

The sparkle in her eye was brighter. "Okay, but look, my full name's Marigold Fields Cohen—don't look at me that way, I was born in 1968 and my parents were living in San Francisco. It's not my fault they gave me a dumb name. Anyway, I'm in the book. West Ninety-fourth Street, just off Amsterdam. When you get out of this mess, you give me a call, okay? Or you could even drop by."

Dave smiled back at her. She was simply delightful. He was utterly beguiled. He was tempted to say something rash. Something very, very rash . . .

Pity you're a happily married man. Or, then again, maybe you're not anymore.

Or perhaps he never was.

"Sure, Marigold." He tried to sound sincere. Maybe he was.

"Don't you dare call me Marigold again."

"Never. I promise. Cross my heart and hope to die. Now there's one last thing."

Marge nodded eagerly.

"The last thing is that I don't want you to get in trouble over this. I don't want anyone suspecting that you helped me. But when they find Greg, there will be questions. So, what we need to do is to give you an alibi. What I have in mind is going to be an absolutely perfect alibi. No one will even think about questioning it. You understand that your alibi has to be bulletproof, don't you?"

"Sure. What is it?"

"This." Dave drove an uppercut into her jaw. He caught her as she slumped unconscious, and gently lowered her to the floor. Then he took all the cash out of her purse. It was only twenty-three dollars, poor girl. He did, however, leave her a subway token so she could get home.

CHAPTER 4
ALL IN THE MIND

1.

Bowing to the silliest sort of superstition, the organization that erected and managed Dave's building had decided that it would have no thirteenth floor. Instead, the floors were numbered 11, 12, 14, 15—as if such gods or demons who mete out bad luck are so dull-witted as to be unable to count.

American Interdyne occupied only two floors—12 and 14. Reception was on 14.

The receptionist was crawling on her hands and knees, squinting at the carpet, and sniffling. Dave gaped at her.

She was a 1980s yuppie caricature. The hemline of her all-natural-fiber, herringbone skirt ended well below her knees. An NFL tackle might envy the shoulder pads of her matching jacket. Her white cotton blouse was so heavily starched that it seemed to crackle as she bent, and the dark burgundy bow around her neck resembled nothing so much as a large dead fowl of a statutorily endangered species. The woman's outfit almost screamed that it had been purchased at Alcott & Andrews—and Alcott & Andrews had been out of business for quite a few years.

"Excuse me." Dave's tones were the politest he could muster under the circumstances. "I'm from the phone company."

She lifted her head, squinting in his approximate direction. "Don't move *(sniff)*. Just stand there and don't move."

"Lost a contact?"

"Both of them *(sniff)*, would you believe?"

"Can I give you a hand?"

"Only if you're careful *(sniff)*."

"I will be."

Squatting down, Dave began studying the carpet. He spotted a glimmer of reflected light near where the woman crawled. "A little to your left, just about eleven o'clock from where your hand is. See it?"

"Yeah, thanks *(sniff)*. One down, one to go."

"The other one is just north of it."

"Oh. Great. I've got it *(sniff)*."

The woman went through her rituals, licking a finger, peeling each eyelid back, tilting her nose at the ceiling, and then popping the contacts in. Dave found the practices of contact lens wearers just slightly less distasteful than those of people who pick their noses in public.

She jerked a tissue out of a box on her desk and dabbed at her eyes. The paper went purple with mascara.

"Get something in your eye?" Even as he asked the question, Dave knew he shouldn't have.

"No." She gulped and sniffed and blotted up a tear. "I was . . . I was . . ."

He loathed being made the confidant of people whom he did not know.

". . . crying."

On the other hand, he needed the woman's help. Trying hard to sound sympathetic, Dave sighed. "Oh. Is something wrong?"

Ten minutes later, Dave knew more than he wanted about the receptionist's life history. At the end of the eighties, she had earned an MBA from one of the better business schools, gone to Wall Street as an investment banker, been let go during the most recent wave of financial industry layoffs, and remained hopelessly unemployed until, in desperation, she applied for and obtained the position of receptionist at American Interdyne Worldwide.

Dave made soothing sounds.

"And so the only place I can get a job is in a dump like this *(sniff)*, and I'm still paying off my student loans *(sniff)*, and I can barely feed my cat *(sniff)*, and my ex is out of work too and can't pay child support *(sniff)*, and I'd make more money as a dental assistant *(sniff)*, and my landlord is on my case *(sniff)*, and . . . and . . ."

Dave touched her hand. "What? You can tell me."

"I got patted on the butt again."

"Who, Greg?" Dave swallowed. That had been a mistake. Fortunately the woman missed it.

"Him too. All of them! From the lousy Chairman of the Board of this lousy company whenever he's in this lousy town all the way down to the lousy office manager!"

Dave folded his arms and closed his eyes.

First Marge, now this woman. There seems to be a distinctive corporate culture at American Interdyne.

"She's a bitch, too."

"Pardon?"

"The office manager."

Later, after he had calmed her down, Dave asked for what he wanted. She smiled trustingly, and gave it to him. He had been so understanding, so helpful, that she didn't even think about it. Besides, he still had a telephone repairman's tool belt around his waist. All she asked was his promise that he return it to her when he was done.

A key.

Dave, lying through his teeth, promised. She glanced at her watch. "Will you be through before 5:00? I go home at 5:00."

Dave smiled at her one last time, saying, "Probably not. But I'll just slip it beneath the blotter on your desk. Will that be okay?"

"Oh, sure. Or drop it in the center drawer."

"Certainly. Oh, one last thing, do you know a woman named Marge Cohen? She works down in the computer department."

The receptionist nodded.

"You might want to give her a call. She's good people, and I think she knows something about dealing with harassment."

"I'll call her at home this evening." She brandished the American Interdyne corporate telephone directory.

Dave turned to leave. "You said the telephone room's on this floor?"

"Right down the hall and to the left."

"Thanks. See you later."

"See you later."

She'd given him the master key to American Interdyne's utility and supply rooms. With any luck, it would fit *every* utility room in the building. Telephone rooms. Janitor's closets. The little nooks and cubbyholes wherein the building manager, the electric company, and a fair number of other organizations stored this, that, or the other thing.

The key was just what he needed.

2.

Dave was inventorying the contents of AIW's supply room when Ransome did, at long last, the unforgivable.

The radio in Dave's shirt pocket hissed alive. Ransome's hauntingly familiar Appalachian drawl came through the speaker. "Mr. Elliot, I have someone here who wants to talk to you."

Dave's jaw tightened. Now what? Another cheap trick. A little psychological warfare to unbalance your prey. Something to destroy his self-confidence or make him question . . .

"I know from your record that loyalty is not one of your personal values. Not to your flag. Nor to your comrades. Nonetheless, it is my hope that you feel a certain bond to your own flesh and blood."

What!

"Dad?"

No!

"Dad, are you there?"

Mark, his son. His only child. His and his first wife's. His and Annie's.

"Dad, it's me, Mark."

He was a junior at Columbia, lived in a dorm on West 110th Street, came down for dinner with his father at least once a week. Jealous Helen never joined them. She knew that Mark was the most important person in Dave's life.

"Dad, listen to me."

The boy wanted to be a philosopher. In his freshman year he'd taken the introductory course. Something in it had touched his soul. He found meaning in Plato, relevance in Kant, and joy in Hegel. On his own, with no prodding from his professors, he had, during his second year, read Martin Heidegger's *Being and Time* from cover to cover, all five hundred densely worded pages of it, and written a critical article that, *mirabile dictu*, had been accepted for publication.

"Please, Dad. This is important."

Oh, Ransome, you sonofabitch, how dare you drag my boy into this? I will see you pay for this. Well and truly shall you pay.

"You've got to listen, Dad."

Dave, who doubted if he himself had even used the word "philosophy" since his undergraduate days, enthusiastically encouraged Mark in his studies. If other fathers might look askance upon a son's desire to invest his college years in a subject not renowned for its relevance to commercial pursuits—well, the more fool they.

"I'm downstairs. Mom is on a plane. She'll be here in a couple of hours."

I'm going to kill you, Ransome. I am going to kill you and wash my hands in your blood.

"Dad, you've got to listen. Agent Ransome told me everything. He's shown me the records, Dad."

What gruesome lie is this?

"It's happened to other people, Dad. You're not the only one. There were twenty or twenty-five of you. They gave you drugs. In Vietnam, Dad, before I was born, they gave you drugs."

I will cut you with my knives. I will brand you with my fires. Oh Ransome, Ransome, you thing of evil, there will be no end to the tortures I will inflict on you.

"It was an experiment, Dad. They didn't know what would happen. But the drug, Dad, the drug has long-term effects. Even after all these years, people get flashbacks. They can go nuts, Dad. They can go nuts even after all this time. The Army is trying to keep it quiet. They are trying to round up everyone who was given the stuff. They say they can treat it. They say . . ."

What? What do they say? This is going to be the worst. This is the one that Ransome hopes will drive me right over the edge.

". . . Dad, they say there are genetic effects. They say that they have to test me too. They say that it's probably why Mom . . . what made Mom have those problems."

Angela. College sweetheart. June bride. One son. Two spontaneous abortions. Deep depression. A bout with the bottle. Divorce. Then psychiatric care, remarriage, two charming daughters, and a life of goodness and grace with another man.

"Dad, you're seeing things, but it's not your fault. It's drugs, Dad. It's bad stuff that's been in your system all of these years. They showed me the records. They showed me the other guys' records, too. It's happening to all of you. Something happens to your body when you get close to being fifty years old. It sets it off. You start imagining things, seeing people come after you with guns and knives and stuff. You begin to believe that everyone is out to get you. So you start trying to get them before they get you. You start trying to get everyone. It's all in your mind, Dad, but they can cure it. If you'll come in, they can cure it. If you don't, it's going to get worse. And fast, Dad, real fast. You've got to let them treat you for it. It's making you see things that aren't there. It's making you want to hurt people. Dad, for God's sake, let Agent Ransome help you. That's what he's here for, Dad. He's your friend. He's here to help."

The gun felt good in his hand. The rake of the butt was comforting. His finger caressed the trigger. It was smooth to the touch. He slid his thumb across the safety and pushed. He moved the select switch from semiautomatic to automatic. He was feeling better with each passing moment.

"Can't you feel it, Dad? The rage? Can't you see that what you are feeling is absolutely out of control rage?"

Goddamned right.

3.

He wanted to kill and kill and kill.

"In the end, gentlemen, it is eminently more useful to destroy an enemy's spirit than it is to destroy an enemy's body."

He could barely wait for the shooting to start.

Good old Professor Robert-call-me-Rob said that.

He was on the third floor.

The other thing he said was, "Do the one, and the other becomes a vastly less complicated task."

He'd traveled there through a crimson fog.

It's what Ransome wants, pal.

The fog was clearing.

You're tying it up with a ribbon and giving it to him in a box.

Soon all would be visible, bathed in a pure light of great clarity.

Christ! Can't you see what he's doing to you?

Dave ejected the magazine from the pistol, and checked it. Full.

Ransome's lied to your wife, he's lied to your son, he's lied to you. It's bait! It's a trap!

He jacked the clip back into the butt, pulled back the slide, and chambered a round. Killing these people was going to feel good.

You're walking straight into it. They're going to be waiting.

Dave wanted them waiting. He was looking forward to it.

"An enemy whose mind is distressed is an uncommonly vulnerable enemy. The demoralized are most easily defeated, the disheartened most readily destroyed. Such is the first principle of psychological warfare, and the first commandment of our honorable profession."

Our honorable profession? Which honorable profession might that be? Ransome's? Mamba Jack's? Sergeant Mullins's? Mine?

His hand was tightly around the banister. It was metal, painted battleship grey, and cold.

Cold. Concentrate on the cold. Don't think about anything else. Just the cold.

Dave stopped. He held himself perfectly still.

Good. Now breathe. Take it long and slow.

He forced himself to inhale as deep as he could, so deep it hurt. He held it until he saw spots before his eyes, then let it out slowly. He blotted sweat off his brow with his shirttail.

That's better, pal.

He held his right hand out. It was trembling.

That's the idea. Guys with shaking hands aren't the best marksmen in the world.

It had been close. Ransome had almost gotten him.

"He who overcomes his enemies by stratagem, is as much to be praised as he who overcomes them by force." Machiavelli said that. Remember? Remember Professor Rob used to quote him all the time?

Dave snapped the safety on and reset the pistol to semiautomatic. He tried to slip the gun back into his belt. It took him three tries.

He'll do it again. He'll do anything to mindfuck you.

Dave's knees went weak. He collapsed on the stairs, motionless and shivering, until his fury ebbed.

It had to have been Ransome's best shot. There was nothing more guilefully evil that the man could do than calling Mark, persuading him to try to seduce his father into a death trap, lying to him . . .

You're sure it was a lie?

No, he was not. That was the special hell of it. Someone—one of his own people—*might* have given him an experimental drug. It wouldn't have been the first time that the intelligence crowd had pulled that particular trick. At least one hapless CIA contractor had been surreptitiously fed a dose of LSD and committed suicide as a result. It took twenty-five years before the Agency admitted to the episode and grudgingly recompensed the man's family.

There had been other incidents as well. During the 1950s, the Army secretly sprayed the skies over San Francisco with an aerosol-borne microbe, *Serratia marcescens*. A decade later a group of covert warfare researchers filled glass bulbs full of moderately nasty germs, dropped them on the tracks of the New York subway system, and then monitored the spread of the resulting sniffles and runny noses. Around the same time, out in Utah, herds of sheep had died when something unspecified got loose from a classified laboratory. Elsewhere there were rumors of biologists, immunologists, and genetic engineers who took an unhealthy interest in the results of prison camp experiments performed by the Axis powers during World War II. Then too there were the American penitentiary inmates who had been injected with infectious viruses, untested medicines, and, most notoriously of all, syphilis spirochetes. Add to that the Army's horrific testing of radioactive substances on members of its own ranks, and it wasn't hard to believe that some dirty tricks specialist might feel motivated to feed a mind-bending drug to a few of his colleagues.

The intelligence establishment had been a law unto itself, more than capable of performing ill-conceived experiments on soldiers and civilians alike. It was, after all, being done in the ultimate best interest of American national security, and thus a necessity if you believed, as everyone did, that the Soviets were doing precisely the same. If a few lab rats, imprisoned felons, or men in uniform suffered along the way—well, was that too high a price to pay for insuring the preservation of democracy? Indeed, when during the 1970s Senate investigators first learned of the operations and voiced their horror, no small number of the people responsible were more than merely indignant. *What's all the uproar about? We're just doing the job you pay us to do. You can't blame us—we're the good guys!*

Ransome had come up with a particularly insidious lie, all the more insidious for being believable. It guaranteed that everyone— *everyone*—who knew Dave and who might help him would now be on Ransome's side. Better still, it would cause Dave to doubt himself.

It could be true, you know.

I know. God help me, I know.

He shivered in the stairwell's half light, his arms wrapped around his knees, despairing in the knowledge that now he was utterly, utterly alone. There was no one to talk to, no one who would listen. Wife, child, friends—everyone who should believe in him believed lies. Every hand would be raised against him, and there was no one he could trust.

Such is the stuff of waking nightmares, incipient madness, the sort of now-bewildered but soon-to-be-deranged thoughts that cause once well-balanced people to peek under their beds at night, suspect that their phones are tapped, and, in time, become certain that sinister forces are monitoring their every move. Maybe it's the government, maybe it's the Trilateral Commission, maybe it's the saucer people. You can't trust anyone because anyone and everyone may be one of Them or one of Their Agents. And pretty soon you begin writing long letters to the editor of *Scientific American*, or maybe you don't because the editors are probably part of the conspiracy too. And you think about lining your room with aluminum foil to keep the radio waves out, and at night you roam the streets spray-painting mystic symbols on the walls to repel strange forces, and all the while you gibber to yourself and what you say makes sense to you if to no one else, and in the end you put your belongings in a shopping bag, better to be mobile, and you look for a dark place you can hide during the daylight hours, because They are out there, and They are searching, and They want you in their crosshairs. . . .

The headshrinkers call it paranoia, and when it gets bad they put you away.

Because, after all, people who think everyone in the world wants to kill them can be dangerous.

CHAPTER 5
SOME FINE JOKE

1.

With any luck Marge—Marigold Fields Cohen, who probably had been conceived the very summer he had ridden into the high Sierra mountains and slept by a lake, perfect and green and never forgotten—Marge would still be unconscious. If so, she wouldn't have heard his son. If so, she'd still use the tape recorder when the time came for Dave to make his escape.

Better have a fallback plan anyway.

Right. Dave wanted nothing more than to avoid Ransome and his people. But if something went wrong before Marge played the tape, he would need geography through which he could pass swiftly, and through which his enemies could not. So far he'd managed to keep one short step ahead of them, and largely played a defensive game. The time had come to change that. Besides, he owed Ransome something for bringing his son into the picture. Indeed, he owed Ransome rather a lot.

1, 2, 3, 5, 7, 11, 13, 17, 19, 23, 29, 31, 37, 41, 43, 47.

Prime numbers. A prime divided by any number other than 1 or itself will produce a fractional number as an answer. Primes are an infinite source of fascination to mathematicians, and easy to calculate—or, rather, easy to calculate if you are only interested in the ones lower than 50.

Professor Rob speaking: "Gentlemen, can you imagine how downright embarrassing it is when a saboteur blunders into his own booby trap? Just think of it. Picture yourself, lying there in the smoldering rubble, a leg blown off perhaps, or possibly with your entrails unraveling before your eyes. Think how chagrined you would feel if you knew that the infernal device that had done the damage was one that you yourself had set. My goodness, but wouldn't your face blush pink? One of life's more nonplussing little experiences, I should say. In order that you may avoid such awkward and humbling moments, it is my mission today to teach you some arithmetic. What I will discuss, and what you will learn, are some few, simple mathematical progressions. Such formulae are quite useful in keeping track of the locales in which you might happen to have prepared a little prank for the edification of your opponents."

There are sixteen prime numbers lower than 50. Dave laid traps in the fire stairs on sixteen floors. Sixteen in the east stairwell, sixteen in the west, and sixteen in the south.

His instructors at Camp P had emphasized the importance of simplicity. A good snare is a plain snare, designed to produce maximum effects with minimal materials. As in almost every field of endeavor, so too in the art of dirty tricks—K.I.S.S. is the greater wisdom.

Dave respected K.I.S.S. His traps—"jokes" the instructors would have called them—included strands of dark green telephone cable strung as tripwires near the top of flights of stairs; buckets of slippery liquid soap (the kind used in bathroom dispensers) set in corners where they might be retrieved easily by a running man; jars of sticky rubber cement ready to be tilted over; containers full of flammable industrial cleaning solvent placed conveniently ready to hand; much heavier gauges of wire, this time carefully coiled around a water pipe and easily unraveled; a handful of cheap letter openers taped in spiky groups of three; power staplers left in various strategic positions; seemingly innocent wads of paper blanketing two platforms in the stairwells; a fire hose unwound from its spool and stretched up five flights of stairs; three canisters of photocopier toner ready to belch out blinding black powder; and other things as well.

His teachers would have been proud of him. K.I.S.S.: Keep It Simple, Stupid.

Dave doubted that all of his traps would be effective. Many wouldn't even be tripped. And as for those that were, at worst they'd cause broken limbs and punctured flesh. Most were merely inconveniences and none were guaranteed mankillers. They didn't need to be. All they needed to do was slow Ransome and his people down.

On the other hand, pal, if you want to cause some real damage . . .

In a janitor's closet he'd found five large cartons—two dozen bottles to the box—of ammonia cleanser.

Ammonia is common stuff. Everyone uses it to wash windows, sanitize toilets, and scrub porcelain. It is an ordinary household ingredient.

At Camp P they had taught him about ordinary household ingredients. They had taught him that, to the knowing, the average kitchen pantry is an arsenal of poisons, incendiaries, and explosives. When combined in the correct ratios, no small numbers of quote ordinary household ingredients unquote are lethal weapons.

Among them ammonia.

When mixed with iodine—the kind found in almost any office emergency medical kit—ammonia produces a precipitate of tiny nitrogen triiodide crystals. Once properly treated and dried, nitrogen triiodide becomes a substance of some commercial value. Indeed, DuPont sells it under a brand name well known in the mining industry—well known as being the perfect tool for blasting open new ore seams. The only problem with the stuff is its instability. A mere sixty pounds of pressure placed on a batch of triiodide crystals and . . .

Dave's guardian angel smirked. *Baby go boom!*

2.

Shortly after 6:00, David Elliot walked into an ambush.

While laying his traps, he'd concluded that Ransome's goons were keeping out of the stairwells. Guarding the ground-floor exits was enough to ensure that their prey did not escape. Besides, occasional smokers—exiled from their offices, lepers of the late twentieth century—snuck out to the stairwells to enjoy secret, shameful cigarettes. While the presence of a telephone repairman carrying spools of wire up and down the stairs was unremarkable to the nicotine addicts, the presence of patrolling thugs would have raised their suspicions.

Had Dave been in Ransome's shoes, he would have ordered his men to steer clear of the stairs until long after the business day had ended. Unfortunately, now the day *had* ended, and some of Ransome's people were getting playful. Dave wondered whether their boss knew what they were up to. Probably not. A man like Ransome would never approve of such an ineptly prepared trap. It was inconsistent with Ransome's professional standards. Dave himself found it sufficiently amateurish as to be offensive.

You just can't get good help anymore.

Two of Ransome's men had positioned themselves in the west stairwell. They were crouched in a corner on the thirty-third floor near the fire door. One of them, doubtless thinking himself cunning, had disconnected the fluorescent lights above the door. The concrete platform, the cold grey walls, and the door itself were masked in shadow.

The shadows were the giveaway. If they'd left the lights on, Dave might not have noticed until it was too late.

The old turn-off-the-lights trick. These guys read too many Robert Ludlum novels.

They couldn't have been in place long. As he'd put the finishing touches on his booby traps, Dave had climbed past the thirty-third floor twice during the last fifteen minutes.

If they have any training at all, there'll be another pair of them on the thirty-second floor, waiting on the other side of the fire door. Standard ambush tactics, straight out of the manual.

The idea would be to trap him between the thirty-second and thirty-third floors. Two men shooting from above, two from below. "Flanking crossfire" was the technical term. It turned your target into shredded beef.

Which means the excitement won't start until you're halfway up the next flight of stairs.

Dave climbed the last few stairs to the thirty-second floor. His shoe heels echoed on the concrete steps. The two men in the shadows knew he was coming. They would have heard him, would have been following his progress, and would have been whispering eagerly into their radios.

How long have they been there? How long have they been listening? Have they had time to summon more men?

The space between the stairs, the empty well that plummeted from the roof of the building to the ground, was wide enough that he could see his waiting enemies. Both were flattened against the wall. Both held stubby, ugly assault rifles to their shoulders.

AR-15s? No, something else. Something with bigger magazines and more rounds.

Dave stopped and puffed hard, as if catching his breath. He untucked his shirttail and swiped it across his face. He blew heavily.

"I hate these goddamned stairs," he muttered in a voice just loud enough to be heard. One of the men above him jiggled a radio closer to his mouth.

Idiot. You can't yammer into a radio and point a rifle at the same time. Don't they teach you people anything?

Dave rolled his shoulders and resumed climbing. The two men on the next floor would not shoot. Not now. They wanted to be sure they got him, and the only way to do that was to take him in a crossfire. They wouldn't fire until he had reached the platform halfway between the thirty-second and thirty-third floors. He was certain of it.

The certainty did not help. His heart hammered, and now, all at once, he *did* feel short of breath. Sweat beaded on his forehead. A small muscle beneath his left eye twitched uncontrollably. His knees felt wobbly. He wanted a cigarette.

There are times when you knowingly walk into a trap. Sometimes you do it because it's the only way to flush out the enemy. Sometimes you do it because the only way to achieve your objective is to spring the trap. But mostly you do it to bait a trap of your own.

Which doesn't make it any easier.

The muscle beneath his left eye was out of control. His wrists, just where the veins are closest to the surface, tingled. It took conscious effort to keep his hands away from his guns.

Dave climbed. One step. Two steps. Three steps. Four . . .

He was, just for this moment, invisible. The men on the thirty-third floor could no longer see him. They would be shifting their aim to the platform eight steps ahead of him, waiting for him to blunder into their sights. The men stationed behind the door would be coiling their muscles, readying themselves to spring out. Both teams thought they knew where their target would be. They were ready for it, looking forward to it, and perhaps even thinking about how, once it was over, they would pat one another on the back, crack rough jokes, light cigarettes, and assure one another that, when all was said and done, the David Elliot affair hadn't been an especially difficult assignment.

Dave put his hand on the stair rail—cold, hollow, tubular.

One deep breath.

He pulled, kicked, pushed, and vaulted.

Thirty-two stories to the ground floor. If he missed, he missed, and that was that.

He cleared the stairwell, cleared the rail opposite, and landed on the balls of his feet. It had been a short, easy jump—only a moment of danger to take him from one flight above the thirty-second floor stairwell to one flight below it.

"Shit!" A voice from above. Silenced bullets pocked the concrete where he had landed. Dave was already gone.

He snatched at the banister, seized it, and hurled himself downward. He took two and three stairs at a time. He had to get past the next platform. If he was still on the stairs leading down from the thirty-second floor . . .

The fire door slammed open. Shoes slapped on concrete.

. . . then the men behind him would have a lovely view of his back.

He swung over the rail and leapt. A hail of bullets cut the air above, behind, and beside him.

A scream of frustration: "Sonofabitch, sonofabitch, sonofabitch!"

David Elliot ran.

"This is Egret! He's on thirty-one, on thirty, headed down! Where are you? What? In the west stairwell, you jackass! Get here, fast!"

Someone, maybe more than one person, emptied a magazine, maybe more than one magazine, down the stairwell. The bullets punched into walls, blasting out rock hard splinters of concrete shrapnel. Dave felt a bee-sting of pain in his shoulder.

They were thundering down the stairs, firing as they ran. Flattened bullets ricocheted all around.

Standard operating procedure. If you can't hit your target with a straight shot, get him on the bounce.

Dave vaulted another banister. A shot, a ricochet, whined under his chin. He flinched. Far away, down—how many?—flights of stairs, another door flew open. Men were running up now. They were trying to catch him in between.

Twenty-sixth floor. One more floor to go.

He slipped, caught himself, pulled himself straight. He was where he wanted to be—on the twenty-fifth floor.

He glanced up the stairs. There it was, snaking up the steps, long and flat, just as he'd left it. It had been surprisingly heavy work to unwind it all the way up to the twenty-ninth floor. He hadn't really expected to have to use it.

Ransome's men were running past its end now. They didn't see it, or if they did, they didn't think about it. An emergency fire hose.

Dave took the red-enameled wheel in both hands, and turned. It was stuck. Dave gave it a panicked jerk. The wheel was frozen.

Aw, God, don't do this to us.

He braced his legs, and strained. The wheel moved. The pipe gurgled and hissed. Water was flowing through it. Dave pulled harder. The wheel turned freely. The hiss mounted to a roar. The fire hose was no longer flat and motionless. It filled, rounded, moved. Water boiled through it, up one flight of stairs, up a second flight, the pressure mounting with each passing inch.

How much water pressure? If memory serves, three hundred pounds. And that, my friend, is one hell of a lot of pressure.

The hose jolted, swayed left to right, and began to rise. It looked alive, like an enormous tan snake shaking itself awake. And if it was shaking here, five flights from its end, then the nozzle would be . . .

A scream echoed down the stairwell.

. . . whipping back and forth uncontrollably. Three hundred pounds of pressure in rapid motion. Six or seven pounds of heavy brass nozzle. One blow would break a strong man's legs.

The scream rose. It was coming closer, and with awful speed. Dave looked up just in time to see the body pass. The man was plummeting down the stairwell, windmilling his arms, trying to seize the banister. His face was white with hopeless terror.

Damn.

Damn, indeed. He hadn't wanted to kill them. He just wanted to slow them down.

From up above there were more screams, more shouts, and no small amount of swearing. Dave ignored it. He had more serious concerns. The men coming up from the lower floors were uncomfortably close. If he shimmed the lock and fled onto the twenty-fifth floor, they'd be right behind him, and he'd be an easy target.

He could hear them—how near?—two or three flights of stairs below. One of them, almost out of breath, gasped, "What's going on up there?"

Another voice, less winded, replied, "Only one way to find out." Shoe soles clattered on concrete. They were running.

A barrage of bullets, automatic fire, stitched across the fire hose. Water geysered as the hose, losing pressure at every bullet hole, slowed its furious undulations. Now, the men racing down the stairs could pass it safely.

Earlier, while laying his traps, Dave had wound double lengths of thick coaxial cable around several standpipes. One of them was on this floor. The cable was anchored firmly and would not come loose. He snatched it up, looping it between his legs.

Tell me you're not going to do this.

Twice around the left leg, twice around the right.

You are utterly fucking insane.

Up over the left shoulder, beneath the crotch, crisscross the back, and over the right and left shoulders.

Pal, let me make this as clear as I can. I do not want to die.

A quick hitch knot. He was done.

He gave the cable a tug. It was secure. And the harness in which he had wrapped himself was a hasty but nonetheless credible imitation of a parachutist's jump rig.

Oh no, pal! No!

A bullet whipped by his chest. He didn't think about it. He took a short step forward, brisk but not hurried, bounced once on his toes, and sprang over the handrail. He dove with a perfection long-practiced, and never forgotten. He dove into the muddy-brown pond of his youth, into a green, green mountain lake. A jackknife, folded at the waist, now turning in the air, the torque of his body rotating him upright. A swimmer into cleanness leaping.

And it felt *good.*

Dave plunged through the empty space between the stairs. As he fell, he caught a glimpse of a face, a man wide-eyed and gaping. "Jesus God!" the man whispered.

A bullet whined somewhere, too far away to be worrisome.

He clutched the cable, bracing himself for the coming jolt. It would be no worse, he guessed, than his first jump. Twenty-five hundred feet over Fort Bragg. One or two men, the company clowns, were cracking weak jokes. Everyone else was solemnly avoiding their comrades' eyes. That sonofabitch Cuban staff sergeant was jumpmaster. He was standing by the open door, screaming above the wind, screaming the countoff, and screaming obscenities. What was that Cuban's name . . . ?

The cable snapped taut. Thinner than the flat canvas straps of a jump rig, the wire sliced into his legs. Unexpected pain drove the breath from his lungs.

Christ! That hurts.

He swung left, arcing up over the twenty-first floor handrail, and slamming into the wall with bruising force. Reflexively, he yanked the hitch knot, tumbled to the concrete, and rolled.

"*Sheee-it!*" someone yelled. "Did you see that sucker?"

Someone else was bellowing, "Down! Get down there! Don't let the bastard get away!"

Dave plucked a pistol from beneath his shirt. His legs were numb and shaking. He forced himself erect. He grinned, showing his teeth, and emptied a twenty round magazine up the stairs.

Are we having fun yet?

Time to move on. Soft bullets pinged and bounced on the stairs above him. Dispassionately, Dave criticized his pursuers' aim. He'd been in clear sight. If they had been better marksmen, they would have gotten him. He guessed his little do-it-yourself bungee stunt had rattled them.

Can we get out of here now?

David Elliot ran. He ran vertically as he had all day, and thus advanced not one step nearer freedom. Nor, in all fairness, did he fall one step closer to capture.

On the nineteenth floor, he lightly vaulted a tripwire. On the seventeenth, he heard a man—perhaps two men—come a cropper of it. Smiling faintly at their screams, he emptied two buckets of slippery soap on the stairs.

His pursuers swore when they reached those stairs. Or rather some swore. Others cried and moaned—they were the ones with broken bones. Dave heard their pain and stifled a laugh.

Now on the fifteenth floor he heard the sputtered but nonetheless gratifying profanities of someone who, up above, had lost his shoes to the sticky embrace of quick-drying rubber cement. His cursing was heartfelt, Dave could tell, and all the more appreciated for its sincerity.

In contrast, the man who had been near the microwave oven at the wrong time didn't swear. He merely whimpered. Dave thought he sounded in shock. Probably needed a medic, and soon. Too bad. Besides, he'd live. It was no big deal, only a small microwave, a countertop model stolen from an employee lounge. Dave had secreted a brace of two liter bottles of diet cola into it, and plugged the machine into an emergency outlet. As he ran past it, he had hit its on switch. Forty-seven seconds later an explosion of scalding cola and the shrapnel of a shattered oven door eliminated yet another of his pursuers.

Dave heard it all—all the outraged wounded, all their obscene invective, all their cries for help—as he ran, and as he ran he giggled.

The thirteenth floor (fourteen by the building manager's logic) was where Dave remembered placing a bottle of cleaning solvent. With no little foresight, he had taped a book of pilfered matches to its side.

Because the men chasing him had cautiously slowed their steps—no reason for that, those seemingly innocent wads of balled up copier paper were no more than they seemed to be—Dave had ample time to empty the bottle, light a match, and, while descending to the twelfth floor, flick it into the puddled cleanser. When it exploded in flame, he could no longer contain himself.

The last thing his pursuers heard was his laughter, deep rolling belly laughs, boundless joy, guffaws of sheerest pleasure, echoing through the stairwell. They stopped, looked questioningly at one another, and shook their heads.

Two pieces of enameled brass ring musically as they bounce across Colonel John James Kreuter's field desk. The colonel picks them up, holds them to the light, and squints. He rolls his tongue around in his mouth, scratches the side of his head, and frowns. "Aw right, Lew-tenant, yew gonna stand there all day lookin' like yew jest et a canary bird or are yew gonna tell me whut these here doohickeys is supposed to be?"

"Ensigns, sir. Those are the insignia of a Russian officer." Dave can't keep the smugness out of his voice. He doesn't even try.

Kreuter rubs his hand across his cheek. He looks up at Dave, and then back down again at the two brass emblems. "Like as not, a field grade officer. A major, meybe."

"Yes, sir. That's precisely what they are." Dave places a folded piece of paper on the colonel's desk. Kreuter looks at it like it was a dead rat. "An' whut's this, yer Christmas list for Santy Claus?"

"No, sir. It's the name of an ARVN captain, one of our loyal allies. The major gave it to me shortly before his untimely demise." He bites his tongue. He has to. If he doesn't, he's going to laugh.

Kreuter unfolds the paper and nods. He taps an unfiltered Camel out of a pack, flicks his thumbnail across a wooden match, frowning as he inhales. "An' jest how is it, young Lew-tenant Elliot, that yew managed to work this here par-tic-u-larly miraculous feat?"

Dave shows his teeth. "Well, sir . . ." He feels the laughter boiling up from his belly. ". . . it's that I figured . . ." His face flushes with the effort to control himself. ". . . living is . . ." He can't bottle it up. ". . . a hell of a lot more fun . . ." No hope for it. ". . . than dying!" The laughter explodes.

Mamba Jack throws his head back and laughs with him. "Well, well, well, Lew-tenant, and ain't yew some piece of work. That's whut I got to say to yew. Jest well, well, well, and meybe yew and me got us here the start of a bee-utiful friendship."

3.

7:03 P.M.

David Elliot stepped out of the elevator and onto the forty-fifth floor.

About time you returned to the scene of the crime. If there are any answers, this is where you're going to find them.

The Senterex executive suite was locked. The receptionist had long since departed, and all the secretaries would have left for home before 6:00. There still might be one or two workaholic executives hanging around at this hour. There usually were. Dave hoped to avoid them, but if he didn't, he was quite prepared to deal with them.

He slid his office key in the lock, turned, and pushed.

Now aren't you glad Bernie didn't have one of those electronic card gizmos installed on this floor? Those suckers automatically log the ID numbers of everyone who comes in and everyone who goes out.

He strode quickly across the reception room, turning left into the corridor leading to Bernie Levy's office. Then, on impulse, he stopped, spun around, and jogged east down the hallway where, twelve hours earlier, he'd cowered beneath Ransome's and Carlucci's bullets.

The repair job was flawless. The bullet holes had been filled in, the gouges papered over; there wasn't a scratch, a dent, or a scar.

No evidence. If you try to show anyone the proof of what happened this morning, they'll just look at you and sadly shake their heads. Poor old Dave, they'll say, it's all in his mind.

He glanced at the carpet, at the spot where Carlucci's blood had spilled. No stain remained, no evidence, no hint that here, at this place, a man had bled to death. The carpet had been replaced with fabric the same shade, the same nap, and even the same wear as every other inch of carpet in the corridor.

A nice professional job. But then would you expect anything less from Mr. John Ransome and company?

He turned back toward Bernie's office and, as he entered the reception room, almost collided with the sartorially resplendent frame of Dr. Frederick L. M. Sandberg, Jr.

Sandberg took a short step back, glanced over his shoulder, and collected himself. With patrician politeness he intoned, "Good evening, David."

"Hi, Doc." Fred Sandberg was the eldest member of Senterex's Board of Directors. He had retired some years earlier as the dean of the Yale medical faculty, but remained active in private practice. His clientele was limited to senior corporate executives, and he was as good as he was expensive. So good, in fact, that he acted as personal physician to Bernie, Dave, and most of the Senterex executive cadre.

"And how are you this evening, David?" Sandberg's tones were soft, smooth, inimitably well-bred.

"I've been better."

Sandberg smiled gently. "So I have heard."

Dave grimaced. "You and everyone else, I presume."

"Quite so. Bernie called a Board meeting late this afternoon. You were, need I say, the sole subject on the agenda." The doctor stroked a perfectly shaved cheek, as if framing a further remark. Dave spoke first.

"Doc, you know me, right? You've been seeing me for at least five years. You know me inside out and five inches up the large intestine."

Sandberg peered over the frames of his gold-rimmed glasses. "Indeed."

"So you know I'm not nuts." ·

Sandberg gave him an exceptionally professional smile. "Of course I do. And, David, I must assure you that neither I nor anyone else thinks that you are actually . . ." He wrinkled his aristocratic nose in anticipation of using an improperly unmedical word. ". . . nuts."

"The story is drug flashback. Right?"

"It is more than a story, David. I have seen proof. Agent Ransome . . ."

"Agent? Is that what he says he is?" Mark had also used the word.

"It is not merely what he says he is. It is what he is, a federal . . ."

"He's lying. He's a paid killer."

The expression on Sandberg's face was both sympathetic and pitying. Beneath a sienna brown sports jacket, he was wearing a canary yellow waistcoat. Not a vest, a waistcoat. Only a man of his style and presence could pull off such sartorial outlandishness. Sandberg fumbled his fingers into one of its pockets.

"Careful, Doc. They should have warned you that I'm violent."

"As indeed they did." He withdrew a white rectangle from his waistcoat. "Ah, here it is. Agent Ransome's business card. Do take a look at it."

Dave snapped the card out of Sandberg's fingers.

John P. Ransome

SPECIAL INVESTIGATIONS OFFICER
Bureau of Veteran's Affairs

There was a phone number, a Washington address, and an embossed official seal.

Dave curled his lip. "Nice print job. But printing's cheap."

"It is not a forgery, David." Sandberg's voice was low, and a little sad.

"When I picked the bastard's pocket this morning he was carrying a different card. The Specialist Consulting Group. It said he was . . ."

"David, I assure you, I have checked Agent Ransome's credentials quite thoroughly. One does not, you know, reach my age and position without developing a certain circle of acquaintances. Accordingly, I made some discreet inquiries among old friends. They assured me that he is very much what he claims to be."

Dave shook his head. "The man's a professional, Fred. He's fooled you and he's fooled your friends. That's what professionals do."

"Very well, David, if you say so. But then tell me, if he is not a government officer, what is he?"

"Damned if I know. All I know is that ever since breakfast, he and a bunch more like him have been trying to kill me."

Sandberg's face wore a look of intense professional interest. It was the sort of expression that said, *Yes, Mr. Elliot, and what did the space aliens do to you after abducting you to Planet X?* It made Dave stutter. "Doc . . . Fred, don't look at me like that. You've got to listen to my side of the story."

"Of course, David. I'll be pleased to. However, I am afraid that I can imagine the substance of your tale. Succinctly stated, your story is that nameless men from a faceless organization want to kill you for reasons which you cannot fathom. You've done nothing. You are an innocent and blameless man. But They—capital 'T' They—want you dead. Does that capture the essence of it, David? Is that the tale you wish to recount?"

Dave's stomach sank. He rubbed his lips and looked at his shoes. Sandberg continued, "David, be so kind as to do me a favor. Think about the yarn you propose to tell me. Consider its credibility. Then tell me if you think that it is not suspect. Tell me that it is not . . . well . . . symptomatic of a certain mental malaise."

Dave frowned, shaking his head. "It's your turn to be so kind as to do *me* a favor. Think about my story. Think about what would happen if it was true. Think about the kind of lies they would tell if they wanted to persuade everybody that I had gone off my rocker."

Sandberg spoke as if gently rebuking a recalcitrant child. "It is not a question of stories, David, it is a question of record. They have shown me the papers. All of the papers. As you know, I sit on the Boards of two defense contractors and I am privileged to hold a rather august security clearance. Consequently, the gentlemen who are seeking to . . . hmm . . . detain you, were rather easily persuaded to share their files with me. I must say, the portrait they paint is not a pretty picture. No blame falls to you, of course. You were merely an innocent victim. Quite horrifyingly innocent, it seems. I fear it was not our nation's finest hour, and what they did to you—to you and your good comrades—goes quite beyond the pale."

Dave spoke through his teeth. "They didn't do anything to me.

They didn't do anything to us. Whatever any of us did, we did to ourselves. Look, Doc . . . Fred, the files they showed you are fake. It's a lie, a swindle—perfect, rounded, symmetrical, complete, colossal."

"Still quoting Mark Twain, are we, David?"

"I wouldn't do that if I was crazy."

"You very well might. David, we have spoken of something relevant to your situation before. I remember your reaction to my concern, and for that reason I hesitate to bring the matter up."

"What?" Dave bit the word off. "Go ahead, Doc. Lay it on me."

"Are you still . . . pardon me, David, I truly dislike asking this . . . are you still hearing voices?"

"Aw cripes, Doc! That's . . . that's nothing. It's just my way of . . . Just like I told you, it's not really a voice, it's just me sort of talking to myself."

Sandberg repeated slowly. "Talking. To. Yourself." He nodded. The nod said it all.

"Damnit, I . . ."

"You will remember when you first spoke to me of this—shall we say—idiosyncrasy, I suggested that it would not be a bad thing were you to see a colleague of mine, a specialist as it were."

"Doc, I said it then and I'll say it now: I don't need to see a shrink. I am as sane as you are."

Sandberg shook his head. "David, David, let me repeat, and it is critical that you understand this—no one claims you are insane. I assure you, you are *not* deranged, not in the usual sense. What has happened, and I have seen irrefutable evidence confirming it, is that you and many of the other men in your Army unit were fed an experimental psychotropic substance. Unforeseen complexities resulted. I am told your own commanding officer . . ."

Dave slammed his palm into the wall. "Oh Christ! Is that what they are saying? That everything that happened was because we all were on drugs? Jesus!"

"David, do be calm." Sandberg reached into his waistcoat pocket again. Dave lifted his pistol. Sandberg withdrew a roll of breath mints. "Please, David, you need not point that thing at me." He removed one from the pack, popped it into his mouth, and proffered the roll to Dave. Dave shook his head. The doctor continued, "David, I do not doubt that you believe that people are trying to kill you. However, you must realize that all the evidence . . ."

"What about this?" Dave brandished his pistol.

"They warned me about that. You wrested it away from a policeman."

"Doc, this is not a policeman's gun. Look at it. It's . . ."

"I know nothing about firearms other than the fact that I despise them."

Dave growled with frustration.

Sandberg lowered his voice, adopting a more intimate tone. "There's another thing, David. Helen has called me."

"Oh hell."

"She is naturally concerned for you, concerned about the effects of such experimental drugs as you were given. And because she feels that for some time your marriage has not been . . ."

"Drop it, Doc. I might need to talk to a marriage counselor, but right now it's not high on my priorities."

"I might argue that a man whose feelings for his wife are not foremost in his mind is in need of more than mere marital counsel." Sandberg slipped the roll of mints back into his pocket.

Dave blew out a long sigh. "Damnit, Doc, I . . ." His voice hardened as he saw what the doctor was up to. "Hand out of the vest pocket, Doc."

"Waistcoat."

"Right. What's in there? What do you have in there other than a pack of Certs?"

Dr. Sandberg smiled sorrowfully. "A small spray dispenser of chemical Mace. They gave them to all of us. The idea, David, is simply to subdue you. I promise you that is all that is intended."

"Doc, you and I—we are friends, aren't we?"

"I sincerely hope so."

"Good, because what I am about to do to you is in the spirit of friendship."

Sandberg tried to step backward. He couldn't. Without his noticing it, Dave had maneuvered him so that his back was against the wall.

4.

The decor of a chief executive's office often discloses more about a company than its annual report. For example, as every stock market analyst knows, it is wise to be wary of any enterprise whose president decorates his inner sanctum with models of jet aircraft— especially Gulfstreams, Learjets, and other high-priced private planes. The presence of such miniatures inevitably means that the corporation owns an awesomely expensive jet fleet, a luxury purchased at shareholder expense because the boss believes it beneath his imperial dignity to travel, like an ordinary commoner, via United, American, or Delta.

By the same token, experienced investors are justifiably suspicious of a corporate leader who subcontracts the decoration of his chambers to an "interior architect" managed by or employing his wife (the second one, the younger one, the blonde one). Usually the results involve opulently upholstered but geometrically odd furniture, ceramic bric-a-brac cast in primary colors by Mercedes-owning folk artists, and lithographs in the styles of Jim Dine, Frank Stella, Sean Scully, or Bruce Nauman, but costing rather more than the genuine works of those modern masters.

At the other end of the spectrum—found less often in New York City than in the high-tech environs of California's Silicon Valley and Massachusetts's Route 128—there are the chief executives whose offices are ostentatiously egalitarian: metal desks, vinyl-covered chairs, uncarpeted floors, nothing on the walls but an erasable whiteboard and, perhaps, a few wiring diagrams. Insiders know that it is wise to be watchful of these officers too. A corporate president is, by definition, the enterprise's ultimate decision-making authority. However, some CEOs find such responsibility fearfully intimidating. To avoid it, they surround themselves with plebeian trappings, cowering behind a mask of democratic corporate governance. Frugal furnishings are the first and most visible sign of an executive who is too timid to make a decision.

Bernie Levy's office bespoke none of these things. Like the man who occupied it, it was subdued and representative of traditional values. Only a little larger than the offices of Senterex's other corporate executives, Bernie's place of business occupied the northeast corner of the forty-fifth floor. Its windows opened on a panorama that included Central Park to the north (on rare clear days he could see far up the Hudson into Westchester County and beyond), and to the east the United Nations building, the East River, Queens, Long Island, and the sharp, slate gleam of the distant Atlantic. Bernie's desk was dark mahogany lovingly carved in classic style; his high-backed leather chair had been purchased from the same craftsmen who provision the Justices of the Supreme Court of the United States; his sofas came from the same source, and were plump and comfortable. Of knickknacks, gimcracks, and souvenirs there were few: a set of Mont Blanc pens in an obsidian holder, an antique abacus given him by his partner in a Chinese joint venture, a single silver-framed photograph of his wife and children, an etched crystal hexahedron paperweight commemorating one of his many charitable efforts, and an enormous, ugly 14.5-millimeter round for a Soviet PTRD antitank gun. The bullet, seven inches long and one inch in diameter, was engraved with Bernie's name and a message reading, "Company B, 3rd Battalion: Inchon to the Chosen Reservoir and back, 1950–1952. *Semper Fidelis.*"

For art Bernie had hung a handful of paintings created by the Wyeth family—N. C. through Andrew—and all paid for out of

Bernie's, rather than Senterex's, pocket. Dave suspected that the artwork had as much to do with Bernie's eclectic tastes as with the fact that one of Senterex's Board members, Scott Thatcher, was an art collector of no small reputation and especially fond of the Brandywine school.

Bernie's office decor exhibited only two eccentricities: his books and his coffee maker. The books were a decade and a half's compilation of a genre that Dave thought of as "executive faith healing"—everything from *In Search of Excellence* to *Reengineering the Corporation*. Senterex's chief executive could not resist a volume that promised to reveal heretofore unknown secrets of improving managerial effectiveness. He bought them all, read them all, believed them all—at least until a new one came along.

Dave ran his finger along their jackets and smiled at the memories they brought.

Then there was Bernie's coffee maker. That too made Dave smile. Somewhere along the line, probably under the influence of one of his California-based motivational gurus, Bernie had decided that Senterex's executive secretaries should not be required to perform coffee duties. No longer would visitors to the executive suite be politely met by a gracious secretary who offered them their choice of coffee, tea, or cocoa. Rather it would become the responsibility of each executive to have his or her own coffee maker, supply of tea bags, and cache of hot chocolate.

No one could fathom why Bernie thought it important that executives drawing six-figure salaries should waste their time fumbling with pots, filters, and grounds, but he was adamant about it. The forty-fifth floor kitchenette was converted to a photocopier room, and every executive office was issued a Toshiba coffee maker.

The results were a catastrophe: stained carpets, coffee grounds splattered on critical documents, expensive credenzas bereft of their glossy finishes—to say nothing of embarrassed visitors who, choking at the wretchedness of the stuff they were served, surreptitiously emptied their cups into potted plants.

After a month of mounting disaster, the secretarial staff rebelled. They started coming in early, sneaking into their bosses' offices, and making the coffee themselves. Shortly peace was restored to the forty-fifth floor, and everyone, from Bernie downward, seemed to have gotten what they wanted.

Bernie, forgetful in such matters and more reliant on his secretary than he was willing to admit, seemed to have left his coffee machine on again. Dave flicked the off switch. "You're welcome, Bernie," he muttered.

The pot was half-full of Bernie's personal blend, the envy of everyone on the floor. Dave poured himself a cup, sipped, and smiled. Bernie asserted that San Francisco was the only American city in which *every* business prides itself on offering guests a great-tasting brew. Consequently, he arranged for a special San Francisco blend—arabica, Kona, and something else—to be air-freighted to Senterex monthly. But he refused to disclose the name of the source from which he purchased it, or to make the beans available to any other Senterex executives. "I want," Bernie smirked, "people should remember the best cup of coffee in New York came from Bernie Levy. That way, maybe they come back to have another cup and we do some business. If you want to do the same, you go find your own coffee."

Bernie. He's got an angle on everything. The last great deal maker.

Dave savored the coffee. It was so absolutely perfect. He wondered if he could find the name of the supplier somewhere in Bernie's files.

Gotten your priorities wrong there, pal. If you're going to check Bernie's files, you should be looking for something else.

Dave placed the coffee cup down carefully on one of Bernie's brass coasters. He spun the chair around so that he was facing Bernie's credenza, and jimmied open its lock.

The top drawer contained the personal and the confidential files of Senterex's chairman—a double row of olive drab Pendaflex Esselte file folders, each bearing a colored tab identifying its contents. Yellow tabs for Board meeting minutes. Green tabs marking the charities nearest to Bernie's heart: Salvation Army, Children's Hospital, United Jewish Appeal, Lighthouse for the Blind, ASPCA. Clear tabs on eight folders bearing the name of each Senterex operating division. One blue tab reading "Lockyear Laboratories." Orange tabs for business projections and forecasts. Purple for the investment bankers' analyses of potential acquisition targets. A dozen red-tabbed folders bearing the names of each of Senterex's most senior executives.

Dave drew out the one with his name.

It was surprisingly thin. It began with, of all things, a photocopy of his original Senterex employment application. The photograph stapled to it showed an eager young man in a two-dollar haircut. The application was followed by a handful of memos to and from the Personnel Department back before its name had been changed to "Human Resources." They dealt with promotions, pay raises, and changes in assignment. There were some insurance forms, an appraisal or two from people who had supervised him in his early days at Senterex, and copies of the various agreements and commitments he had signed as he moved up the corporate ladder. Toward the very end of the file he found some correspondence between Senterex's chief counsel and the Securities and Exchange Commission. As soon as Dave had been made an officer of the company, any trades he might make in its stock became a subject of interest to that agency.

The last piece of paper in the folder was a letter on FBI stationery.

Dave's stomach did a somersault.

"Dear Mr. Levy," it read, "In reference Mr. David P. Elliot, an individual known to you and in your employ, this will apprise you that this office has been charged with conducting a background investigation of the aforenamed individual, with said investigation being deemed necessary and appropriate under the conditions provided for by the Defense Supplier and Contractor Act of 1953, as amended, and pertaining to the issuance of security clearances to executives and directors of corporations engaged in business operations involving classified, restricted, privileged and/or other secure affairs. The requester of said investigation has directed the undersigned to coordinate with you as relates to specifics to be discussed at your earliest convenience. Your cooperation in this matter is appreciated."

Uh-oh.

Defense Supplier and Contractor Act? But Senterex didn't do any defense work. In fact, it didn't do any government work at all.

Or does it?

Dave read the letter over twice. It really didn't say much.

What about the date?

Three days ago. The letter was dated just three days ago. Now what the devil did that mean? And why—*why, why, why*—after all of these years was someone trying to renew security clearance that had been canceled the day he was discharged from the Army?

Worse yet . . .

Worse yet, unless the letter was a forgery, Dave was the subject of a federal investigation. And Ransome was telling everyone that he was a federal officer.

Suppose Doc Sandberg was right: Ransome really is a Fed!

That didn't make sense. The government doesn't put out contracts on innocent civilians. It doesn't dispatch teams of hard case hitmen to assassinate forty-seven year old businessmen. That was movie stuff, pulp fiction, conspiracy theory. Oliver Stone, Geraldo Rivera, Rush Limbaugh.

There have been allegations—Lee Harvey Oswald, Jack Ruby, Bill Casey, Martha Mitchell . . .

Only the lunatic fringe made those kinds of claims. Besides, even if the conspiracy buffs were right, the people who had been assassinated were killed for a reason. They knew something. They were involved in something. They had secrets.

What have you seen, what have you heard, what do you know?

Nothing. Dave had no secrets—no state secrets. There wasn't . . .

Those court-martials were secret. They sealed the records. They made you sign a promise never to disclose what happened.

No, no, no. That was too long ago. Besides, Dave wasn't the only person who knew. There had been other witnesses. And everyone, *everyone*, who had been involved in the trials knew—board members, prosecutors, defenders, steno clerks. It was crazy even to think that . . .

Crazy.

He took one more look at the FBI letter. Was it real? Was it a forgery? Was there some way to find out why it had been sent?

He lifted Bernie's telephone and tapped the number printed beneath the name of the man who had signed the thing. The phone was answered on the first ring. "You have reached the Federal Bureau of Investigation, New York City. Our office hours are 8:30 A.M. to 5:30 P.M. If you know the extension of the person you are trying to reach, please enter it now. If you do not, please touch the star key now."

Dave hated these damned robotized telephone systems. He punched the star key. "If you wish to leave a message for the switchboard attendant, please touch the pound key now. If you wish to access the voice mail system, please touch the '0' key now."

He hit "0."

"Please enter the last name of the individual whose voice mailbox you wish to reach, using the keypad on your telephone. For the letter 'Q,' please substitute '0.' "

Dave looked at the signature on the letter. He pecked in the name.

"No one with the name you have entered is accessible through this voice mail system. If you have mis-entered the name or wish to try again, please touch the star key now."

He hung up.

Maybe the man who sent the letter wasn't with the FBI. Maybe he was, but his name hadn't been entered in the goddamned telephone system's database. Maybe, maybe, maybe. Dave didn't know. He had no answers. There were no answers anywhere.

Or were there?

He needed to think. There was something that he had forgotten or put out of his mind. It was the key to what was going on. But first . . .

He studied the files in Bernie's credenza. Personnel, Charities, Forecasts, Board Meetings, Acquisition Candidates, Division Operations. One of them might hold a clue. He reached for the first in the drawer. As he did, Bernie backed into the room.

Bernie entered not from his secretary's foyer, but rather from a door to the west. It connected his office with the Senterex corporate boardroom. As he walked backward, he spoke to somebody who was still in the boardroom. ". . . Don't you know it?"

Dave jumped, gasped, was certain that his heart had stopped.

Bernie continued, "Wait a minute. That's yours, isn't it, the portfolio back there?" He stepped back into the boardroom.

Dave hurled himself out of Bernie's chair, scrambling for the closet. It was, like the closet in his own office, a spacious walk-in. Bernie used it to store a miscellany of meeting supplies—oversized easel pads, marking pens, tape, and a half dozen tripod-mounted easel stands. Senterex's chairman was incapable of holding a business meeting without writing something on an easel.

Dave flattened himself against the far wall, pulling the door almost but not quite closed.

Bernie came back into the office. ". . . like a knife to my heart, that's what it is."

Another voice answered, "You're not alone. Olivia and I are quite fond of David."

Dave knew the voice. Its distinctive New England twang belonged to Scott C. Thatcher, a member of Senterex's Board of Directors, chief executive of his own company, and one of Dave's few intimate friends.

"So maybe it will all work out in the end," Bernie said. "This Ransome, he's no schmuck."

"Emmm." Dave could picture Thatcher. He'd be stroking his bushy, Mark Twain moustache or running his fingers through his unruly, long white hair. "Bernard, on the subject of your Mr. Ransome, I wonder if you have been a little less than forthcoming."

Go out. Go out there right now. Thatcher will believe you. He's the only person in the world who will.

"Me? What do you mean?"

"Today is not the first time I have encountered the man. I do not forget faces. I have seen him before, and I have seen him in this building."

Now. Do it now. Thatcher will be on your side.

"Uh . . ."

"In the reception room some four or five weeks ago, I should say. He was leaving as I was entering. Indeed, I distinctly remember asking you about him."

Just walk out of the closet, pal. "Hi, Scotty! Boy, am I glad to see you!"

He couldn't. It would draw Thatcher into the thing. It would put Thatcher's life in as much jeopardy as his own.

Idiot! Thatcher is the CEO of the second largest computer company in the world. They put his picture on the cover of Forbes, Fortune, Business Week. *No one is going to mess with him.*

"Nonsense. *Mishegaas.*"

"Not at all. He gave me an uncommonly arrogant look. I remarked upon it to you. You replied that he was an executive of a company you planned to acquire. Given the man's demeanor, I thought your answer improbable."

Dave put his hand on the closet's doorknob.

Do it! Do it!

"Not me. It's something with somebody else, you're remembering."

"Bernard, though aged and feeble and far beyond the springtime of my buoyant youth, I am not yet senile. That man was here, and you were his host."

Dave turned the knob slowly, gently pushing at the door.

"Bernie Levy does not lie."

"A misstatement. Better put, one would say, 'Bernard Levy *rarely* lies because he knows himself to be frightfully inept at it.' "

"Scotty, my friend . . ."

Through the widening crack Dave saw Bernie spread his hands in a false gesture of openness.

"We are friends, Bernard, and have been for forty years and more. I am a member of your Board, and you a member of mine. There is a trust between us. If it happens that there is more to this problem with David than you are willing to disclose, then I must respect that—as I must assume that your reasons are good."

It's now or never, pal.

Dave pressed his palm against the door. The radio in his pocket hissed awake. Thatcher said, "If you need a hand, you can call me at any time." Dave pushed. Bernie said, "It's tougher than you know." Ransome's voice came over the radio, calling, "Mr. Elliot? Do you copy?" Thatcher said, "Just bear in mind that David is as much my friend as you are." Ransome said, "I have authority to offer you a mutually acceptable compromise solution, Mr. Elliot." Dave took his hand from the door. Bernie said, "He's like a son to me." Thatcher replied, "I'll say good night, then. Olivia's expecting me home." Ransome said, "Mr. Elliot, I truly would appreciate your answering me." Bernie said, "Good night." Dave's voice said, "Forget it, turkey. By now you've got your tracers and your triangulation equipment set up all over the building, right, Ransome? So tell them to take a fix on me. Tell them to find what floor I'm on. Guess what, buddy, I'm not on any floor. I'm outside, and I'm not coming back. Hey, Ransome, you can run and run as fast as you can, but you can't catch me, I'm the gingerbread man!" Ransome's voice was flat as ice, and as cold. "Mr. Elliot, this is unacceptably immature behavior." Bernie spoke from near the door, "You'll be at the audit committee meeting next week?" A second voice, Partridge's voice, came over the radio. "He's telling the truth. He's somewhere on the Upper West Side." Thatcher, now outside Bernie's office, answered, "Sorry. I've got to be in Singapore. An issue with our largest supplier."

Somewhere in Manhattan, Marge Cohen switched off a tape recorder.

Partridge whispered, "He's gone. We're all dead men."

Dave stood motionless, turning that last remark over in his mind.

5.

He stepped out of the closet, his pistol held lightly at waist level. "If you move, Bernie, I'll shoot you." He tried to sound like he meant it.

Bernie was sitting at his desk, shuffling through papers. He looked up with an expression of desolate weariness on his face. "Hello, Davy. It's good to see you." He sounded like a man who was a million years old.

"Bernie, I want you to keep your hands on the desk. I don't want you pulling another gun . . ."

"No more guns." Bernie gave him the ghost of a smile.

". . . or a can of Mace."

Bernie nodded. "You know about that?"

"I know." Dave walked closer. "I know some other things too. But I want to know more."

Bernie's face was a model of sadness. He turned his hands

palms-down on the desk. When he spoke, Dave sensed that his words were meant more for himself than for anyone else. "Yeah. So go figure. You spend all of your life trying to be a *mensch*, you know, a real *mensch*. Work hard, play fair, tell the truth, do the right thing, be a patriot. When it's all over, you know what? I'll tell you what. To them you're still nothing but a lousy little Jew. Here, Jew, do this. Here, Jew, do that. Thanks, you're a good American. For a Jew, that is."

He shook his head slowly, sadly, all the weight of the world on his shoulders. "They gave me the Silver Star. Me. Bernie Levy. Did you know that, Davy?"

Dave replied with such gentleness as he could muster, "No, Bernie, I didn't."

"Scotty, he got one. Me, I got one too. Damnedest thing you ever saw. Two crazy soldiers, completely *fartootst*, Lieutenant Thatcher and Corporal Levy. Charged a North Korean tank, is what we did. Him with a .45 and a hand grenade, me with an M-1 rifle. Totally insane, I'm telling you. Dead is what we should have been. Instead we both get the Silver Star. MacArthur, he's the one who pinned them on. Oh, but you should have seen it, Davy, you should have seen it. Scotty is lying in bed with a shot-up leg. Bernie Levy is standing next to him. The old man comes in. There's a photographer from *Life* magazine taking pictures. I tell you, it was some moment, Davy, maybe the best I ever had. And so MacArthur starts to pin on the medal, and you know what? Scotty, he's nothing but a lowly lieutenant, Scotty starts chewing out the general. The general! Can you believe? It was wonderful. It was a miracle. No one has ever seen anything like it. I was—I was in awe. Did he ever tell you about that, Scotty, I mean?"

Dave shook his head.

"Amazed. Bernie Levy was amazed. You see, Scotty's father, he was this doctor on MacArthur's staff. In Japan, I mean, just after the war. He and this Russian and this OSS guy are investigating the war crimes. So they find out something and they bring it to the general and the general says hush it up. But they say no way and so the general fires everyone home and gets himself a new doctor. So—you gotta picture this—so five or six years later, there is this nothing lieutenant lying in his bed with the most important general in the world—in the world!—pinning the Silver Star on his pajamas, and the photographer is taking pictures, and all of a sudden the lieutenant is telling off the general for firing his father. Oh, Davy, you should have seen it. Such *chutzpah*! Bernie Levy has never seen its like!"

Dave grinned. "That's a pretty good story, Bernie."

A small smile flitted across Bernie's lips. "I know," he said, looking Dave in the eye and nodding. Suddenly the smile disappeared. Bernie looked weary again. "Okay, okay. So you want to talk, Davy, we talk. Maybe I tell you something, maybe I don't. A man's still got his honor, you know. That, they cannot take away from me. So sit down, make yourself comfortable."

"I'll stand."

"Sit, stand, what's the difference?" Bernie wrapped a pudgy hand around a coffee cup, lifted it to his lips, and took a sip. "You want I should pour you a nice cup of coffee, Davy?"

"That's my coffee you're drinking, Bernie."

Bernie's face changed. "Your coffee?"

"Yeah. I poured it while I was looking through your files."

"You've been drinking my coffee?" Bernie suddenly leaned back in his chair. The worn expression on his face was replaced by an ironic smile. The smile widened. Bernie laughed. "How wonderful. You drink *my* coffee. Now, I'm drinking *your* coffee. Isn't that wonderful? Davy, it is so wonderful, you don't know."

He laughed harder, the guffaws growing into whoops.

Dave frowned. "I don't get the joke."

"The joke? It's a wonderful joke, Davy! Wonderful! And best of all, the joke's on Bernie Levy!" Shaking with laughter, Bernie rose and, coffee cup in hand, walked across the office. A circular worktable and four straight-backed chairs sat by the northern window.

Bernie put a pudgy hand down on the back of one of the chairs, gripped it tightly, and turned to Dave. "It's the most wonderful joke in the world!"

Suddenly, with surprising strength, Bernie lifted the chair and hurled it through the window. Glass exploded outward, spinning in the night, wind-whipped and looking for a moment like a jeweled storm, an ice blizzard, white light reflected and refracted and sparkling among diamond shards. A gust spun glass needles back into the office. One splinter opened a surgically straight line of red on Bernie's left cheek. Dave took a halting step forward. Bernie held up his palm, as if to tell him to come no closer. All the sadness in his face had disappeared, and he seemed as happy as a child. "Bernie Levy has only Bernie Levy to blame. Turnabout is fair play. That's some fine joke, Davy, that's the best joke of all. Let me tell you, only God Himself could come up with a joke like that."

Bernie took one last sip of coffee, and, still clutching his cup, stepped into space.

6.

It takes an object six seconds to fall a thousand feet. Dave reached the window in plenty of time to see Bernie die. In Vietnam he had, of course, observed enough wet death. It had taken him more time than most to become hardened to it, but hardened he became, and hardened he remained. Nonetheless, the sight of Bernie's end, even from a height, was bad. Very bad.

Poor pudgy Bernie exploded.

Orphaned limbs, pink strings of flesh, slick grey organs burst onto the street. Blood, quite black under the harsh glare of streetlights, splashed streamers. A car speeding east on Fiftieth Street veered up on the sidewalk, laid a trail of sparks as it careened along a building, and rolled steaming on its side. A woman washed in gore collapsed. Her male companion knelt retching where she lay. People farther away screamed. A lump of Bernie Levy the size of a soccer ball tumbled out into the Park Avenue intersection, there to cause brakes to shriek and fenders to crumple. A dog pulled free of its master's slackly held leash and trotted eagerly toward the entrancing odor of fresh offal.

Forty-five stories aboveground, David Elliot leaned out a broken window, looked away, felt the wind cold and brisk, and was thankful that the air was so fresh. Speaking to the sky rather than the street, he whispered, "Aw Jesus, Bernie, why the hell did you do that? Christ, it can't have been that bad. Whatever it was, I would have forgiven you. We could have worked it out, Bernie. You didn't have to . . ."

Noises.

Not only in the street below, but also in the halls outside Bernie's office. Feet running on carpet. The chunky metal sound of pump shotgun chambering a shell. A cool voice, an Appalachian voice: "Careful up there."

Christ almighty! He's been on this floor the whole time!

Dave wheeled away from the window, raced across the office, flung himself into the closet, cowered in the dark. The door to Bernie's office flew open. Dave heard a thump and a shuffle. His mind's eye formed a picture of the scene—standard assault tactics: one man prone in the doorway, his trigger finger tense; another kneeling, drawing a wide arc with a shotgun or automatic rifle as he searched out targets; a third man crouched behind and above, doing the same.

"Clear?" Ransome speaking from outside the office.

"Clear. But we got a problem."

"What?"

"The Yid's scragged himself. Done the dive."

A burst of sirens from the street muffled the first half of Ransome's answer. All Dave could hear was, ". . . should have known he couldn't take the heat."

"We've got minutes before the local law arrives." Ransome was in the office now, in control, issuing orders with a soft, cool drawl. "Wren, take three men and move our gear down to base. Use the stairs."

Base? Have they set up a base of operations on another floor?

"Bluejay, get on the horn—use a scrambler—tell pathology I want the subject's blood sample ASAP. Tell them to put it in an ambulance and siren it up here double time."

Blood sample? Where the hell did they get a blood sample? You haven't had a blood sample taken in months, not since Doc Sandberg . . . uh-oh. Oh yes you have . . .

"Sir?"

"DNA fingerprinting, Bluejay. I intend to sprinkle a little of the subject's blood on that broken glass."

"I read you, sir. Nice going."

"Move it."

"Yes, sir."

Another voice, duller, older. "I don't get it, chief."

"Bluejay and I will arrive a few minutes after the law. It will be suggested that this was not a simple suicide. Who the prime suspect is will also be suggested. Forensics will find two blood types at the scene of the crime. Bingo, it's murder. And when they autopsy the subject, it will be bingo again."

Autopsy? Now we know the kind of deal he wanted to offer you.

Ransome continued, "Greylag, I want you to open the spigot with the media. Maximum exposure. Radio, television, the papers. Lunatic throws boss out window. Maniac murderer on the loose. Mad dog. Shoot to kill. By 8:30 we'll have every law enforcement officer in New York looking for him."

"What if he decides to leave the city?"

"Contra-psychological. He's one of us. He won't cut and run."

"Still . . ."

"Point taken. We've got coverage of everybody he knows or might try to contact, correct?"

"Yes, sir. Double teams."

Jesus! How many regiments does this guy command?

"Okay. How many ways are there off this island?"

Greylag paused to think: "Four auto tunnels. Sixteen or seventeen bridges, I guess. Three heliports. Four or five subway routes, maybe more. The Ferry. Four airports counting Newark and Westchester. Three train lines. Oh yeah, he could take the cable car to Roosevelt Island and then . . ."

"Too much. We don't have the resources to cover it all."

"I could call Washington."

Washington? Oh God, are these bastards from the government after all?

"At the moment, that is not a desirable option." There was a new note in Ransome's voice—slightly querulous, slightly uneasy. "Not desirable at all. Just put some men on the major arteries and at the airports. That's the best we can do. The rest of you men, pass the word—if anyone bumps into the local law, keep it cool. These are New York cops, not the kind of Speedy Gonzales greasers you're used to dealing with. They don't bribe cheap. Keep your lips zipped and avoid confrontation. Okay, let's move out."

"Radio, sir. Incoming message for you. Urgent."

"Give . . . Robin here . . . He what? . . . Beautiful, just beautiful. . . . Acknowledged. Robin out. Okay, you men, listen up. Wren is down on the seventeenth floor with a punji stake through his carotid." His voice was as emotionless as a robot's.

Dave, crouching in the closet, gnawed his lip. *Thought those letter openers weren't lethal, did you, pal?*

Ransome's frosty monotone continued, "Gentlemen, this is slovenly. I asked for a full sweep of those stairwells after this afternoon's incompetent attempt to lure the subject into a firefight. I am disappointed in the results. Let us try to behave a bit more professionally from now on. Given our subject's uncooperative attitude, caution is called for."

"Sir, are we going to get him?"

"Affirmative, Greylag. If we don't get him on the streets, we'll get him when he comes back here. He *will* come back, you know."

Like hell!

"Good. I'd like a little private time with Mr. Elliot."

"Negative. I'm first on the chow line. There won't be any left-overs."

2.
DÉJÀ VU

"... he did not feel that war consisted of killing your opponents. There is a contradiction here."

—Patrick O'Brian, *H.M.S. Surprise*

CHAPTER 6
DAVE GOES FOR A RIDE

1.

Admit it, pal, you've always wanted to do this.

Absolutely.

More fun than you've ever had in your entire life.

Close. Very close.

The guy in the BMW isn't taking you seriously. Flash him.

Dave hit his high beams. The BMW's driver had his ear glued to a cellular telephone. He refused to move, straddling two lanes, and blocking Dave's passage. Dave snatched the microphone off the dashboard, flicked a toggle switch, and angrily growled. "You in the Beemer, this is a police emergency. Either you get out of the road or you go to jail."

The amplified sound of his voice echoed through the crowded streets. The BMW's driver glanced over his shoulder, gave a disgusted look, and pulled to the side. Dave stepped on the accelerator. Accompanied solely by his sardonic guardian angel, he roared through the Manhattan night in a stolen police car.

Yeah!

The keys had been in the policeman's pocket. They were conveniently tagged with the number and license plate of the vehicle to which they belonged. Dave had glanced at them warily, and was prepared to drop them on the tiled men's room floor when his inner voice whispered, *Hey, pal, you've just flattened a uniformed law officer during the performance of his duties—or at least whilst taking a bladder break—and duct-taped him to the handicapped toilet. Add to that the fact that you have stolen his clothes, his badge, his sidearm, and his hat.*

But not his shoes.

Only because they didn't fit. Plus you've killed five, maybe six guys who just might be federal agents, stolen money from everyone you've met, phoned in a bomb threat, placed life-endangering traps on the fire stairs of a Park Avenue office tower, perpetrated countless aggravated assaults and felonious breakings and enterings, cooked up a batch of home brew explosive, and boosted telephone company property. Oh yeah, also you are wanted for the murder of Bernie Levy. So what are they going to do to you if you steal a police car too? Worst case, maybe they add another few centuries to what's already going to be ten thousand years in Sing Sing.

Dave shrugged and pocketed the keys. He strolled out of the forty-fifth floor lavatory just as another officer was entering. Dave nodded at him.

"Whadadeal," the policeman grumbled. "Guy's got his own private can and he turns leaper. Kee-rist, can ya believe it?"

Dave replied, "So I tell the lieutenant I wanna take a dump, just once in my life, in a private Park Avenue can, and he says no, there might be evidence in it."

"Said the same to me. Kee-rist, can ya believe it?"

Five minutes later Dave was on the ground floor, pushing his way through the crowd of police and camera crews in the lobby. No one so much as looked at him. As he'd expected, the patrolman's blues made him even more invisible than his telephone repairman's disguise.

The patrol car was right by the curb. Dave slipped in, started the ignition, grinned broadly, and drove into the night.

At Eighty-seventh Street and Broadway, Dave yanked the wheel left, gleefully sending the police car into a four-wheel drift, and gunning his way west. In the middle of the next block he switched off the siren and flasher. He slowed, pulled right, and eased the vehicle up to the curb. There was just enough space for it next to a fire hydrant.

There may not be a law on the books you haven't broken today.

Marge Cohen said she lived on Ninety-fourth Street. Dave planned to walk the rest of the way. Keeping the patrol car—or even being near it—was too risky. Someone would be noticing its absence soon.

With a paper-wrapped bundle containing Greg's clothes beneath his arm, Dave began walking back east on Eighty-seventh. The sight of a cop on foot was sufficiently uncommon that some few people glanced at him. Most didn't.

He turned north on Broadway. It had been years since he had been in this part of town. Yuppie gentrification had infested the neighborhood. The bars he passed sported potted ferns and campy names. What used to be junk stores now sold antiques. The clothing shops' mannequins looked like Cher on a bad night. The streets were still dirty, though, littered with the very special detritus that only accumulates on Manhattan's Upper West Side.

Walk like a cop, pal, not like a tourist.

Dave slowed his steps, forced himself into a rolling John Wayne gait, and made a point of looking watchful.

That's more like it.

He was north of Ninety-first Street before he found what he wanted. Green neon above the entrance announced "McAnn's Bar and Grill."

If you can't trust an Irish pub, what can you trust?

He pushed the door open. The place was dim. It smelled of draft suds, old sawdust, and hot corned beef. The joint's patrons weren't yuppies, never had been and never would be. They looked like they'd been at their tables a long time. One or two gave him the eye, and then went back to nursing their beers.

He walked to the bar. The bartender was already pulling him a Ballantine. Dave hated the brand. He accepted it anyway.

"Can I help you, officer?"

Dave lifted his mug. "This is help enough." He took a sip. The slightly metallic taste reminded him . . . so long ago . . . reminded him . . .

Ballantine was Taffy Weiler's favorite beer. The redheaded refugee from New York had carted who-knows-how-many cases of the stuff up into the Sierras. Afterward, just before they left, Dave had made him collect all the empties. Taffy wanted to leave them where they lay. Dave had been furious at the idea of the least blemish marring the beauty of . . .

"Want a shot to go with it?"

"Pardon?" The bartender had broken Dave's chain of thought.

"I asked if you wanted a shot to go with your beer?"

"Not on duty."

The bartender snorted. "That hasn't stopped your partners. Say, you're new on the beat, aren't you?"

"Temporary duty. Usually I'm out in Astoria."

"My name's Dunne. Call me Jack."

Uh . . . right, pal, so what's the name on that nameplate you're wearing? No peeking!

"Hutchinson. Everyone calls me Hutch."

"Figures."

"You got a phone book, Jack?"

"Sure." The bartender reached beneath the bar and lifted a thick Manhattan White Pages. He watched while Dave flipped through the C's. Cogan, Coggin, Cohan, Cohee, Cohen . . . Lots of Cohens. Pages of them. Cohen, Marge? No listing. Cohen, Marigold? Ditto.

Cohen, M.? A couple of dozen. But only one on Ninety-fourth Street. Just off of Amsterdam. It had to be her.

He passed the directory back to the bartender. "Thanks. Is there a phone—a private phone I can use?"

"In the back. Local call, I presume."

"Very."

"Be my guest."

It wasn't Marge Cohen that he called, and it wasn't a local number. It was AT&T International information. Dave wanted a telephone number in Switzerland.

2.

Marge's building was a four-story brownstone, the sort that native New Yorkers find charming, but that reminds out-of-towners of the Great Depression. No lights shone through its grime-streaked windows. A flight of pitted concrete stairs led to its grilled front door. Dave heard the sound of snoring. Someone seemed to be sleeping among the trash cans beneath the stairs.

According to the bank of tarnished mailboxes in the foyer, M. F. Cohen's apartment was on the ground floor and in the rear. Apartment 1B.

Dave looked for the buzzer and intercom system. Somebody had ripped it out of its mountings. He shrugged, and shimmed the lock with his credit card.

Inside the walls were grey with inattention. The carpet was worn and stained, the hall lights dim. The building smelled of age, mold, and indifference. The landlord didn't spend much on up-keep, and probably wouldn't until the tenants threatened a rent strike.

Dave knocked on the door to apartment 1B.

Light winked through the peephole in the door. Somebody was looking out. A lock clicked, the latch turned, the door swung open, Marge Cohen sprang at him hissing like a cat. "You sonofabitch!"

What fresh hell is this?

Her hands were hooked into claws; her nails—neither long nor enameled—were aimed at his eyes. Dave jerked back. She missed, but not by much. He held up a palm, "Now wait a minute . . ."

Marge crouched, ready to spring. "You rotten prick!" She leapt. Her nails came at his eyes again. Dave snatched her wrists, and held her rigid. This was the last thing he had expected.

"Bastard, bastard, bastard!" She writhed in his grip, and landed a hard kick on his shin. Dave knew he'd have a bruise.

Strong for such a little thing, isn't she?

Marge screamed, "How dare you! How dare you fucking people!" Dave lifted her, pushed back, forced her into the apartment. She kicked him again.

He shoved the door closed with his hip. "Who do you fuckers think you are, just who the fuck do you think you are!" Twisting furiously, she tried to pull away from him. Dave tightened his grasp, drawing her close. She spat in his face.

"Marge? Hey, look, I don't . . ." White fire, Indiana summer sheet lightning, scorching pain. Dave's lungs emptied. He slumped to his knees, fighting for consciousness.

Marge had driven her knee into his groin.

Ransome and his thugs are one thing, pal, but 110 pounds' worth of infuriated New York womanhood is another thing entirely.

Dave put a hand on the floor to steady himself, and tried to shake his vision clear. It didn't work. He lifted his head, drawing deep shivering breaths. Marge came at him with a vase heavy enough to kill. As she brought it down, he fell left, sweeping her feet out from under her. She tumbled beside him, cursing. He rolled over on top of her, using his weight to hold her down. She screamed and swore and promised to kill him.

Shouldn't have swiped her cash like that, pal.

"Mrfpf ahmm serrie . . ." Dave forced his mind away from the agony between his legs, concentrated on breathing, concentrated on having enough breath to sound coherent. "Marge, I'm sorry about taking your money. I thought it would make it look more authentic and . . ."

"Money?" she screamed. "Money! You sick bastard, I'd forgotten all about that, you and your goddamned sick perverted friends, I'll tear your balls off you, you . . ."

It took him ten minutes to calm her down. By then she was weeping, wretched, trembling like a terrified bird.

Four men, big men, had been waiting at her door. One of them flashed a badge. Fifteen minutes earlier she had ditched the radio Dave had given her, leaving it in a litter bin outside the neighborhood D'Agostino's. She thought she had nothing to worry about.

"Can we come in and talk to you, Miz Cohen? We want to follow up on the mugging today at your office."

"Sure. How long will it take?"

"Not long. Here, let me carry that grocery bag for you."

When she opened her apartment door, only three of them came in. The fourth stood in the hall outside. One of the three turned, fastened all her locks, and rested with his back against the door.

That door was the only way out. Marge backed away, putting a sofa between her slight body and the other two men. One of them carried a black leather satchel. He set it on the coffee table.

The second man, the one with the badge, spoke. "I'm Officer Canady. This is Doctor Pierce."

"Doctor?"

"A gynecologist."

". . . ?"

"We have reason to believe that the man who assaulted you this afternoon may have raped you while you were unconscious."

"No. Don't be silly. I'd know . . ."

"We are here to make a determination. The doctor will now examine you."

The doctor pulled on a pair of latex gloves.

Marge's face was clean, she'd washed her makeup off earlier. Her tears flowed clear, each transparent and bright. "Swabs," she gasped. "Specimen bottles. A needle. The other two watching. Their faces didn't move. The big one . . ." She shuddered and sobbed in Dave's arms.

"Easy, Marge." Dave couldn't think of anything else to say. "It's over. Just take a deep breath and . . ."

"He held me down. He had his hand over my mouth. He pulled off my things. The other one, the one who said he was a doctor, oh God, it was as bad as, it was worse than . . ." Her whole body shook, racked with sobs and humiliation.

Dave wrapped his arms around her, nestling her head against his chest. It seemed to comfort her. Besides, it was better that she didn't see his face, white with rage and bearing the look of a man who was planning vengeance.

9:23 P.M.

Dave had been with her more than an hour. He'd found a bottle of brandy, cheap stuff, Christian Brothers. The liquor had calmed her down. Apart from the bruised circles beneath her green, emerald green, eyes, she was again the pertly attractive woman he'd met that afternoon.

They were no longer talking about the men who had violated her. She couldn't talk about that. It might be months before she could. Now, they spoke of Dave, trying to find some sense in what had been happening to him.

"I don't know," he said. "I can make some guesses, but guesses are all they are."

She was wearing some sort of powder blue smock. Dave wasn't

quite sure precisely what it was supposed to be—a nightie perhaps, or more likely a top to be worn loosely over slacks. But she wasn't wearing slacks. And her legs were nice. Dave forced his eyes to focus on her face.

"What? Give me a for instance." She held a Salem Ultra Light 100 between her fingers. Blue smoke curled up to the ceiling. Dave almost asked her for one. He really wanted a cigarette.

"Okay, first point. It's the government, or something to do with the government."

"That's the looniest thing I've ever heard. Hey, I saw this movie on HBO last month. Secret chambers underneath the Pentagon, shadowy men in anonymous uniforms, spooky no-name organizations with ties to Odessa. Lousy movie. I canceled HBO."

"But it has to be . . ."

"Don't be silly. That stuff doesn't happen—secret plots, fiendish conspiracies . . ."

"Conspiracies happen. If you don't believe me, ask Julius Caesar."

"Oh come on! That was two thousand years ago."

"How about Iran-Contra or Whitewater or Watergate? Yeah, Watergate. Remember Gordon Liddy?"

Marge studied him. Her eyes were large and bright, her lips pursed. Dave liked the way her lips looked. He thought . . . He shook his head. He didn't know what he thought.

Oh yes you do.

"Who? Watergate? Hey, how old do you think I am? That thing was over before I was in grade school." She waved her hand. A streamer of smoke hung in the air.

"Liddy was one of the Watergate conspirators. He wrote a book after he got out of jail. In it he said that for awhile he was sure he was going to be silenced. He said he was ready for it. And Liddy was a Fed. He was an insider. He knew how things worked."

"Sounds like a nut case to me."

Dave sighed. When he inhaled he tasted the smoke from her cigarette. "Other covert operations people were involved. Hell, even the courts and the judges called Watergate a conspiracy. Conspiracies are real."

She shook her head.

"The other thing . . ." Dave swallowed. ". . . Aw hell, the guys who do these things, the Gordon Liddys and the Oliver Norths and all the rest, believe, really and truly believe, they're on the side of the angels. Just like they believe that the guys who are against them are the enemies of truth, justice, and the American way. I'd bet money that if you asked Ransome, he'd tell you that he's the good guy and that I'm the villain. And he'd be sincere. Hell, I know I was . . ." Dave dropped into silence.

Marge tilted her head, eyes a little wider. But she was too smart to speak.

"Look, Marge, a long time ago, almost before you were born, I was one of them. They took me away from the Army . . . No, that's a lie. They didn't take me. The truth is, I volunteered. I thought it was the right thing. I thought a lot of things were right back then." Dave closed his eyes. These were not good memories, and it hurt to bring them back. "Anyway, they sent me to a place in Virginia. I was there for months. Special training. Special weapons. Special intelligence. Special warfare. For awhile we thought we were being trained to work with the ARVN, the army of South Vietnam . . ."

"Vietnam?" The expression on her face changed. He couldn't read it.

"My war, Marge. I was in it."

"Was it as bad . . ."

"Yeah. Worse, actually." Dave decided the look she was giving him was genuine concern. He was grateful for that. She was too young to remember the war, and too young to be among the ranks of those who hated everyone and everything associated with it.

Likewise too young for you.

He emptied his brandy glass, and poured himself another two

fingers. There had been plenty of haters in the old days. Going to war had been bad. In some ways coming back was worse.

"Dave?" She was leaning forward. He could see her breasts shift beneath her smock. She wasn't wearing a bra and . . .

Put it out of your mind, buddy.

"Sorry. Old memories." Dave smiled faintly. "Anyway, I was saying that they trained us for all sorts of dirty work—hundreds of us. Camp P had been in business for ten or twenty years when I was there. It probably still is. Thousands of people have gone through it, a whole army of secret warriors. And now they're out there somewhere. Maybe they don't work for the government. Maybe they don't even work for the outfits who work for the outfits who work for the government. But if you know the right people, you can find them, and they'll do any job they're paid to do."

She frowned. "No way. The government doesn't kill taxpayers. The deficit is too big. Besides, I can't believe anyone would give an explicit order . . ."

Dave spat, "They don't give orders. They just drop hints. Remember Becket? The king says, 'Who will free me of this turbulent priest?' and next thing you've got a dead bishop on the floor."

She nodded, but she wasn't believing him. "Okay. Suppose it's possible. What's your evidence?"

"There isn't any. Not real evidence. It's all circumstantial—the way they talk, the high-tech gear they carry, how easy it is for them to order telephones tapped, the fact that Ransome read my Army personnel jacket, the fact that everyone on his side seems to have a Beltway address. And the other thing is Harry Halliwell. My friend Harry, who tried to brain me with a coffee pitcher. He's a big kahuna, a real political rain-maker. If he's on Ransome's team, it has to mean that important people are involved."

"I still don't buy it . . . unless . . . Do you think it could be something to do with Vietnam?"

"Yes. No. Hell, I don't know. Something happened there. I was in the middle of it. But I wasn't the only one involved. If they wanted to silence us, they'd have to come after all of us. Besides, they covered it up—another conspiracy, by the way, a conspiracy of silence. And anyway, it was too long ago. There's nothing left, there's nobody that cares. Nobody ever really did."

"Can you . . . will you tell me? I mean, maybe you've forgotten something."

Dave's voice dropped. He almost growled. "Forgotten? Not very goddamned likely. I haven't forgotten a thing. I wish I could."

"But . . ."

"No, Marge. You don't want to know, and I don't want to tell you. Just take my word for it. It doesn't have anything to do with what's been going on today. It can't."

"If you say so. But then why do these people, why would anyone want to kill you?"

Dave threw his arms up at the ceiling. "That's the sixty-four dollar question. My guess is that I've seen or heard something I shouldn't have. Damned if I know what. But whatever it is, the idea of my knowing it scares the living daylights out of some very powerful people."

"Scares?" She took a deep drag on the cigarette. Dave sighed.

"Exactly. Scared that I'll go public. Scared that once I figure out what it is that I know, I'll blow the whistle. I did that once—blew the whistle. They never forget you if you do that. They never forgive you either."

"Is that what you're saying? That they're afraid you'll expose . . . expose whatever it is they're doing? That they want to kill you because you're a whistle-blower?"

"Maybe, only they'd use stronger words than 'whistle-blower.' But, yes, it's possible. In the Army—in the old days—we used the phrase 'plausible deniability.' That meant that the senior officers could deny they knew what we were doing. It meant that whatever shenanigans we pulled off, we had to make sure our bosses had the option of saying, 'Hey, this was a rogue operation. Totally unauthorized. Contrary to orders. Don't blame us. We didn't know a thing about it.' "

" 'Your mission, Jim, should you choose to accept it . . .' "

"Something like that. I'll tell you one other thing. Whatever it is, it's something that no one is supposed to know about. Something that no one can afford to have disclosed. The kind of something that makes angry congressmen hold public hearings and reporters from *The Washington Post* bay at the moon."

"Iran-Contra."

"For example."

His eyes had drifted away from Marge's face. As if they had a will of their own, they were . . .

You're looking at her legs again, pal. You really shouldn't do that.

"Then the reason they're after you and the reason they're scared is that you can destroy their cover, their ability to disavow all knowledge of . . . knowledge of . . . whatever it is."

Dave took another sip of brandy. He was feeling warmer now, and a little loose. He set the glass down. Getting tipsy would not be a good thing. "You know what's weird? What's weird is that they were going to make me a part of it. I mean if that letter was real, not a forgery I mean, then the FBI was doing a check on me because someone wanted to reactivate my old security clearance."

"But if they were doing that, why are they trying to kill you now?" She shifted her posture, tucking one leg beneath another. Dave caught a glimpse of pale pink panties.

Speaking personally, it is probably a good thing your balls are black and blue.

"That's the other sixty-four dollar question. Maybe they found something in their background check that made them think I'm a bad risk. Maybe by the time they found it, someone had said something to me that I wasn't supposed to hear. I don't know. All I can say is that it had to have happened within the past few days. Maybe within the past twenty-four hours. Bernie was exhausted. He hadn't gotten any sleep. Ransome and Carlucci hadn't shaved.

They'd been up all night. And everything they've done to catch me has been on the fly—a seat of the pants operation. They're making it up as they go. There isn't any plan. That's the only reason I'm still alive. Ransome is no rookie. If he'd had the time to lay out a nice detailed plan of operations, I would have been bagged and tagged before breakfast."

She gave him a sympathetic look, and pointed a finger at his empty glass. "Would you like another drink?"

Dave thought, Yes! You have one too!

"No."

"So what have you done the past few days? What have you seen? Who have you talked to?"

"Marge, I've racked my brains. There is nothing. Absolutely nothing. I spent the weekend out on Long Island with Scotty and Olivia Thatcher. Sunday night I picked Helen up at the airport. She'd . . ."

"Helen?"

"My wife."

"Your wife." Her voice was as neutral as the look she gave him. She tucked both legs away out of sight.

You took off your wedding ring, pal. Remember? The lady's been oper-ating under a misconception.

"Ahh . . . she'd been out in California for an old college friend's wedding. Monday, Tuesday, Wednesday, I went to the office. Business as usual. Meetings, conferences, papers to review, decisions to make, calls to return. All routine except that I had to go back out to Long Island on Wednesday for a meeting, and on Monday night I had to play host to some visitors from Japan."

"Excuse me for a minute." Marge stood up and slipped out of the living room. She left her cigarette burning in an ashtray. Dave looked at it hungrily. He reached for it, felt guilty, stopped himself, reached again, and felt guiltier still.

Let's try to resist temptation, pal. By which I mean all temptations the flesh is heir to.

The smoke hung in the air. Dave salivated and suffered until Marge came back.

She was wearing a pair of blue jeans, and was holding a long-haired tabby cat in her arms. Earlier Marge had sat curled on the sofa next to him. Now she perched in an easy chair, discreetly separated from Dave by a cheap glass-topped coffee table.

"Nice cat," Dave said, suddenly feeling uncomfortable. "What's her name?"

"It's a he. His name is Tito. He comes from Colorado."

"Tito?"

"My older sister married into this enormous extended family. I was out at their ranch this summer. The family patriarch fought with the Yugoslav partisans during World War II. He gave me the cat and named him for me." She put the animal down on the floor.

Dave stretched out a hand to stroke it. The cat hissed, snapped its fangs, and took a wobbly step out of his reach.

"Careful—I just had the vet fix him," Marge said. "He's still in a bad mood from the operation."

"Oh. Sure. That explains . . ."

Yup, that explains it, doesn't it?

Ice formed in Dave's veins.

There it is. Right in front of your nose. That has to be it, pal. It couldn't be anything else.

No, it wasn't possible.

"Are you all right?" Marge's voice was concerned.

Dave looked doubtfully at the brandy glass in his hand. He tossed the dregs down his throat, stood, and quite carefully dropped the glass so that it shattered on the floor.

3.

David Elliot sped east on the Long Island Expressway. He passed the exit to Great Neck, home of the overly amorous Greg, whose clothes he was again wearing. Dave suspected that Greg might currently be viewing monogamous family life as a more desirable—or at least less risky—alternative to being the office Casanova.

He rubbed his hand across the top of his newly smooth head. While Marge, who unlike many New Yorkers had a driver's license, went to get a rental car, he had snipped, then shaved himself a new hairline. Then he had bathed his remaining hair in peroxide. The effect was curious. Now blond and balding, he thought he looked to be a wholly different man, albeit not one whose appearance he much liked. The hairdo was a bit on the effeminate side. If there had been any of Ransome's watchers stationed on the Triborough Bridge, they had ignored him.

He wondered if Marge had left yet. He hoped so. And he hoped she would forgive him for stealing her rent-a-car keys and the contents of her wallet while she was in the bathroom. He had decided he had to betray her one more time while she'd been out at the Hertz office. While waiting for her return he had hastily pecked out an explanation on her old electric typewriter:

```
Dear Marge:

I am sorry that I did this, but I had to. I came here because
I wanted a place to hide, and I thought you'd let me sleep
with you on your sofa for a few days until it was safe for me
to leave. But now I think I've put your life in danger.

I'm leaving my watch. It's a solid gold Rolex. They retail
for $15 or $20 thousand. Sell it or pawn it. Keep the money.
Get out of town. Take your cat and catch the first airplane
you can. If you don't, they may hurt you. Go out to your
relative's ranch in Colorado. I looked in your address book.
If I live through this I will contact you there when this is
over.

Now please pack a bag and get out of your apartment. Don't
use your credit cards because they can trace them. You have
to do this Marge. Believe me. I am not lying.
```

Again I am sorry for taking even more of your cash. The watch will more than pay you back. Marge, please, do what I tell you. <u>RUN AWAY BEFORE IT IS TOO LATE.</u>

Dave

The one thing he hadn't mentioned in the note was his fear that, if he hadn't run out on her, she would insist on answers, or worse, insist on coming with him. It was better she didn't know anything. Ignorance would be her best protection.

He glanced at the odometer. The car, a low-priced Korean import, was new. It had 215 miles on it when Dave pulled away from Marge's apartment. Now it had 247. He had another thirty or so miles to go.

A voice on the radio announced that it was time for the headlines. Dave turned up the volume. "At the top of the news this hour, a citywide manhunt is under way for David Perry Elliot, alleged killer of New York businessman Bernard J. Levy. Levy, president of the multi-billion dollar conglomerate Senterex, was hurled from his forty-fifth story Park Avenue window earlier this evening. Law enforcement sources report that Elliot is the prime suspect, and state that Levy had recently raised questions about financial affairs that Elliot was responsible for."

That's a new wrinkle.

"Authorities also suspect Elliot of having assaulted police officer William Hutchinson and stolen his uniform and vehicle. Elliot is described as being a white male, six foot one inch tall, weighing 170 pounds, having light brown hair and brown eyes, and in good physical condition. He is described as armed and highly dangerous. Citizens are asked to immediately notify the police if they observe anyone answering to the description. In other news today . . ."

Dave lowered the volume.

Up ahead a road sign announced PATCHOGUE—24 MILES. His exit.

He'd been there only the day before. He'd traveled in a chauffeur-driven limousine, one of the four kept ready for the use of Senterex executives. Given the midday traffic, it had taken him nearly two hours to get from Senterex's offices to Lockyear Laboratories. Now, late in the evening, it would take less than an hour.

It has to be Lockyear Laboratories, doesn't it? That's the only place Ransome could have gotten your blood sample.

Divisional facilities tours are one of the more wearisome burdens of executive life. A visiting prince from the corporate castle is dispatched to an outlying fiefdom, there to be greeted in a musty reception area by a nervously smiling plant manager. This manager shepherds the travel-worn visitor into a freshly scrubbed conference room. He offers his guest a cup of ill-tasting coffee. Courtesy demands it be taken and sipped. Shortly the division's four or five most senior people troop into the room. Today their shirts are fresh, their collars buttoned, and their tie knots tight. They are wearing suit jackets, which on all occasions other than ones like this slowly wrinkle behind their office doors. The guest stands, shakes hands, and tries unsuccessfully to memorize their names. The local manager walks to the head of the conference table, fumbles with a projection screen and turns on an overhead projector. He says that he has a few transparencies that will describe his operation. He rarely gets to talk to corporate management, and intends to make the most of this opportunity. The visitor tries to look interested. He's not. Someone dims the lights. The visitor no longer needs to look interested because now no one can see his face. The local manager drones through an interminable presentation about his operation. Founded after World War II by the elder son of an emigrant tinker; graphs illustrating a forty year history of steady growth; organizational chart in tiny print; process schematics of smooth and efficient operations; lists of satisfied customers; more graphs forecasting ambitious growth plans—in summary a family of happy employees, pleased to have been acquired by a prestigious corporate parent, see a relationship that can only be mutually beneficial. The visitor sits in silence throughout this sermon, either enjoying a relaxing catnap or desperately trying to concoct an intelligent question or two.

"Now, unless you have any questions, let's take a short break before we begin the walking tour."

"What about competition?" Dave had asked. Most of the presentation had revolved around immune biology—receptor molecules, antigens, lymphocyte attributes, T cells, B cells, histocompatibility complexes, polypeptides, CD 8 coreceptors, macrophages, and the like. A question about competition was the best Dave could muster.

He didn't understand much of the answer. It had a lot to do with "unique classes of MHC molecules," "new approaches to the clonal deletion hypothesis," "SCID and TCR transgenic laboratory animals," and "special relationships with the National Institutes of Health and certain other federally funded research organizations."

Dave, knowing nothing, nodded knowingly. He resented Bernie assigning him responsibility for Lockyear, and was more than merely irritated that he would, once again, have to learn a whole new language and industry so that he could oversee yet another of Bernie's off-the-wall acquisitions. What the blazes was Senterex doing buying a biotech company anyway?

After a side trip to the washroom, they'd begun their walking tour. The administrative offices; the computer center with Sun workstations running the Molecular Design Laboratories suite of database software; Lab number one with shining chrome equipment doing something Dave couldn't pronounce; Lab number two with its walls lined with cages full of pink-eyed white mice; Lab number three so cold that Dave could see his breath; Lab four where people were dissecting cats; Lab five . . .

RESTRICTED
VOICEPRINT ACCESS ONLY
PROTECTIVE WEAR MANDATORY

"And this is Lab five. I don't think we have time to show it to you today . . ."

Thank God!

". . . besides, you have to get suited up to . . ."

The door to Lab five flew open. Someone in a snow white "spacesuit"—that bulky form of protective garb that cloaks the wearer from head to heel—started out, glanced over his shoulder, and swore. "Goddamnit, close that cage!" A writhing ball of brown fur bounced into his chest. He stumbled. The brown thing leapt up. Acting on reflex, Dave grabbed at it, caught it. Pain seared through his hand. It was a monkey, a small, reddish brown monkey. Its long canine teeth were locked to his left hand.

A few seconds of confusion followed. Various people muttered, "Sorry. Small accident. Never happens." Then they led him to the medical station. A nurse cleaned his wound, applied greasy antiseptic, and dressed it with gauze bandages.

"I'll just take a blood sample now, Mr. Elliot. No, there's nothing wrong, no chance of rabies or anything like that. But better safe than sorry. That's our golden rule at Lockyear Laboratories. Better safe than sorry. Oh—and an ounce of prevention is worth a pound of cure. That's the other thing we say all the time."

The blood sample.

Yeah. I know. That's where Ransome got it.

And the painting.

What painting?

Old creepy whatshisname Lockyear, the guy who founded the company.

Dave remembered. There had been a gilt-framed oil painting of Lockyear in the conference room. He'd barely given it a glance. But . . . there was something about it. It showed an older man, perhaps

in his early sixties. Now what the devil was so odd . . . ? It was a
. . . No. The man in the picture . . . Aha! He was in uniform, an
Army uniform. Why would the founder of a biotechnology re-
search laboratory pose in uniform?

Not just any uniform.

The uniform was not a contemporary one, nor even the style
Dave had worn during his time in the service. Lockyear had been
wearing an Eisenhower jacket, a ridiculously short black tie, and a
World War II-style garrison cap.

What did Bernie say about the acquisition?

Lockyear had died a few years earlier. There were problems with
his estate. That's why the company was for sale, and that's why it
was—he claimed—a bargain.

*So we've got a sixty, maybe seventy year old guy, and a company that's
four decades old. So when he founded it he was maybe in his thirties. But
when he's older, and it comes time to get his memorial portrait painted,
what does he do?*

Chief executives and company founders pose for their official
portraits in blue pinstripe suits. White shirt, dark tie, maybe a vest.
But not Lockyear. Lockyear posed in a forty year old military rig.

Odd.

Very odd indeed.

4.

At the Patchogue exit, Dave turned south toward the ocean shore.
A few minutes later he turned east again.

It was farmland out here, rolling meadows, potato fields, some
few stands of trees. The narrow blacktop was empty at this hour.
Dave's rental car was the only thing on the road, his headlights the
only light to be seen. He closed his right eye, and held it shut.

You know there's more to it than the blood sample.

Dave felt uneasy driving at night. He didn't like the way the trees looked. Leaves, green and warm in daylight, were blanched dead by the glare of headlights.

Come on, admit it.

He hated the pale color. It reminded him of corpses. And trees should be lit from above, casting their shadows below. Night driving reversed the natural order. It made him queasy.

You're ignoring me, pal.

An animal with incandescent eyes darted across the road. Dave's heart leapt into his throat. Before he could touch the brakes it was out of sight.

You don't want to face the facts.

Right turn. Toward the ocean again. It was a moonless night. That would help.

Hey, pal! Listen to me. . . .

There it was. A long stretch of mesh fence, topped with a coil of razor wire. A gate and a guard shack. A small sign:

LOCKYEAR LABORATORIES, INC.
EMPLOYEES SHOW ID
VISITORS <u>MUST</u> REGISTER BEFORE ENTERING

Dave drove past, keeping a steady speed. There was no one to be seen. The guard shack was empty, not a watcher in sight.

Was it possible that Ransome blundered, that some of his men weren't stationed out here?

No way.

Or that Dave was wrong, and that Lockyear did not lie at the center of things?

Likewise, no way.

Dave cruised a mile beyond the southernmost border of the Lockyear fence before switching off his headlights. As he pulled off the road he opened his right eye. It had become dark-adjusted. It was an old infantryman's trick, keeping one eye closed while the flares were going off. Once the dark returned, your night vision was better than your enemy's.

Still behind the steering wheel, he struggled out of Greg's loose clothes and into his policeman's uniform. Dark blue trousers, dark blue blouse, the colors of the night.

One last thing. The interior light.

Dave used his pistol to shatter the bulb. Then he opened the car door, leaning out to scoop a handful of dirt from the side of the road. It was good thick soil, farm soil, just right for darkening his face, hands, and newly bald scalp.

He backed up, turned, and, headlights off, drove slowly toward Lockyear. A hundred yards from the property line, he switched off the ignition, coasting to a stop near the property's south boundary.

During the drive across Long Island he'd thought about what he had seen the day before, reconstructing, as best he could, the layout of the Lockyear property. The grounds were a half mile square, with the office complex sitting in the center. For the most part the land was flat and featureless, although there was a slight rise south of the main building. Stands of trees, very nearly forest, surrounded the outer peripheries, concealing the fences.

If Ransome's men were there, they'd be in the trees, in the shadows, out of sight.

Dave slipped off his shoes. They were no good for what he had in mind. Their leather soles would slip on the grass and fallen leaves, and tap too loudly on linoleum flooring.

Somewhere, somehow, you've got to get a decent pair of shoes.

He'd taken two chocolate brown hand towels from Marge's bathroom. Now he wound them around his feet, binding them with twine. Clumsy, but it would have to do.

He started across the road.

What an absolute goddamned pathetic excuse for a professional! Ransome would be furious. Jesus, you just can't get good help anymore.

Dave tightened his lips in disapproval. He shook his head. The watcher was thirty feet ahead of him, crouched beneath a low Chinese elm. Dave wouldn't have seen him if the man hadn't chosen just that moment to light a cigarette.

No discipline left in the world. Mamba Jack would have de-balled anyone who fired up a butt on night watch.

Moments later Dave thrust the muzzle of his pistol behind the man's ear and whispered, "Surprise." The man jerked, groaned, and dropped his weapon. The stench of evacuated bowels arose from him.

"How many?" Dave whispered.

"Uh . . ."

"Listen up, meathead. I've got nothing to lose. If I paint the landscape with your brains they aren't going to do anything to me that they didn't already plan to do. So tell me, how many of you are there?"

"Man, no one believed you'd make it out here."

"I'm going to count to three. One . . ."

"Five, man, five. Two on this side, two on the other side, and one in the building."

"I don't believe you."

"No lie, man. Honest to God, it's no . . ."

The temptation to shoot him was overwhelming. He owed it to them, to Ransome and to all of them. They'd tried to kill him. They'd brought his son into it, his wife, and Annie. They'd used their lies to make his friends into enemies. Maybe worst of all, they'd treated poor Marge Cohen like a piece of livestock. They deserved to die. All of them. Starting with this one.

He didn't do it. But he did pistol whip him more than was necessary. And when he found another man, some hundred yards north, he did it again. Then, because he felt the need to make a statement, he used his pistol butt to hammer the second man's ankles into splinters.

————

The first man had not been lying. There were only two watchers on the south side of the property. Dave took them easily. For the next several months, they would need casts and crutches.

Dave scouted the west side, behind the building complex. No one there—it was going to be a piece of cake.

There was a low, rolling rise to the south. Dave crouched and dashed forward, hidden from sight by the contour of the land. A hundred feet from the rear entrance, he dropped to the ground, and belly-crawled the rest of the way.

One person in the building? That's what the man had said. Maybe true, maybe false. Only one way to find out.

Dave slid his hand up to the doorknob. It turned easily. Unlocked. A bad sign.

What was inside was a worse sign yet.

5.

Lockyear Laboratories was empty. Everything was gone. They'd taken the furniture, the lab benches, the equipment, and the pictures on the wall. Even the light fixtures had been removed. What used to be Lockyear Laboratories was now a hollow shell.

Dave pulled off the towels he'd wrapped around his feet. He padded silently through the barren corridors on stocking feet, trying to remember the route to the research labs.

The building reeked of disinfectant. Every room, every office, every foot of hallway smelled of bactericide. In one or two places the floor was still wet with it. Dave touched it with his hand, brought his fingers to his nose, and winced. Strong stuff.

The day before, he remembered, his tour had taken him past a men's room, a water fountain, a women's room, and an employee lounge. The laboratories—numbers one through five—were spaced down a long hallway to the left of the lounge.

It's not something you saw, it's not something you heard, it's not something you did. It's none of those things.

There. The toilets, the lounge. And . . .

A click of bootheels on the floor. Someone was coming up the hall, coming from where the laboratories were.

Dave backed around the corner, bringing a pistol up and ready.

Only the faintest light, barely enough to see by, shone through the windows.

The steps reached the end of the corridor, and paused. Then they started again, coming in his direction. Dave coiled his finger around the trigger, seated the pistol firmly in two hands. At this range, it would punch a hole straight through his target. He rather looked forward to that.

Now wraith not man, though without sex or magic, Lieutenant David Elliot has spent this humid day in hell not as predator but as prey, a role for which he is ill-suited.

He has been running a run that has taken him not one step farther from his pursuers, a run that has left him frustrated and vengeful, a run filled with fear.

No more.

Now it has changed. He is the hunter. His pursuers are the quarry. This, he knows, is the proper order of things.

His senses alter, his perceptions shift, he focuses on the landscape ahead, ignores what may lurk behind.

His skin tingles. His eyes dart left and right. His vision is astonishingly sharp, his hearing preternaturally acute. He sniffs the air, and can taste—he swears he can taste—rivulets of sweat running down his hidden enemy's cheeks.

Hunter.

And, dear God, he has never felt so alive.

The walker stepped into view, profiled against a window. Dave leveled his sights. His hands were steady. His target was about five foot five inches tall and slightly built. He drew a bead on the center of the torso. The guard carried an M16A1 assault rifle held at port arms. He was wearing a baseball cap. There was a fall of hair beneath it. It was a woman.

In the days immediately following the 1991 Iraq war, there had been heated debate—in Senterex's offices as elsewhere—about the role of women in combat. Should women fight? Should they kill? What effect would fighting shoulder-to-shoulder with women have on men? How would the enemy react? David Elliot voiced no opinion, refused to participate in the discussions, feigned disinterest, and tried to change the subject. His experience with the Vietcong had taught him that female soldiers were quite as lethal as males. Nor did any soldier whom he'd ever known hesitate, even for a second, to think about the sex of the enemy firing at him.

She didn't turn. She passed by, slowly patrolling the hallway, a bored soldier on boring duty. Her steps faded. Soon she was gone.

Dave worked his jaw back and forth. He'd almost killed her just for the hell of it.

Made enough statements for the night, have we?

This business was turning him into something he didn't want to be. It was taking him back twenty-five years. He had almost gone over the line then. Now he was close to going over it again.

Ransome keeps saying that you're still one of them, cut from the same cloth.

He shook his head. He wasn't going to let them do it to him. The price was too high. He remembered the price; he remembered the look of damnation and despair on Mamba Jack Kreuter's face when Jack realized what he'd done, and knew that he'd gone so far that there was no coming back.

Okay, pal, so cool it. You already know what you're going to find, so let's just get this over with and then get the hell out of Dodge.

Dave frowned. He didn't know what he was going to find.

Oh yes you do.

He started up the hall, turned into the laboratory corridor, and stepped past what had been Laboratory one. It had been, like every other room in the building, stripped bare.

It's not Lab one. You've got to quit pretending that you still don't know what it is.

Lab two was in the same condition. Likewise Labs three and four.

Lab five.

Even the door was gone. They'd not only removed the furniture and fixtures from Lab five, but they'd even taken the door. And inside it was . . .

The linoleum had been ripped up. The ceiling tiles were removed. They had attacked the walls, the ceiling struts, the concrete floor with a flame gun. They had sterilized every inch of plaster, concrete, and steel with fire. Nothing, not a fly, not a flea, not a microbe, could have survived in Lab five.

David Elliot doubled over, and fell to his knees. For the second time that day, he vomited.

CHAPTER 7
NIGHT LIFE

1.

Ransome had been right—Dave would be coming back. He had no choice. He had to see the file on Lockyear, the file in Bernie's credenza that held the secret about why Bernie—Bernie and everyone else—wanted David Elliot dead.

He was back on the Long Island Expressway, racing west toward New York. The rental car was whining at the speed. Dave pressed the accelerator to the floor. The speedometer registered 85 mph. It was all the car could take. Any more and it would blow apart. He cursed Hertz and he cursed the Korean car industry.

And he cursed Bernie Levy. He knew now what Bernie had done—at least in general terms. He knew because Scott Thatcher had told him.

It had been a year and a half earlier. Scott and his wife, Olivia, had invited Dave and Helen to Thursday night dinner at their Sutton Place *pied-à-terre.*

Thatcher's Thursday night dinners were legendary. You never

knew who the other guests would be. Visiting heads of state, political pundits, Nobel laureates, artists, writers, musicians, and once a troupe of circus performers—Thatcher hosted them all, or at least the interesting ones.

There had been five couples that night: the Thatchers, the Elliots, a much lionized novelist and his undergrad inamorata, a senator and his wife from one of the western states, and Mike and Louise Ash—the latter executives of Thatcher's company, married and warring as only people deeply in love can war.

Dinner ended. The dishes were cleared. Thatcher rose and walked to the sideboard. He lifted a bottle of Fonseca's port and an ebony box. He placed both on the dinner table, and opened the box.

"Cigars, anyone?"

The women fled.

Thatcher withdrew a long, brown Monte Cristo. He sliced its tip with a Buck pocketknife, and, igniting it with a wooden match, grinned a foxy grin. "The last weapon left to the male race, gentlemen." Thick blue smoke rolled slowly out of his mouth. He passed the humidor to Mike Ash. "All of our other arms are defeated, our stratagems overthrown, our armor pierced. Only the cigar remains, the last tattered banner of manhood, still waving over a battlefield otherwise fallen to Amazons."

Ash lit his own cigar, passing the box to the senator. "If Justine were here . . ."

"Ms. Gold, Senator, ever dear to my crotchety heart and surely the only woman in the world who rivals me for sheer wickedness. She handles my public relations—the labors of Hercules, that—and would be here this evening had she not been called out of town on business. A fine woman, with as keen an appreciation of a good Havana as any man I've ever met."

The senator declined to take a cigar, pushing the box across the table to Dave. Dave chose one, rolling it lovingly through his fingers. While he had long ago given up cigarettes, a good cigar was not to be resisted.

The novelist made his apologies and left. Cigar smoke made him sick.

Thatcher leered like a wolf. "Now that the women and the wimps have departed, in what bestial male viciousness might we indulge? Politically incorrect language? Salaciously demeaning stories? Conspiracies to restore female-kind to subjugation? Plots to corrupt children, pillage the environment, plunder minorities, oppress the weak, exploit the poor, and humiliate the handi-capped? Or alternatively, perhaps we might wallow in the subject women most despise and speak of sports?"

Mike Ash smiled at Dave. "He's in one of his moods again." Ash turned to Thatcher. "What's got your goat today, chief?"

Thatcher glowered. "Have you observed that in these decadent times, it is no longer enough to feel good yourself?" His voice rose, reverberating with indignation. "Self-esteem is not enough. A sense of achievement is not enough. Dignity and self-respect are not enough. No, sir, not at all. Rather it has become the case that I cannot feel good unless you feel bad!"

"The California Commission on Self-Esteem . . ." began the sena-tor.

Thatcher walked right over him. "I cannot feel good about being a woman unless you feel bad about being a man. I cannot be proud of being black unless you are ashamed of being white. I cannot re-spect myself for being gay unless you are embarrassed that you are straight. Tolerance has been put by the boards; it is a stale and bit-ter thing and we will have none of it. Equality, likewise; it is conde-scending at best and in truth intended to demean. If I am to achieve the inner harmony and self-respect that is my due, it will not suffice for you and I to be equals. No! Nothing less than superi-ority will make me happy. And to ensure that I make my point, I shall commend your libraries to the flames, rewrite your histories, purge your dictionaries, and arm the thought police with power to enforce political correctness in all speech and apprehension. Oh, whole new vocabularies and crafty code words have they . . ."

Ash interrupted. "You accepted that invitation to speak at the university, didn't you? Damn it, Scott, I told you not to do it. Dealing with academicians is bad for your blood pressure."

"As indeed it is. Those slinking worms of sophistry dared to carp at my using the word 'Indian,' sneering me bigot and boor for not using 'Native American,' which is as sly and snooty a racist neologism as was ever coined, implying that those of us sprung from generations of honest New England yeoman aren't *real* Americans . . ."

"You're ranting, Scott."

Thatcher flourished his cigar and showed his teeth. "Of course I am ranting. It is the prerogative of my years, one of the few joys left to me in the autumn of my days, and indeed, given my white hairs and black reputation, it is expected of me. I am a curmudgeon, after all, and have a certain illiberal reputation to maintain."

"You voted Democrat in the last election."

Thatcher shot him a sour look. "A moment of weakness, a mistake that shall not be repeated. The man has since exhibited all the character of a stuffed squirrel, or so I might say did it not slander a noble animal, lacking in neither resolve nor mother wit." Thatcher leaned back, took another long pull on his cigar, and exhaled. "But change the subject if you will. I am only a poor old man, and best ignored by youth."

Ash looked at the ceiling and spread his hands in open prayer for inspiration.

Dave offered up a distraction: "Did I ever tell you the story of the Dong Hoi cathouse?"

Thatcher arched a bushy white eyebrow. "Something to do with the Vietnam War?"

"Yes."

"A lamentable business. My opposition to it resulted in Mr.

Nixon putting me on the White House enemies list. Did I ever tell you that?"

"Fifty or sixty times."

"There are so few accomplishments in life in which one can justly take pride. But I interrupt. Please, David, tell your tale."

Because Scott Claymore Thatcher III was something of a puritan and much disliked obscene language, Dave had to be circumspect in describing how the CIA, learning that a meeting of top Vietcong and North Vietnamese commanders would be held in the Cambodian border town of Dong Hoi, surreptitiously purchased the town's bordellos, populating them with legions of remarkably contagious prostitutes. Recognizing that the scheme was a violation of Geneva Convention prohibitions against biological warfare, the Agency had clapped ("no pun intended," Dave added) a strict security seal on the operation, advising no one—not even the military high command—of its scheme. Unfortunately, the Army learned through its own intelligence channels of the impending enemy conference. It reacted by launching a preemptive strike, seizing and garrisoning the town before the enemy arrived.

"Oh no," gasped Thatcher, who guessed the punchline.

"Oh yes," Dave said. "Six hundred hormonal young GIs, far from home, with nothing to do on a Saturday night."

"Dear me!" Thatcher laughed so hard that tears streamed down his cheeks. "Is this true, David? You are not making it up?"

"It's very true. I knew the CIA agent who ran the operation." Dave did not mention that the man shortly fled the country because a group of Special Operations officers, led by Mamba Jack Kreuter, had put a price on his head.

Thatcher wiped his eyes. "Ah, the intelligence establishment. They are such rascals. But so dedicated, so sincere. One almost might admire them, had they the merest scintilla of morality. I have my own spy story, by the way. Should you like to hear it?"

"Of course."

"Well, you are aware that from time to time they approach us—

business people, I mean, executives of a certain stature and seniority?"

Dave and the senator nodded. Mike Ash looked perplexed. "Ahh . . . ?"

"Oh, not at PegaSys. I won't have it in my company. But elsewhere? Why, there has not been an American businessman returned from Moscow since Mike Todd and his bride honeymooned there in the 1950s who was not debriefed by the naughty boys from Langley. It is hard to turn them down, you know. One does have a certain patriotic duty. Unfortunately, and I speak from experience here, gentlemen, a little cooperation is but the beginning. Give them an inch and they will take a mile. Unless you are careful, your executive cadre will be suborned into tattling to Washington on the affairs of your foreign suppliers and customers. Worse, you will have your balance sheet weighed down with unproductive Agency assets. In these days of budget deficits and with the Soviet Union gone to its just reward, the spies and the spooks desperately need to find corporate angels to sponsor their grubby little projects. They have too many front operations, too many shell corporations, and now that the cold war has ended, too little money. Therefore they come to you, wrapping themselves in the flag, and asking in the nicest way, 'Oh, sir, might you do a favor for your country? There is a certain skunkworks that will be closed for lack of funds. If you could find it in your heart to fold it into your corporation so that it might be kept alive, we would be forever in your debt.' "

Thatcher snorted. "Rascals! But that's by the by, and not germane. More port, David? Help yourself. Well then, to begin at the beginning . . ."

Would Bernie Levy do that? Would he allow Senterex to provide cover for an intelligence operation? Of course he would. Bernie was an ex-Marine. Fiercely patriotic, he wouldn't have given it a second thought. *Semper Fidelis*—always loyal.

A front. It would be a going business like any good front. It would have employees, products, services, and customers. There would be an audited balance sheet, a profit and loss statement, and a credible earnings history. From the outside it would be indistinguishable from any other business. Only the insiders—and usually only a handful of them—would know that somewhere in a back room something wasn't quite kosher. Something like Laboratory number five.

Dave spotted a sign above the freeway exit: GAS, FOOD, LODGING. He cut across two lanes, and sped onto the off-ramp. Behind him a big-rig driver leaned on his horn.

The gas station was just up the road—an all-night station with two pay phones plainly in sight. Dave turned in, switched off the ignition, and tumbled out of the car.

He snatched a phone, dialed Marge's number, waited while it rang. No answer. Three more rings. Still no answer. On the fifth ring, he heard it pick up. "Hi, you've reached 555-6503. We can't come to the phone right now, so please leave a message at the sound of the tone."

Smart girl. Her answering machine message contained no names. And she said "we" not "I." Too many single women didn't take those simple precautions. And regretted it.

Had she done what he told her to do, and run for cover? "This is Dave. If you haven't . . ."

Stop! Just shut up, you goddamned idiot!

Dave gulped. Leaving a message on Marge's machine was a mistake, a bad one. It would be like Ransome to tap Marge's phone—he was the sort of man who covered all his bases. And if he overheard Dave making a call to her, then Marge would be in even greater danger than she already was.

"Err . . . sorry, wrong number." It was weak, but it was the best he could do. He hung up the phone, and glanced at his wrist.

No watch. You gave it to your lady friend.

He called out to the gas station attendant, "Excuse me, can you tell me the time?"

The attendant pointed mutely at a large-faced clock hanging above the cashier's shack. 1:12.

Six hours' time difference between New York and Switzerland. Nobody would be in the office yet. He'd have to wait at least an hour and a half before calling.

You're really going to call him aren't you? Bernie has—had—*a word for that, pal.* Chutzpah.

Ransome thought he'd gotten to everyone Dave knew, lied to them, convinced them that Dave had gone dangerously insane. He had tapped every telephone, and put watchers on every doorstep. There was no place Dave could go, and no one to whom he could turn. Ransome wanted David Elliot to be alone, without a friend in the world.

Maybe, Dave thought, he was. Then again, maybe he wasn't. Maybe there was one person whom Ransome had overlooked, one person whom Ransome didn't view as a threat because he knew Dave would never call him, never in a million years.

Mamba Jack Kreuter.

2.

Six general court-martials. Kreuter's is the last.

For reasons of its own, the Army decides to try each man separately. Each faces a separate Board of officers, each is confronted with a different prosecutor, each is defended by a different Judge Advocate General attorney. Only the witnesses are the same.

The Uniform Code of Military Justice puts a premium on procedural efficiency. The same officers serve as both judge and jury. Delaying tactics and legal posturing are not allowed. Convictions are the expected outcome.

The first five court-martials take four days apiece, and are spaced two weeks apart. Their outcomes are as expected.

Dave spends his days and nights alone in the Bachelor Officers' Quarters. The one time he visits the Officer's Club, the bartender refuses to serve him. His fellow officers will not speak to him. When he goes out for his morning run, everyone in uniform moves to the other side of the street. He is completely isolated, cut off from human contact, except when he is in the courtroom.

COLONEL NEWTON, PROSECUTOR: Lieutenant, you are still under oath.
FIRST LIEUTENANT ELLIOT, WITNESS: Yes, sir, I'm aware of that.
PROSECUTOR: You have testified in this matter before?
WITNESS: Yes, sir, five times.
PROSECUTOR: Lieutenant, you have heard the Board read the charge sheet against Colonel Kreuter, have you not?
WITNESS: Yes, sir.
PROSECUTOR: On the date in question, on or about 1100 hours, you were in or near the village of Loc Ban, Republic of Vietnam.
WITNESS: Yes, sir.
PROSECUTOR: Who was in command of your unit?
WITNESS: Colonel Kreuter, sir.
PROSECUTOR: Describe the chain of command, Lieutenant.
WITNESS: We had taken casualties, sir. Captain Feldman and First Lieutenant Fuller had been air-evac'd a day earlier along with three NCOs. The colonel and I were the only officers left. Colonel Kreuter ordered me to take command of team alpha and he led the baker team himself. First Sergeant Mullins was the ranking noncom, so he took the con for team charlie.
PROSECUTOR: When you arrived at Loc Ban, what did you find?
WITNESS: Very little, sir. It was barely a village, just a dozen huts in the middle of a rice paddy. Our helicopters had just dusted off the LZ and we . . .

LIEUTENANT GENERAL FISHER, PRESIDING OFFICER: Twelve hooches, Lieutenant?

WITNESS: Sorry, sir. Actually we counted fifteen.

PRESIDING OFFICER: Be precise, Lieutenant. We're dealing with capital charges.

PROSECUTOR: Continue.

WITNESS: Most of the villagers were out in the fields working. They didn't pay much attention when we landed. Like they'd seen it all before. So then Sergeant Mullins and his men rounded them up, brought them back to the huts. We knew an enemy patrol . . .

PRESIDING OFFICER: Insurgents or North Vietnamese?

WITNESS: At the time it was reported as Vietcong, sir. We knew that a VC patrol had been seen in the area the day before. So we questioned the villagers as to any enemy activity they might have seen.

PROSECUTOR: What response were you given?

WITNESS: A negative, sir. Everyone denied having seen any troops other than our own.

PROSECUTOR: How did Colonel Kreuter react to that?

WITNESS: He thanked them, and gave the village headman a carton of Winstons, sir.

PROSECUTOR: What about First Sergeant Mullins?

WITNESS: First Sergeant Mullins was angry, sir. He wanted to apply stronger interrogation techniques. When Colonel Kreuter ordered him not to, he recommended torching—I mean burning the village.

COLONEL ADAMSON, BOARD OFFICER: Lieutenant, you used the phrase "stronger interrogation techniques." Can you be more explicit?

WITNESS: Torture, sir.

PROSECUTOR: Lieutenant, were these quote stronger interrogation techniques unquote common in your unit?

WITNESS: Common, sir? No, sir, I wouldn't say that.

PROSECUTOR: But used?

WITNESS: Yes, sir, on occasion.

PROSECUTOR: By whom?

WITNESS: First Sergeant Mullins, sir.

PROSECUTOR: Under Colonel Kreuter's orders?

WITNESS: No, sir. Nor with his permission. Sergeant Mullins, sir, well, he often exceeded his orders. Colonel Kreuter had reprimanded him a number of times, and for some weeks prior to the episode at Loc Ban had been trying to get the sergeant reassigned to non-combat responsibilities. I think he was worried that the sergeant was getting pretty close to Section 8.

PRESIDING OFFICER: For the record, Section 8 addresses general discharge from the service by reason of mental instability or incapability, untreatable in the context of active duty.

PROSECUTOR: Do you remember and can you quote for this board the words exchanged by Colonel Kreuter and First Sergeant Mullins at the time?

WITNESS: Not word for word, sir. But I do recollect the sense of the argument. Sergeant Mullins was convinced that the villagers were lying, and that they were collaborating with the VC. Colonel Kreuter replied that there was no evidence to that effect, and that the people looked like peaceful farmers to him. The sergeant said they were all liars the same as every Vietnamese was a liar. He said that if he could take his K-Bar knife to the village headman's wife, the headman would tell the truth. The colonel ordered him to belay that, and then gave the command for everyone to move out. While we were leaving the village, First Sergeant Mullins said that if the villagers were lying, he would come back. He said he would crucify them one by one to the walls of their hooches. He screamed it at them, sir. He screamed it over and over until we were out of earshot.

PROSECUTOR: Before we move on to the events of the evening, Lieutenant, I wish to ask you whether you experienced any friction with Colonel Kreuter on the occasion in question or any other occasion.

WITNESS: No friction, sir. If I may say so, I consider the colonel to be a fine man and fine soldier. I honor him, sir, and I always will.

PROSECUTOR: Then there was no bad blood—

MAJOR WATERSON, DEFENSE OFFICER: My client wishes to make a statement.

PRESIDING OFFICER: The accused officer will not—

COLONEL KREUTER, ACCUSED: I got me something to say.

PRESIDING OFFICER: Sit down, Colonel. That's an order.

ACCUSED: What you going to do, court-martial me?

PRESIDING OFFICER: Colonel—

ACCUSED: I'm going to say this one thing, General, whether you like it or not. Lieutenant Elliot is as honorable an officer as ever served under my command.

PRESIDING OFFICER: You do yourself no service, Colonel. Be at ease.

ACCUSED: No bad blood between us. There wasn't then. There isn't now. There never will be.

PRESIDING OFFICER: I said at ease, Colonel.

ACCUSED: And another thing—

PRESIDING OFFICER: This court is adjourned for an hour. Major Waterson, counsel your client. Turn off that damned steno machine, Corporal.

3.

Dave cruised along the avenues west of Times Square. During the twenty years that he had lived in New York, every mayor who had taken office had begun his administration with a pledge to renovate the area, drive out the riffraff, and bring decency and dignity back to the neighborhood.

Somehow or another, none of them ever quite got around to it. Not that it mattered. No one believes the mayor of New York anyway.

At this late hour the action was slowing down. The hookers

were no longer patrolling their beats. Instead, they had gathered in small packs, leaning wearily against graffiti-coated walls, sharing cigarettes, and boasting of their pimps. The pimps themselves were out of their flashy cars, standing in their own circles, and negotiating such barters and trades as the day's business conditions demanded.

The "Triple X-X-X" movie houses were closed, but the bars were still open, their garish neon brightly inviting imprudent fools to enter. Doors periodically opened to admit or eject hunted-looking nighthawks who might make it home safely to bed—but only because the predators were too glutted with earlier prey to stalk them.

Most of the drug hawkers were gone. The touts for the "Girls! Girls! Girls!" and "Live Sex Acts on Stage!" joints were off the streets too. A few sailors, clustered together for protection, stumbled drunkenly down the sidewalk. Three teenage boys circled a trio of bored prostitutes. One boy finally worked up his nerve, and stepped forward. The prostitutes smiled. Dave drove on.

He stopped at a red light. A blue and white patrol car pulled up beside him. The driver glanced his way, and then turned to study the street.

Good. He didn't even give you a second look. Shaving and dyeing your hair was an inspired piece of work. Even if I do say so myself.

Dave's stomach grumbled. It had been fourteen hours since his last meal. He was hungry. Worse, exhaustion was catching up with him. He needed coffee, the stronger the better.

There was an all-night cafeteria in the middle of the Forty-fourth Street block. Dave pulled out of traffic and squeezed the rent-a-car between a dumpster and a candy-flake, tangerine orange pimpmobile. He climbed out and stretched.

Three years earlier he and Helen had gone on a photo safari to Tanzania. It had been a luxury affair, managed by the exceptionally competent (and exceptionally expensive) firm of Abercrombie & Kent. Safely seated in mammoth Toyota Land Cruisers, Dave and the other tourists had oohed and ahhed as they passed by hunting lions, stalking leopards, and leering hyenas speckled with blood. As the Land Cruisers approached, the animals cheerfully went about their gory business, not paying the least attention to the sightseers. Nor would they—unless one of the plump pink bipeds left the protection of the truck. Leaving the truck changed the nature of the relationship. Leaving the truck made you meat. *Meat!*

Dave barely had placed his foot on the sidewalk when a pair of prostitutes moved in on him. One wore a see-through net blouse and hotpants the color of lemon meringue pie. The other wore a Mickey Mouse tank top and a lime green miniskirt.

Citrus colors must be this year's fashion among the demimonde.

The one in the hotpants began to speak. The second hooker touched her on the shoulder and whispered something in her ear. Hotpants nodded, giving Dave a slightly pitying look. "Sweetie, you're on the wrong side of town. The kind of trick you want hangs out over on Third Avenue in the lower Fifties."

Dave gaped. The two turned to walk away.

It's your new hairdo. It makes you look a little, well . . .

Dave rubbed his hand across his newly bald dome and smiled.

The air inside the cafeteria was thick and humid. An odor of strong coffee hung in the air, mingling with the smell of greasy meat and cigarette smoke. Most of the tables were occupied, and the place buzzed with low conversation.

Dave walked to the counter. "Large cheese danish, please." The counterman needed a shave. His eyes were red, and he seemed to think his night would never end. "Outta cheese. They don't deliver until 6:00, maybe 6:30."

Dave nodded. "Have you got anything else?"

"Apple. But it's stale. Like I say, they don't deliver until 6:00 or 6:30."

"I'll take one."

"No returns. No refunds."

"Make it two. I need the carbohydrates. And give me a coffee. Black." Dave paused, then added, "In a paper cup, okay?"

"All I got is styrofoam."

"Whatever." Styrofoam would be as easy to get rid of as paper. All he had to do was tear it into tiny shreds.

The counterman slapped two stiff-looking pastries on a chipped plate and filled a large styrofoam cup with coffee. "Four-fifty with the tax."

The first danish and coffee Dave had ever purchased in New York City had cost him a quarter.

Dave handed him a five dollar bill. "Keep it." He slid his wallet into his rear pocket.

Someone bumped into his back. Dave knifed his elbow backward. It drove into something soft. There was a gasp of pain. Dave turned. The pickpocket was doubled over, clutching his chest. Dave retrieved his wallet from the man's fingers and smiled. "Thanks, I guess I dropped it."

The pickpocket muttered, "No problem, man." He backed away.

One or two people looked at Dave. Their eyes were expressionless.

He took a table by the window, wolfed down his pastries, and savored his coffee. The pastries tasted dry but good. You can't get a bad danish in New York. Dave went to the counter for a second serving.

When he returned to his table, he glanced out the window. His jaw dropped. The rental car had disappeared. How long had it taken for someone to steal it? Ninety seconds at the outside.

Africa, he thought. It's like a tourist leaving the safety of his truck and stepping out onto the veldt. . . .

Three giggly black women were sitting at the next table. One tapped a cigarette from a pack of Virginia Slims. As Dave watched her, hungrily remembering all the pleasure that tobacco brings, an idea came to mind. Virginia Slims . . .

He leaned across the aisle. "Excuse me, miss, might I ask you for a smoke?" The woman's eyes widened. Dave added, "I'll pay. In fact, I'll give you a buck for a pack."

"Chil', coffin nails cost two-fifty a pack in this city, an' what planet do you come from?"

Dave handed her a five. She reached in her purse and removed a fresh pack of Virginia Slims. "Profit's profit, honey, and you don't look like anyone I can make money off of the usual way."

The other women at her table found her comment hilarious. They dissolved into gales of laughter. "Here. Best take these matches, too."

Dave broke open the pack, drew out a cigarette, and, for the first time in twelve years, lit up a smoke.

What the hell, pal. You're going to die anyway.

4.

Grand Central Station spooked him. At this late hour it was another place entirely—eerie, almost eldritch. The building was almost empty, and that alone was both unnatural and unnerving.

No more than five people were in sight . . . a teenage boy and girl slumped sleeping on their backpacks . . . a lone patrolman circling the perimeter of the main floor . . . a tired-looking mechanic, greasy in grey-and-blue-striped overalls, tramping wearily out from one of the platforms. Only one of the ticket booths seemed to be manned. The lights above the Off Track Betting windows were dark. The news kiosks were closed and shuttered.

Spookiest of all, the floors were clean.

Dave's shoes clicked hollowly on the marble. No one seemed to be paying attention to him. Nonetheless, he felt eyes watching. Not hostile. Not even curious. Just watchful.

Cave dwellers. They say this part of town is riddled with tunnels and underground passageways. People live in them, keeping guard through holes and grilles, only coming out when there's no one around.

The hair on the back of his neck prickled. New York is strange. Deep in the night, it is stranger still.

Dave turned east. There was, he recollected, an instant photo booth not far from the Lexington Avenue exit.

He studied the instructions. "PHOTOGRAPHS. Four pictures for $1. Adjust seat height. Insert $1 bill in tray, face up. Push in. No change returned. Green light illuminates when ready. Red light illuminates when complete. Wait 1 minute. Remove pictures from slot."

Dave fed a dollar into the machine. The red light winked green. Click. Click. Click. Click. *Whirrrrrr*. The light turned red again. He counted off sixty seconds, and withdrew a strip of photographs that made his eyebrows arch querulously.

Jesus, pal, that hairdo makes you look queer as a plaid rabbit. Let's not talk to any strangers, huh?

Dave held the strip of photographs between his fingers, blowing softly until it was completely dry. Then he drew a small pocket-knife out of his slacks, using it to trim one of the photographs to the size of the picture on the stolen ID card: "American Interdyne Worldwide. M. F. Cohen, Computer Systems Analyst." He spoiled the first photo. The second was a perfect fit, precisely the same size and dimensions as Marge's picture.

He needed something to fasten the photo to the card. His options were few. Indeed, he had no choice in the matter.

Oh no! Yecch! Ugh! Gross me out!

He felt around beneath the seat in the photo booth. Sure enough, there were several pieces of chewing gum stuck to it.

Typhoid! Herpes! Gingivitis!

He pried one loose, tried not to think about what he was going to do, and popped it in his mouth.

You are a truly disgusting individual.

The flavor was gone. No matter. He chewed it soft, stretched out a thin strand, and used it to glue his photograph over Marge's. He slid the result into a plastic window in his wallet, formerly the home of a driver's license now as useless as his credit cards.

And now, he needed to make one last phone call.

Well, not needed.

Wanted.

Marge Cohen was on his mind. Marigold Fields Cohen. He liked "Marigold" better than "Marge." And he needed to be sure she was safe.

Just a quick call, just to make sure she'd left. She had to be gone, long gone, by now.

But still, he wanted to check one more time.

There were five pay phones in a row, right next to the photo booth. Four of them were out of order. One of them worked. Dave dialed. One ring, two rings.

She has her answering machine set to answer after five rings.

Three rings, but not a fourth. "Hi, you've reached 555-6503. We can't comI've got her, Mr. Elliot, and if you want her, you know where to find her."

There were now five out of order phones next to the photo booth.

Dave gripped the handset, torn from its wire, though he didn't entirely remember doing so. He turned it over, studied it with an empty mind, and placed it back on its now useless cradle.

It was a lie, of course. Ransome up to his goddamned tricks again. Psychological warfare. Mindfucking his prey. Trying to weaken him, frighten him, make him act rashly; it is eminently more useful to destroy an enemy's spirit . . .

It could not be true. Dave had called earlier. Marge's regular message, a single woman's thoughtful message, was on the machine then. That could mean only one thing. Marge had made it. She'd gotten free and fled. Then Ransome's men had returned. They found her gone.

Dave cursed himself for wrecking the phone. If he hadn't he could call back, call Marge's number again. There was something to the way Ransome's voice sounded . . . as if it had been coming from too far away. Through a radio? Yes, almost certainly. That's what had happened. Ransome's little friends had found Marge missing and radioed for instructions. Ransome, cunning Ransome, had used the radio link to record the message.

That was it. It had to be.

It was a shot in the dark. Ransome did not know, could not possibly know, that Dave felt . . . felt what? . . . felt something that men should not feel about women who are twenty years their junior. Ransome was just guessing, hoping that Dave was foolish enough to feel some sense of obligation to a woman he'd only met twice, and whom, if the ugly truth were told, he'd exploited on both occasions.

Yeah, a shot in the dark, and a long shot at that. The act of a man who was running out of time, running out of ideas, and getting desperate. It was just a cheap trick.

But if it wasn't . . .

If it wasn't, he was going back to Senterex anyway. The secret locked in Bernie's credenza was reason enough. And if Ransome really did have Marge . . . well, he'd have to do something about that, wouldn't he?

Escalators led out of Grand Central and into the old Pan Am building, newly renamed for its current owner, Metropolitan Life Insurance, but more commonly known to cynical New Yorkers as the Snoopy Building—a sarcastic tribute to Met Life's advertising spokes-beagle. At this late hour the escalators had been turned off. Dave climbed them anyway, then walked swiftly through a darkened lobby and out onto Forty-fifth Street.

Park Avenue was above him, an elevated roadway that left ground level a block north at Forty-sixth Street. Two dark pedestrian tunnels led from where Dave stood to the corner of Forty-sixth and Park, and Dave could see sleeping bodies stretched out in their shadows. He needed to get to Park Avenue. He didn't need any incidents.

Disturbing the homeless, annoying the crazies, caused incidents.

Maybe you ought to think about moving to a safer city. You know, Sarajevo, Beirut . . .

Dave chose the tunnel that looked emptiest, and tried to walk as softly as he could.

He almost made it, but not quite. Just short of Forty-sixth Street something plucked at his foot. Adrenaline spiked his heart. He kicked hard, simultaneously snatching a pistol from his belt. "I'll fucking blow you away!" The loudness of his own voice scared him.

A surprised rat spun through the air, collided with a wall, and squeaked with indignation. Dave stood, breathing hard, sweating, cursing himself. The rat trotted back toward Forty-fifth Street.

Getting a little hyper, aren't we, pal?

He slipped the pistol back beneath his shirt, and jogged out to Park Avenue.

The sight stunned him. He had never seen Park Avenue so beautiful, had never thought that it could be. By night, the traffic gone, the sidewalks empty, it possessed a certain peace, a gentleness. Noisily frenetic by day, it now seemed to him to be a woman, dark-haired, napping lightly, and wearing the faintest of slumbering smiles.

He stood momentarily transfixed, wondering how it was that he had never noticed how heartbreakingly gorgeous this city could be.

The central median, dividing the northbound and southbound lanes, sparkled with flowers—not the tulips of spring, but the asters of fall. The colors were muted by the streetlights, turned to soft pastels. To the north the traffic lights changed, blinking their circuit from green to yellow to red and back to green. The buildings were mosaics of light and dark, indigo blue and deep sea green dominating.

Green . . .

Emerald green . . . green as a green bottle . . . green as a small, perfect lake nestled in a high Sierra valley . . . in the magic evening of a hot summer day . . . Taffy Weiler wearing a loopy grin . . . horses standing bowed as if praying to an equine God . . . David Elliot, his heart near enough to bursting, knowing that no matter how sour his later life might turn . . .

In the dark behind him someone cursed. A bottle arced out of the shadows and exploded at his feet.

The moment was gone. The Sierras disappeared. The city returned, and night.

In New York, only imbeciles stand still after sundown.

The hair on the back of his neck prickled again. Someone was watching him, sizing him up, wondering about the contents of his wallet. It was time to move on.

Dave trotted north. Four more blocks would bring him to the corner of Fiftieth Street.

The nightowls had long since departed the Avenue, the workaholics left for home at last. Some few random office windows were still lit—largely, Dave thought, the offices of people who had not gone home until after the janitors were through with their chores.

Nonetheless, there were still people in every building, including his own.

He stood across the street, studying its windows floor by floor. On the eleventh floor most of the lights were lit. That particular floor was occupied by the mergers and acquisitions department of Lee, Bach & Wachutt, one of the city's most notoriously predatory investment bankers. Up higher, on floors 34 to 39, many of McKinley-Allan's lights were still on. Doubtless, legions of eager young management consultants were toiling the night away, striving to satisfy the perfectionist partners who had long since gone home to bed.

Elsewhere the building was a checkerboard of light and dark, albeit mostly dark. No one floor seemed to be showing more . . .

Thirty-one.

Dave squinted. The thirty-first floor's windows were neither bright nor dark. They were merely dim. The curtains had been drawn closed on every window facing Park Avenue.

What's on thirty-one?

Dave didn't remember. A reinsurance company? No, that wasn't right. A trading company? That was it. A trading company with the word "Trans" in its name. Trans-Pacific? Trans-Oceanic? Trans- . . . something or another.

Promising, very promising. Just the kind of anonymous enterprise the intelligence crowd likes.

"Hi. Wanna date?"

Dave spun, his fist drawn for a punch.

"Whoa, honey! I ain't no trouble."

She—he?—was the most improbable transvestite Dave had ever seen. Too tall, too thin, dressed in a silvered Chinese cheongsam, and dripping with rhinestone jewelry.

Dave growled, "Two things. One, don't sneak up behind people. Two, go away."

He—she?—the creature cocked its head, placed an electric pink fingernail against its cheek, and smirked. "Aw, don't be that way, baby. I can tell from just lookin' at you, you like what I got to offer."

See, I warned you about your new hairdo.

Dave felt himself blush. He didn't like the experience. "Get out of my face."

"Lighten up, hon. Tell you what, seein' as you gonna be my last customer of the business day, I give you a special price."

Dave bit his words, one by one: "I. Am. Going. To. Say. This. Only. Once. *Go! Away!*"

"Oooh. A rough one. Don't look so rough, but I guess appearances can . . ."

Dave took a step forward, put his flattened palm against the man's chest, and pushed. The transvestite stumbled back over the curb and sat down hard.

"Awww!" He pointed at his high-heeled, shiny patent leather sandals. One of his five inch spikes had snapped. "Now look what you've done, you animal! Those cost me forty dollars a pair from Frederick's! Plus shipping and handling!" He started blubbering.

My, my. Turning into a fag basher now, are we?

Dave winced. What he had just done had been too natural, too instinctual—the same as it was twenty-five years earlier. Got a problem? No problem. Just lock and load, my friend, and shortly all of life's ambiguous complexities will be simplified. And never forget, anyone who's a little different, anyone who isn't just like you, well hell, son, in this man's Army we call that kind of person "target."

Dave gritted his teeth and started to frame an apology.

A voice came out of the shadows. "Kimberly, you all right, child?" Another luridly dressed prostitute clattered into view. This one seemed to be a woman (or at least a more authentic-looking cross-dresser). She was wearing a black ciré skirt that barely hid her panties, a blood red Victorian bustier, and heels that were as high as the fallen Kimberly's.

Jesus, where are these people coming from?

"Ohhh, Charlene, he hit me." This from the crying transvestite.

"I did not. All I did . . ."

Charlene advanced on Dave. "You some sort of rough trade, huh? Beat up on a helpless little faggot? That your thing, ain't it, whuppin' up on 'em? Poor boy Kimberly the nicest boy in the life, mister. He don't need no business from your kind."

Dave backpedaled. "Now look, lady . . ."

"I ain't no lady. I's a whore." Something bright and sharp snapped open in her hand. "An' whores take care of their friends."

5.

Dave looked around wildly. There wasn't a cab in sight. No police cars. A lone Toyota sped north on Park Avenue. Its driver glanced in his direction, looked away, and increased his speed. The transvestite named Kimberly was tottering to his feet. His eyes were bright with feral hunger.

Charlene crouched, circling Dave. The thing in her hand was a straight razor, and she held it in a wholly businesslike fashion.

"Now look . . ."

Kimberly urged her on. "Cut him, Charlene."

"Yeah, get him!" Another voice. "Take his balls off!" And another.

A pack of them. Seven or eight. Black and white. Dressed to kill, and looking for all the world like a pride of hunting cats. *Meat!*

Charlene's eyes sparkled. Her pupils were wide. Dave guessed she was high on some drug. "White man, you about to have the worst experience in your faggot life."

A gun would solve the problem. All he had to do was pull one out from beneath his shirt. Showing it would probably do the trick.

But if it doesn't . . . ?

If it didn't, then it would only make matters worse. And if matters became worse, he'd have to use it.

Charlene's razor sliced the air beside his cheek. He dodged left. She was a little off balance. He could have taken her easily.

Then you'd have all the rest of them to deal with. Let her go. The others will stay back as long as they think she can handle you.

Charlene hissed. "You move fast for a pussy queer." She came in again. He felt the wind as the razor flashed past him at eye level.

Not bad, she almost got you that time.

The woman was good. He was going to have to do something about her.

The razor weaved and flashed. A three inch cut snicked open on his shirt.

He couldn't risk pulling a gun. If she made him shoot her, he wouldn't be able to go into the building. The corner of Fiftieth Street and Park Avenue had been the center of too much excitement today—bomb scares, twelfth floor muggings, Bernie's suicide. One more incident, and the police would be all over the place.

While New York City's finest are willing to overlook a lot, a bullet-riddled corpse on Park Avenue usually gets their attention.

Dave edged back, slowly luring Charlene forward. He heard steps shuffle nearby. Someone was getting ready to give her a hand.

Now or never.

He lurched left, as if trying to flee. Charlene moved in with the grace and speed of a tango dancer. The razor arced down, shining in the streetlights, cutting for his face. He slid under her arm. Her wrist slammed down on his shoulder. The razor clattered on the sidewalk.

Your next move has to be flashy, a real crowd-pleaser.

Dave dropped into a crouch. The woman's momentum carried her over his shoulder. He cocked his right leg behind her ankle, kicking it forward while he thrust his body upward. Charlene's feet left the ground. She began to tumble. Dave snatched her arm and twisted, adding velocity.

It was perfect. It was spectacular. She spun like a propeller, turned 270 degrees in the air, and smashed face down on the sidewalk. She lifted her head, spitting blood.

Dave ran. The gang behind him howled.

He sprinted across Park Avenue, reaching the median before Charlene's friends worked up the courage to follow. Someone hurled a can at him. It bounced off his hip and clattered on the asphalt. Dave kept running.

To the disgust of the construction industry and the irritation of the developers, New York City requires that high-rises have ample outdoor public space. For this reason, and this reason only, Dave's building was fronted by an open plaza. The plaza was surrounded by marble-faced planters. Every now and then the landlord tried to grow shrubbery in them. The plants died, poisoned by the air and choked by trash.

Dave vaulted a planter and dashed toward the entrance.

There were—or rather had been—a pair of fountains on either side of the plaza. However, by the end of the eighties, the city's homeless population had begun treating such decorative amenities as open-air bathrooms. The building management drained them, and erected chain-link fences around their borders.

Behind him someone stumbled into the fence. Dave sprinted toward the steps, cleared them in one leap, and bounced off a window. He saw the night guard inside look up at the sound. The man started to rise from his desk.

Two glass panes had been shattered during the morning's evacuation. They'd been replaced with plywood. Dave ran by them. There were revolving doors ahead. The first one was closed, a yellow-striped safety barricade set in front of it. Dave flung himself into the second.

He pushed. Nothing happened. There was a sign on the glass: USE CENTER DOORS FOR ENTRY AFTER 9:00 P.M.

Dave darted out. The pack was close. One woman was out ahead of the others. She brandished a broken bottle, and was shrieking like a banshee.

Dave threw the center door open. The guard was up. He had a radio in his hand. It was one of Ransome's radios, and the guard was one of Ransome's men.

Dave let his voice rise in fear. It wasn't difficult. "Help! I'm being . . ." He ran toward the guard station.

He glanced over his shoulder. There were more than a dozen of them now. They boiled into the lobby behind him.

Dave fumbled for his wallet, flinging it open in front of the guard. "*Please!* I work here! I'm supposed to be on duty! These *animals* want to kill me!"

The guard's eyes flitted from Dave's face to the approaching mob. When he looked at Dave, he didn't like what he saw. When he looked at the mob, he liked it even less. He reached beneath the desk. His hands came out holding a shotgun, an autoloader with an oddly shaped choke.

Ithaca model 37. Complete with duckbill choke. Long time no see, old friend.

A popular weapon in Vietnam. Fully automatic. Loads and ejects through the same underside port. The duckbill spreads the shot horizontally, in a nice wide arc. If there's somebody hiding in the bushes, all you have to do is point in their general direction. A charge of number 4 shot does the rest. The grunts who carry the guns call them "Hamburger helpers."

Of course if there was a camera crew in the neighborhood, you made sure that your Ithaca was out of sight. Couldn't have the folks back home know that their baby boys were toting around great big nasty meat shredders.

The guard leveled the shotgun on the crowd. Things went quiet.

"Street-sweeper," someone muttered, using the Tactical Police Force's nickname for a duckbilled 12-gauge.

Dave's inner voice urged him, *Ham it up, pal. Ham it up.*

He took the advice. "My *God*! Thank you, *officer*! Those *creatures* were going to tear me apart!"

The guard glared at Dave, his face a mask of homophobic loathing. All at once, and for the first time in his life, David Elliot knew what it was to be hated not as an individual, but rather as a member of a class.

"Don't you listen to that faggot!" A tall Hispanic woman stepped forward.

The guard growled, "What's your gripe, lady?"

"He beatin' up on people. He just whupped the hell out of my frien' Charlene and a poor transvestite boy."

The guard gave Dave a malevolent stare, his eyes hot with abhorrence of homosexuals. Dave played to the man's repugnance; it was the only thing to do. "They tried to take my *wallet*! I *pushed* her away. I didn't want to hurt *anybody*! Do I look like some sort of *brute*?" He fumbled his cigarettes out of his jacket and nervously lit one.

The guard scowled at the pack. Virginia Slims. That settled it for him. "No, mister . . ." He glanced at Dave's doctored ID card. ". . . Mister Cohen, you most certainly do not." He turned to the mob. "You people get the hell out of here. Go back on the street where you belong."

The Hispanic woman looked over her shoulder. Several of her cohorts nodded encouragement. She rounded on the guard, screaming: "We gonna kill you, prick! You and your faggot boyfriend!"

The guard's face went bright red. He put the shotgun to his shoulder. "People like you don't call people like me queer."

Oh Christ! He's another goddamn Mullins.

The late First Shirt had once broken the jaw of a buck sergeant who had jokingly called him a "homo." Too many career military men were the same way.

We definitely do not need a midnight shotgun massacre.

"Queer lover! Pansy boy!" The mob wasn't helping things.

Dave forced his voice into a high-pitched giggle—Norman Bates sharing a joke with his mother. "Kill them! Nasty *whores*!" He strutted two steps toward the pack. "He's going to turn you into Gaines Burger, you *bitches*!" The Hispanic woman stopped short, let her hands fall, and shook her head. Dave whirled to face the guard. He opened his eyes wide, hoping they glittered with appropriate insanity. "Well, *do it*!"

The guard's eyes flicked left and right between Dave and the crowd. Dave swiped at his lips, as if brushing away a fleck of saliva. He jiggled on his feet impatiently, turned and stepped back to the guard desk.

Someone behind him muttered, "Aw, shit. This ain't worth it."

The guard's posture changed slightly. Just enough. He was calming down. "I'm counting to ten."

Now, while he's distracted . . .

Dave drew back another step, moving out of the guard's field of vision, stretching his hand to where the man's radio lay.

"Can't count to twenty-one. Ain't got enough digits." The whores began to laugh. The guard snorted. The trouble was over.

Nope. The trouble's just begun.

CHAPTER 8

ONE OF OUR OWN

1.

Dave was back in the American Interdyne computer room. He had been tempted to make his first stop the thirty-first floor, the place where all the lights were on and the curtains were drawn. If Ransome really had taken Marge Cohen prisoner, that would be where he'd keep her.

But Ransome didn't have Marge. Dave was sure of it.

Almost sure.

Besides, if the thirty-first floor was Ransome's base of operations, there would be guards at the elevator and watchers by every stairwell. Trying to break in was too risky, and it would buy him nothing.

And anyway, he had work to do at American Interdyne. He remembered he had seen an old Mead Data Services Nexis terminal sitting right next to AIW's mainframe. It might be just what he needed.

Mead, like Dow Jones and a handful of others, maintains a massive on-line database of articles, extracts, and facts assembled from a legion of sources. For a price, anyone can dial in and retrieve information on almost any subject. All you need is the phone number, an ID, and a password.

Consistent with the highest standards of corporate computer security, someone from American Interdyne had Scotch-taped a TymeNet dial-up number, user ID code, and password to the Nexis terminal's keyboard.

Dave flexed his fingers over the keys, and logged on. He'd never used any of the news retrieval services himself. That was a job he delegated to his aides. Nonetheless, he didn't think it would be difficult.

A line of characters printed slowly across the screen. Running at 1200 baud, a glacial speed, the terminal was, like everything else in AIW's computer room, an antiquity. Dave scanned the instructions as they appeared, entering the American Interdyne ID and password in the proper places.

The system menu appeared. It offered him a choice of topics—general news, business news, scientific databases, financial statistics, and a half dozen other categories. The last menu choice read, "ALL." That was the one he wanted.

Next, the terminal asked how far back in time he wanted to search. Dave pecked in "20 YEARS."

"INVALID PARAMETER. TRY AGAIN."

"10 YEARS." That worked.

The system asked: "KEYWORD OR SEARCH ARGUMENT?"

Dave typed, "LOCKYEAR," and hit the "enter" key.

The machine told him it was working. After a few moments it displayed, "12 MATCHES FOUND. USE <ENTER> TO REVIEW. USE <DELETE> TO CHANGE SEARCH CRITERIA."

Dave stroked the "enter" key again.

"FULL <F> OR ABSTRACT <A>?"

Dave touched the "A" key.

The first four stories were recent articles from *The New York*

Times, The Wall Street Journal, Business Week, and *Newsday* about Senterex's acquisition of Lockyear. Dave didn't bother to retrieve the full stories. He'd already seen them.

The fifth abstract read, "LOCKYEAR AWARDED PATENT FOR D-RECEPTOR ANTI-IMMUNE DRUG." Dave touched the "F" key. The full story scrolled down the screen. It didn't say very much. Nor did the sixth, seventh, eighth, or ninth story. The tenth, however, was what he'd been looking for:

RANDOLPH LOCKYEAR OBITUARY. C-NEW YORK TIMES. 12/14/91. PAGE C22. W/PHOTOG. 270 WORDS.

HEADLINE: Randolph J. Lockyear, research scientist, dead at age 74.

Dr. Randolph J. Lockyear, respected medical researcher and chief executive of Lockyear Laboratories, the company he founded, died today at his home on Long Island. A company spokesperson reported that Dr. Lockyear had been ill for some time. The cause of death was congestive heart failure.

Dr. Lockyear was born in Parsippany, N.J., on May 11, 1917. He attended Dartmouth and took his medical degree at the Columbia School of Medicine. He served on active duty in the Pacific theater during World War II. In 1947, General Douglas MacArthur appointed Dr. Lockyear as medical advisor to the Allied Commission on Japan. Dr. Lockyear was discharged from the military in 1949.

In 1950, he founded the company that bore his name, headquartering it near Patchogue, Long Island. Privately held, Lockyear Laboratories is an independent research and pharmaceutical development organization. It was among the earliest corporations to be awarded a patent for a synthetic human biochemical. Since the 1980s, the company has been cited frequently as one of the leaders in immune studies.

In 1964, Dr. Lockyear was elected to the Board of Directors of Kitsuné Ltd., a Japanese conglomerate and pharmaceutical manufacturer. He also was a member of the Boards of Nor-Beco Pharmaceuticals and Gyre A.G., a Swiss manufacturer of laboratory instruments. From 1969 to 1973, he acted as special advisor on tropical medicine to the Joint Chiefs of Staff. In later years, President Reagan sponsored Dr. Lockyear's appointment as chairman of the United Nations' Advisory Panel on Pandemic Diseases.

He is survived by a son, Douglas M. Lockyear, and by a daughter, Philippa Lockyear Kincaid. Services are scheduled to be held at the family home on Saturday.

It was a short obituary, four or five column inches at most. It didn't say much. All it really did was raise questions.

Like what?

How did he get to be an aide to MacArthur? He couldn't have been more than thirty-three or thirty-four years old at the time. You would have thought someone like MacArthur would have wanted a more senior man.

It was wartime, pal. You remember what that's like. Everyone *is young except the generals.*

He was a member of the Board of a Japanese company. The Japanese don't invite foreigners to sit on their Boards.

It was probably a trade. Some sort of technology licensing deal. Lockyear gave them some patent rights, they gave him a Board seat. No big deal.

And he had government connections. Pretty high ones.

Who doesn't? Once you've achieved a certain seniority, you get those kinds of offers. Hell, Doc Sandberg has been on a dozen government panels.

Yeah, but . . .

"Myna, this is Robin. Where's your quarter hour check-in?" Ransome sounded as laconically self-controlled as ever.

The radio hissed. "Sorry, Robin." The voice belonged to the lobby guard. "This goddamned radio's fucked. It wiped its codes and I had to reset. Plus I had some company."

Dave licked his lips. Swapping the radios had been a risky move. If the guard had noticed . . .

"Company? Expatiate."

"Some fruit got in dutch with a bunch of prosties. They . . ."

"Who's the pixie?"

Dave glanced at the remaining abstracts on the Nexis terminal. More patent stories. They wouldn't tell him anything. He switched the machine off.

"Just some computer guy. Works for American Interdyne. He . . ."

"Name?"

"Ah . . ."

"Look at the sign-in log, Myna."

There was an embarrassed silence. The guard finally muttered, "Well, er, with all the excitement, I forgot to make him sign in. But, I remember . . . yeah. It's . . . I saw his ID . . . it's . . . shit, I forget."

Ransome growled, "Fourteenth floor?"

"No, twelve. That's the computer room. I checked. Look, Robin, he was a real three dollar bill. Didn't fit the subject's description, and . . ."

"Snipe, are you reading this?"

"Affirmative."

"Get down to twelve. Check him out. Maintain radio contact at all times."

"On my way, Robin."

Dave had been expecting that. He'd already turned on a half dozen monitors, and spread sheaves of printouts around one of the desks in the computer room. He loosened his tie, and tried to look busy tracing through a line of programming code with a red felt-tip pen.

"Myna."

"Yes, sir."

"Give it to me line by line."

"Yes, sir. It was just after I came on duty. I observed the pansy running toward the entrance. Half the whores in New York were after him. He came in. They followed. He claimed they were trying to mug him. I think he was right. Those broads were out for blood."

"What was their gripe?"

"They said he was a fag basher. No way, sir. The guy is a cupcake. If he tried to duke it out with a Smurf, I'd put my money on the blue . . ."

"No editorials."

"Yes, sir. Well, there was some shouting and whatnot. So I had to show them my piece. They backed off. End of story."

"And the queer?"

"Sick as they come, sir. My gun was giving him a hard-on. He wanted me to blow the prosties away. Anyway when he left, I watched the elevator monitor. He went straight to twelve just like he said."

Better be careful how you travel, pal, they're tracking every move the elevators make.

"Description."

"Ah . . . tall and skinny. Half-bald with blond hair. You know, with one of those swishy haircuts, how they trim it short and brush it forward. I'd say he gave Mother Nature a hand with the coloring, too, sir. Had eyes like Bambi, all big and wet."

Eyes like Bambi, eh? I like that.

"Snipe, what's your status?"

"On twelve, sir. Computer room ahead."

"Keep the channel live."

Dave snapped the radio off and slid it into a desk drawer. A moment later there was a tap on the computer room door. He called out, "It's open."

The man called Snipe walked in. He was young and cut from the same cloth as the rest of Ransome's men—bulky, muscular, and hard in the eyes. He wore a blue rent-a-cop uniform. It was too tight across the shoulders.

"Good evening, sir."

Dave glanced up. He'd found another pair of glasses, wire-rimmed. He peered over their tops, eyes wide and looking, he hoped, precisely like Bambi's. "Well, *hello.* Come to keep me *company,* officer?"

Snipe studied him, making no connection between David Elliot's description and the prissy-looking man before him. "No, sir," he growled. "I'm just making the rounds. You're working late tonight, aren't you?"

Dave nodded. "I *know.* What a *bore.* I was just heading home from the Village when they beeped me. There was this *gorgeous . . .* well . . . someone I met."

Ransome's man pursed his lips and gave Dave a sour look. "Em."

Dave sighed. "At night we're slaved off of the corporate DP center in Missouri. There was a system crash. I'm on night call this week, so they buzzed my beeper. So much for *my* sex life." He paused two beats, simpered, and asked, "How's *yours*?"

The man glared at him, blushing.

Dave waved his pen over the printout. "Well, I'd just *love* to sit here and chitchat with you, but . . ."

The guard nodded, mumbled, "Good night," and turned to leave.

"Good night to you. But why don't you stop back in an hour or so. I should be finished then. I'll brew up some herbal tea, and we could have a *little* talk."

"I'm a coffee man, myself." The door slammed shut behind him.

Dave pulled the radio out of the desk and snapped it on, the volume set to low.

"... catch that, Robin?"

"Affirmative, Snipe. Why didn't you card him?"

"I was in the lobby this morning, sir. I got a look at the subject. This one isn't him."

Dave leaned back and blew through his cheeks.

"Okay, Snipe. You'd better know what you're doing. Robin out."

"Sir?"

"What is it, Snipe?"

"Sir, are you sure about his coming back? I mean it's almost 2:30 and ..."

"He'll be here. There's nowhere else for him to go. He'll be here. And we'll get him."

"With all respect, sir, we've been saying that ..."

Ransome's voice changed. He sounded weary. "I know, Snipe. God knows, we've been saying that all day long." Ransome paused as if thinking something over. Then, quite contemplative, he continued: "Let me tell you something: more than once today I've had second thoughts about the subject. Wondered about his record, about what he did in 'Nam. Most people would say what he did was cowardly. But, you know, you could look at it differently. You could look at it and say the man had guts. To do what he did took courage—a different sort of courage, but courage nonetheless."

"What, sir?"

"That's classified information. However, I'll tell you one thing, if he did what he did because he's a brave man rather than a coward, then I have been operating under a misimpression. And, gentlemen, it is a misimpression I intend to remedy."

Ransome hesitated. Dave heard the snap of a cigarette lighter. Ransome inhaled, blew out. "Experience, that's the key. The subject's experienced—too experienced for the sort of maneuvers we've been trying to run on him. Listen, Snipe. Listen up, all of you. We've been treating Mr. Elliot like one of our usual subjects.

Well, he's not one of those, he's not even close. Same as you and same as me, this man has been out there at the dirty end of the stick, down at the business end of the chain of command. He's seen real life real close and doesn't have any illusions. Oh, Snipe, let me tell you who this man is: this man, he's one of us, he's one of our own."

We have met the enemy and he is us.

Ransome went silent again. Dave heard him draw on his cigarette. "That's where this has gone wrong. As per orders, we've been treating him like one of them rather than one of us. An easy target. The usual procedures. And if he got lucky the first time, then all we'd have to do was apply a little psych-warfare. Bring in his wife, his kid, his friends. Shake him up. Slow him down. Make him an easy mark."

He grunted. "Damn!—it just rolls off his back. I could stake his mother out for bait, and he'd just shrug and grease another couple of men. I'm telling you, the usual procedures won't work with the man. He already knows them. We taught them to him. No, Snipe, the customary ceremonies of our trade are not going to succeed with this subject. Ordinary solutions don't solve extraordinary problems. It's going to take something special."

"Sir?"

"I'm setting it up now. This will do him, Snipe. Nothing else will, but this will turn the trick."

"What, sir?"

The weariness faded from Ransome's voice. A tone of triumph took its place. "I'm reinterpreting our orders, Snipe. You don't want to know how. Suffice it to say that this one is a masterpiece, my pièce de résistance. They're going to put this beauty in the textbooks, I guarantee you. And I guarantee you that this time is the last time Mr. David Elliot is going to mess with this cadet. Before I'm through with him, the subject will be begging me to kill him!"

Ransome laughed. It was the first time Dave had heard him laugh. He didn't like the way it sounded.

2.

Showtime!

Dave had not planned on making his move quite yet. However, Ransome's words had changed things. His guard was down, and whatever hellish trap he was preparing had made him smug and overconfident.

The phrase "target of opportunity" comes to mind. Likewise the phrase "counting your chickens before they're hatched."

Dave kicked off his shoes and ran out of the computer room.

The corridor was long, anonymous, lit from above with fluorescent light. A few cheap art posters were hung along its cream-colored walls. Dave's stocking feet made no sound as he raced toward the elevators.

Snipe was standing in the elevator lobby, his back turned. He had his finger shoved against the elevator button, impatient for its arrival.

Dave moved in. Snipe sensed that something was wrong, and began to turn. It was too late. Dave shouldered him into the wall and thrust the muzzle of his pistol against his neck. Blood ran down the plaster; Dave's back slam had broken Snipe's nose against the wall.

Dave twisted the gun left and right, burrowing its business end into the man's flesh. "It's thirty-one, right?"

"Uh . . ."

"Don't screw with me, buddy. Remember what Ransome told you. I'm not an ordinary civilian. I'd do you for the price of a subway token. Now, tell me, your base is on thirty-one, isn't it?"

"Yeth, thir." Dave wrapped his fingers in the man's hair, pulling his head back. "Again."

"Yes, sir."

"The whole floor?"

"Park Avenue side."

"How many men?"

"Uh . . ."

"How long have you been in the service, son?"

"Uh, four years, uh . . ."

"They don't give your family full survivors' benefits unless it's six."

Something in Dave's voice did it. Snipe knew he was serious. He broke into a wail. "I don't know! Maybe twenty or twenty-five!"

" 'Maybe' isn't good enough."

Snipe was barely more than a boy, too young for Ransome's kind of work, and a lot softer than he looked. He bawled, "Jesus! Don't shoot! I really don't know!"

The boy was shivering with terror. Dave twisted the gun again. "Okay, next question. Why are you bastards after me?"

"Aw Christ! They don't tell people like me, mister! I'm just a grunt! Robin and Partridge—they know, but they haven't said, won't tell anyone."

"What have they told you?"

Snipe was babbling now. "Nothing. On my mother, nothing! Just that you had to be . . . uh . . . dead. Fast. And that if we . . . ahh . . . like, you know . . . if we got you, we shouldn't touch the body unless we're wearing, ahh . . . you know . . . rubber gloves."

Dave gritted his teeth. It was getting worse and worse.

"Where's Ransome?"

"Forty-five! He's in that dead guy's office, the Levy guy!"

"What's he doing up there?"

"Don't know! Word of Christ, I don't know! I haven't been up there! I was just . . ."

"Guess." Dave was feeling cold, lethally cold.

"Jesus, I don't know! I really don't! When we snatched that Jewish broad . . ."

Dave smashed Snipe's face into the wall. He did it more than once. He didn't keep count of the number of times.

"Speak to me, son. Tell me about the 'Jewish broad.' "

A bloody froth bubbled out of the man's lips. "Aw Christ! Aw, shit!"

Dave did it again. "Speak up, I can't hear you."

"The Cohen broad. She was making a run for it. We got her—me and Bobby and Georgo—just as she was leaving her digs. She's a fucking animal, man. She bit poor Bobby's nose off. All the way off. The poor bastard will be wearing plastic for the rest of his life."

"So?" Dave was ice.

"Nobody hurt her, man. Not bad. Just . . ." He was in an absolute funk.

Dave bounced Snipe's face into the wall again.

"How bad?"

"Bruises. That's all. I swear!"

"Where is she now?"

"That's what I was trying to tell you, man. We had her on thirty-one. Then Ransome took her up to forty-five. I don't know, maybe fifteen, maybe twenty minutes ago."

Dave shuddered with rage. The message Ransome left on Marge's answering machine was no lie. And if Dave had gone to the thirty-first floor first rather than AIW's computer room . . .

"What else, you little prick? Tell me everything."

"That's all I know. Honest to God, that's all I know."

Dave spoke gently. "Say that again."

"Uh . . . what? Say what?"

"God's name. You want to die with it on your lips."

"Huh? What? Oh shit, no, man, don't . . . !"

Dave dropped him, took three quick steps back to avoid the backsplash, and leveled his pistol on the man's head.

This is the way it's going to be, huh?

This is the way.

So far it's been self-defense. Except for those guys whose ankles you broke.

Passive resistance hasn't worked very well today.

And besides, you never exactly identified with Gandhi.

Never. Didn't like the movie either.

Snipe slumped to his hands and knees. He turned toward Dave weeping. "Please, oh God, please . . ."

Dave pulled the trigger. Plaster exploded from the wall. Snipe collapsed. His face was chalk white. He had fainted.

3.

No, Ransome, I am not one of you, although I might have been. It wouldn't have been hard. In fact, it would have been easy. It was one of those things that you can just let happen. It's no work at all. It's the path of least resistance. All you have to do is shrug and smile at the corpses and say, "Sorry 'bout that." And, the more you shrug at it, the easier it becomes. After a while, the sight of blood doesn't bother you so much. Those things you used to think of as dead people undergo a sea change, and now they're merely meat. You don't call them human, you call them gooks, slopes, rice heads, Victor Charlie, chopstick Charlie. The men are dinks and the women are slants, and the only reason God made them was so that you could have fun with moving targets in a free-fire zone. Look at these animals. You call what they do "living"? It's not living. You're doing them a favor when you blow them away. They're better off dead, better dead than red. It's that easy, Ransome, really, really easy. You quit thinking of yourself as a soldier, which is an honorable profession. Instead you're just a mechanic, which is not. That was me, Ransome, or pretty close to being me. Out in the boonies, things had started becoming very simple, very clear. It was all turning into physics—the arc of trajectory, the calculus of ballistics, the equations of force and mass applied at a distance against physical objects that happened to have legs. It wasn't about war, it wasn't about politics, it wasn't about our noble allies and stemming the rising tide of atheistic communism. It was about target practice. When I went over there, I thought that the war was Right with a capital "R." Maybe I don't anymore, but that's not the point. The point, Ransome, is that you and all the people like you didn't give a damn one way or another. And you didn't want the rest of us to either. You wanted us to become machines. That's all, just machines. You almost did it to me. I would have gone over the line, Ransome, over to your side. I already had one foot there. But one day Jack Kreuter did something, and all of a sudden I saw where I was, and saw that I had to step back from the line. I saw that people are people, and you can kill them if you have to, but you can't kill them if it's fun. That's when it has to stop, Ransome. Once you start enjoying your work, you have to stop. Otherwise, you turn into someone like you, and the world would be a better place if you'd been born dead. That's why I'm not killing this poor kid you've named Snipe. Because I'm me, not you. You said I was one of yours, Ransome, one of your own. You've been saying that all day long. Dave Elliot is one of us. He's ours. Beneath the skin we're brothers. Well, Ransome, I've got a point of view on that. Here it is: Kiss my ass.

The temptation had been overpowering. A full frontal assault. Gunfire, blood, and the satisfaction that the sight of dead enemies brings. He could have done it. Ransome was off guard. His men were relaxed. No one knew their target was in the building. The element of surprise was on Dave's side. He would be able to take out half of them before they knew what was happening.

It would be gratifying, you gotta admit.

It also would be stupid. His enemies' resources were endless. No matter how hard he hit them, someone would live long enough to use his radio and summon more troops. A lot more. Enough to man a floor by floor sweep.

He who turns and runs away lives to fight another day.

He couldn't run. He had to have the answers, and there was only one place he could find them—in Bernie's credenza, in the file marked "Lockyear Laboratories." But that meant going to the forty-fifth floor, straight into the trap Ransome was so boastfully preparing.

The files—Bernie's goddamned files—there was no way to get them except through Ransome.

Or around him.

Or around him. Right. There might be a way around him. It was crazy as hell, but it could be done.

The toughest part was Marge Cohen. Ransome had her up there, and whatever he had in mind for the woman would not be pleasant. She was part of Ransome's game now. He'd already used Dave's wife and son as psychological weapons. He'd use Marge the same way. Ransome would do anything he could to torment Dave, anything to distract him and anything to provoke him. "In the end, gentlemen, it is eminently more gratifying to destroy an enemy's spirit than it is to destroy an enemy's body."

Besides, once you've blown your opponent's mind, blowing off his head is hardly any work at all.

He couldn't try to rescue her. It was exactly what Ransom expected him to do. It would play to his strength. He'd have every route into and every route out of the forty-fifth floor covered. All of his resources would be focused on just that one point. It would be certain death to go after her. It was stupid even to think about it. Besides, he hadn't spent more than two hours in her company. He hardly knew her. He owed her nothing. Why should he care what Ransome was cooking up for someone like that? It was stupid even to think about her. She was nothing to him, nothing at all, and she never would be. Ransome was very badly mistaken if he thought he could use a woman Dave had barely met to bait a trap. Dave was no fool, and only a fool would fall for bait like that.

No doubt about it. He was going to have to go get her.

4.

Dave glanced at the wall clock: 3:03 A.M. Everything was in place.

The nitrogen triiodide he'd precipitated earlier in the day had dried nicely. He'd passed the liquid through filter paper—the kind American Interdyne Worldwide used in its coffee brewers—and left the crystals to dry in the American Interdyne telephone room. He had fewer than twenty ounces of the explosive. It wasn't much, but it would do the job. In an enclosed area, it most certainly would do the job.

The triiodide was not the only joke he had in mind. He had spent the past half hour in the west and south stairwells—floors forty-five to fifty—setting new booby traps to replace the ones Ransome's men had disarmed. Of necessity, the new traps were cruder than the ones he'd laboriously set earlier in the day. Pretty slapdash stuff, he thought.

Now, he was back in the American Interdyne computer room. He was waiting for Ransome to come on the radio again. Once Ransome had finished laying his trap—whatever it was—he'd order his men into place. They'd be distracted then, as they tried to settle into position. That was when Dave would make his move.

But first, he had something to do. There was no avoiding it, painful though it might be. He winced at the thought of it, but it had to be done. If there was anyone in the world who might be able to tell Dave about Lockyear or about a.k.a. John Ransome, it would be Mamba Jack Kreuter.

He reached out for the telephone. He noticed his hand was shaking. He stopped, tapped a cigarette out of his pack, and lit it. His hands still shook. Talking to Jack was not going to be easy. The man would neither have forgiven nor forgotten. Jack Kreuter wasn't the forgiving kind. He had to hate Dave more than he hated anyone in the world.

Dave took another drag. The nicotine wasn't helping.

Making this call was going to be the hardest thing he'd ever done in his life.

Lieutenant David Elliot loved Colonel Jack Kreuter. Lieutenant David Elliot betrayed Colonel Jack Kreuter.

Servicemen do that—fall in love with one another. It has nothing to do with sex. Sexual attraction is a feeble imitation of the love a man-at-arms feels for his comrades. The emotions go deeper than those between father and son, between brother and brother, between husband and wife. The bond that forms, soldier-to-soldier, is old, old, old—primitive stuff, the instincts of earliest evolution, slope-browed protohumans banded together, all for one, one for all. It is in the blood, and cannot be resisted.

One can lie, cheat, steal, and murder, and do so with an untroubled conscience. David Elliot did not doubt that a.k.a. John Ransome, to take but one example, slept well at night, and was not troubled in his dreams. Anyone can break the commandments, each and every one of them, and not feel the worse for it. There is no depravity or sin so vicious for which a man, given time and the proper attitude, cannot pardon himself—and for which others, in the end, will not absolve him . . . but for one exception, the sole offense that is never forgiven, never forgotten. No soldier will forgive a comrade-in-arms who has betrayed him.

No betrayer will forgive himself.

David Elliot forced himself to pick up the phone. It wasn't easy.

He tapped "9" for an outside line and dialed "001" for an AT&T International line. The telephone clicked and gave him a triple-beep. "Enter ID code now."

What?

He hung up and tried again. The same thing happened. American Interdyne appeared to have installed one of the modern world's more obnoxious technologies, a phone system that required an individual identification code for every long distance call. Big Brother is alive and well and living in the phone company.

Dave slammed down the phone, and swore.

He took a last drag on his cigarette and stubbed it out. The call had to be made, and it had to be made soon. He needed to find another phone.

5.

Dave slammed down the phone and swore.

He was as furious with the technology as he was with himself. All the risks he had taken, and it was another goddamned restricted phone system the same as American Interdyne's.

He'd been careless—worse, thoughtless. Desperate to find a usable telephone, he'd left the American Interdyne computer room, run down one flight of stairs, shimmed the fire door lock, and started looking for an open office.

You clown. Are you totally brain dead?

He'd forgotten what he had seen from the street—that the eleventh floor was the most brightly lit in the building. The mergers and acquisitions department of Lee, Bach & Wachutt never slept. There were people all around. He had been stopped and questioned three times. Every time, he'd been forced deeper into the investment banker's offices, and further away from the fire stairs and elevators.

It had been a nightmare.

"Excuse me, can I help you?" A short, sallow-looking man in an expensive suit. He had a ginger moustache and a warty complexion the color of putty, and spoke with a softly lisping British accent. Dave hated him on sight.

"Ah, yes," Dave stammered, "I'm from the printers."

"Right," the Englishman said. "That'll be the I.P.O. team you're looking for. They've a Red Herring due tomorrow."

Dave nodded briskly. "The S.E.C. will want it before noon, I presume." It was important to demonstrate an understanding of the lingo. Any financial printer would know the ins and outs of Initial

Public Offerings, and how critical it was that a Red Herring—a preliminary stock offering prospectus—comply with Securities and Exchange Commission requirements.

The Englishman replied, "Quite right." He pointed Dave down a hallway and told him to turn left. He watched while Dave departed.

Dave had persuaded the next person he bumped into, a tall, distracted-looking man with luridly flowered suspenders, that he was a courier from a law firm. He'd told the third that he was a network service technician called in to troubleshoot a problem on the Ethernet.

Each encounter drove him toward the outer peripheries of the office, and away from the safety of the building core, elevators, and fire stairs. He was ready to scream with frustration.

In the end he found himself herded past a darkened corridor leading to the northeast. He glanced over his shoulder, made sure no one was watching, then dove into it.

The hall dead-ended in a secretarial area. No, not entirely a dead end. There was one last door at the far side of the secretary's desk. Dave turned the knob. The door opened on a darkened office. Reflected streetlights from Park Avenue showed its dimensions—it was enormous, vastly larger than Bernie's.

Dave made out a desk at the distant end. He stepped toward it, promptly barking his left shin on a low table. He cursed and rubbed his leg. He took the next several steps cautiously.

There was a brass Stiffel lamp on the desk. Dave switched it on. A small, circular pool of light opened across the desk and illuminated a massive, multiline telephone. He picked up the handset and dialed. It beeped, and requested him to: "Enter authorization code now."

Damn. He hurled the handset back in the cradle.

Sit down, pal. Take a breather. Think it through. Let's not make any more dumb mistakes.

Good advice. He took it, sat down, lit a cigarette, looked around. The faint light thrown by the desk lamp was enough for him to make out the furnishings. He was awestruck.

The desk at which he sat was hewn of glowing mahogany and topped with white marble. Its projecting ends bowed out in graceful curves, and it sat on six symmetrical, cylindrical pillars. Dave was certain that it was a Duncan Phyfe, and easily worth $75,000. Opposite the desk there were a quartet of serpentine-backed, inlaid, Federal lolling chairs—$6,000 each. A cherrywood high chest of drawers was placed against the wall, just next to the door. It would bring $50,000 if it was Chippendale, and Dave was reasonably sure that it was. A mahogany tall-case clock stood opposite the chest—a Manheim, Dave guessed, dating from the early 1800s. Someone had paid $35,000 to own it.

And there was more, much more. The contents of the office would bring tears to an antique dealer's eye. The whole lot would be worth a million dollars, or near enough that it didn't matter.

It was odd, he reflected, how those who added the least value to the national economy had, during the past decade or so, accumulated the most money. It wasn't the companies who produced things that had gotten rich, not the automobile makers, nor the appliance manufacturers, nor any of the other industrial organizations. If anything, they had become poorer. Rather, it had been the predators who prospered, the doers of deals, the structurers of leveraged buyouts, the floaters of junk bonds, the takeover artists, and the raiders. People like Bernie Levy and Scott Thatcher would never squander a million bucks to furnish their offices. But people like Lee, Bach & Wachutt . . .

Out of the corner of his eye he spotted a second telephone. It was resting on top of a gilt-trimmed huntboard behind the desk. It was a plain black telephone, and Dave recognized it for what it was—a private line bypassing the switchboard. Bernie had one and so did a dozen other executives whom Dave knew. It was more than a status symbol—it was a tool that allowed its owner to make and receive especially confidential calls without worrying that the switchboard operators might eavesdrop.

Dave spun his chair around, and lifted the handset. Dial tone. He punched in the number for the international operator. "Thank you for calling AT&T International. This is Suzanne. How can I help you?"

Success!

Dave asked the operator to place a person-to-person call.

"What is the party's name?"

"Mam . . . Mr. Kreuter. Mr. Jack Kreuter."

"Residence or business?"

"Business."

"And your name, sir?"

"David Elliot."

A male voice behind him echoed, "David Elliot. Indeed."

6.

Every nerve in Dave's body screamed, ordering that he fling himself behind cover and start shooting. He didn't. Instead he placed the handset back on its cradle, and leaned back, rotating his chair.

The man was silhouetted in the doorway. An exquisitely cut suit exquisitely draped his tall, lean form. He had one hand casually in his pants pocket. He gestured with the other. "What magnificent self-control. A weaker man might have fainted. Even the most stouthearted should have jumped. Or so one might think. I am most impressed, sir."

Dave simply looked at him.

"Might I come in? It is my office, you know." His voice was baritone, perfectly pitched, and as musical as an opera singer's.

"Certainly," Dave replied. His back had been turned. The man had to have been standing there for more than a few moments. He easily could have crept away to call for help. He didn't. Whoever he was, he wasn't a danger—at least not a danger of the conventional sort. "Please close the door behind you."

"Of course. By the by, have you occasion to employ my office again, and wish privacy, all you need do is rotate this lever." He twisted the lever. "Perfect security. A system of deadbolts. One requires it in my trade. Perfect security, I mean." He stepped forward into the pool of light.

Dave studied his features. The man looked to be the very devil himself, as darkly handsome as Lucifer Morningstar ever was. With the grace of a hunting cat, he dropped into one of the lolling chairs and smiled. "Let me introduce myself." His smile widened. His teeth showed. "Whenever I begin a sentence thus, I almost feel obliged to add I am a man of wealth and et cetera. Nicholas Lee, at your service. Do call me Nick."

The chief executive of Lee, Bach & Wachutt. Dave had never met him, but he recognized both the name and the face. The face in particular—it had graced the cover of *Institutional Investor, Business Week, Fortune,* and a half dozen other magazines during the eighties. However, during the nineties it was more often to be found on the front page of *The New York Times* business section, usually beneath a headline containing the words "Federal Indictment."

"Dave Elliot."

"So I gather, and I must say that I am both charmed and delighted to make your acquaintance."

Dave lifted a questioning eyebrow.

"Well, one always feels a certain frisson upon encountering a celebrity, doesn't one?"

"Am I that famous?"

"Most assuredly, sir. The statutory fifteen minutes of fame promised by Mr. Warhol's bromide is surely come upon you. Even now, the bulldog editions of the tabloids blazon your photograph. Not that one man in a thousand would recognize you. The change you've wrought in your appearance is most startling. By the by, the tabloids have dubbed you the 'Amok Exec,' a not uneuphonious sobriquet, you'll agree. Further, certain sources kept by me on retainer report that tomorrow's *Wall Street Journal* prominently displays your face in one of those oh-so-complimentary stippled drawings of which its editors are so fond. The headline associated therewith is, I fear, rather less so. Complimentary, I mean."

Dave groaned. "What are they accusing me of?"

"Accusations, none. Implications, many. In this era of libel lawyers grown plumply prosperous, no publisher of balanced mind accuses anyone of anything. Instead they pose questions, raise hypotheses, and strew their sentences with words such as 'alleged,' 'speculated,' and 'supposed.' For example, it is *alleged* that you hurled the unhappy chief executive of Senterex through a window forty-five stories above street level. It is *speculated* that you did so because he'd caught your spoor in the vicinity of the financial cookie jar. It is *supposed* that you'd been doing something naughty with corporate currency trade. That's usually what it is, isn't it? Dubious currency trading, I mean."

"Usually."

"Well, tell me, sir, did you do it? Diddle the dollars, I mean. No need to be shy. We are friends here, and I am most accustomed to keeping confidences. Do tell me, how much did you pilfer, and why? Was it one of the three R's? Rum, redheads, and racehorses, I mean. Come, come, sir, midlife crisis visits us all. Do not be ashamed to admit its taint. You can tell me. I shall be most discreet."

Lee's coal black eyes sparkled. His skin glowed. He was, Dave thought, *too* interested.

"It's not important now."

Nick Lee leaned forward. Dave observed a small band of sweat beaded on his upper lip. "Of course it isn't. It's the merest curiosity on my part. Nonetheless, I should consider it a kindness if you would gratify it. My curiosity, I mean."

Dave shook his head. He had just deduced why Lee was so interested in his and Senterex's affairs. Now he planned to have some fun.

Lee simpered. "Perhaps we could work a trade. Trading is my profession, after all. One buys; one sells; one hopes for a modest profit. It is the soul of capitalism. Trading, I mean. Thus, if you will be so kind as to give me a hint or two as to the factors underlying your current situation, then I, perhaps, might be able to do some small service for you."

"It would have to be a rather large service."

Lee steepled his fingers. "Ah, how cunning of you. You understand."

"Sure I do. Tomorrow morning Senterex's stock is going into the toilet. The news of Bernie's death and the rumors of financial impropriety will do that. And if I . . ." His inner voice offered advice, *Bait the trap.* "If I or someone else . . ."—Lee licked his lips— ". . . have been playing fast and loose with Senterex's corporate cash, then the company's stock will dive even further. On the other hand, if all is well—or if the damage is only modest—then the stock will rebound. In either event, a man who knew the truth would be in a good position to make a killing."

Lee was hooked. Dave was afraid that the man was going to drool. "Just so. Puts and calls—the leverage in options trading is so attractive."

"Someone who had inside information might make $5 for every $1 he invested."

Lee sniffed. "I tend to think in terms of making $5 million for every $1 million invested."

"Whatever."

"Well, sir, will you strike a bargain with me? The hour's already late enough. Shortly trading in London, Frankfurt, Amsterdam, Zurich, and Milan commences. If we are to strike a bargain, let us strike it now so that I can go about my business."

"What's your offer?"

"I make you my best. The lamentable fates of such peers and colleagues as Messrs. Boesky, Keating, Levine, Milken, and et cetera have persuaded me to make provision for hasty travel. One never can tell but that one might need to decamp on rather short notice. Hence, across the Hudson at the Teterboro airport, I keep a Gulf-stream fully fueled and prepared at all times. It is stocked with all the necessities, including, I might add, some several bundles of Deutsche marks, Swiss francs, yen, pounds sterling, and, if memory serves, a roll or two of Krugerrands. The range of the jet is such that you might choose as your place of refuge any of the traditional South American bolt-holes, or if you wish, and as I might recommend, sunny Spain, balmy Portugal, or even carefree Greece. The cost of living in such places is low, the climate clement, and the authorities inexpensively pacified. My limousine is parked on Fiftieth Street, sir. The chauffeur waits. You can be airborne in an hour's time, and all your troubles behind you. What do you say to that?"

"That you'd trade me to the authorities as soon as I was out of your office." Dave brought a pistol up level with Lee's chest. "According to the newspapers, you're facing prosecution for every crime in the book. You'd offer them me in return for dropping a few charges. You're a dealer, Mr. Lee, a trader. You've said so yourself. You couldn't pass up a deal like that."

Lee's face fell. "No, really, I do not . . ."

"Shut up. I've got two things to tell you. The first thing is that I wasn't looting Senterex's corporate treasury. At least not alone. Bernie was in with me. Actually, it was his idea. We stripped the pension fund, the ESOP, and the treasury. And, we got it all. There isn't a dime left. Senterex is bankrupt. Bernie couldn't take the pressure anymore. That's why he jumped out the window."

Lee nodded furiously, his eyes aflame with greed. "Yes, oh, yes!"

"The second thing is this: You're going to sleep."

Lee's head jerked. "Oh no. You can't. The foreign markets open any minute now. I can sell short . . ."

"Too bad. But not to worry, I'm sure you'll be awake in time for the New York opening."

"Please," he whined. "Please. Let me at least call Frankfurt. . . ."

"Well . . ." Dave stood. Lee looked up eagerly. He reached for his telephone. Dave liked the angle at which he held his chin. Lee caught the look in his eye and squealed, "Don't hit me! I bruise! In my bathroom. In the cabinet. Drugs. Sedatives. Sleeping pills. I have chloral hydrate. Just don't hit me!"

The weight of Nicholas Lee's gold watch felt good on his wrist. Dave needed a watch, and was pleased to discover that Lee wore the same heavy Rolex as he did.

On the other hand, Nick Lee's wallet was useless. All he carried in it were his credit cards. However, there was an 18 karat Tiffany money clip in his pants pocket. It held a sheaf of twenties, fifties, and hundreds. Best of all, there were some $500 bills. Rather a lot of them, as it turned out.

First you feed him a poisoned stock market tip, then you swipe all his pocket change. I like your style.

Dave tucked a pillow under Lee's head. It was the least he could do.

The radio in his pocket stuttered. Ransome's voice came on. "Okay, people, it's time to rock and roll."

CHAPTER 9
JACK

1.

A combat unit is at its most vulnerable when moving into position. For the next few moments, Ransome's men would be off guard and distracted as they climbed stairs, opened doors, and took cover. Dave would have the advantage.

"Myna, I've sent some more bodies down to the lobby."

"They're here."

A few brief minutes of confusion—he couldn't let the opportunity slip away. He had to get to the forty-fifth floor—to Bernie's credenza and Marge Cohen—ahead of them.

"Good enough. I want them out of sight, and I want them on full alert."

"We're locked and loaded, Robin."

The elevators were out of the question. There were two separate banks, one serving the lower twenty-five floors, and one serving the top twenty-five. He couldn't take an elevator to Senterex without first returning to the lobby. The man called Myna was monitoring the elevator control panel. He'd know the moment Dave pushed the button for 45.

"Alpha team. Partridge, you've got the con. Don't disappoint me."

"Affirmative, Robin."

The only thing to do was to run for it. Run up thirty-four flights of stairs.

"Parrot, you're in charge of baker team. It's reserve duty for you. Forty-third floor outside the south stairwell."

"Aye, aye, Robin. We'll be on post in three minutes."

But he hadn't called Kreuter yet. He looked at Lee's private telephone. He took a step toward it.

"Pigeon, you've got delta. Kingfisher, you and charlie team are with me."

"Aw, boss, I's regurgitated. Sapphire's mama done . . ."

"One more Amos and Andy joke, Kingfisher, and your next tour of duty is Antarctica."

Dave stopped and shook his head. Kreuter wouldn't talk to him. Trying to call him would be a waste of time.

"Now all of you, listen up. Keep away from the entry points. I want no one visible near the stairs or elevators. The only way this thing will work is for the subject to have a very easy time getting in."

"A roach motel?"

"You've got it, Pigeon. He checks in, but he doesn't check out."

Dave turned toward the door. He stopped, and looked toward the telephone. He didn't know what to do.

"One last thing. It is my strong preference that the subject not be killed. I would consider it a personal favor if you aimed for the legs. Stop him. Feel free to mess him up. But do not kill him unless you have no alternative."

Dave frowned. Ransome's order was puzzling. Had the situation changed, or . . .

The man called Kingfisher spoke again. "What have you got in mind, chief?"

"Revisions to this afternoon's orders have come in. We're instructed to put the subject in an acid bath when we're finished. However, I find in these orders no requirement that he be dead when we do it."

"Gotchya, chief."

Dave grimaced. Got you, Ransome.

"Head 'em up and move 'em out."

Dave looked at the door. He looked at the phone. He had to make a decision.

2.

"*Bitte?*"

Dave wanted to rip the telephone out of its socket. The goddamned woman didn't speak English. "Kreuter," he hissed. "I want to speak to Mr. Jack Kreuter. Kreuter. Please."

For the third time she answered, "*Nien, nein, ich verstehe nicht.*"

It was infuriating. The seconds were ticking away, and the damned woman refused to understand him. How could she not understand Kreuter's name? Goddamn her to hell!

The Swiss are supposed to be bilingual. Dave tried some sophomore French, "*Mademoiselle, je désire à parler avec monsieur Kreuter, votre président.*"

"*Bitte?*"

Dave went pink with fury. "Kreuter. Kreu-ter. You dumb kraut, don't you know your own boss's name?"

The woman replied politely, "*Eins augenblick, bitte,*" and put him on hold.

A few seconds later another woman's voice came over the line. She spoke with that lilting singsong accent so common among English-speaking German women. "Yes. This is Solvig. May I help you, please?"

Thank God! "I'm calling for Colonel Kreuter."

"Ah." Dave could tell that she had covered her phone's mouthpiece with her hand. He heard her rattle off a stream of German. Then she spoke to him again. "Sorry for the confusion. We say 'crew-TER' and you say 'CROY-ter.' Sorry."

Dave ground his teeth. She continued, "Herr Kreuter is not in the *büro*, how do you say, the office yet. I expect him any time. May I take a message so that he can return your call?"

"I'm not reachable. I'll call back. Tell him that Dave Elliot called, and that I'll call back . . ."

The phone clicked. Dave's heart fell. "Hello!" he shouted. "Hello! Are you still there?"

After a moment's silence, a slow, sly drawl: "Well, I'll be switched. Jest tie me up an' tickle my fanny with a feather."

"Uh, is this . . ." He stumbled. He knew who it was.

"Son, it sure as hell has taken yew the longest damn time to get around to callin' me. I'd kinda given up hope on the subject." The connection between New York and Basel was clear and perfect. It sounded like a local call.

Jack seemed ready enough to speak to him. It wasn't quite the reaction Dave had expected. He wasn't quite sure how to handle it. "Well . . . you know . . . uh . . ."

"Sure. Yup, sure do. Suppose I mighta called yew, but I figured the time an' place of it was more for yer choosin' than mine."

He wasn't sure how to interpret Jack's words. He stuttered lamely, "So, er . . . Jack, how are you?"

"Largely unchanged, son. The good Lord seen fit to let me keep my hair an' keep my health. Can't ask more than that. An' whut about yew? Yew doin' well and feelin' fit?"

"After a fashion."

"An' yer family? How's that li'l blonde honey whose picture yew was always a-moonin' after?"

"Annie. Fine, but we . . . Well, I've got another wife now."

"Yeah, well don't we all. Speakin' personal, I done burned

through pretty near a six-pack of 'em. Like the man sez, shit happens. So whut about yer career? Yew doin' well—bein' a big time lawyer an' makin' lots of money?"

"I didn't go to law school. I'm just another New York businessman. But, yes, I guess I'm doing okay. Or at least I was. I sort of . . . well . . . you could say I've lost my job."

"Sorry to hear that, son. Truly sorry. Now me, I'm a-rollin' in it. Ol' company I got me here, she jest mints money. Damnedest thing yew ever seen. Gonna get me one of them great big vaults like ol' Scrooge McDuck. Yew wouldn't think that the ancient an' honorable callin' of combat warrior could be run at a profit, but she surely is. Son, I tell yew, mercenaries an' arms tradin' is the growth business of the nineties."

"I'm pleased for you, Jack."

"So yew says you've lost yer job, does yew?"

"Well . . ."

"Hell, son, then why don't yew put yer butt on the great silver bird, an' fly on over here. We'll sit an' jaw some. Meybe I got a job openin' lyin' loose somewheres."

"Uh . . ."

"Come on, son. Yew was always my favorite, yew know that. Never met none better than yew."

"Jack, I . . . oh hell, Jack . . ." No, this wasn't what he expected. It wasn't even close.

"Aw, come on, boy. Whut is it? Is yew still all knotted up over whut happened back in 'Nam?"

"It's not that." For some odd reason, Dave felt his eyes tingle. "Or it is. But, Christ, Jack, I turned you in!"

"Yeah, so whut?" Wrong answer. It wasn't what Dave wanted to hear.

"You were court-martialed."

"So whut again?"

Speechless, Dave worked his jaw back and forth.

"Bein' court-martialed weren't such a bad price to pay. Them were evil men and needed killin', and when they was gone, the earth was a somewhut better place."

Dave could barely manage the words: "Jack, I blew the whistle on you."

"Aw, shee-it, that's why yew ain't bothered to call me all these years. Yew figured I was still p.o.'d or somethin'. Dumb, son, that was purebred dumb. Ain't never been mad at yew 'cept meybe for a little bit. After all, yew only did whut was right. Now, son, yew ever see me once complain 'bout a man doin' the right thing? Nope, it ain't in me. Sure, I was a mite worried 'bout the proceedin's. But not all that much. Figured they wouldn't have the nerve to put me in the brig whut with everythin' I knew an' all. An' they didn't. So whut the hell, they booted my buns out of the Army. Now I got me a fat ol' Swiss bank account, an' I tool my bony behind around in a great big Mercedes car, an' when I drive up they send their flunkies runnin' out to open up the door for me. Heh! So yew tell me, son, yew tell me, jest whut the holy hell have I got to be pissed at yew about?"

David Elliot had spent twenty-five years punishing himself for what he had thought to be a sin. However, the victim didn't blame him. The victim thanked him. It was worse than forgiveness.

He drove a fist into a wall.

"Yew there, son?"

"I'm here." Dave glanced at his hand. Blood was beading on his knuckles.

"Well, now. Must be—whut?—'round 'bout 0300 hours over there. I gotta figure yew ain't callin' jest to be sociable."

"Right." He shook the pain out of his fingers. The pain was not a bad thing.

"Okay, then yew wanna tell me whut's on yer mind?"

Dave started to say something. He bit his tongue, took a deep breath, and started over. "Jack, do you know . . . have you ever heard of a guy named John Ransome?"

Kreuter's voice lit up. "Johnny Ransome? Sure I do. He wuz a master sergeant in the unit oh, lemme see, meybe eight, meybe nine months 'fore yew showed up."

Dave's heart pounded. Ransome *had* been one of Kreuter's men. Maybe the two still kept in contact. "Where is he now?"

"Ain't nowhere 'cept that his name's on that big black wall they got down Washington way."

"Dead?" Dave gnawed his lip.

"Sure 'nuff. Walked into a bouncin' betty. I'm the one who tagged and bagged him. Why yew askin'?"

"There's somebody who's using his name. He says he served with you."

"Lots of folks did. Whut's he look like?"

"Big, blocky, lots of muscle. Sandy grey hair. Square face. Five-ten or five-eleven. Has an Appalachian accent, sounds like . . . someone we both knew."

"Could be any one of a dozen different men. Whut else can yew tell me 'bout him?"

"Not much. Except . . . maybe, just maybe his real name's Donald. I overheard . . ."

"Well, hell. There wuz two Donalds in the unit same time as Sergeant Johnny, one a buck lieutenant, other a captain. The men called the second looey 'Iceman,' the other wuz 'Captain Cold'— the both of 'em bad asses same as yew."

"I was *not* a bad ass."

Jack drew the word out: "Bulllll-*sheeeet!* Only difference 'tween yew and them two dudes is yew had yerself a sense of humor."

Uh-uh, Dave thought. No. Not true. I'm not, I wasn't, I'm not . . .

"So, son, whut else can yew tell me 'bout yer very own personal Donald-damn-Donald?"

"He carries a lot of ID. One says he's with the Veteran's Department. Another says he works for something called The Specialist Consulting Group."

Dave heard Jack inhale sharply. "Whut yew got to do with that crowd?"

Dave ignored his question. "Who are they, Jack?"

Kreuter's voice had an edge of disapproval. "Contractors. Per diem boys. Does the kind of work people like me won't touch with a manure fork."

"What . . ."

Kreuter snorted. "Guess I sounds a mite sanctimonious. Like that joke 'bout the lawyer man and the Tijuana donkey lady. Professional standards and all. But, no, they's some kind of jobs I just won't do. Specialist Consultin', howsomever, don't seem to have no moral qualms at all. Leastways, none as yew'd notice."

"Who do they work for?"

"Anybody with the cash. Anybody who wants someone to do their dirty work for them, and is willin' to pay the price."

"The government?"

"Not these days, and that's fer shure. Specialist Consultin's been long time eighty-sixed from U.S. gov'mint work. Twenty years or more. No one in Washington would touch 'em. Which ain't to say that meybe somewhere, somehow, they still don't got theirselves a relationship or two. Not a direct relationship, yew know, not as a prime contractor and not as a subcontractor. Meybe sub-subcontractor or somethin' like that. They's an outfit as been around a coon's age, way back since my daddy came home from his war. Stands to reason they got friends. Now, yew wanna tell me why yew askin' about those there boys, which ain't exactly questions whut a prudent kinda citizen would ask?"

"I have my reasons. Tell me about them, Jack. Who are they and what do they do?"

"Aw, hell, I don't know a one of 'em. Don't want to neither. An' as for what they do, well, generally speakin' outfits like Specialist, they's just into all sorts of businesses. You know, fundamental intelligence and analysis, a li'l light bribery and subornin' of foreign officials, subcontractin' merc operations, dirty work R&D, arms sales, plus yer basic breakin' and enterin' and buggin' an' burglin' an' other miscellaneous dirty tricks."

"Dirty work R&D?"

"Yeah, you know, the kinda devil's work that only yer genuine lowlifes even think 'bout. Yer Sad-damnable Husseins and yer Colonel Ka-Daffy-Ducks."

"You mean . . ."

"Son, I don't 'specially cotton to the drift of this here conversation."

Dave took a deep breath. "Jack, I have to know. *Have to!*"

Kreuter sighed. "Can't say as I know enough to do more than speculate." His accent carved the word into three distinct parts: Spec. You. Late. "Alls I can tell you is that the rumors been goin' 'round a long damn time—long as I can remember. Yew see, at the end of World War II, the Rooskies wound up occupyin' the eastern half of Germany where the Krauts had most of them death camps, an' where they did most of their quote-unquote medical experiments. Occupyin' that, you gotta figure Joe Stalin, who was as crazy as a shithouse rat, got his hands on suchever nastiness them Krauts was a-workin' on. An' so you gotta figure soon as our folks found out, they says if the Rooskies got that stuff, then we gotta get that stuff too."

"Stuff, Jack?"

"Bugs, son, bugs. Plague and pestilence. Germs an' viruses an' biological weapons. Rumor was lots of enemy scientists were a-workin' on it then. Rumor is that some folks still are."

There was a long silence. Dave fired up a cigarette.

"Yew bein' mighty quiet, son." Jack's voice was soft. There was an undertone of concern in his words.

"Just thinking, Jack."

"Thinkin' whut?"

"What would happen if fifty years ago someone, say an Army doctor on MacArthur's staff, came across a Japanese biological weapons research facility."

"Easy question, son. It'd get crated up and shipped home. Same way as they crated up all them Nazi rocket science labs, an' all the people to go with them."

"Then what?"

"Yew gotta remember, biological weapons is just as illegal as hell. Banned by Congress and condemned by treaty. So whut they'd do is they'd do everythin' they could to keep it secret. Like as not they'd subcontract it out—maybe to yer friends from Specialist Consultin' or somebody like 'em. An' such few people as needed to know about it, they'd get told that the whole she-bang was strictly research—jest to keep up with what the Rooskies was a-doing. Them Rooskies got this thing called Biopreparat whut's on an island in the Aral Sea. Ain't nobody much allowed to visit that island. Thems as does never comes back. So you can figure that if them Roosky boys is engaged in a little illicit R&D, then some Yankee boys is too. An' of course if any of 'em—our gang or theirs—thought someone was gonna blow the whistle on 'em, they would initiate whut is technically called 'appropriate sanctions,' a term not defined to exclude the takin' of certain regrettable but necessary steps with which both yew and I are sadly familiar."

"One last question, Jack. What would happen to someone who got infected by one of those weapons?"

"Son, you'd likely die."

The monkey. The goddamned stupid monkey.

He'd suspected from the moment Marge's cat had snapped at him, known from the moment he saw the gutted interior of Bernie Levy's very last acquisition, spent every moment since praying he was wrong.

Lockyear fronted for a biological weapons research lab. One that had been around since the end of the Second World War. One that had been founded by a man who saw fit to pose for his portrait in a fifty year old Army uniform.

A weapons lab. From the outside it looked like an ordinary

biotech company. But on the inside—in Laboratory number five—
it was far from ordinary. Nor was the monkey an ordinary lab animal. It had been infected with a test substance. And it had escaped
and bitten . . .

The late David Elliot.

Bernie had been conned into buying Lockyear. Who knew how
or why? Maybe Harry Halliwell, honest broker, set up the deal.
Maybe somebody else. It didn't matter. All that mattered was that
they had appealed to Bernie's sense of duty. He'd fallen for whatever lies they'd told him. That was why he was willing to play ball.
It wouldn't have been a problem for him. Not if they'd appealed to
his patriotism. *Semper Fidelis.*

Poor Bernie. He wouldn't have known the truth about Lockyear.
They wouldn't have told him. Not until after . . .

*He assigned a notorious ex-whistle-blower to manage the deal. And the
whistle-blower got infected.*

Sooner or later Dave would have started exhibiting symptoms.
He would have gone to a doctor. There would have been tests. The
tests would have revealed something inexplicable. All hell would
have broken loose.

*Calls to the Centers for Disease Control. Consultations with the World
Health Organization. Questions, questions, and more questions.*

Questions asked of people who don't like questions.

It's contagious, you know. Really, really contagious.

Dave had poured himself a cup of coffee while he was in
Bernie's office. Bernie had drunk from the same cup. Then he had
killed himself. "Bernie Levy has got only Bernie Levy to blame.
That's some fine joke, Davy. Turnabout is fair play. . . ."

He took the cup with him. Forty-five stories down.

Whatever infection Dave had was so bad that Bernie would
rather kill himself than endure it. And when Partridge thought that
Dave had escaped from the building, he had said, "We're all dead
men."

Marge.

That was why they had taken vaginal smears and blood samples. They were afraid that Dave had . . .

If you had so much as kissed her.

Whatever disease he had caught from the monkey was more than merely serious.

Curable, you think?

If there was a remedy, why wouldn't they simply give it to him?

Easier to kill you and be done with it. You were a whistle-blower, remember? Suppose they gave you the cure. Would you show the proper gratitude and keep your big mouth shut? Or would you go public? And if you were them, bad ass that you are, would you be willing to take the risk?

At the other end of a four thousand mile long telephone connection, Mamba Jack Kreuter asked, "Yew worked out yer situation yet, son?"

"Pretty much, Jack."

"Yew wanna tell me about it?"

Dave blew a long sigh. "Thanks, Jack. But it would be best not to."

"I believe I can say I understand. Ol' Kraut preacher man I know over here done give me the right word for it. She's a four-bit word, she is: 'eschatology.' That's what we been a-jawing about, eschatology. But still, if there's anything I can do . . ."

"You've done enough. You've told me what I needed to know. And I appreciate it."

"No problem-o. An' look, if yew manage to get past these here troubles of yours, yew give me a call. Hell, man, we was friends, and we still should be."

"I'll do that if I can, Jack."

"Well, son, I purely hope you will."

"Okay. Look, Jack, I've got to go."

"Fair 'nuff. But now yew listen, yew put that business in 'Nam out of yer mind. She was a long time ago, an' it ain't no good to brood on it."

"Sure, Jack."

"An' keep yer pecker up, yew hear?"

"I will."

"Sayonara, boy."

"Sayonara, Jack."

3.

A biological weapon. Silent, invisible, and lethal. The stuff of nightmares and Stephen King novels. It wasn't the kind of weapon you used to kill an individual enemy, nor even an enemy regiment. You didn't even use it to kill an enemy army. There was only one use for such a weapon—killing an entire nation.

Now it was on the loose in his body.

And he was on the loose in New York.

No wonder they were after him.

And no wonder Ransome thought Dave was the bad guy.

You are!

He should run. They didn't know he was in the building. Ransome had ordered his men to keep away from the stairs and the elevators. The man called Myna, the one in charge of the lobby, thought that he was a gay computer worker from American Interdyne Worldwide. Dave could get past him.

If he ran, he would be safe. Once on the streets he could escape to . . . to . . .

. . . to wherever he wanted. It wouldn't be hard. He'd flag down a cab and tell the driver to take him across the Hudson River to New Jersey. The Newark train station would be as good a place as any. From there, he could catch an Amtrak Express to Philadelphia or Washington. Then he could take a plane. He had stolen enough money to fly anywhere in the world.

Once in hiding, he'd want to make some phone calls. The medical authorities. The press. Maybe even a congressman or two.

If there was a treatment for what they'd given him, the publicity would force them to administer it. And if there wasn't . . . well, he'd cross that bridge when he came to it.

He should run. There wasn't any reason to stay. Much less reason to walk into a firefight.

Well, maybe one reason.

Marge.

Maybe two reasons.

Ransome. It's time to settle his bill.

4.

3:36 A.M.—an hour and a half before the first faint glow of day in the east; three hours before sunrise.

Dave took one last long look at the sky. Nearest the horizon, the sky was pale, the color of weak beer, and the stars were erased by the haze of a million streetlights. Higher, some few stars, only the brightest, burned through the city's shroud of dirt. But overhead, straight up, the night was black and pure, the stars painfully sharp, luminously clear—Perseus in perpetual pursuit of Andromeda, whom he must rescue; Orion stalking the Great Bear through and beyond all time; the Pleiades dancing behind a veil of radiant blue.

How beautiful is the sky at night, how sad that electric lights blind city dwellers to its glories. When was the last time he had looked, *really* looked at the stars? So long ago . . . camped beneath their canopy in the high Sierras, Taffy drunkenly snoring, Dave awake and looking up in awe at the . . .

Waxing philosophical, are we?

Dave sighed. Well, at least the skies were clear. Thunderstorms had been predicted—Dave had heard the forecast on the rent-a-car's radio. But, the storm hadn't come, at least not yet.

Thank God for small favors.

All around him the cityscape was still. In the far distance, south of the Battery and beyond the harbor, he could make out the lights of the Verrazano Bridge. It suddenly struck him that he had never once been on that bridge. He'd spent more than twenty years in the city of New York and never set foot on Staten Island. Odd—the island was part of the city. People lived there. It had restaurants, theaters, and probably even a museum or two. But he'd never been there. The idea of going had never crossed his mind. Now, of all times and in all places, he was wondering what it was like.

Peculiar what passes through your mind when you're about to die.

The other odd thing was that, in all of his years working at Senterex, he had never once been on the roof of the building. The roofs of other buildings, yes. There was a roof garden atop his apartment building; in the summer, on Sunday mornings, he went there to read *The New York Times*. Helen had arranged their wedding reception on the roof of another building—somewhere in midtown; he could probably see it from where he stood if he knew where to look. And other roofs, too. He'd just never been on this one before.

It was a cluttered place. Its center was occupied by the building's air system, an enormous, grey piece of machinery. Even at this hour, set on low power for the evening, it rumbled noisily. Elsewhere there were standpipes, an emergency water reservoir for the building's fire sprinklers, a miscellany of ducts, and, of course, the cement blockhouse in which the fire stairs terminated.

Future generations will call that blockhouse "Elliot's last stand." Maybe they'll even put up a plaque, same as for Custer.

A double row of metal rails surrounded the periphery of the

roof. They were sturdy and firmly mounted. He checked and double-checked their strength before deciding to use them.

He leaned over the railing and looked down. The street was far away. One splotch of asphalt was blacker than the rest.

Bernie.

He didn't want to think about that. Not given what he was about to do. Besides, it was time to get this business over with.

He tugged on the coaxial cable—the same sort that had saved his life earlier in the day. He had found another two hundred and fifty foot spool of it in one of the telephone rooms. It was strong stuff; he knew it was more than capable of bearing his weight. Unfortunately it was rubber-sheathed—too slick and too thin for a proper climbing rope. Still, it was all he had, and so, at the cost of some time and even more irritation, he had carefully doubled it over, and tied thick, hefty knots every three feet. The knots would give his hands purchase.

He slipped on his telephone repairman's work gloves, tightened the jury-rigged harness around his thighs, tested the cable one last time, and stepped over the railing.

He listened for his inner voice. Nothing. Dave's invisible guardian angel had gone completely silent. It was as if it was too stunned to comment on what he was about to do.

Come on, say something.

You're going to die.

So what?

You're going to take me with you.

That's life, pal.

He shook the cable. It fell loose, free of tangles.

Time to go.

He gripped the cable, easing his feet over the edge of the roof, stretching the cable tense with his weight. One foot beneath the other, one hand above the other, one knot at a time, David Elliot started walking backward down a fifty story wall.

It had been twenty-five years since he had done this sort of thing. At Fort Bragg, they had made all the trainees scale a 150 foot tall smokestack, then rappel back down. Two of the men in Dave's training unit refused to do it. A third made it to the top and then froze. All three had been washed out. No green beret for them. Dave joined everyone else in laughing about their cowardliness.

Not laughing now, are we?

The cable-rigged harness cut his thighs brutally. Unless he descended quickly, it was going to make his legs numb.

Sheets of speckled granite stonework were hung between the windows. Dave kept his feet to them. His shoes were tucked into his belt. The granite was rough and pitted, and cold through his stockings.

The building had been erected in the early sixties. Now, after thirty years of wind, weather, and pollution, the stone had begun to decay. Some cracks were thick enough to insert a pencil. It wouldn't be long now, a few years at most, before the stonework began to crumble. Then chunks of rock would start raining on the street. Dave wondered how many other buildings in New York were in the same condition.

He passed the fiftieth floor. The lights were out. He should have checked the lights before starting down. It would not do for some late night worker to glance out his window and see a man with a brace of pistols in his belt dangling fifty stories above street level.

He peered down. No lights until 45. He was safe.

You call this safe?

The coaxial cable was a poor substitute for rope. It was slippery; grasping its thinness strained his hands. Too much of this and he would get a cramp. And that would be a problem.

Between the forty-seventh and forty-sixth floors, Dave's heel knocked a pebble-sized piece of granite loose from the building's facing. Six seconds later it detonated on a green trash dumpster, making a noise that sounded, for all the world, like a mortar shell exploding. Unless Myna, the man in the lobby, was an utter fool, he'd send people out to investigate.

On the other hand, New York is full of odd and inexplicable noises. At all hours of the day things growl and whine and sometimes sound like bomb blasts. People get used to it. Maybe Myna would ignore the sound.

Forty-fifth floor coming up. Last stop—last in more ways than one if Ransome and his goons are in Bernie's office.

He had left the roof of the building near the northeast corner. When he reached 45, he would be just to the left of the window that Bernie had smashed open.

They would have covered the window. The building management would insist, and so would the police. With the weather forecast calling for rain, neither would want the office open to water damage. The only question was whether they'd use canvas or—as they'd used for the shattered lobby windows—plywood.

The broken windows down there—that's what gave you the idea for this, right? You knew you couldn't go through Ransome. You had to go around him. And yeah, I agree. This idea is crazy as hell.

He came level with the window. It was sealed with canvas.

He had misjudged the length of cable he needed. Three or four yards of slack dangled below him. It could be dangerous if he had to leave Bernie's office in a hurry.

Dave braced his feet against the stone and twisted his right arm, wrapping the cable around it. Once, twice, three turns. He released the grip he held with his left hand. The cable sliced into the flesh. Grimacing, he coiled up the few yards of slack beneath him, fastened it, and then wound his right arm free.

And now for something truly dangerous. He asked his inner voice, are you ready for this?

Why not just make yourself a noose and get it over with?

Forty-five stories above the street—*but only six seconds to fall that far*—David Elliot pushed away from the side of the building and flung himself toward the canvas covered window. At the height of his arc, he leaned his torso back, stretched his legs, and pumped like a child on a swing.

He swung away from the covered window, pumped again, and swooped back. The cable creaked. He wondered what its tensile strength was.

Isn't it a little late in the game to be asking that particular question?

He was oscillating like a pendulum. The curve of his flight carried him past the canvas covered window. He almost reached the glass window beyond it. Almost, but not quite. He swung back.

The windows were set in aluminum curtainwall. Curtainwall . . . For nine grim hours a night, five days a week, every week of his college years, he had worked in an aluminum extrusion plant, being paid seventy-five cents an hour, making curtainwall. Maybe the people who built this building had bought their curtainwall from the very plant he had worked at. The timing would be about right. Wouldn't that be a coincidence?

He reached the top of his backward swing. He pulled and pumped and started back down.

This time he would make it. The curtainwall protruded two inches from the granite stonework. He would be able to hook his fingers around the metal, stop his swing, and pull himself forward. Then he could look through the window. If Ransome had left any little surprises in Bernie's office, he'd be able to see them.

The ridged edge of the glass window was coming up. Dave snatched at it, wrapped his fingers around it. The momentum of his flight reversed itself. The force nearly tore his grasp loose. He held fast, gritting his teeth.

Blew it. You shortened the cable too much.

He could make it. He tensed, drew himself forward, almost there, fingers slick with sweat, heels trying to find purchase on the granite, slender cable slicing his thigh muscles . . .

He was there—clutching the narrow sill, pressed against window glass, looking into Bernie's office.

The lights were lit. What Ransome had left for him was on display. And, yes, the thing that Ransome had called his masterpiece was precisely that.

Dave's fingers slipped from the curtainwall. He tumbled away from the window. For some several moments he swung back and forth until the motion damped.

No longer entirely conscious, David Elliot hung limp and still above the streets.

5.

Emerald green.

With ruby eyes.

A centipede like a jewel.

On a leaf like jade.

He hears a whistling come down through the sky. He knows the sound. It's a Soviet made RPG-7 rocket. He closes his eyes.

The rocket explodes. He opens his eyes. The leaf is shaking. The centipede seems impervious to the bombardment. It goes on eating.

Someone is screaming orders. They don't make sense.

The centipede is toxic. In survival training they teach you which insects you can eat and which you cannot. This one will give you severe cramps.

He isn't hungry anyway.

An AK-47 empties its magazine. The bullets whip through the brush. Several thump into a nearby tree. Someone is yelling, "Fall back!" It's Kreuter. What he says makes sense after all.

It's not the Vietcong, and it's not a patrol. Whoever said it was a patrol didn't know what he was talking about. It's two full North Vietnamese brigades. They have armor and they have artillery. It is part of a major offensive. It is not the kind of thing three under-manned fire teams want to deal with.

"Fall back! Fall back!"

Falling back is not quite what's called for. Running like hell is what is called for.

His rifle is lying in the mud. He stretches out his left hand to pick it up. He can't get a grip on it. It slips through his fingers. That's odd. There seems to be something wrong with his hand. Maybe it has something to do with the piece of metal that juts from his upper arm. It's the length of a railroad spike, but thinner and twisted. It seems to go in one side and out the other. There's not much blood.

Using his right arm, he takes the rifle, a CAR-15, and pushes himself up. He is shaky and almost falls.

Over to the left, two people are hobbling through the undergrowth. He can't quite focus on them. Oh, now he sees who they are. Latourneau and Pasceault. They enlisted together out of some New Hampshire mill town, and are best buddies. Latourneau seems to be helping Pasceault, who is having trouble walking. His right leg is missing. That would account for his not being able to walk very well.

An actinic flash blinds Dave. When he can see again, Latourneau and Pasceault are gone. There's only a muddy crater, and smoke.

"In line! Fall back!"

That's ridiculous. People who've walked into a meat grinder do not form up for an orderly retreat.

He stumbles toward Kreuter's voice.

The sound made by a Kalashnikov AK-47 is quite distinctive. You never forget it. Several of the North Vietnamese seem to be carrying the Type 56 modification with 40 round box magazines. They fire at a cyclic rate of about 350 rounds per minute. There's a lot of lead in the air.

Sparky Henderson is on the radio crying for air support. Kreuter wrenches the handset out of his fingers and coolly gives their coordinates. Dave trips at his feet.

Jack pulls him up. "Need a medic?"

"Feeling no pain." Just like they tell you. It can be hours before it begins to hurt.

Jack and Sparky and Dave run.

Above them the skies fill with the roaring of great waters. Behind them the jungle is swallowed in flame. The very drums of God thunder and boom. An air strike is under way.

Dave's head is almost clear now. He knows where he is, what has happened, and where he is going. There will be an air evac near the village they'd passed earlier in the day. It's the only place the copters can set down. They're scheduled to arrive at 19:15 hours.

He pushes through the brush. The great green leaves are heavy and wet. Tangled vines snatch at his feet. He's far away from the fighting. The shriek of fighter-bombers is distant, the sound of explosions mere thumps.

He's managed to get separated from the others. Or, perhaps they've managed to get separated from him. In either event, this particular retreat is not being conducted with military precision, sound off, by the numbers. It's a rout. Everyone is fleeing in panic. Kreuter will be furious.

It was the surprise and the ferocity of the Vietnamese attack that did it. The patrol walked right into it. The enemy was waiting, flanking fire positions nicely set up, an ambush calculated to annihilate.

They'd known an American patrol was coming.

Dave stops and glances at his arm. It's aching now. There will be a large scar and maybe some muscle damage. He's going to be on the noncombatant roster for awhile.

He gingerly pulls a plastic box out of his shirt pocket. There is a pack of Winstons and a butane lighter in it. He fumbles the box open with his mouth, taps a butt between his lips, and lights it. The nicotine helps.

He carefully closes the box and puts it back in his fatigues.

There's a lensatic compass in his left pocket. He doesn't have the use of his left hand. It takes him some time to fish it out. He pops the compass's lid, takes a reading, and adjusts his course. He thinks he has another hour or so to go. He has all the time in the world.

He comes out of the jungle by a rice paddy. The village is over there, to his right, about two hundred meters away. He can hear wailing and crying coming from it. He can't imagine what's causing it.

He glances at his watch. Twelve dollars from the PX at Cam Ranh Bay. Twelve dollars he had to spend after he'd blown his old watch to fragments. He'd like to blow this watch to fragments too. 18:30 hours. Forty-five minutes before the choppers are due at the LZ.

The wailing rises and falls in ululating waves. Dave wonders what's going on. Maybe someone's fragged an ox. He starts slogging through the rice paddies, heading toward the village.

He comes into the place from the south. All the crying and shrieking are at the north end.

His rifle is slung over his shoulder. He can't use it anyway, not with his left arm out of order. He tugs his pistol out of his holster, a good old standard issue .45 caliber Army model 1911A.

He eases past the hooches. Very carefully, he peeks around the corner of the last one. What passes for the town square is right ahead of him. What he sees there doesn't entirely register.

Behind him a voice whispers, *Hey, pal, if I were you, I'd just turn around and walk the other way.*

Dave spins. There is no one there.

He shakes his head. Must be shock. Hearing voices.

He turns back to look at the village square.

He still doesn't quite understand what he sees. Exhaustion. Confusion. The inner shivering of combat not yet manifest in exterior form. He shakes his head again, tries to clear his mind.

Sergeant Mullins is there, and a handful of men. Kreuter and the majority of the unit haven't come in yet.

For a second, he asks himself what the majority of the unit is these days. How many casualties did they take back there?

He looks closer. The villagers are huddled by the side of a dike. Two American soldiers hold their rifles, covering them, keeping them back. The villagers aren't the only ones they are holding back. There are a dozen American GIs standing with them. Their weapons are gone and their hands are in the air.

Curious.

Mullins is doing something. He's kneeling on the ground with his back to Dave. Three men are with him, two on hands and knees, and one standing.

Mullins is working his arm back and forth. The villagers are bawling.

Mullins stands. He has something in his hands. He is walking toward the crowd.

There are some poles stuck in the ground there, right in front of the dike. Some of them have sharpened points. Others don't seem to. Instead they have objects sitting on them.

No, not sitting. "Sitting" is the wrong word. The right word is "impaled."

Mullins places another woman's head on a pole.

6.

Ransome, having neither sharpened stakes nor soft ground into which to set them, had used tripods—the ones that Bernie kept in his closet.

His cutting work was neater too, almost surgical, not anywhere near as messy as the hasty butchery of Sergeant Mullins and his trusty K-Bar knife. All in all, Ransome had done a clean and tidy job, precisely as one would expect of a highly skilled professional.

Ransome had, of course, placed them facing the door. They'd produce their best effect that way.

He might even have sewn their eyelids open.

Marge Cohen with open eyes. That would be a nice touch.

That surely would have made Dave scream.

7.

Dave screams.

Mullins whirls. The men with him hit the dirt. Dave aims his pistol at Mullins's chest. Mullins steps toward him. Dave yells something at him, he's not sure what. Mullins marches forward, right into the barrel of Dave's gun. Dave squeezes the trigger. The chamber is empty. With his arm shattered he is unable to work the slide. He shouts something. He's not sure what. It might not even have been words.

Mullins snatches the pistol away from him, and slaps his face. "Shut up! Just shut up, you fucking faggot college boy!"

Two men seize him and throw him to the ground. Mullins stands over him with his knife. "You fucking cunt, you were going to fucking grease me! Weren't you, college boy? Weren't you? Gun down one of your own men, you cocksucker!"

Mullins looks like a mad animal. His lip is curled and quivering. His eyes blink in and out of focus. Flecks of saliva fly from his mouth.

Mullins squats. He pushes the tip of his knife into Dave's neck. "The objective, motherfucker, is to kill the fucking enemy! All of the fucking enemy. Including the fucking people who help the fucking enemy. You kill the fuckers, and you kill their fucking women, and you kill their fucking kids, and then when each and every fucking one of them is dead, everybody's happy except the fucking dead people about which no one gives a fuck, and we all get to go home. That is the fucking objective, you little shit. You remember it, you remember it good, and you never point a fucking piece at me again." He turns to the others and growls, "Put this asshole with the other assholes. I'll deal with them when I'm finished with the gooks."

He and his men pull another woman out of the crowd of weeping villagers. Mullins leers in Dave's direction. "What we've got here is an object lesson, by God, an object lesson."

They push the woman down and hold her. She lies quite still while Mullins saws at her throat. A rooster tail of blood geysers four or five feet into the air, splashes into the mud ten or twelve feet away. Mullins lifts her head by the hair and shows it to the village. He howls like a wolf, and his eyes are mad beyond all redemption. "Tell 'em," he shrieks at the translator, "tell 'em this is what happens to people who collaborate! Tell 'em this is what they can expect! Tell 'em that you do not fuck with America and you do not fuck with the U.S. Army and least of all do you fuck with First Sergeant Michael J. Mullins."

The translator rattles off some French. Mullins barks, "Bring me another one."

They grab her around the waist. She screams and kicks. She manages to break from their grasp and plunges back into the crowd. For reasons that Dave does not understand, she flings herself on him, kneels, and wraps her arms around his knees. Her tears are bright and large. Although he speaks a little French, he can't make out her words.

They come for her. Dave turns pale with rage. He roars, "Mullins, you're going to hang! Do you hear me? I'll see you hang for this!"

Mullins looks at him, merely curious, or so it would seem. His look is steady; his voice is cool and calm and reflective, and thus infinitely more terrifying than his deranged screaming. "Turn me in? Rat on me? You would, wouldn't you, college boy?" He orders his men, "Bring the colonel's pet over here."

One of them wrenches Dave's wounded left arm up behind his back. He shrieks and nearly faints. Mullins calls him a coward.

They hurl him face down. Mullins kneels beside him, rolls him over, and wipes his knife blade across Dave's fatigue shirt. It leaves a rusty stain. Mamba Jack Kreuter's voice booms, "Freeze! Freeze and belay that and freeze, soldier!"

Mullins rises. His men stand aside. Dave pushes himself up to his knees.

Jack is standing there. Twenty or so men are behind him. They have their rifles up. Jack holds his against his hip. His eyes are wide. He stares at the villagers standing by the dike, at the soldiers among them still with raised hands, at the headless corpses, at the stakes, and at the severed heads atop them. "Oh, God," he whispers. "What obscene shit is this?"

Dave notices that his accent is gone. He no longer sounds like an East Texas peckerwood.

"Mullins, oh Mullins, you thing of evil . . ." Kreuter's voice fades into silence.

Mullins merely looks at him. His eyes are childlike in their innocence.

Jack looks at the carnage, and shakes his head. He croaks, "Why, man, why?"

Mullins smirks. "I needed to make a statement."

One of his men echoes him, "Yeah. A statement. No board in the world will convict us."

The light and life go out of Jack Kreuter's eyes. He turns his rifle on the man who has just spoken, and fires. The weapon is set on full automatic; it cuts the target in two. A soldier at his shoulder leans forward and asks, "Sir?"

Kreuter nods. The soldier guns down the man standing nearest to Mullins. He walks over to the corpse and empties a full clip into its face.

Another of the men with Kreuter fires. And another.

Six men had been helping Mullins with his work. Kreuter has killed one. The rest are killed by five of the soldiers accompanying Kreuter. It's all over in seconds.

Mullins is still alive, sneering. His chest is puffed out, and he holds himself braced at full attention.

Kreuter drops his rifle. He slides a .45 automatic out of its holster. He takes three quick steps forward. Mullins spits at him. Kreuter clips his chin with the pistol, and then lays the muzzle against Mullins's right temple.

Dave stands. "Jack!" he yells.

Kreuter turns his eyes, which are horribly cold and empty, toward Dave. "What?" is all he says.

Dave can't meet his stare. He can't look Jack in the eyes. He mutters, "Nothing."

First Sergeant Michael J. Mullins, late of Hamilton, Tennessee, snarls, "Fucking pussy cunt."

Jack looks away from Dave, back at Mullins. The greater portion of Mullins's face disappears.

In the distance Dave hears the beating of helicopter rotors. The air evac is arriving a little early. The air evac is arriving a little late.

Dangling limp above Fiftieth Street, Dave relived the day, once again confronting the fact that he himself would have killed them—Mullins and all of them. It was accident, happenstance, that he was unable to. If his arm had not been paralyzed, if he'd been able to chamber a round in his .45, he would have done it. He wanted to. He would have liked it and felt no regrets.

Or would he?

Eris, the goddess of chance, chaos, and destiny, had seen fit to give him a second chance to find out.

CHAPTER 10
ESCHATOLOGY

The heads, all but one, had come straight from the morgue. Some appeared almost fresh, others less so. They were all women, of course. Long ago and far away that was what Michael J. Mullins had used—people like Ransome and Mullins always used women when they felt the need to "make a statement."

Some were young, one little more than teenaged. Others were older, though none quite as ancient as the village headman's wife had been. Most were in their early middle years. They should have had more time.

How had they died? Dave did not know. Nor did he have the inclination to make up little stories about them. They were, all of them, dead and gone to marble.

All but Marge Cohen, whose bruised, grey skin—now the color of putty, not blushed with life—might still glow a fading hint of warmth.

Dave thought he should stroke her cheek with his fingers to feel that warmth, the last she would ever radiate. But his fingers were cold, so cold. He could not do it. He could not even bring himself to look closely. . . .

For a moment, hanging above the street, he had thought that Ransome had taken Helen's head too, and Annie's, and even that of the poor myopic receptionist from the fourteenth floor.

But no. They were all strangers, all but Marge.

And Ransome had been right all along—he had known Dave better than Dave knew himself. The sight of those impaled heads *had* paralyzed him, precisely as Ransome planned. If Dave had come through the office door, he would have frozen—and frozen he would have stayed until Ransome's men brought him down.

Ransome's plan was a good one. He'd be sorry when he learned that it hadn't worked.

Quite sorry.

Bernie's file folder on Lockyear was marked with a blue tab. It was right where Dave remembered it, just behind the clear-tabbed files on Senterex's operating divisions, and just before the orange-tabbed folders containing corporate business projections and forecasts.

The Lockyear file was, however, less thick than it had been a few hours earlier. Now it contained only a single sheet of paper, a note scrawled on Bernie's personal stationery. "Mr. Elliot, I didn't think you would make it this far. If you have you're smartter than I thought. If you were really smart you would give up now. J.R."

Dave used Bernie's Mont Blanc pen to scribble a reply below Ransome's initials: "J.R., you illiterate buffoon, there is only one 't' in 'smarter.' By the way, if you were really smart, you would give up now (note punctuation). D.P.E."

Dave left the folder open on Bernie's desk. It wasn't very likely that Ransome would see what Dave had written, but if he did, it would nettle him—a petty revenge, but nonetheless satisfying.

There was something new in Bernie's office, something that hadn't been there earlier in the day. It was a small grey box, hung above the door. A contact alarm, Dave guessed, and probably radio-based. If so, he had a use for it.

Keeping his eyes averted from the center of the office, Dave walked to Bernie's closet, and inventoried the supplies Bernie had kept stored there: easel pads, colored markers, thumbtacks, and . . . yes, there it was . . . "Scotch 3M #665 double-coated tape. Attaches riders, photos, samples and swatches, quickly and neatly. Ready to use! Sticks and holds instantly; no drying time needed. 1 Roll 1/2 in x 1296 in (36 yd)."

Thirty-six yards. One hundred and eight feet. He'd need two boxes.

He studied the grey box hanging above the office door. A nearly invisible wire extended from the box's base to the gap between the door and its frame. The wire would be glued to the door; if the door was opened, the wire would break, triggering a silent signal. It was a simple alarm, inexpensive and foolproof, guaranteed to alert a hunter that his quarry had fallen into his trap.

Unless the quarry already was in the trap, and planning to get out.

Gently, very gently, Dave wound tape around the fragile wire trigger—one, two, three loops, making certain that it was quite secure.

Then, walking backward and carefully unspooling the tape, he made his way to the broken window.

He reached through the window, stretching for his climbing harness. For a brief moment he thought of turning back. There were two last things that he might do. One was to plant a kiss on . . .

Give it up, pal. You outgrew making dramatic gestures a long time ago.

There was one other thing he thought of doing.

Senterex's corporate boardroom was connected to Bernie's office by a pale oak door. Dave knew that Ransome would have stationed men there, would have told them to lie in wait with their weapons at the ready.

And, therefore, the one other thing David Elliot thought of doing was going into the boardroom. He thought of killing whomever he found there. It wouldn't take long, and it would feel good.

He shook his head again, then carefully wound the cable around his thighs, re-rigging his climbing harness. Without looking back, without wanting to look back, he swung into the night.

As he did, Ransome's voice came over the radio: "It's 3:45, people. Sound off."

Three forty-five? Had it only been nine minutes? How could it be nine minutes? It had felt like all eternity.

Slow time.

"Myna here. All quiet. Petrel, Killdeer, and Raven are all on station." The man in the lobby, the one with the problem about homosexuals, was checking in.

Four men on the ground floor. It'll be a piece of cake, pal.

"Partridge reporting, Robin. Greylag, Ovenbird, Loon, Bluejay, and Condor are in position. If he comes up the east stairwell he's my meat."

Six men along the hallway leading to the east fire stairs.

"Parrot here. Stork, Finch, Darter, Buzzard, Macaw, and Warbler are with me."

The reserve team on the forty-third floor.

"Pigeon reporting. On the west side we've got Ringdove, Cockatiel, Catbird, Egret, and Whippoorwill, all checked in."

At least twelve men on the forty-fifth floor. How many more?

"Dis is de Kingfish, an' Calhoun an' me an' our three friends . . ."

"Hold it!" Ransome's voice rose. "Pigeon, give me your count again."

"Affirmative, Robin. Ringdove, Cockatiel, Catbird, Egret, and Whippoorwill."

Ransome's voice hardened. "That's five men. You're supposed to have six. Where's Snipe?"

"I thought he was with Kingfisher."

The man named Kingfisher dropped his Amos and Andy accent. "No, he was supposed to be on your team, Pigeon."

There was a raggedness to Ransome's words. "Snipe? Snipe, report. Where are you?"

Dave knew where he was. Snipe was chewing duct tape on the twelfth floor.

Ransome called for Snipe again. Again there was no response.

"Oh damn," Ransome hissed shakily. "Oh goddamn." For a moment, Dave thought Ransome was shivering with fear. Then he realized that it was not fright making the man's voice tremble, but rather exultation. "He's back! He got past Myna! He's here!"

Partridge, Ransome's second-in-command and link to the outside world, whispered prayerfully, "We're going to make it, aren't we, sir?"

"Affirmative." Whatever emotion that had lifted Ransome's voice was gone. He coolly issued an order. "Call HQ. Tell them to put the heavy back on hold."

Heavy? Dave asked himself. What does that mean? For some reason the word triggered distant memories of the cigar-chomping General Curtis LeMay. LeMay had been commander in chief of the United States Air Force during the sixties. Now why, Dave wondered, did I suddenly remember him?

"Excuse me, sir." The voice belonged to Kingfisher, and it was rising. "Did you say 'heavy'?"

Ransome replied softly, "Belay that question, Kingfisher. It was only a contingency."

"Headquarters says they're in pattern!" Partridge was very nearly shouting.

"Partridge, advise them to return to base."

"A heavy! Jesus, man. How the fuck . . ."

A heavy? Curtis LeMay? They reminded Dave of an old movie. What movie was that . . . ?

"At ease," Ransome said conversationally. "If you've got a problem, Kingfisher, we'll discuss it at the appropriate time."

Kingfisher was screeching, "A fucking heavy! Oh man, you've got to be shitting me!"

Ransome sighed. "You knew the job was dangerous when you took it. Now, be at ease."

"Oh shit, shit, shit . . ."

"You're relieved of duty, Kingfisher. Report to Parrot on 43. Kestrel, take over the team."

"You fuck, Robin! You gigantic fucking asshole . . ."

"Kestrel, kindly get that man off the air."

There was a scuffling sound. The radio squawked. Someone, Kestrel, Dave presumed, growled, "Kingfisher's on the casualty list, Robin."

Ransome, his voice smooth as ice, and as cold, said, "The rest of you men, listen up. No determination, I repeat, no final determination was reached on this . . . this little issue that has so disturbed Kingfisher. However, I trust you will recognize that certain eventualities have been prepared for. Perhaps those of you who have underestimated the gravity of the situation now have a better perspective."

General LeMay was the model for a character in that old movie. George C. Scott played him. What was the name of that film? Peter Sellers was in it too. Oh yeah. *Dr. Strangelove.*

"In any event, the alternative only would have been invoked had the subject not come back to this building."

Dave braced his feet against the wall. Maybe, he thought, climbing back to the roof was not the best way to make his escape. Maybe triggering the alarm and dashing down the stairs while Ransome and company converged on Bernie's office was not the best solution. Maybe there was a better way.

He heard a snap and the sound of inhalation. Ransome had lit another cigarette. "Gentlemen, the requirements of security have . . . well, several of you have asked why we are in pursuit of the elusive Mr. Elliot, and why we are obliged to implement uncommon procedures. Heretofore I have not disclosed all the facts. Now I am prepared to."

Ransome took a drag and blew it out. The sound made Dave want a cigarette himself.

Go ahead, indulge yourself.

Dave fumbled his pack of Virginia Slims out of his pocket. He tapped one into his mouth and reached for his matches. The cigarette pack slipped from his fingers. He snatched for it. It tumbled away, softly fluttering forty-five stories down to the street.

It's just as well. Those things will kill you.

"Now I shall tell you. And because it is without question that our subject, Mr. Elliot, is in possession of Snipe's radio, I will tell him too. Listen up, people. Listen up, Mr. Elliot. Listen very closely."

Dave filled his lungs with smoke. Ransome was making a mistake. He was talking when he should be taking action. He was distracting his men from their mission. Their attention would be focused on his words and not on the possibility that Dave . . .

"It seems that our Mr. Elliot has caught a bug. Not an ordinary bug. Far from it. On the contrary, it's something rather special. The bug is what the lab boys call 'tri-phased,' a term meaning that it is highly mutagenic. It changes, it evolves through three quite separate and distinct phases. Much as the caterpillar evolves into the pupa, and the pupa into the butterfly, Mr. Elliot's bug transforms from being one kind of entity into another, wholly different kind of entity, and then into a third and totally distinct creature."

. . . was in motion.

He flicked his cigarette away, and began pumping his body into a swing, arcing back toward Bernie's window. He knew what he was going to do. He knew—he thought he knew—precisely how Ransome had deployed his men. If they were positioned as they should be, he could neutralize them.

With luck, he might not even have to kill anyone. Anyone, that is, except Ransome.

"Or the frog spawn to tadpole, and the tadpole to frog, three quite different creatures, each with unique behavioral attributes. So too the unfortunate Mr. Elliot's bug."

Dave unfastened his harness, and slipped back through the office window. He drew a pistol from beneath his belt and ejected the clip. Full. He pulled back the slide. A round leapt out. He retrieved it from the floor and put it back in the firing chamber. He replaced the magazine, released the safety, and set the selector for full automatic.

There would be at least two men in the conference room. Maybe more. Ransome's roll call had gotten as far as Kingfisher—twenty-eight men. Four of them were in the lobby, and another seven were in reserve on the forty-third floor. Kingfisher himself out of action. That left sixteen men, plus Ransome. Dave tallied the calculus of a well-laid ambush. He knew how he would allocate his forces if he was in command. And if Ransome had done the same, then there would be . . .

"At first, this bug is a harmless little fellow. His only distinguishing attribute is that he holds primates in great esteem. Monkeys, chimps, apes, orangutans I suppose, and humans. Only primates, gentlemen. Our bug, Mr. Elliot's bug, is a finicky bug—he will accept no other species as host."

. . . three men. They all had their backs to the door. They were so engrossed by Ransome's words that they did not hear it open, did not notice it close.

Dave gripped the pistol in both hands, combat style, and edged forward. The men were ordinary grunts, cannon fodder like Snipe, and very far from being in Ransome's class. They didn't even carry the same high-tech weaponry as Ransome. Two had Finnish Jati-Matics, lightweight 9 mm submachine guns with 40 round magazines and factory silencers. Dave frowned in disapproval. A 40 round magazine is amateurish. Its weight drags the muzzle down. A trained professional would know that. A professional would only use a 20 round clip.

The third man had an Ingram MAC with a WerBell Sionics suppressor, the state of the art in Dave's day, but now merely an interesting antiquity. The poor idiot had laid the gun on the conference table. Dave stretched out his left hand and . . .

"As I said, a tri-phased bug. During the first phase nothing much happens except that the bug rides around in your bloodstream where it's warm and cozy, and there's plenty to eat. The bug likes it there, so he decides to settle in. And once he does that, he starts a family. A large family. That's what stage one is all about—breeding. Every forty-five minutes the bug splits itself down the middle. Where there was one bug, now there are two. Forty-five minutes later, where there were two, there are four. Forty-five minutes after that, eight. And so forth and so on for a period of roughly twenty-four hours. And when stage one ends, gentlemen, that one little bug has sired more than four billion offspring, gentlemen, more than four billion."

. . . flipped the machine pistol onto the floor. "Heads up, guys," Dave whispered. "Likewise hands."

One turned, bringing up his Jati-Matic. Dave swung his pistol. The man's mouth sprayed shattered teeth and bloody saliva. Dave was speaking before the body hit the floor. "Don't move and you won't die. I don't want . . ."

The man—a boy really—who had been carrying the MAC went pale. His eyes rolled in terror. Words and saliva bubbled out of his mouth. "He's got something. AIDS, some disease, Jesus, keep away from me!" He stumbled toward the door.

Dave aimed his pistol on the boy's thighs. He didn't want to kill him. He didn't want to kill anyone. If he stitched the boy's legs, he would bring him down . . .

"After about twenty-four hours is when the second stage begins. The second stage lasts about seventy-two hours—three days. That's the stage your bug is in now, Mr. Elliot. It has changed, evolved, mutated from its earlier, harmless, and quite passive stage into something else. The caterpillar has evolved into the pupa, and the pupa has an attitude."

. . . screaming. The screams would alert the rest of Ransome's men. Dave couldn't afford that. He lifted the muzzle, fired, and looked away, sickened. The third man's gun clattered to the floor.

His hands were in the air. He flattened his back against one of Bernie's prized Pissarros, a dark painting of a cottage at the end of a distant lane. "Just don't touch me, man," he begged. "I'll do whatever you want, but just don't fuckin' touch me!"

Dave nodded. He reached into his pocket and pulled out the vial of pills he'd taken from Nick Lee's medicine cabinet. "Okay, son, I want to see you swallow five of these. There's a carafe of water behind you. Pick it up, pour a glass, and then wash them down."

There was a worried look on the boy's face. Dave tried to muster a friendly smile. He couldn't quite manage it. "Just sleeping pills."

The boy . . .

"Once mutated, the bug becomes mobile. It begins to migrate out of the bloodstream and into other organs. Now it's infectious. After the twenty-four hour mark, the carrier—that's you, Mr. Elliot—can pass it on to other people. But only via his bodily fluids—semen, saliva, urine, or blood. It's been about thirty-six hours or so since our Mr. Elliot caught this bug, and so that is his current and highly contagious condition. You men will recollect that at 3:30 this afternoon, just before the twenty-fourth hour of his infection, I issued new orders regarding the handling of his remains. You now appreciate the rationale for those orders."

. . . shook his head and said, "I'm not eating anything you've touched."

Dave answered, "Read the label. It's not my prescription. I haven't touched those pills. Besides, if you don't take them . . ." He gestured with the pistol. The boy understood, opened the vial, and gulped down a half dozen powerful soporifics. "Now what?" he asked.

"Now you turn around and face the wall."

"Don't hit me too hard, okay?"

"I'll do my best." Dave . . .

"Mr. Elliot, I want you to pay attention to this. Listen closely. The bug can be spread—will be spread—to anyone who drinks out of the same glass as the carrier, anyone who kisses the carrier, anyone he gives a little love bite to, anyone he fucks, anyone who gives him a blow job."

. . . clipped him behind the ear with his pistol. The boy yelped and staggered, but did not fall. Dave hit him again, harder.

He looked back at the door leading to Bernie's office, picturing how the bodies should lie. One of the three would be a real corpse. He hated that. He would have done almost anything to avoid it.

He slipped his hands beneath the arms of the dead man. There was too much blood. If Ransome or one of his people looked into the conference room, looked at the floor and the wall, they'd know what had happened.

Too late to worry about it now.

He dragged the corpse the length of the conference room, dropping it face up near the door. He lay one of the Jati-Matics across its chest. Then he went back for the second man.

In less than a minute, he had arranged the bodies so that they looked . . .

"Of course the carrier won't know that he's contagious, that he's spreading disease right and left. He thinks he's still healthy because the bug isn't producing any harmful effects. At least not yet. That doesn't start to happen until well into the fourth day. By that time the bug has mutated again. What was a pupa is now a butterfly. It is ready to go airborne."

. . . like they had died charging out of the conference room. If the alarm over Bernie's door sounded, they would have been the first into his office.

For final effect, he stepped to the center of the office and pumped a dozen silenced rounds into the walls and floor. Now the room looked like the scene of a firefight.

His time was running out. Ransome *(God, he loves the sound of his own voice!)* wouldn't run off at the mouth forever. Dave had to set up the rest of his illusion quickly. Two doors opened into the conference room—one from Bernie's office and one . . .

"Technically speaking, in stage three, the bug becomes what the medics call 'pneumatic.' That means that the carrier spreads the infection simply by breathing. Every time he exhales he spits out six million spores—I repeat, gentlemen—six million. He breathes in, he breathes out. If he does that fifty times, he will have released enough bugs to infect every man, woman, and child in the United States. He does that a thousand times and he's unleashed enough bugs for everyone, every living soul, on God's green earth."

. . . from the hall connecting Bernie's side of the building with the reception area. There were only three offices on that corridor—one belonged to Mark Whiting, Senterex's chief financial officer, the second to Sylvester Lucas, the company's vice chairman, and the third to Howie Fine, the chief counsel. Ransome would have stationed men in all those offices. They, like the three people in the conference room, would reach Bernie's suite ahead of the others if the alarm was tripped.

Dave crouched, flung the door open, and rolled into the hallway. He drew a circle with his pistol, searching for a target.

No one was there. Just as it should be.

The interesting question was Ransome's location. Dave wasn't sure whether he would station himself close to Bernie's suite—say, for example, in Whiting's or Lucas's office—or farther away. Either alternative would be militarily correct: close to lead the attack; far to redirect forces as battlefield conditions required. Which would Ransome choose?

Which would you choose?

A toss of the coin. Farther, I think.

He slipped up to Whiting's door and placed his ear against it. He could hear nothing except for the whisper of Ransome's frosty voice over the radio. He lifted his pistol . . .

"However, I overstate the case. You see, the bug in question is a delicate little fellow. Once he's been expelled from the carrier's body, he doesn't live very long. Ten minutes, maybe fifteen at the high side. Unless he finds a new carrier before then, he dies."

. . . braced his legs, and shouldered the door open. A single black man, an older one, was sitting behind Whiting's desk. His weapon, another Jati-Matic, was propped butt up on Whiting's credenza. The man looked at Dave, opened his eyes wide, and raised his hands. The expression on his face said that he was far too experienced to offer any resistance.

Dave nudged the door shut with his foot.

The man said, "Mister, I just want to say that I'm sorry. I accidentally seen what the man done there in Mr. Levy's office, but I didn't have nothing to do with it, and it just made me sick." His eyes were sad and a little watery. He wore a moustache that had begun to go grey. He was getting old, and becoming weary.

Dave asked, "You a vet?"

"Yes, sir. Drafted in '66. I was CO, a conscientious objector, assigned to the 546 Med. But we took 93 percent casualties in Tet. Wasn't a CO after that. I re-upped infantry. RA all the way. Retired just two years ago. Should have stayed retired, I guess."

Dave nodded. "I guess."

"So, sir, I'd be obliged if you'd consider me a noncombatant."

"No can do." Dave fumbled the pill vial out of his pocket.

The man's sad look showed that he understood, and that he was resigned to whatever fate Dave planned for him.

"Take the cap off this bottle, pour out five or six pills, and dry swallow them."

The black man lifted the bottle from where Dave had placed it. With infinite sadness, he said, "The man's gone insane. Cuttin' heads. Calling in a heavy. Can you believe that? Oh, mister, I was half-ways to running when I heard that. You hadn't come through that door, I probably would have run. 'Nother thing, sir, there's another thing. You know the code name he gives me? 'Crow.' That's what he gives me. And me the only black man on this job. Can you believe that?"

There were six yellow tablets in the palm of his hand. He studied them, sighed, and choked them down. "These sleeping pills, aren't they? How long they going to take?"

"Too long. I'm going to have to speed it up."

"You want me to turn around?" Resigned and passive.

"Please."

"Okay, but you just remember that I'm sorry. Mister, I'm sorry and I wished I was out of here a long time ago." Dave brought his pistol butt down on the back of the man's skull. "Me too," he muttered.

Next stop, Sly Lucas's office. Would Ransome be . . .

"However, our initial carrier, Mr. Elliot, still won't know what's going on. He still won't feel ill. All he'll feel is a little odd, and oddly a little more alive. Colors will seem brighter to him, sounds more musical, tastes and smells sharper. He will start dreaming Day-Glo dreams. Depending on his metabolism, he might even see a vision or two."

. . . in there, yammering on the radio? Dave hoped he wasn't. He wanted Ransome to keep talking, wanted him to tell his men the truth. Because, once they knew the truth, they would start to sweat. One or two might run. All of them would make mistakes.

He kicked through Lucas's door.

Two men, neither of them Ransome.

One was standing guard at the door, the other gazing out the window. The guard was fast. He was firing before the door was fully open.

He shot too high, overcompensating for his 40 round magazine. The bullets ripped into plaster above Dave's head. The guard fought the Jati-Matic's muzzle down. Dave fell to his knees. He released a short burst into the man's chest. The silenced automatic's soft thump, thump, thump seemed too gentle a sound for the results it produced. Fired from close range, the slugs lifted the man off his feet and sent him spinning backward over a chair. A backwash of blood spattered into Dave's eyes. Plaster dust powdered into his nose. He lurched back into the corridor, flattening his back against the wall, out of sight.

The man by the window sent two bursts into the hallway. Dave rubbed his shirtsleeve across his eyes. Another burst of fire exploded into the wall. The sound of the slugs ripping through plaster was louder than the muffled thump of the Jati-Matic.

Dave slapped a fresh clip into the butt of his pistol. He had to act before the man used his radio. He tugged off his shoe, readied himself, and tossed it through the doorway. A hail of bullets caught it in mid-air. Dave rolled through the door.

His opponent had positioned himself in a corner. He had the Jati-Matic braced against his shoulder. It was aimed left of the door, and above floor level. He started to bring his sights down to where Dave lay.

Dave's shot clipped his leg. The man grunted. His gun wavered. "You son of a bitch," he said.

Dave drew a bead on the center of his chest. "Don't do it."

The man swung his weapon toward Dave . . .

"You may ask how we know these things. Well, gentlemen, the answer is yes. Yes, Mr. Elliot is not the first person to have been infected with this bug. Of course, the other cases were all under rather more controlled conditions. That's how we know, gentlemen, and that's how we know that there is no cure."

. . . who took him with a single shot.

He hissed through his teeth. He hadn't wanted this. He only wanted Ransome. There was no need for it, not for the deaths, not for anything else. Ransome's words were proving that.

And Dave felt so cold.

But he couldn't stop. Not now. There was one more office, a third office, where Ransome's goons would be waiting . . .

"Or rather, there is one single cure. If you kill the carrier, the infected man, before the bug reaches its final stage, then you can stop the spread of the disease. And that, gentlemen, is the only way to stop it. Do you understand me, Mr. Elliot?"

. . . Howie Fine's office. Howie was Senterex's chief counsel. There was a Thomas Eakins oil hung over his credenza. It portrayed a famous trial, the judge on his bench, a distraught witness in the box, a starched-collar attorney thundering at a jury. Dave had never liked the painting. He'd never liked anything dealing with courtrooms.

He kicked the door open. The room was empty. No, it wasn't. It was . . .

How . . . ? What . . . ?

The strength went out of his legs. He slumped, no longer able to keep upright, to his knees, but so weak that he might fall utterly helpless, prone to the floor. The room was completely empty; no one there but for Marigold Fields, call-me-Marge, Cohen. Nylon rope—it looked like parachute cord—had been used to tie her to Howie Fine's large leather chair. She was alive, awake, gagged, looking at him, her eyes so wide, as wide as his must be. Which was very wide indeed.

She was trying to say something to him. He couldn't make it out. Her mouth was taped shut. Her words were unintelligible mumbles.

Dave swallowed. Hard. Twice. This was not possible . . . she, the others . . . their heads . . . Ransome's theater of brutality . . . She was dead. He'd seen it with his own eyes.

He breathed through his gaping mouth, taking great gulps of air. Marge's muffled voice seemed to be begging him to untie her.

Why? What had Ransome . . . wait a minute. Of course. It was obvious. Ransome . . .

"Do you understand that this is the only way to stop the disease, Mr. Elliot? And it is critical to stop the disease. Why? Why is because the *real* symptoms won't begin for a few days after the bug mutates into its third stage. Are you listening to this, Mr. Elliot? A few days of inhaling, a few days of exhaling. A few days of spitting out six million deaths with every breath you take. Then you'll begin to feel it, Mr. Elliot. First a fever. Then the sweats. Chills, nausea, deep painful aches. In seventy-two hours you'll die."

. . . was a pro. He'd have a fallback plan. And a fallback to his fallback. That's why he hadn't killed Marge. She was useless to him dead. Alive, however, she'd be another weapon, one last weapon, he could use against his prey. He had to keep her alive, ready to bring out if, against all odds, Dave survived the death traps prepared for him. Then and only then—if he knew Dave was escaping—would Ransome have put one of his radios to Marge's mouth, and hoped that her screams stopped Dave from fleeing.

It probably would have worked.

The same as the sight of her severed head *should* have worked.

That head . . . a nice piece of craftsmanship. Almost something he could admire. He had to admit, it was masterfully done, just like you'd expect from a virtuoso like Ransome. Was it clay or wax or a rubber cast or a dead woman with enough of a resemblance and enough makeup to make her look like Marge? Dave didn't know. He didn't care. All he cared about was that Marge was still alive.

He intended to see that she stayed that way.

Dave stumbled to his feet. "Sorry, Marge. I've got to go."

She shook her head furiously. Louder sounds, shrieks if she could open her mouth, bubbled beneath her gag.

"You're safer here than you would be if I cut you loose. There's going to be trouble out in the halls pretty soon now. I don't want you in the middle of it."

There was red murder in her eyes. She'd rip his throat out if she was free.

He wheeled her into Howie's closet, out of sight. "But I'll be back. I promise you. I promise I'll come back for you. Marge, don't look at me like that. Goddamnit, I'm running out of time and I don't have a choice."

He left her, knowing that she'd not forgive him, and returning to the hallways to do . . .

"Seventy-two hours. That's all you will have. And then you die. For most of those hours you will wish you were already dead. Twenty or thirty days after that, everyone's dead. Everyone who's been close enough to inhale your breath. And everyone who has come in contact with the people you've infected, and everyone who has come in contact with them. In other words, everyone in the world, Mr. Elliot, absolutely everyone in the world."

. . . what he had to do. Dragging the two corpses into position took only a moment. Once the bodies were in place, the hallway outside Bernie's office looked a scene of carnage. Copper-smelling blood pooled on the carpet, acrid cordite smoke hung in the air, dead men sprawled, as dead men always seem to do, in uncomfortable postures, wearing painfully surprised expressions on their faces. Those not dead, but only unconscious, looked less authentic.

Dave was in his stocking feet. One of his shoes had been shredded by gunfire. He'd discarded the other. The black man's shoes were large, comfortable-looking brogans; they seemed to be his size; Dave looked at them greedily.

Better not. Someone might notice.

Right.

'Bout time to get the party started, isn't it?

Right again.

Dave lifted one of the Jati-Matics, checked its clip, and tightened its strap. He slung it . . .

"Forget about ordinary murderers, and forget about armies and war, and forget about Hitler and Stalin and every mad dog despot who was ever born. However many notches those people had on their guns is nothing to the number our Mr. Elliot is going to rack up on the scoreboard. He's in a league of his own. There's no word for what he is, they haven't coined one."

. . . around his left shoulder. He trotted back down the corridor to the boardroom. He paused at its doorway.

After triggering the alarm he'd have three choices—he could run for a stairwell, hide in Bernie's closet, or conceal himself in the boardroom.

The closet, he thought, would be best. He could reach it faster than any of the stairwells. Ransome's men wouldn't look in the closet. They'd see the bodies, see the cable hanging by the open window, and conclude he'd escaped to the roof.

Or so you hope.

Or so I hope.

He wheeled into the conference room, jogged its length, and, for what he hoped would be the last time in his life, entered Bernie Levy's office.

The scene hadn't changed. Ransome's knife work was still on display.

Madness. Sheer lunacy. As unnecessary as it was unspeakable. All they had to do was explain it to him. He would have understood. He would not have been happy, but he would not have run. If they had told him what Ransome was telling him now, he would have cooperated. They could have offered to take him somewhere to a clean room, sterile, isolated from the outside world. Or they could have put him on a deserted island, or some other safe place. All they would have had to do was let him die with a little dignity. He wouldn't have resisted. How could he have resisted? Knowing the truth, he would have surrendered.

But instead, they decided to treat him like a rabid animal. We're licensed operatives, Mr. Elliot, highly trained professionals, and we know what's best. Besides, we don't trust you enough to tell you the truth. We don't trust anyone enough to tell them that. We'll lie to you, and we'll lie to your friends, and we'll lie to the people who pay us. That's our way, Mr. Elliot, and if you aren't used to it by now, you never will be. So kindly be a good little citizen, and don't give us any trouble while we clear up our problem in the traditional way.

You still could offer to surrender. Maybe you could talk Ransome into letting Marge go. . . .

Too late. Things have gone too far. There are debts to be settled . . .

"All right, you men, all right, Mr. Elliot, here's the bottom line: once the bug mutates to the third stage, and once it gets out into the general population, it can't be stopped. The only way to stop it is to stop it before it reaches the third stage. That means stopping the man who's carrying it. So you kill him before it's too late. And if you have to kill some other people along the way, it's a bargain. Maybe even if you have to kill the whole city of New York, it's still a bargain. That's a viable alternative, you know that, men. Dropping a heavy is a rational alternative."

. . . and accounts to be closed. Next year a.k.a. John Ransome's name does *not* appear in the telephone book.

Dave clutched his fingers open and closed. He looked at the tape. It stretched from the alarm box to the shattered window.

Let's get it over with.

Dave jerked the tape.

Ransome was still speaking. The words were coming out of his mouth just a little more rapidly than they should. He had said too much, knew that everything he said made it worse, but couldn't quite stop himself. "You think AIDS is contagious. Well, men, the AIDS infection rate doubles only once a year. But this . . ." Ransome drew a short, sharp breath. "He's here! The Jew's office! Go! Go, go, go!"

Dave flung Bernie's office door open, spun, and raced for the closet. From the corridor he could hear other doors slamming and the sound of men running.

"Robin, this is Parrot . . ."

"At ease. Reserve and perimeter teams keep on station."

Dave was in the closet. He eased the door closed.

They were in the hallway, just on the other side of the wall. Dave heard them moving. Someone stumbled and thudded into the Sheetrock. There was another sound. Dave couldn't quite identify it. A gurgling, and a splash. Whoever was nearest the wall whispered loud enough that Dave could hear, "Get that lame bastard out of here until he stops puking."

Ransome hiccupped an expletive: "Shit!" It wasn't like him to swear in surprise.

From the radio, Parrot's voice: "Robin, what's going on?"

"At ease, I repeat, at ease. I'll get back to you."

The voice on the other side of the wall: "How many? Who?"

Another voice: "Buzzard, Macaw, and Crow."

Ransome was not whispering. He spoke in his normal, coolly conversational tones. "Loon, Bluejay, and Condor were in the conference room. They'll be down too. Six men. Mr. Elliot is beginning to get on my nerves."

"He's still in there, sir?"

"Affirmative. Where else would he be? If he'd come into the halls, we'd have him by now." Ransome's tone of voice shifted. "Or . . . or . . ." He sounded puzzled. Dave wondered why.

"Sir, should we . . . ?"

"Should we what, soldier? Earn our pay? I think we should. All right, ladies, on the count. Set your weapons to rock and roll, and if Mr. David Elliot happens to be within your field of fire, do us all a favor and aerate him. Now, one . . ."

Dave could hear bolts snap. Men who knew they had live rounds in their chambers were chambering another round, just to be sure. It was always that way. He'd done it himself.

". . . two . . ."

Their hearts would be feeling too big for their chests. It would actually hurt. The last spike of adrenaline before the shooting starts is terrifying. The first time Dave felt it, he thought he was having a coronary.

". . . three!"

A hail of silenced bullets sounds little different from the flurry of a flock of surprised pigeons, beating their wings in panicky escape from a stalking cat.

Hot brass pinged onto the floor. Glass shattered. Something crackled with the percussion of bursting popcorn. An object collapsed with a crash. Dave could feel the vibration of slugs tearing into the walls, the floor, the ceiling.

He could picture what was going on in Bernie's office. He'd seen it before. There was a ville just thirty klicks north of the DMZ, and on its outskirts an old French plantation house that was supposed to be an enemy HQ. Dave's men put so many rounds into it that one of the walls crumbled. Once the shooting stopped, Dave had been the first to enter. The interior of the house—every stick of furniture—had been turned to confetti.

It was quiet. Just for a second there was no more noise. Then a man began to gibber.

"What the hell! Christ, man! These are women! I didn't sign up for . . ."

"At ease." Ransome's voice had as sharp an edge as Dave had ever heard.

"I'm going to puke. Let me out of here."

"Take one step, and you're meat."

"Aw, shit! That's the Cohen broad. Jesus! Are you some sort of fucking psycho . . ."

Dave heard the gentle cough of a silenced weapon. Something limp bumped against the closet, and slid to the floor.

Ransome, his voice soft and serene, whispered, "When I say at ease, I mean at ease. Now, ladies, let's get back to work. The issue at hand is not these women, the issue is the subject, who appears to have eluded us again . . ."

"The window, sir . . ."

"Someone, check out that conference room . . ."

"No, sir, the window . . ."

Ransome's voice drowned out the others. "Stand aside. Let me see what's . . . ah, God. Wouldn't you know it?"

He's at the window, Dave thought. He's seen the cable. They're all with him. Their backs are turned, and it would be so easy.

Ransome barked into the radio. "The roof! Elliot's got a rope! Parrot, get the backup team up the stairs! Move! Move!"

Parrot yelled back, "West stairwell, sir! That's the only access to the roof!"

"Do it!"

Seconds later the silence returned. Dave took a long breath. His shoulders slumped, and he loosened his grip on the Jati-Matic's stock. The whole business had barely taken a minute. They'd come and they'd gone, and not one of them had suspected that it was all a ruse.

The bodies, the blood, the bullet holes, the canvas drawn back from Bernie's shattered window, the cable dangling outside—it had been a perfect illusion. Ransome bought it lock, stock, and barrel.

Careful. Remember what Mamba Jack used to say about overconfidence.

A down payment on a body bag.

For a minute there, wasn't there something funny about Ransome's voice?

Maybe. For just that one moment it changed. It sounded puzzled.

So?

Better safe than sorry.

Dave slid prone to the closet floor. He wiped his hand across his shirt and gripped the Jati-Matic. He seated its butt against his shoulder.

Forty round magazine. Compensate for the weight.

He tickled the closet door with the tip of his finger. It opened a fraction of an inch.

Dave paused and listened. Silence. Not the least hint that there was anyone on the other side. He nudged the door again.

Still nothing.

And again. And open all the way.

Dave stepped over the body of the man whom Ransome had shot.

Bernie's office was empty.

Another window was shattered, blown into the night by Ransome's men. A section of Bernie's fine mahogany desk, the quarter nearest the door, was in splinters. Five or six lines of bullet holes traced across the wall behind it. One Wyeth painting was destroyed; two others were untouched. Bernie's sofa was now merely shreds of fabric, fiber, and wood. His credenza leaned drunkenly. The lamps were porcelain shards. And as for the impaled heads . . .

He gulped a deep breath, forcing nausea to become anger. Someone had stolen the engraved antitank round commemorating Bernie's service in Korea. Dave thought that if he found the man who had taken it, he would kill him too.

He belly-crawled to the door, now smashed from its hinges, and rolled into the corridor. He swung left, jutting the Jati-Matic forward, aiming it at the height of a standing man's waist. He let off a burst of silenced fire, and somersaulted, bringing the still chugging rifle to the right.

The bullets thudded into the walls. There was no one there. The hallway was empty, cool beneath fluorescent light. The understated wallpaper, the discreet beige carpet, the muted, tasteful framed art were as they ever were—corporate America, marred only by a few bullet holes and three bodies bathed in blood.

Dave spun left, and spun again.

God loves ya, pal. Ransome actually did *fall for it.*

Yeah.

Now let's wrap it up.

Right.

Dave ejected the Jati-Matic's magazine and slapped a fresh one in. He brought the weapon up to port arms and began to run. Ransome was going up the west stairwell, Ransome and *all* of his men except the four on the ground floor.

Dave sprinted for the east stairwell. He was cool now, in control. He had been since taking the three men in the conference room. The old calm had come over him, the relaxed poise of a professional doing a professional's job. No rage, no terror, no second thoughts. Only the job. Just do the job.

He reached the door, flung it open, and dashed up the stairs.

Forty-ninth floor.

The fire door was locked. There was no time to shim it. He shot it open.

He ran. He had only seconds left now. Ransome would be on the roof any moment. It wouldn't take him long to realize he'd been lured into doing the one thing no commander ever should do—concentrating his troops in a location with only one way in and only one way out.

Dave ran.

Down a corridor. Right turn. Faster. Another turn coming up.

His momentum carried him into the wall. He bounced off it, stumbled, and picked up his pace. His shoeless feet thudded on the carpet. He wasn't breathing hard. He was tranquil, collected, at peace. In less than thirty seconds, everything would be settled.

The fire door to the west stairway.

Dave pulled himself to a stop. It was almost an effort. It was almost that he hadn't wanted to stop running. He thought he might have kept running forever.

He pressed his ear against the door. He heard nothing. His enemies were not there.

He pushed the door open, propping it ajar with one of his pistols.

The concrete was cold beneath his stockinged feet. Above him he could hear the muffled click of shoe heels. Some few men were still on the stairs, not yet out on the roof.

Too bad.

He took four quick steps forward and looked down. The stairway spiraled away for forty-nine floors. Two flights of stairs per

floor, ninety-eight flights in total. A platform at every floor, and another in between each floor. You could see all the way down. You
could see all the way up.

And if you looked up, and if you knew where to look, you could
see where the stairwell gave access to the roof. You could see the
bottom of the platform inside the roof bunker. You could see where
Dave had taped a brown bottle of crystalline nitrogen triiodide.

Baby go boom!

Dave lifted the Jati-Matic. A tricky shot. He glanced back at the
door, judging his tolerances. Seven feet. It was going to be close.
He'd make it if his timing was right. If it wasn't, he'd never know.

He steadied his sights. Someone was still up there climbing toward the roof. Dave waited for him to get out of danger.

The radio crackled. Ransome was shouting. "Myna! Myna, seal
the . . ."

Time's up!

Dave fired.

The Jati-Matic recoiled against his shoulder. He was in the air,
diving for the door. His finger was still on the trigger. Bullets
sprayed through the stairwell, ricocheting off concrete. The door,
the hall, safety was only a few feet away.

His eyes were squeezed shut. There was a white brightness, so
white, so bright. The blood vessels in his eyelids glowed incandescent red.

And neon heat, hot as the heart of God.

And a thunder, not the thunder of a lightning storm in distant
farmlands, not the slow boom and long roll heard from a young
boy's bedroom window, not wait for the flash and count the seconds until you hear the sound and then multiply by 0.2 so that you
know how many miles away the lightning struck.

Not far thunder. Not near thunder.

Interior thunder, thunder heard from inside the lightning.

Most of his body was through the doorway when the blast
struck. Its force did not punch him down, but rather lifted him, ro-

tated him, and slammed him upside down into a wall. It held him for a second, pushing so hard that the breath left his lungs, and then dropped him to the floor.

He felt as though a street gang had bludgeoned him with clubs. Every muscle ached. Every inch of skin felt bruised.

He pulled himself away from the gaping door, now twisted metal on bent hinges. Chunks of concrete rubble rained down from above, bounced, and rolled across the carpet. A choking cloud of dust powdered his face. He gagged for breath and crawled away.

Water.

There was a fountain down the hall. Dave reached it, pulled himself erect, and pushed the lever. He drank deep, and then let water run over his face. Behind him metal shrieked. An I-beam smashed through the ceiling and impaled the floor where, seconds earlier, he had been lying.

Jesus, pal, are you sure you didn't use a bit too much of that triiodide?

Nope.

He took another drink of water.

Noise—static? a voice?—crackled out of the radio. Dave's ears were ringing. He couldn't quite make out . . . He worked his jaw back and forth, swallowing, and trying to clear his ears. There was a pop, and he could hear again.

". . . there? Repeat, what the holy hell was that? Come in, Robin. Come in, Partridge. Repeat, what's going on up there? Somebody answer." It was Myna, the man stationed in the lobby.

Dave hit the transmit button. "Myna, give me a status. What did it sound like down there?"

"Like a goddamn train wreck."

"Did anyone hear it on the street? Is there any activity out there?"

"Negative. Anyone outside who heard it probably thinks it's just another Con Ed manhole explosion. But there are other people in this building, and I'll bet they're all dialing 911."

Right. Whatever happens next has to happen fast.

"Stand by, Myna. Don't do anything."

"Affirmative. Who is this anyway?"

"I'll tell you who it is." Ransome. His voice was as scratchy as an old 78 rpm record.

Dave pushed his thumb down. "David Elliot speaking, Myna. Keep cool, and don't do anything rash if you want to make it home today."

Ransome spoke softly, "You astonish me, Mr. Elliot. It is quite unlikely that any of us will make it home."

"They will if they listen and do what I say. Myna, Partridge, the rest of you people, pay close attention to me. First, let me give you what I think the status is. Myna, you've got three men with you. There are six men down on the forty-fifth floor . . ."

"Dead," Ransome shot.

"Not all of them. You should have looked closer. I only shot the ones who didn't give me any choice. Think about it, guys, I've spent the whole day trying my damnedest to *not* kill you people."

"With a regrettable lack of success."

Dave ground his teeth. Score one point for a.k.a. John Ransome. He couldn't let the bastard score again—not if, as he hoped, he was going to be able to win Ransome's men away from him. "Okay, on the roof, Ransome, you've got, what, a dozen people left."

"You don't really expect me to tell you, do you?"

"Fewer. Anyone who was on the stairs, anyone who was near the door is on the casualty list. Myna, FYI, the noise you heard was me blowing the stairs. Everyone on the roof stays on the roof."

"This is Robin. Myna, notify HQ immediately."

"Belay that, Myna," Dave snapped. "If you notify headquarters one of two things will happen. One, they send more men, or two, they say to hell with it and drop a heavy. Either way, you die."

"Don't listen to him, Myna."

"Myna, if they send more men, they won't get me. Not right away. Even if they send a whole goddamned regiment and run an office-by-office check, it will take hours. By then it will be past sunup. People will be in the streets. Commuters will be arriving. The city will be awake."

"Myna, I have given you a direct order. Call HQ."

"And you know what I'll do? I'll wait until the peak of rush hour. Then I'll put a chair through a window and take a high dive. Maybe I'll go out a ten story window. Maybe a forty story window. It doesn't matter which, because when I hit the concrete my blood will be all over the place. Did you take a look at the street after poor Bernie Levy jumped, Myna? It will be the same with me."

"Myna, I don't have to remind you of the penalty for refusing a direct order, do I?"

"You heard what your boss said about my blood awhile back, didn't you? It's full of germs or viruses or whatever hellbrew I'm infested with. Anyone who ingests it gets the disease. Think about it, Myna, think of how far Bernie's blood spattered. Think of how many people will get my blood in their mouths and up their noses if I go out a window during rush hour."

"Do your duty, Myna, call . . ."

Myna cut Ransome off. "What's my alternative? I'm dead if you jump. I'm dead if they bomb us. And I'm dead if I let you walk out of here 'cause your germs will kill everyone in the world."

"I don't walk. That's the deal."

Myna didn't answer. After a moment's silence, Ransome laughed softly. "I want to hear this. Oh yes indeedy, I do. Tell me, Mr. Elliot, just what do you have in mind? Surely you don't believe that, at this late hour, you have thought of a *new* solution to this little predicament of ours?"

"I have. Do you want to hear it?"

Ransome snorted. "Speak on."

"First, I want to ask Myna something. Myna, do you know what your friend Robin, my friend Ransome, has done? What kind of a little treat he left for me in Bernard Levy's office?"

"Uh . . ."

"How about you, Parrot? Did you ever get up there and take a looksee?"

"No. I was two floors down on reserve duty. Why do you ask?"

"Tell them, Ransome. You were so damned proud of it, so go ahead and tell them."

Dave heard a hiss and a snap. Ransome's cigarettes and lighter had survived the explosion. "I see no reason to do that, Mr. Elliot. Nor does someone like me take orders from someone like you."

"Fine. I'll do it for you. Parrot, Myna, the rest of you, what your boss did was cut off some heads and stick them on poles." Dave paused for effect. "Women's heads."

Someone, Dave didn't know who, muttered an obscenity of disbelief.

Ransome's voice hardened, not by much, but perceptibly. "You've made a mistake, Mr. Elliot. More than one. If you'd looked closely, you would have observed . . ."

"That you were holding Marge Cohen hostage? Well, you aren't. I've found her, and I freed her, and she's been a long time out of here."

Ransome whispered, "Son. Of. A. Bitch."

"Okay, let's get down to brass tacks." Dave was speaking through his teeth, working hard to control his voice. "I want you men to know that your boss has been staking out women's heads. You got that, people? Do you read me loud and clear? Do you understand what your sick twisted bastard of a C.O. has been doing in his spare time? Let me say it one more time—your boss has been beheading women."

"Psychological warfare. Approved practices . . ."

"Can it, Ransome. That's just an excuse. Men, he wants you to believe that the reason why he did it was to freak me out. I was in 'Nam. You men know that. And while I was there somebody did the same thing to some Vietnamese women—took their heads off. I freaked then, so your boss figured that I'd freak now. That's the reason Ransome wants to give you. But it's not the only reason. It's not the real reason. The real reason, the reason why he did it . . ."

"At ease, Elliot. Who gave you a license to practice psychiatry?"

". . . is because he likes . . ."

"Lieutenant Elliot betrayed his own men and his own C.O."

". . ." Dave gasped.

"That's what he did in 'Nam. He ratted on his commander. Turned him in. Sent him in front of a general court-martial, him and five of his own men. You can't believe him. You can't trust a word he says. He's a Judas."

"Right." Dave, his knuckles white, squeezed the radio as tightly as he could. "Right you are, Ransome. And I'm willing to bet that at least one of your men—maybe more than one—will do the same." Dave lowered his voice and continued earnestly. "One of you men *will* turn in Ransome. You'll do it because it's the right thing to do, or you'll do it because you can't sleep at night, or you'll do it because you know that if anyone in authority ever finds out what happened here, then you'll be in just as much shit as your boss is. And that, my friends, will be very deep shit indeed."

Ransome snorted. "Drivel. I have authorization . . ."

"To decapitate women, to mutilate women? Hey, you men, if Ransome has those kinds of orders, I'd want to see them in writing. I mean, if I were you . . ."

"You men are covered. I'm the senior officer here, fully accountable, and . . ."

Dave shot back, "It's the senior officer who gets off with a suspended sentence. The grunts are the ones who hang. That's the way it always has been, and that's the way it always will be. I never met a combat soldier who didn't know that, Ransome."

"Mr. Elliot, I have had enough of you. Myna, I have ordered you to call headquarters. Now make it so."

"Don't, Myna. Listen to my offer. It's either that or you die."

The radio went silent. Seconds ticked off. Dave's hands were sweating. He didn't dare set down the radio to wipe them dry.

Finally, Myna spoke. "Go ahead, sir. I mean, I think we ought to hear your deal. I mean if no one has any objections."

"You disappoint me, Myna," Ransome whispered. "Let me remind you that if he had wanted to make a deal, he could have done so any time this morning."

You've got him on the run, pal.

Dave snapped, "Partridge, do you believe that? You've been closest to Ransome. Come on, Partridge, tell us, tell your buddies, what would have happened if I tried to deal."

Ransome's tones rose, although only slightly. "At ease, Partridge! I'll handle this. As every one of you men know, if Mr. Elliot had been the least bit accommodating, if he had shown any sign of being willing to cooperate, if he'd behaved maturely as we have every right to expect . . ."

Partridge interrupted. "You would have blown his heart out."

Ransome's voice broke. "Partridge, goddamn you, trooper! And Myna, I gave you a fucking order, and you'd fucking well better obey it!"

Dave held his voice level. It wasn't easy. "My deal is simple. All I want is Ransome. You give him to me, let me have him for a couple of minutes of quality time, and when I'm through . . ."

"Liar! Goddamned sniveling ratfuck liar!"

"When I'm through with what I have to do—the same thing any one of you would do—then I put away the guns, and turn myself in."

"This is bullshit! Bullshit! Don't listen to it!"

Dave forced himself to sound weary and resigned. "The elevators were probably wrecked by the explosion, Myna. I'll come down these stairs, the north stairs. No guns. No tricks. Hands in the air. Then it's up to you. You want to grease me, fine. I guess I'm a dead man anyway. You want to call headquarters, that's fine too.

Whatever you want, that's what you do. I don't care. All I care about is sharing a few intimate moments with your boss."

"You prick! You think these men are so stupid . . ."

Another voice cut Ransome off. It was Partridge, speaking quietly. "How do you get him? He's up here. You're down there."

"I'm on my way back to Bernie Levy's office. I'll be there in a minute. There's rope. Cable actually. It's on the north side of the roof. Tie Ransome up and lower him down to Levy's window—the one that's broken open. But first get his clothes off. I want him buck naked."

Ransome snarled, "Why, Mr. Elliot, I never knew you felt *that* way about me."

Dave ignored him. "Partridge, Myna? Have I got a deal?"

There was silence at the other end of the radio link. Dave held his breath. Now it all hinged on loyalty. How loyal were Ransome's men to their leader? How much did they love him; how secure was the bond? There was a steadfastness in some soldiers' souls that was more than mere obedience. If the man they followed was the right kind of man, nothing could break their bond to him. They would die first.

But the officer to whom they pledged their faithfulness had to earn it. Dave didn't think Ransome had.

Neither did Partridge.

"You got it." There was a military crispness to Partridge's voice. Dave knew he was telling the truth.

Ransome roared, "GET YOUR FUCKING HANDS OFF OF ME I'LL SEE YOU IN FRONT OF A FIRING SQUAD YOU PUSSY CUNT DON'T YOU FUCKING DARE TOUCH ME MOTHERFUCKER OR I'LL NAIL YOUR COCK TO THE . . ."

Dave heard grunting and muffled obscenity. Ransome's radio made a sound like crumpled cellophane.

"Partridge," Dave asked, "Partridge, are you there?"

"Here, Mr. Elliot. Where are you?"

"Almost in Levy's office. I'm in the hallway now."

"We're ready to lower him down."

"Wait a minute, Partridge. What size shoes does he wear?"

"Twelve, I'd say. Wide. Twelve B or C."

Dave stepped into Bernie's office. Carnage and meaningless horror, the stuff of every war in history. Best to ignore it. Ignoring it was the only way a soldier could stay sane.

"Perfect. Leave his shoes on. Nothing else. Not even his socks. Only his shoes. You got that, Partridge?"

"I read you, Mr. Elliot."

"Call me Dave."

"He's on his way down . . . Mr. Elliot."

Dave walked to the window and tugged back the canvas. He looked up. Ransome's body had just been put over the edge of the parapet. He was naked, white, and his muscularity was, in some brutal way, beautiful. Even at the distance, Dave could see that his torso bore a network of twisting scars.

The man's won a Purple Heart. Maybe more than one.

Ransome had recovered his self-control. He no longer screamed, he no longer swore. His voice was calm, flat, modulated only by his faint Appalachian accent. "I am very disappointed in you men. You are not handling this situation with the responsibility one expects of skilled professionals. However, there is still time . . ."

Dave pressed the radio's transmit button. "Partridge, I don't want him lowered all the way. I'll tell you when to stop. And see if you can jog him left a little, so I can reach him."

"Roger, Mr. Elliot."

". . . still time to turn this situation around. You people know me. You know that I'm a fair-minded man. I'm prepared to forget about this unfortunate deviation from duty. Otherwise, what you are doing will be called mutiny. I want you men . . ."

Ransome twisted in his descent. His body scraped against the building's pitted granite facing. He left a streak of abraded skin against the stone. Dave flinched. Ransome didn't.

". . . to think about mutiny. And, I want you to think about your duty. I have every confidence, men, that if you think about your duty, you will do the appropriate and intelligent thing."

Dave snapped on the radio. "Partridge, about another five feet and then stop."

"I read you."

Partridge and the men on the roof had not been gentle with Ransome. His ankles were fastened tight with cable. His circulation had been cut, and his legs were turning an ugly purple. Higher, his arms were locked behind his back. The cable was wound so taut about his midriff that flesh bulged out between the strands. Ransome had to be in pain, but, of course, he didn't show it. Men like Ransome never did.

Dave stepped back from the window. Ransome's shoed feet appeared. Then his bare calves. "Hold it," Dave said.

"Holding."

Ransome chuckled. "You've got it wrong, Mr. Elliot. They'll have to let me down another foot or two before you'll be able to suck my cock."

Dave ignored him. He reached out into the air, took Ransome's left foot, and unfastened the shoelaces.

"What is it, Mr. Elliot, do you think I'm hiding a .50 caliber machine gun in there?"

Dave slipped off Ransome's right shoe, and slid it onto his own foot. It was a perfect fit, the same as the left shoe.

Ransome laughed as if enjoying a private joke. "Well, goodie for you. You've spent all day pretending to be the kind of man who could fill my shoes. Now, you think you've made your case. But you haven't."

Dave bent over and tied the laces.

"While you're relishing your little *temporary* moment of triumph, let me advise you that if you think you're embarrassing me, you've got it wrong. And if you think you can break me, you're wrong about that too."

Dave straightened. He leaned out the window, taking one of

Ransome's calves in his hand. He spoke into the radio. "Partridge, did you hear Ransome's explanation of my situation?"

Partridge sounded a little perplexed. "Yes, sir. Why do you ask?"

"All of it?"

"Yes, sir."

"All about the three phases of the disease. First in the blood, then in the bodily fluids, and then in the respiratory system?"

"Yes, sir. I am aware of that."

"And you're sure you understood it all?"

"I am, sir."

"And you know I'm in the second phase? That the disease can be communicated through my blood, urine, and saliva? And the business about drinking out of the same glass, and love bites, and kissing, and all of that?"

"Absolutely affirmative, sir. Now can you tell me why you're asking these questions?"

"Sure," Dave said. "Or better yet, just look over the side, and watch."

David Elliot looked up into his enemy's face. He no longer hated the man. He felt, if anything, some small sympathy for him.

Ransome glared back.

Dave smiled. Curiously enough, it was a sincere smile, warm and not unfriendly.

Ransome's eyes burned with almost palpable hatred. "Are you ready to get it on now, Elliot. Come on, man, come on. I can hardly wait to see what kind of twisted shit is on your mind."

Dave's smile widened. He lifted his voice, making sure that the men on the roof could hear him. "What's on my mind, pal? Kisses are on my mind. That's all. Just kisses and little love bites."

As David Elliot lowered Marge Cohen out of a shattered second story window, above him, distant but quite clear, he heard Ransome insane with terror and keening in the night.

And kept hearing him, as they fled into the dawn.

EPILOGUE

Sleep; and if life was bitter to thee, pardon,
If sweet, give thanks; thou hast no more to live;
And to give thanks is good, and to forgive.

Algernon Charles Swinburne,
"Ave atque Vale"

A lone man on horseback.

His name is David Elliot. He is lanky and dark, his complexion not yet whitened by the onset of final disease.

This ride is his last journey. Death, he knows, awaits him at its end.

His eyes are brown, and might appear solemn were it not for the smile that crinkles their corners.

He knows that he will die alone, and has made his peace with that inevitability. Autumn is near, winter not far away; his body will not be found until the summer comes again.

This knowledge accounts, in part, for his smile. The microbe that will shortly enter its third, killing stage needs a living host. And so, by dying far from any other human, he will slay that which has slain him.

There are other reasons why he smiles, but they are private things.

Today, he's more than two hundred miles east of San Francisco, in the Sierras. He crossed the mountain divide yesterday, and picked up his horse from a leathered man who seemed not to have aged a single year since Dave had last seen him.

Dave gave the man money and a handful of letters. The letters were addressed to a *pied-à-terre* on Sutton Place, to an office in Basel, to a dormitory at Columbia University, and to a ranch in Colorado. The man counted the money, smiled in a leathery way, folded the letters into a shirt pocket, and promised not to mail them until after the first snow of the season.

Now David Elliot is riding west into the high mountain fastness, up a cobbled slope, toward a small valley he visited once and has never forgotten. There is no trail, but he knows where to go. Every foot of ground—granite, grey and shot with streaks of black—is fresh in his mind, as though he'd been here only yesterday.

He hasn't shaved. Three days of stubble speckle his cheeks, chin, and upper lip. He wishes it would grow faster. It would be good to have a moustache at the end.

Dave pulls out a handkerchief. He lifts the brim of his floppy straw hat and wipes away a line of sweat. He knows how much further his destination is. There's only another hour to go.

It is nearly sunset when he arrives. The air is filled with golden light. He breasts a small rise, looks down, and catches his breath. The valley's loveliness is heart-stopping. At its center, greener than a green bottle, there is the emerald lake that he has always remembered, just as he has remembered the soft evening shadows that of necessity lie across it. Nothing moves. And yes, the air is wine.

This one moment has been the finest in his life, the finest that can be experienced. He knows that, of all men, he is privileged to have experienced it twice. And the knowledge fills his heart with joy.

Projects Administration Office
Mail Drop 172, LFMDUSA 20817

TO: Distribution List, via fax
FROM: Project Administrator, Project 79-1-18
SUBJECT: Status

This office advises you that:

1.   New test results indicate that microbe 138.12.b survivability is dependent on a highly oxygenate-permeated host. Microbic efficacy declines logarithmically as a function of the formula $f(x) = -2.17E+5 * \ln(x) + 4.71E+5$, where x is the atmospheric pressure in milllibars. Microbe 138.12.b enters dormancy at an altitude of 4,200 feet ± 5% above sea level. 100% microbic mortality occurs above an altitude of 6,800 feet ± 5%. R&D staff emphasize that these results are unanticipated, and apologize for any inconvenience that may have been caused by the oversight. Staff further emphasize that microbic efficacy remains at established parameters below an altitude of 2,000 feet ± 5%.

2.   Field investigation confirms that subject ELLIOT, David Perry, reached a camp site below Mount Excelsior, state of California (latitude 38°07'N and longitude 118°53W) on 29 September this year. USGS maps indicate an altitude for this camp site of 9,434 feet above sea level. Accordingly, there is a high degree of certainty that subject ELLIOT is, at the present time, operating in a non-deceased mode. Further data regarding subject ELLIOT's subsequent movements and present whereabouts are not forthcoming at this time.

3.   Subject KREUTER, John James, Colonel, US Army Ret., departed his Basel, Switzerland office on 14 October this year. Further data regarding subject KREUTER's movements and present whereabouts are not forthcoming at this time.

4.   Passport records indicate subject COHEN, Marigold Fields, cleared Swiss immigration on 28 September this year. Subject COHEN was resident at the Hotel Mercure, Lucerne, Switzerland until 14 October this year. Further data regarding subject COHEN's movements and present whereabouts are not forthcoming at this time.

5.   This office judges the potential for retributory initiatives on the part of subject ELLIOT, prospectively in collaboration with subject KREUTER, to be above acceptable risk levels. All affected personnel are herewith directed to adopt level 3 defensive procedure.

6.   Keep your heads down, gentlemen. We appear to have a situation on our hands.

        LTF
        /mj

AUTHOR'S NOTE

In 1946 Allied war crimes investigators discovered that Dr. Shiro Ishii, a general of the Japanese Imperial Army and commander of a military organization known as Unit 731, had constructed the world's largest and most advanced biological weapons laboratory in Manchuria. Satellite laboratories were later found in Tokyo and elsewhere. Evidence assembled by investigators demonstrated that throughout the course of the war, Ishii and his assistants had conducted extensive biological weaponry tests on Chinese civilians and on American and British POWs held at various camps in Southeast Asia.

Inexplicably Dr. Ishii (whose crimes far exceeded those of his German counterpart, Dr. Josef Mengele) was never brought to trial. Rather, he was allowed a long and prosperous retirement, enjoying a sizable pension from the Japanese government as well as income from other sources that remained anonymous until, just as this novel was being sent to the typesetters, *The New York Times* revealed that the U.S. government had paid Dr. Ishii a handsome stipend.

Such few records as are publicly available are ambiguous as to the ultimate disposition of the extensive body of research reports prepared by Dr. Ishii and his staff.